The Door in the Sky

By Sandy Klein Bernstein

First published by Dog Ear Publishing
4010 W. 86th Street, Ste H
Indianapolis, IN 46268
www.dogearpublishing.net

ISBN: 978-1-4575-1111-0

This book is printed on acid-free paper.

This book is a work of fiction. Places, events, and situations in
this book are purely fictional and any resemblance to actual
persons, living or dead, is coincidental.

Printed in the United States of America

To the real King Shevre and Queen Jacqueline,
and to the real Allie and Ricky—without you,
these pages would be empty, as would my life.

Prologue

Two glittering balls of light streaked out of the inky sky and skidded to a halt just above the Chicago skyline. Had anyone bothered to look up, they might have thought that the stars were shining especially bright that night. And they may have wondered why two stars seemed to hang so low in the frosty air. But it was just after five o'clock, and the people on the streets of Chicago were much too busy racing home after a hard day's work to notice two stars twinkling far beneath a dark and wintry sky.

The glittering objects stared at the city below. The bigger one suddenly spotted what he'd been looking for and nudged the littler one, pointing toward the Space Museum. Clouds of purple stardust tumbled to the ground as the smaller star twirled in the air, cheering loudly.

"Shhhh," the larger one cautioned.

The two stars flew closer to the museum, staring intently at its entrance. As an ordinary-looking boy ran up the marble steps toward the museum's front door, the little star could not contain his excitement.

"Is that him? Is it? Is it, Uncle Shimmer? Huh? Is it?"

The elder star smiled and nodded. His little nephew was so excited he began spinning out of control. He bounced off a telescope jutting out of the museum's roof, skidded backwards across the air, and got tangled in a web of wires hanging off a nearby antenna. The elder star shook his head and sighed as he soared across the rooftop to untangle his nephew. A sheepish grin spread across the little star's face as he spun helplessly in the wintry winds.

Down below, the boy they had been watching raced up the stairs. As he stepped into the Space Museum, he never could have guessed that two magical beings hovered on the roof above. And he never could have dreamed that they had traveled several galaxies just to meet him. And as his older sister ran to catch up with him, he certainly couldn't have known that a retired witch in a faraway kingdom had just conjured his image in a cauldron that smelled surprisingly of chocolate.

Across a sea of stars, an old man hobbled into his study. He closed the door behind him and locked it, as was his habit. Passing a gilded mirror on the wall, he smiled at the handsome young man reflected back at him. Years before, he had enchanted all the mirrors in his home to only reflect him as he had looked in the prime of his life.

He stopped and peered into the glass. Sighing, he ran his hand across the top of his head. The mirror, reflecting the same movement, showed a strong hand moving across a thick mop of glossy brown hair. In reality, an age-spotted hand swept across a balding head, save for a few wisps of silver hair.

He shuffled across the room to his desk and slowly eased himself into a creaking chair. Wrinkling his nose at the bowl of mashed dinner his cook had prepared for him, he wriggled a finger and recited a spell he had committed to memory years before when she first began serving him old-man slop like this. The bowl of mush wobbled, then suddenly transformed into a slice of chocolate fudge cake. He lifted his spoon and smiled.

"Ah, such are the advantages of being an Alchemist of the Highest Order," he chortled, digging into the cake.

When he finished eating, he perused the stack of mail sitting on his desk that he had postponed reading all day.

"Bill, bill, bill," he muttered, wriggling his finger at each and delightedly watching them explode in mid-air.

But the next letter in the stack was not a bill. It was an elegantly engraved envelope bearing the return address of the king's personal assistant, Roberts.

He tugged thoughtfully on his long white beard (over time, Magnus had grudgingly accepted that an alchemist of his rank must also look the part, complete with flowing robes and a snow-white beard). With an annoyed sigh, he reached for a silver letter opener and slid it under the royal seal. A single sheet of vellum floated out of the envelope and started to soar away. He snatched the letter before it could fly across the room and began to read, although he already knew what it would say. It was the third such letter he'd received in as many months.

Dear Alchemist Magnus,

I hope all is well at your cozy forest cottage. All is well here at the castle, minus a recent incident involving a kitchen maid and the royal shoemaker. Their romance was short-lived, to say the least. To put it bluntly, the king was furious when he choked on a shoelace in his mashed potatoes.

I am writing once again to urge you to name your successor. It was with a heavy heart that King Shevre accepted your resignation six months ago. He understood that your advanced years made it difficult to get around the sprawling castle and agreed it was in your best interest to move back into your old cottage. However, the king grows impatient for a new Royal Alchemist to be appointed, and I am afraid I must agree. The castle needs a master magician to reside within its walls.

Only last week a passing unicorn got his horn stuck in some fresh mortar on the northwest turret. As there was no alchemist within the castle to cast a rescue spell, King Shevre decided to save the poor creature himself. He dragged his old magic carpet out of storage and attempted to fly it. As the carpet hadn't been serviced in years, its sense of direction was in dire need of repair. The king wound up on the rooftop of a local tavern and had to hitch a ride with a passing witch atop a very worn broomstick (eighteen splinters had to be removed from the Royal Buttocks).

Thus, I must implore you to name an alchemist to succeed you. Your inventive spells and quirky sense of humor served the Royal Family well for many years (who could forget the scepter-juggling hamsters?). It is out of respect for you that King Shevre continues to await your decision. However, I feel duty-bound to inform you that if you have not reached a decision by month's end, King Shevre will be forced to appoint someone himself to fill the position of Royal Alchemist.

Best Regards,
Roberts

Magnus folded the letter into a paper airplane and sent it flying across the room. He knew that the most qualified alchemist for the job was a man named Agrippa Thoth. Normally, he disliked the expression "hated his guts," but that was exactly how he felt about Thoth. To be precise, he hated not only his guts, but his intestines and liver as well. He had detested the man for years, ever since Thoth had trained under him as an apprentice alchemist.

That was why he had been working so feverishly to train his newest apprentice, a lad of seventeen named Henry. Henry was a farm boy Magnus had found quite by chance the year before when he lost his way in the countryside. Recognizing the boy's extraordinary powers at once, Magnus had hired him on the spot. The boy, of course, had no idea that he was gifted with an abundance of magical talent, but Magnus had no doubt that Henry would one day become a powerful alchemist, perhaps the most powerful of all. To his delight, he soon discovered that Henry had all the qualities he admired most in a person—he was kind, brave, loyal and trustworthy.

But it was obvious from Roberts's letter that King Shevre could not be put off any longer. With a weary sigh, Magnus vowed to train Henry even harder and explain to the king that despite his youth, the boy was the best candidate for the job. Glancing at the clock, he realized his apprentice was already late. *Strange,* he thought, *the lad is always on time for his evening lesson.*

"Well, time to get to work." He whistled a familiar call and waited for his cane to come and help him out of his chair. Drumming his fingers impatiently on the desk, he looked around the room and narrowed his eyes when he saw it flirting with a lacy white umbrella in the corner. The umbrella turned three shades of red as the cane looped its handle around hers. Magnus cleared his throat loudly and the cane quickly untangled itself from the blushing umbrella, then hopped across the room and helped him up from his chair.

He ambled over to his bookshelves, determined to teach Henry an enchantment so complex that King Shevre couldn't help but be impressed. He went right past the *Encyclopedia Magicka,* as its pages were only filled with ordinary fluff such as jinxes, curses and charms. He stopped to flip through some of the volumes within *The Alchemist's Books of Knowledge* and then tossed them to the floor, muttering, "Even a toddler could cast these!"

Rubbing his hands together, a smile began to play at the corners of his mouth. "It seems there's no choice," he mused, "I'll just have to teach him one of my own." Confident that his pupil was gifted enough to learn any magic spell, he began looking for his private collection. Like any other sorcerer, Magnus kept a detailed list of the spells he invented, writing them down in a secret book he kept hidden away. Having achieved the rank of Royal Alchemist, Magnus's spells were so powerful that they needed safekeeping lest they fall into the wrong hands.

He leaned against the mysterious slab of emerald that graced every alchemist's study and muttered, "Now, where did I hide that spell book?" Glancing at the numerous inscriptions engraved upon the green stone, one of the verses caught his eye: "*It ascends from the earth to the heavens and again it descends back down.*" Snapping his fingers he shouted, "That's it!"

Humming a few bars of "Rain, rain, go away," he hobbled over to the coat rack and unzipped a battered old raincloak. He felt around inside its sleeves, but they were empty. Suddenly, his fingertips started to sparkle. He tugged on the glitter, and pulled a hidden object from out of the air. Momentarily elated, his shoulders slumped when he saw that it was only a goldfish bowl. Looking more closely, he noticed that the goldfish was floating belly-up atop the murky water. "Oh dear," he muttered. "I was wondering where I had put you." Tapping on the cloudy glass he mumbled, "Sorry, old friend."

He put the bowl down and crossed the room to the small laboratory in the back. His spirits rose when he spied a mortar and pestle sandwiched between a beaker of enchanted crystals and a deck of playing cards. He peeked beneath them, but all he found was a torn receipt for a magic harp and a ticket stub from the *Four Fairies Floating Follies.*

Frustrated, Magnus snapped, "Where could it be?" His eyes then fell upon the Wand of Hermes leaning against a dusty scrying table. A silver serpent was entwined around the brass wand. Thinking at last he found where he had hidden his book of spells, he opened the serpent's mouth, but all he saw was an old breath mint.

Determined to find his spell book before Henry's arrival, he paced back and forth across the worn, wooden floor. He stopped to stare at an old photograph of himself as a young apprentice, beaming proudly at the pieces of gold he had just transformed from lead. Blowing the dust off the picture he muttered, "Don't know why everyone is so impressed by that ridiculous parlor trick. All it takes is a bit of quicksilver, a simple incantation and—poof—you have gold.

"Gold ...," he murmured. His eyes grew wide as he suddenly remembered. Turning toward a wobbly drink cart, he grabbed a decanter filled with golden liquid. He pulled the stopper out, sniffed the contents and smiled. "One never tires of the smell of old leather," he said, inhaling deeply. When he turned the decanter upside down and poured, a golden book oozed out of the bottle and fell with a soft thud onto the floor below. Magnus grinned with satisfaction as he picked the book up and ran his fingers across the cover: *My Incantations and Spells, by Theobald Magnus, Alchemist of the First Order.*

Lowering himself once again into the creaky chair, he flipped through the pages, searching for an outrageously flamboyant spell. He made a mental note to tell Henry where he kept his spell book hidden, lest he forget again. After all, the book was both priceless and irreplaceable. It was his life's work; a treasury of every spell he had ever invented.

While the old sorcerer busied himself with finding the perfect showy spell, a misty fog blew out of the dark woods bordering his cottage. The black vapor rolled across the moonlit grass, then seeped under the alchemist's locked front door. It hovered in the entryway for a moment and listened. Hearing movement from the room above, it floated up the rickety stairs and drifted down the dark hallway until it came upon a closed door. Easily slipping beneath it, the mist quietly crept across the room toward the hunched figure seated behind the desk.

"She'll never get her hands on it, you know," Magnus suddenly said, snapping his book shut and turning to face the black smoke hovering before him. "Oh, she may find where the king has hidden it, but she will never wear the Serpent's Eye, I promise you that!" The swirling vapor rose in the air, slowly transforming into the dark shadow of a man, made entirely of mist.

As if sprung from a child's nightmare, two black eyes gleamed from the depths of the shadow's sunken sockets, half-hidden behind the hood of his cloak. Through the smoky haze of his face, a pair of lips twisted into a demented imitation of a mouth. And as he moved forward, his cloak left a trail of black mist on the floor.

Noting the shocked expression crossing the shadow's face, Magnus's eyes twinkled. "Come now, Shadow, did you honestly think you could sneak up on *me*? I may be old, I'll grant you that, but I am still an Alchemist of the First Order!" As the shadow growled, he stroked his chin thoughtfully. "So, how did you escape anyway? Pardon my curiosity, but I thought you and your mistress were sentenced to spend the rest of your miserable lives rotting away in that desolate wasteland. Surely you weren't released early for good behavior?"

With a vicious snarl, the shadow lunged for the spell book in Magnus's hands. Belying his years, the old man tossed it in the air while shouting an incantation. The book instantly vanished amidst a handful of glittering dust.

Pulling a jagged knife from within the folds of his cloak, the shadow spoke with a deep, throaty rasp, "If you wish to live another day, return your spell book, *now!*"

"I've lived enough days in my time," Magnus said with a resigned sigh.

Shadow pressed the tip of his blade against a vein in the alchemist's wrinkled neck.

Magnus laughed as he wriggled a finger. The knife glittered then faded from sight. "Do you seriously think you can intimidate *me?* I do not take orders from mere *servants*. And I especially do not take orders from *your* mistress. How is Queen Glacidia, by the way? Still enjoying her banishment to Windermere?"

The shadow hissed and a pool of black smoke crawled out of his mouth and began twisting around the alchemist's body. "Bring it back *now!*"

Magnus calmly met his enemy's eyes. "Never."

Shadow's claw-like fingers melted into the smoke already circling the old man's throat, and began to squeeze. Magnus's eyes bulged as he gasped for breath, but he would die before giving that madwoman's minion his life's work. He had already guessed the spell Queen Glacidia was after, and he knew that the entire kingdom of Galdoren would be in grave danger if it came into her possession. *Henry*, he thought, *where are you?*

From out of nowhere, Magnus's cane hurled itself against the dark mist, attacking him from behind. The shadow cursed violently, never letting go of the alchemist's neck. As the cane continued to pummel him, Shadow gave it a savage kick. With a loud crack, the loyal walking stick broke in two and clattered to the floor.

A movement in the mirror caught the shadow's attention. Golden liquid the exact shade of Magnus's spell book suddenly sloshed inside a crystal decanter. A cruel smile split his hollow face. "Clever," he whispered. "I never would have thought to look there."

Magnus saw the decanter reflected in the shadow's gleaming eyes and his blood turned cold with terror. No matter the cost, Glacidia could not be allowed to get her hands on his spell book! As the life drained from his body, he focused all his power on the one incantation he never dreamed he would cast—destroying his life's work. Tears stung his eyes as he summoned this last bit of magic with his dying breath.

"*Abrestan scinncraeft boc,*" he choked through bluish lips.

Streams of golden smoke billowed inside the decanter as red-hot sparks shot against the glass. The molten liquid bubbled and sputtered then burst into flames, exploding the crystal cork right out of its top. The cork shot up to the ceiling and shattered, raining shards of broken glass.

Shadow screamed with rage, violently snapping the old man's neck. He dropped the alchemist's body to the floor, then flew across the room. But even as he reached the crystal container, the fire inside began to weaken. Suddenly, all of the spells within the room began to unravel, as if they had died along with the alchemist. The image in the mirror blurred, then instead of reflecting a young man crumpled on the floor, the glass reflected the lifeless body of an old sorcerer. The plate that had held the chocolate cake wobbled and the few remaining crumbs turned back into bits of gruel. Finally, the burning embers within the crystal began to burn less brightly, until at last they flickered and died.

Shadow flipped the decanter upside down and shook. The smoking liquid slowly oozed past the neck of the bottle until a sizzling spell book squeezed into the shadow's waiting hands. He flipped through the book's scorched pages until he found the spell he had been sent to retrieve. His lips twisted into a perverse smile. "Soon," he breathed, stroking the charred page.

A loud knock on the front door startled him. "Alchemist Magnus," a young man's voice called. "It's me, Henry! Sorry I'm late, but the homework you gave me exploded and I had to change clothes."

Shadow ripped the page from its binding and dropped the spell book on the floor. It bounced off the wood planks and slid under the desk. He hurriedly scanned the list of ingredients scrawled across the page, knowing his queen would have all but one. He streaked across the room to the alchemist's fully stocked potion shelves. Bottles crashed to the floor as he knocked everything over, searching for that one rare ingredient. He finally found a near-empty bottle of it hidden behind an old dragon's egg. Carefully slipping both the spell and the bottle into the pocket of his cloak, he slid out the open window and slithered down the stone wall, cloaking himself within the ordinary shadows of the house.

"Hello?" Henry shouted. "Alchemist Magnus? Is this another one of your tests?" With an annoyed sigh, the young man muttered an incantation. Nothing happened. Cursing under his breath, he tried again. Finally, the front door creaked open. "Okay, do I pass?" he called, stepping inside.

The shadow silently slipped across the lawn and disappeared into the dark woods. He moved swiftly through the trees, eager to deliver the spell to his waiting queen. Nothing in the forest took note of him as he melted into all the other shadows on this moonless night.

In a small house not far away, a silver-haired witch stood before a steaming cauldron and lifted her wand. Swirling the image of the Earth boy that floated within the bubbling brew, she shook her head and sighed. "And so it begins."

Chapter One

THE DOOR IN THE SKY

The Chicago Space Museum had closed to the public promptly at five p.m., and it was already nearly nine. The only people left in the vast, three-story building were pajama-clad kids between the ages of ten and seventeen, some chaperones, and a handful of security guards. The museum's annual "Sleep Under the Stars" was one of the city's biggest events, and now that Ricky was eleven, he was finally old enough to go.

His sister Allie, older by four years, had little interest in this cosmic slumber party, thinking it was only for geeks and nerds. Besides, she would much rather be at the mall with her friends. What she didn't know was that Ricky had been having strange premonitions about the museum. Misty dreams clung to his waking hours, urging him to go. That very morning, he had been daydreaming in math class when he began hearing phantom whispers in his head—*the Space Museum, Ricky … tonight.* A cold chill ran down his spine at the memory.

When Ricky had finally worked up the nerve to ask his mother for permission to go to the museum's sleepover, the words had spilled out of his mouth in a frantic jumble. She had replied, "Only if your big sister goes with." Allie had looked up from her magazine and almost laughed out loud. She was about to say, "No way," when she made the mistake of looking into her little brother's pleading eyes. Suddenly, she heard herself mumble, "Okay, sure, whatever." And that was how she now found herself sitting in a small theater getting ready to watch a show about the constellations.

All of the seats in the theater tilted back, so the audience had to look up. Staring at the dark ceiling, Allie swallowed a yawn, wishing her mom had let her bring her laptop.

Ricky shifted nervously in his chair as the lights slowly dimmed and the show began. Thousands of glittering stars suddenly twinkled across the huge domed ceiling. Symphony music swelled in the background as a monotone voice began to describe the stars above.

Suddenly, a brilliant streak of blue flashed across the artificial sky, followed by a smaller streak of purple. Ricky jumped in his seat. "What was THAT?!?" he whispered to his sister.

She turned to him and whispered back, "That was Orion. Honestly, Ricky, are you even listening?"

"No, I'm not talking about Orion. I mean, what was that flash of light?"

"Those are stars," she snapped.

"No, not the stars! The other flash!"

"What other flash?"

"Shhhhh!" a kid hissed from behind them.

Ricky crossed his arms angrily. He knew he had seen something. *TWO* somethings, in fact! Just then, the brilliant blue light flashed again. Only, this time, instead of disappearing, a shape began to form. It was the shape of a star. But this star looked completely different from any of the other stars dancing across the ceiling. It had a classic five-point shape instead of just being a dot of light. Plus, it glowed so brightly that the other stars seemed dim by comparison. And where the other stars were white, this one was a shiny robin's egg blue.

The bright star began to move at lightning speed, leaving a trail of letters in its wake. Ricky's jaw dropped open when he saw the glittering message written across the artificial sky: *Good evening, Ricky.*

He tugged on his sister's arm. "How'd they know my name?" he asked in a hushed voice.

"How did WHO know your name?" she answered, annoyed.

He pointed at the ceiling, where the message still hovered brightly.

"Are you delirious?" his sister hissed at him.

Couldn't she see it? How could she not? But just then, the words began to fade to nothingness. Suddenly, a new sentence formed in the sky above him.

Come back here at midnight, Ricky, the star spelled out in the sky. Ricky stole a glance at his sister. It was obvious from her bored expression that she could not see this message either.

Ricky's jaw couldn't have dropped any lower without hitting the ground. "What do you see now?" he asked in a shaky voice.

Turning to him she answered, "I see a moron."

"No! What's in the sky?"

"Do you need glasses?"

"Just tell me what you see!" he hissed.

Looking back at the ceiling she sighed, "I see the Big Dipper and the Little Dipper." Turning to her brother she added, "And the biggest dip in the room."

He couldn't believe it. She couldn't see it! That meant the message was just for him. Or that his sister was right and he really was nuts.

Then the little flash of purple he had seen earlier zoomed across the sky. When it finally stopped moving, he could clearly see that it, too, was a star. But this little purple star was much smaller than the blue one.

The little star began to race back and forth, scribbling letters across the ceiling. In what looked like a child's scrawl, the words *Bring Jello* flickered on and off.

The blue star zipped across the message, neatly erasing it. Then, in glittering blue letters it added, *Never mind about the Jello.*

Just then, the show ended and the lights began to come back on. For an instant, the word *midnight* glittered in the air. And then it was gone.

"That was unbelievable!" Ricky stammered, shaking in his seat.

"It sure was," Allie answered. "It was the most unbelievably boring thing I've ever seen in my life." Turning to her brother, she cocked her head. "Are you okay? You're not going to puke, are you? 'Cause Mom's not here, and I am so not cleaning it up."

As the clock ticked toward midnight, all of the kids in the museum were snuggled deep in their sleeping bags. Some were sleeping, some were reading by flashlight and some were whispering to their friends.

In a dimly lit room far from the crowd, Ricky was pinching himself to stay awake. He kept glancing at his sister, hoping she would fall asleep. It was nearly midnight, and he knew she would never let him go back inside that theater by himself. She probably wouldn't let him go at all. And if he told her about the star's message, she would just think that he was making it up. After all, *she* hadn't seen anything. *If only she would turn off her flashlight and shut her stupid book!*

"Allie," Ricky whispered. Desperate for any excuse to get her to go to sleep, he fibbed, "I can't sleep with your flashlight on. It's too bright."

"So turn the other way!" she whispered back, flipping to the next page.

"Um, the pages are too loud. They're keeping me up!"

"Are you serious?" she snapped.

He faked a yawn. "Just as I'm about to fall asleep, you turn a page, and WHAM, my eyes fly open! That's gotta be the loudest book in history!"

"You've gotta be the weirdest brother in history." She slammed her book shut, and turned her flashlight off. "Goodnight," she muttered.

Ricky's eyes flicked back and forth between the clock on his cellphone and his sister. Soon, it was five minutes to midnight and she was still awake, shifting in her sleeping bag trying to get comfortable. He needn't have worried, though, for at that very moment, a familiar blue star hovered in the sky above the museum. It took a deep breath, puffed up its chest and began to spin. As it did, millions of specks of blue stardust fell across the Earth. From America to Africa, from Europe to Asia, from the North Pole to the South Pole, glittering pools of stardust fell gently from the skies. And as it landed, everything on Earth fell into a deep sleep. At precisely 11:59, all of the clocks in all of the world stopped ticking and time stood still. On the entire planet, there was only one thing that was completely unaffected. And that one thing was an eleven-year-old boy named Ricky.

"Are you up?" Ricky whispered to his sister. He was surprised by how quickly she had fallen asleep. He quietly climbed out of his sleeping bag, grabbed his robe and tiptoed down the hallway toward the theater.

His pulse quickened as he pushed open the door and stepped inside. There was a sudden explosion of light and Ricky's hands flew to his eyes, shielding them from the blinding glare. His heart hammered wildly as the door swung shut behind him, causing him to jump in the air. *Be brave,* he told himself, *you're eleven years old … almost a man!* But it was easier to think the words than to actually feel them. Taking a deep breath, he slowly peeled his fingers from his eyes and blinked against the spectacular display of lights bouncing across the room.

His attention was drawn upward to the theater's domed ceiling. Ricky's mouth fell open when he saw an enormous door dangling in the artificial sky. Millions of twinkling stars formed the shape of the closed door. It sparkled so brightly that had he looked in a mirror, he would have seen starlight blowing through his hair and dancing down his pajamas.

"Good evening! I'm so glad you came!" a friendly voice called.

Ricky whipped around to see a glittering blue star, about his size, floating behind a row of seats. The soft glow of the smiling star cast glistening shadows as he sailed above the chairs toward the stunned boy. When at last he reached him, the star cleared his throat. "Please allow me to introduce myself," he said, bowing deeply. "I am Shimmerius Perseus Orion. But you may call me Shimmer." He arched a brow, waiting for a response.

Ricky just stood there, too astonished to speak. He finally managed to stammer, "Um, er, hello." Gaping at the star hovering in the air before him, he continued to stumble over his words. "I'm, er, um … Ricky."

"Oh, I know, dear boy. I know." The star's eyes twinkled with amusement.

Remembering how his name had glittered in the sky during the constellation show, Ricky narrowed his eyes and asked, "Oh, yeah. How *do* you know my name?"

"Because it's written on this invitation, of course," Shimmer answered, pulling something from a seemingly invisible pocket on his leg. It was a neatly rolled piece of parchment. Clearly written on the outside of the scroll, in extremely elegant handwriting, were the words:

Mr. Ricky Austin
Space Museum
Chicago, Illinois
Planet Earth
The Milky Way Galaxy

Just as surprising was the return address on the left side of the scroll:

King Shevre
Galdoren Castle
Galdoren by the Sea

"Well, go ahead," the star urged, pressing the parchment into Ricky's shaking hands. "Open it!"

The impatient scroll began pushing itself against Ricky's fingers, eager to be read. It startled Ricky so much that he dropped it. But instead of falling to the floor, the scroll remained floating in the air. It fluttered open and golden words flew off the page to hover in front of the stunned boy's wide eyes.

Ricky continued to stand there, blinking dumbly, until the blank parchment tapped him on the shoulder and pointed to the hovering words. But just as he began to read his magical message, a little purple star streaked out of nowhere, smashing through the golden letters. The star skidded to a stop, did a double flip then crashed through the words a second time, jumbling them even more. Ricky could barely make out the first sentence, which now read:

Royal forbidden hereby Proclamation Galdoren invited the By

"TWINKLE!" Shimmer yelled at the little star.

Screeching to a halt, the purple star smiled crookedly at Ricky. "Didja bring the Jello?"

"I told you a hundred times, Twinkle, forget about the Jello!" Shimmer sputtered. "Just look at what you've done to his invitation!"

The tiny star glanced at the mixed-up words bouncing in the air and clapped a hand-point over his mouth, stifling a giggle. "Oops, sorry," he hiccuped. The irate parchment began smacking him on the head. "Ouch! I said I was sorry!"

Shimmer pushed his way through the tangle of words and pried the furious parchment off the other star's head. "Ricky," he sighed. "Meet my nephew, Twinkle."

The little star winced at the use of his formal name. "Uncle Shimmer, no one calls me that but *you!*" Turning to Ricky he said, "Hi, I'm Twink!" Then he politely added, "I like your planet."

"Er, thanks," Ricky replied, sizing up the friendly-looking star floating in the air before him. He was about the size of a basketball.

"Sorry about your invitation." Twink said, staring at the tumble of words drifting in every direction.

"That's okay, I guess," Ricky muttered.

Twink zoomed across a row of chairs, and began tugging on a word caught between two armrests. "Got it!" he called, zooming back to the boy. "You can still have dessert," he joked, dropping the word "*Dessert*" into Ricky's hands.

"Um, thanks?" Ricky replied, cupping the hovering word in his palm.

Shimmer tapped his foot-point in the air, an irritated expression crossing his face. "Step back, please." Ricky and Twink moved into the aisle as Shimmer spun through the words, neatly reassembling them. After checking to ensure that they were in the correct order, he shot his nephew a reproachful look. Plastering a smile back on his face, he turned to Ricky. "Now, please read your invitation. After all, I've traveled across three galaxies just to deliver it!"

Tingling with excitement, Ricky read the golden words floating in the air:

By Royal Proclamation, Ricky Austin is hereby invited to spend three Earth days exploring all of Galdoren by the Sea (except for the Windermere border, which is expressly forbidden).

On the evening of his last day, a banquet will be held in Ricky's honor at Galdoren Castle.

Banquet Itinerary:
6:00 pm: Appetizers —Blue Throne Room
7:00 pm: Six-Course Dinner — Great Hall
9:00 pm: Endless   Buffet — Castle Buttery

Twink tapped Ricky on the shoulder and pointed to the word still clenched tightly in his fist. "Oh, yeah," Ricky smiled, opening his palm to let the word "*Dessert*" fly out. The lone word floated into the space between the words "*Endless*" and "*Buffet*," so that the sentence now read:

9:00 pm: Endless Dessert Buffet — Castle Buttery

Ricky took a deep breath, then continued reading:

10:00 pm: "The Four Fairies Floating Follies"
(Presented in Fly-O-Vision)—Warlock Towers
11:00 pm: Wizard's Wand Ceremony—Solar Suite
12:00 am: Royal Send-Off with Fireworks
Eagerly Awaiting Your Arrival,
His Royal Highness,

King Shevre

Ricky was so astonished that he flopped into the nearest seat. The worn springs beneath the chair squeaked loudly as he leaned back to look at the door sparkling in the sky above. Scarcely believing that this wasn't a dream, he turned to the stars and asked, "Who's King Shevre?"

"Who's King Shevre?!" Twink repeated. Flying up above Ricky he chirped, "He's only the ruler of our entire kingdom!"

"Twinkle, Ricky couldn't possibly know that," Shimmer scolded his nephew. "Stop being condescending."

The little star flipped in the air. "I can't be *condescending*. I don't even know what it means!"

Shimmer smiled at his young nephew. "It means, talking down to someone."

"Oh," Twink said, hovering above Ricky. Thinking fast, he zoomed down so that he was now hovering just *beneath* Ricky. "King Shevre is only the ruler of our entire kingdom!" he repeated. Then, beaming proudly, he added, "See Uncle Shimmer? I'm not being condescending anymore!"

Scanning the words still floating in the air, Ricky asked, "Why can't I go to the Windermere border?"

Shimmer and Twink exchanged nervous glances. "It's a long story," Shimmer began.

"No it's not!" Twink interrupted. Turning to Ricky he said, "Once upon a time, there was an evil witch who ruled over an icy kingdom named Windermere. Her name was Queen Glacidia. She tried to take over Galdoren and nearly killed every living thing, but she was defeated." He paused for a moment then chirped, "The end."

"Twinkle," Shimmer said, his lips twitching in amusement. "I think there's a little more to it than that."

"Oh yeah," Twink replied. "The king ordered the most powerful witches in the kingdom to put a spell on the entire border of Windermere. The Border Spell is an invisible wall that keeps the evil queen and her creepy servant, Shadow, locked inside Windermere forever." He waited a beat then squealed, "The end."

A smile tugged at the corner of Shimmer's lips. "Yes, well, I don't believe I've ever heard it told quite that concisely, but I suppose, in a nutshell, that is what happened."

"Told ya it wasn't a long story," Twink bragged.

Shimmer was about to comment, when a small black rock slipped through a crack beneath the door in the sky, hitting him on the head. "Ouch!" he gasped, rubbing the top of his point.

"Meteorite," Twink giggled.

"It's not funny," Shimmer snapped, bending down to pick up the glowing rock. A moment later, another one dropped from the sky and bounced off his rear end. The two boys locked eyes, trying to swallow their laughter.

"That reminds me," Twink grinned, turning to Ricky. "I brought you a present!"

Ricky blinked in surprise. "Wow, thanks!"

"I've just gotta find it," he muttered, slipping a hand-point down his leg. Half of his hand suddenly vanished!

"What happened to your hand?" Ricky cried out in alarm.

"Huh?" Twink answered, looking down. "Nothing happened to it. It's just in my pocket." He pulled his point back up, and the tip reappeared. Seeing the surprised look on Ricky's face, he pushed his entire hand back into his invisible pocket. Ricky paled as he watched it seemingly disappear.

Twink grinned. "I guess you don't have invisible pockets where you live, huh?" Ricky shook his head *no*, amazed at the existence of such a thing. Twink stuck his hand back into his pocket, searched around, then pulled out a small, black object. "Here it is! I brought you this all the way from Galdoren!"

Ricky took the object from the little star, then stared at what he was holding. He didn't want to offend Twink, but he already had one of these. It was a meteor ball, just like the one he had bought in the museum's gift shop. "Um, well, thanks," he mumbled.

"You're welcome," Twink replied, distracted by a nearby photograph of the constellations. "Hey! Is that *me?*" he squealed, pointing to a twinkling light behind Gemini.

Shimmer flew over to the picture in question, squinting to get a better look. "No, I don't think so. Although it does look like your cousin, Castor."

Ricky was about to shove Twink's gift into his pajama pocket when he noticed a tag with instructions hanging off the meteor ball. He tried to keep from laughing, as he didn't want to hurt Twink's feelings, but he couldn't help stifling a giggle at the ridiculousness of having directions on a ball. What could it say other than "*toss*" or "*bounce*"? He was surprised when he flipped the tag over and read:

Ages 10 and up. Adult supervision recommended.
1. *Do not bounce on any surface other than ground or bottom floor of a building.*
2. *Do not throw meteor at or near anyone's head.*
3. *Use extreme caution when throwing.*
            Warning: Do not use near open flame!

"Go ahead, try it!" Twink urged.

Shrugging, Ricky ripped off the tag, and bounced it on the floor. The moment the ball left his fingers, it began glowing red, and a flame burst from its tail. It ripped through the floor in a blur of fire, easily tearing through the concrete. Only a trail of smoke was left blowing in its path.

Ricky's mouth hung open as Twink sighed, "That's the only thing I hate about playing with meteors. You can only throw 'em once."

Shimmer stared at the smoking hole in the floor, shaking his head.

"Sorry," Ricky apologized. "I didn't know it would do that!"

"Think nothing of it," Shimmer replied. "The employees must be used to it by now. After all, this *is* a space museum. Must happen every day."

Ricky wasn't about to explain the difference between the museum's meteor balls and Twink's. Shimmer clapped his points together, eagerly announcing, "It's time to begin your adventure, Ricky. Soon, you will be standing in the gleaming halls of Galdoren Castle."

"Wait!" Ricky cried in alarm. "I want to know more. Like, why was *I* chosen? I mean, out of all the kids on Earth, why'd the king pick *me*?"

Shimmer contemplated Ricky's question then carefully said, "Well, first of all, you weren't just picked out of all the children on *Earth*, you were chosen from all of the children in the *universe*." Ricky's eyes widened in surprise as Shimmer continued. "And as to why King Shevre chose you, well, er, actually, he didn't." When Ricky's face began to fall, Shimmer quickly added, "A very powerful and high-ranking witch named Edna chose you! Quite unusual, really, as normally the Bureau of Interstellar Visitation handles these invitations. You see, every decade, one child from another planet is invited to spend three days in Galdoren. But this year, since Edna was nearing retirement, she was quite insistent that she get to choose the child." Smiling kindly at Ricky he added, "And she chose *you*."

"But, why?" Ricky pressed.

Shimmer shrugged. "I couldn't even begin to guess." Once again, Shimmer couldn't shake the feeling that something was not quite right. Only the evening before, his heart had nearly stopped when he went to brush his teeth and an image of Edna was floating in the water in his bathroom sink. She had insisted that he leave immediately and fetch the Earth child a full day earlier than scheduled.

Remembering the urgency of Edna's request, he clapped his hand-points together and announced, "Time to go! We don't want to get caught in traffic."

"There's traffic in outer space?" Ricky asked.

"Only during rush hour," Shimmer explained. "Now, I'll just zip up and open that door. It shouldn't take but a minute."

Alarmed, Ricky's head snapped up. "What? I can't leave NOW!"

The two stars exchanged curious glances. "But ... why ever not?" Shimmer asked.

Ricky paced up and down the long aisle, trying to figure out how to explain why he couldn't just fly off to another universe at a moment's notice. Sitting on the edge of a nearby armrest he began, "My sister will go ballistic if she wakes up and I'm not here! And my mom..." He shuddered, thinking of his mother's panicked reaction to his vanishing into thin air.

Shimmer smiled warmly. "Dear boy," he chortled. "No one will miss you, because I stopped time on Earth!"

"You stopped *time*?!?" he gasped.

Shimmer blushed a deep shade of blue then modestly replied, "It was nothing, really. Something every star learns when he's just knee high to the moon."

"Yeah," added Twink. "And I'm almost old enough to try it!" Turning to his uncle he began to plead, but Shimmer merely held up a point and firmly said, "Not yet, Twinkle. I told you, when you're eleven, and not a day before."

Twink muttered something under his breath and kicked a speck of stardust.

"Now, as I was saying," Shimmer continued. "I stopped time on Earth, and every living thing is under a powerful sleeping spell. They will not awaken until I return you three days from now and start time ticking again. So you don't have to worry," he assured Ricky. "No one will ever even know that you were gone."

Ricky pulled his cell phone from the pocket of his robe. He was astonished to see that it still said 11:59, even though at least twenty minutes had passed since he had come into the theater.

Twink's eyes widened when he saw what Ricky was holding. "What's *that?*" he gasped.

Ricky gave Twink a sideways glance. "A cell phone," he shrugged.

Twink hovered in the air, staring open-mouthed at the image of a video game that Ricky had set as his background. "How does it work?"

Ricky looked at the little star curiously and asked, "Don't you have cell phones in Galdoren?"

Twink shook his head *no*, unable to tear his eyes away from the amazing gadget. "I'll trade you for it!"

"No way!" Ricky answered, slipping the phone back into his robe. "I saved my allowance for months to get this!"

Shimmer rolled his eyes. "Twinkle, we really don't have time for this."

Ignoring his uncle, Twink reached inside his invisible pocket and dug around. When he pulled his hand-point out, it was wrapped tightly around a tiny green pixie, who was writhing furiously and sputtering like mad. Her wings were mashed down where Twink was clutching her, and her face was splotched bright green with rage.

"It's a pixie!" Twink announced proudly. Then he wrinkled his nose. His eyes began to water and he sneezed. And sneezed. And sneezed again.

"Bless you," Ricky automatically responded.

"Thanks," Twink said wiping his nose with his free point. "Pixie dust. I'm allergic."

The miniature pixie continued writhing and kicking and Twink had to talk loudly to be heard above her ear-splitting screeches. "So, wanna trade?"

Ricky backed up a pace, "Um, no thanks."

"Come on, she won't bite!" Twink coaxed. With that, the pixie leaned over and bit him.

"OW!" Twink yelled, dropping the pixie.

She zipped over to Ricky's face and angrily screeched, "Zeee zaxx zixellzee zerx zax!!!!" Then she smacked him on the nose with her wand.

"Ouch!" Ricky yelped, rubbing his nose. "What'd *I* do?"

The teeny fairie stuck a green tongue out at him then streaked up to the sky, slipping under the slimmest of cracks beneath the glittering door.

"Hey!" Twink shouted. "Come back! I won you fair and square!" But it was too late; the pixie had vanished.

"Hang on," Twink pleaded, searching another invisible pocket. "I may have something else to trade you."

"Um, no thanks," Ricky answered.

"As you can see, Ricky," Shimmer interrupted, flying between the boys, "there isn't a single problem with leaving now."

Ricky stared down at his feet, wriggling his toes. His head snapped up as he exclaimed, "Yes there is!" Curling his fingers around the bottom of his star-patterned shirt he blurted, "I'm in my pajamas!"

Chapter Two

THE ICE QUEEN

A pair of owls in a pool of silver moonlight hooted softly, show-ing little interest in the strange black fog blowing through Gal-doren Woods. Had they cared enough to look, they might have noticed a pair of ebony eyes gleaming darkly within that ominous-looking fog.

The mist blew quickly in and around the twisting branches until it came to Galdoren's border at the edge of the woods. Then it sud-denly stilled, its watchful eyes darting back and forth. It floated qui-etly above the shadowy moss, stopping when it bumped against an invisible wall. The mist flowed across the wall of magic until it felt a trickle of cold air.

"Windermere," the mist whispered, melting into the arctic draft leaking out of a hidden crack. Swirling into a thin line of vapor, it poured itself into the narrow opening. As the black smoke flowed into Windermere, it rose in the air, transforming into a dark and misty shadow. His filmy cloak left a trail of black mist as he moved silently over the pristine snow.

Shadow turned his face from the subzero winds, the bitter gusts stinging his sensitive eyes. Unlike his mistress, he despised the brutal cold of this desolate land. Their banishment to Windermere had been much harder on him than on his queen.

He stared through the invisible wall of magic known as the Bor-der Spell, longing for the lush landscapes and balmy breezes on the

Galdoren side. Not for the first time, he cursed the witches who had cast the spell so many years before. Meant to keep Shadow and his queen locked inside Windermere forever, the Border Spell had been neglected for several years now. And in that time, a tiny crack had begun to form—just wide enough for a trickle of air to escape. But what was a shadow if not air and mist?

"Did you bring it?" hissed an icy voice.

Shadow glided across the frozen sleet, stopping to bow at the feet of the woman before him. "Of course, your majesty," he replied. Yearning to stroke the creamy skin of her deathly-pale cheek, he instead knelt in a snowdrift, staring obediently down at the fur boots of his mistress.

"Were you followed?" she demanded, her gaze darting to the green trees on the other side of the spell.

"No, Your Highness, I traveled in my vaporous form." Shadow looked up and his breath quickened, as it often did when he looked into his queen's luminous grey eye. On the other side of her face was an empty eye socket, covered in a milky white membrane.

Queen Glacidia slipped her hand from the warmth of a fur muff. Holding her palm wide open, she commanded, "Give me the spell!"

Shadow reached inside his cloak, retrieving the prize he had brought his mistress. A delighted shiver crept up his spine as he recalled how easily he had slaughtered the alchemist and stolen this powerful enchantment.

As Glacidia reached for the charred page, a howling wind ripped the velvet hood from her head. As always, Shadow's heart pounded at the sight of his queen's magnificent hair. Sparkling braids of ice dangled from her scalp to her waist. Adorning her head was a crown made of frozen crystal that glistened in the moonlight.

"Allow *me*, Your Majesty," he panted, eager to feel those icy locks slide against the cool mist of his hands. As he tucked her glorious hair back inside her hood, he could almost feel a heart beating inside each frost-glazed strand.

"The Spell of Spilled Secrets," she breathed, caressing the parchment. But as she scanned the list of ingredients, her brow twitched angrily. Pointing a finger at the paper she snarled, "You *fool!* The spell is useless without this ingredient! Do you have any idea how rare this is?!"

Shadow opened his mouth to reply, but before he could utter a sound, she uncurled a finger and pointed it at him. Streaks of ice shot out from under her fingernail, stabbing the mist that formed Shadow's arm. He cried out in pain as his wound began oozing black smoke.

"BUT, MY QUEEN, LOOK!" he begged. With shaking hands, he reached into another pocket and retrieved a bottle.

Her lips curled into a twisted smile as she took it from him. "Powdered Centaur Hoof," she purred, reading the label. "How ever did you find it, my pet?"

"The alchemist," he breathed. "It was hidden amongst his potions."

She clicked a sharp nail against the bottle. "Fascinating," she drawled. "The king's own alchemist, harboring illegal spell ingredients? Then I suppose we did Galdoren a service by disposing of that monstrous criminal."

Shadow snickered, his hot breath forming white puffs in the arctic air.

Examining the contents of the bottle more closely she snapped, "Was there no more? This is barely even enough to conjure one spell!"

The shadow turned his face to the stinging winds. "No, my queen. That is all there was."

Stroking his wispy cheek she whispered, "Then you'd better pray the spell works the first time, my pet, as there isn't enough powdered centaur hoof to try it again, and centaurs don't live in Windermere ... *anymore*." She held her hand out to admire her shiny fingernails. "Pity. The fresher the ingredient, the more powerful the spell."

"Yes, Mistress."

Chapter Three

LOVE AT FIRST SIGHT

"I still don't understand why you want to change your clothes," Shimmer said, admiring Ricky's plaid robe and star-covered pajamas. They had just come out of the theater and were moving down the hallway toward Ricky's overnight gear so he could grab a tee shirt and jeans.

But before Ricky could answer, Shimmer scowled down at his nephew. "Twinkle! Will you PLEASE stop fiddling with those gadgets!"

Twink had been sidetracked by a display of early nineteenth century telescopes. Peering through the wrong end of one, the little star blinked in confusion. "This is a dumb invention," he said, tapping the glass repeatedly. "All it does is make everything look *smaller!*"

Ricky plucked him out of the air and dropped him on the other side of the telescope. "You look through *this* end."

"Never mind," Shimmer insisted. "Twinkle, stop playing with that thing! We're in a hurry, remember?"

Twink huffed then sped up to the ceiling, zooming past his uncle.

"There it is," Ricky whispered, pointing to his duffel bag.

"You don't have to whisper!" Twink called loudly. "Everyone on Earth is under a sleeping spell! Remem ...," Twink skidded to a halt in mid-air, speechless. He gasped as he looked down upon Ricky's sleeping sister. Her golden hair was fanned out across the pillow, her lovely face peaceful as she dreamed away, lost in a magical sleep. He sucked in his breath, feeling like he'd been struck by a bolt of lightning. He had never seen anyone so beautiful in his entire life. Speechless, he just dangled helplessly above her, his mouth hanging open.

Ricky grabbed his overnight bag and pulled out a pair of jeans and a tee shirt. He moved behind a large model of the moon to change in privacy.

Twink shook his head to clear it, then, still gazing adoringly at Allie, he asked, "What's her name, Ricky?"

"Huh?" Ricky poked his head out from behind a crater.

"The girl who's sleeping," Twink explained.

"Oh, that's just my sister, Allie," he answered, pulling an orange shirt over his head.

Twink twirled in the air, sighing dreamily. "Ellie? Ellie is the most beautiful name in the whole entire universe."

"Not Ellie, *Allie!*" Ricky corrected, zipping his jeans.

A dopey smile spread across the little star's face. "Oh, yeah, *Ellie's* okay, but *ALLIE* is definitely the most beautiful name in the whole entire universe!"

Shimmer shook his head at his nephew, then turned to Ricky, who was just emerging from behind the moon. "Do you have comfortable shoes?" he asked. "Because, obviously, Twink and I don't need them, but I have heard that it is very important for creatures without the gift of flight to have good walking shoes. Isn't that right, Twinkle?"

"What color are her eyes, Ricky?" Twink asked, looking down at the sleeping girl with a lovesick expression.

Ricky turned to Shimmer. "Don't worry," he said, shoving his feet into a pair of Nikes. "I've got awesome sneakers."

Twink zipped to Ricky's side and tugged on his sleeve. "Hey, Ricky! What color are your sister's eyes?"

Shimmer flew closer to examine the swirl on the sides of Ricky's shoes. "Is that some sort of ancient symbol?"

Ricky laughed as he began tying the laces. "Yeah, it's the ancient symbol for expensive shoes!"

Twink circled Ricky's head. "What color are they, Ricky? Are they blue? Huh? I'll bet they're blue! Blue's my favorite color!"

"What?" Ricky asked, confused.

Shimmer sighed, remembering his first crush. He gently nudged his nephew, "She's very beautiful, Twinkle, but we need to get a move on. King Shevre is waiting, remember?"

Ricky finished tying his shoes, took a deep breath, then announced, "Okay, I'm ready."

"Wonderful!" Shimmer beamed. Escorting Ricky down the long hallway, he turned back to his nephew. "Coming, Twink?"

"In a minute," Twink mumbled, unable to tear his eyes away from Allie.

As Ricky walked toward the theater, he began to grin—he was about to fly through a door in the sky to an enchanted kingdom in a faraway world! He shook his head in disbelief. Up until now, the farthest he'd been from Chicago was the Wisconsin Dells. And he'd thought *that* was exciting!

Shimmer stopped in mid-air and turned back to the sleeping bags where his nephew still hovered. Narrowing his eyes, he snapped, "Twinkle! It's time to go!"

Twink was torn. He knew he should go, but he couldn't seem to make himself leave. He thought he could happily hang there staring at Allie forever. Besides, he just had to know what color her eyes were. Chewing his lip nervously, he called back to his uncle, "Um, I'll be there in a minute. I have to use the little star's room."

Shimmer tapped his point impatiently in the air. "I told you to go before we left Galdoren!"

"I didn't have to go then." Twink whined convincingly. Crossing his hand-points behind his back he lied, "but I have to go *now*."

Shimmer let out an exasperated breath. "Very well. But hurry up!"

"I will, Uncle Shimmer! I promise!"

As soon as his uncle and Ricky were out of sight, Twink began pacing back and forth in the air, questioning his decision. But when he gazed down at the beautiful sleeping girl, he knew what he had to do.

He squeezed his eyes shut, twirled two times then concentrated with all his might. A tiny shower of purple stardust rained down upon Allie. She stirred and slowly stretched her arms above her head. As her eyes fluttered open, Twink squealed, "I KNEW IT! THEY'RE BLUE!"

Chapter Four

THE SPELL OF SPILLED SECRETS

Henry called up to the alchemist for the umpteenth time. Annoyed by the inexplicable silence, Henry bounded up the stairs two at a time. When he finally reached the alchemist's study, he knocked loudly, and was puzzled when no one answered. He tried turning the doorknob, but it was locked.

"Alchemist Magnus? Sir, is everything all right in there?"

Hearing no reply, he began to worry. He rattled off an incantation, bursting through the door the moment it opened. Surveying the room, his eyes fell upon the crumpled body of his teacher.

At his side in an instant, Henry listened for a heartbeat. Hearing none, he slowly stood and ran his hands through his shaggy brown hair, unsure of what to do. His eyes darted around the room again, stopping on *The Alchemist's Books of Knowledge.* He charged toward the bookshelves and started rifling through the volumes, looking for a spell to bring his teacher back to life. Momentarily elated when he found an entry on "reanimation," his heart sank when he saw the spell was designed for enchanted objects only. He continued to search through all of the spell books in Magnus's collection before finally giving up

Choking back a sob, he knelt at the alchemist's side. Unable to look at his teacher's deathly white face, he turned away from the corpse and noticed a gold leather book peeking out from under the desk. Curious, he reached around the legs of the desk chair and picked the book up off the floor. His eyes grew wide when he saw what he was holding: *My Incantations and Spells, by Theobald Magnus, Alchemist of the First Order.*

Tears blurred his vision as he turned back to the old man. He set the book aside and gently lifted the alchemist's head onto a cushion. As he did, Magnus's head wobbled unnaturally to one side. Henry jerked back when he saw the cruel red marks along the sorcerer's neck. Breathing hard, he stared wide-eyed at the corpse. His teacher hadn't died of old age … he had been murdered!

"Who did this?" he whispered. Shaking his head in disbelief, he tried to figure out why the murderer hadn't stolen Magnus's priceless book of magic spells. He was astonished that it had been left behind. *And why was the book scorched?*

He took a deep breath and wondered what his teacher would do in such a situation. *He would cast a spell to find out who did this,* he thought angrily. Determined to bring the murderer to justice, he stormed back to the small library of books and yanked Volume Six of the *Encyclopedia Magicka* off the shelf. There was a spell in there he had mastered recently that would help solve this mystery.

He flipped through the ivory pages until he came upon the spell he sought. "Revelation Enchantment," he muttered, as he scanned the list of ingredients. He was furious when he went to the laboratory at the back of the room and saw the broken potion bottles scattered across the floor. He carefully sifted through the shattered glass, gathering what he needed by scraping the loose powders into a spoon he had found on the alchemist's desk.

When the potion was finally finished, he shook it over the top of the mirror and loudly commanded, "Reveal to me the murder that happened in this room."

The mirror misted over, and as the fog began to clear, Henry could start to make out images. He was momentarily surprised when he saw a young Alchemist Magnus with a full head of brown hair and a cleanly shaved face. He had forgotten how the old man had enchanted all the mirrors to reflect him as he had been in his youth. He continued to watch the gruesome scene replay in the glass, sucking in his breath when he saw a dark fog rise up from under the door. "No," he whispered. "It can't be." He watched with growing dread as the black mist transformed into the shadowy image of a man. Frustrated that the mirror could not reflect sound, he nearly went mad wondering what the alchemist was saying. He clenched his fist angrily when he saw the shadow hold a jagged knife to Magnus's throat. The horrific scene continued to unfold before him, like a nightmare he couldn't wake up from, ending with the silent snap of his teacher's neck.

The mirror misted over again just as Shadow was reaching for a burning decanter. *At least the monster didn't get his hands on Magnus's spell book,* he thought with a sigh of relief, glancing at the golden book sitting on the desk.

King Shevre would need to be told at once. But would the king believe him? He barely believed it himself. How could Shadow have escaped? His blood ran cold as he wondered, *has Queen Glacidia escaped as well?*

It suddenly dawned on him that he would soon be speaking to the King of Galdoren. Who was *he* to talk to a king? He was nothing but a lowly farm boy studying to be an alchemist.

His hands shook as he reached for the bottle of travel dust that Magnus always kept by the window. He took a deep breath and wiped his sweaty palms across his frayed pants. He had to at least *appear* to be confident. After all, Galdoren's future might depend on the information he carried.

He was about to leave when a terrifying possibility crossed his mind. He grabbed the alchemist's spell book and began flipping through its charred pages. His mouth went dry when he came upon the ripped bits of paper near the end of the book. *Shadow had stolen a spell!* His heart pounded wildly as he tried to puzzle out which one. He closed his eyes, concentrating on all of the spells the alchemist had told him about. With each one he remembered, he tried to imagine how it would benefit the Queen of Windermere. His eyes suddenly popped open. "I know the spell you took!" he roared angrily, his fingers curling around the worn, leather binding. Just to be sure, he searched through the book two more times then slammed it shut, certain he knew what spell was missing.

As the sun rose over the horizon, he threw a handful of travel dust out the open window, calling, "Galdoren Castle!" Swirls of color began to twirl outside the window. Henry slipped Magnus's spell book into his pocket as he waited impatiently for the swirls to subside. When they finally did, the image of a castle floated in the air. Henry lifted the window a little higher then leaped onto the castle bobbing in the wind. His image sparkled, and within moments, both the castle and Henry had vanished.

It was dawn when Queen Glacidia finally completed her potion. She kissed the bottle of green liquid as it hissed and sparked inside. "The Spell of Spilled Secrets," she whispered.

Turning to the rays of sunshine peeking over the horizon, she spat, "For twenty years, I have been locked in this frozen wasteland! For twenty years, I have dreamt of *nothing* but escape!" A strand of ice slithered out of her hood. Standing straight up from her scalp, it hissed at the sky.

The witch swirled the bottle clutched in her hand, watching the potion fizz with green foam. Shadow shuddered with pleasure when she squeezed his shoulder. "But tonight, my pet, when you bring me the Serpent's Eye ... *tonight I shall finally break free!*" Her good eye glazed with a burning madness as she rose in the air. She brushed a finger along her empty socket, imagining herself pressing the gem into the folds of her flesh and seeing the world through those glittering facets. She could almost feel the power of the Eye coursing through her veins.

"That gem is rightfully mine!" she cried, spinning in the air. "And the moment I get it, every living creature in Galdoren will begin to *suffer* as I have *suffered* these twenty long years!" A blizzard howled in the distance as her cloak billowed in the shrieking wind.

And there, under the rays of the rising sun, Queen Glacidia chanted the incantation scrawled across the page torn from the alchemist's spell book. And as she chanted, she poured the green potion into the air before her. Sparks of green hissed and sizzled in the wind as she commanded, "Reveal to me King Shevre's secret—where has he hidden the Serpent's Eye?"

The empty bottle she was holding cracked under the pressure of her squeezing hand, showering the snow below with shards of broken glass. And although the skin across her palm was split wide open, not even a single drop of blood poured forth.

Within moments, thousands of tiny green specks sparkled in the sunlight as an image slowly formed in the air. A glowing green forest hovered in the breeze. Dark green footprints appeared in the air, moving forward through the tiny, floating forest. The footprints suddenly stopped before an enormous tree trunk. The massive tree sparkled and spun in the air before the queen's wide eyes. Within moments, the trunk itself opened, and the glittering footprints disappeared inside. The image showed with perfect clarity exactly how to access the secret passageways in and out of the tree.

Glacidia threw her head back and laughed. "King Shevre, you fool! Hiding the gem within an ancient tree? Did you think I wouldn't find it? And did you really think your pathetic Invisible Knights could thwart *me*? I AM THE QUEEN OF WINDER-MERE!" The winds shrieked and howled as she screamed to be heard above them. "And soon, King Shevre, *I* shall rule over Galdoren! AND YOU SHALL BOW DOWN TO *ME*!"

She lowered herself to the ground and turned her attention to the shadow quivering with excitement before her. "Assemble a squadron of assassins!" Pointing to the glittering forest still hovering in the air, she ordered, "Find this ancient tree and kill everyone inside. And do not return without my gem!"

"Yes, my Queen," Shadow bowed. He turned to mist and slipped through the crack in the Border Spell.

Queen Glacidia raised her hands to the sky, shooting icicles from her fingertips, laughing maniacally at the rising sun.

Chapter Five

THE INTERSTELLAR HIGHWAY

llie stretched in her sleeping bag, rubbing her eyes. She opened her mouth in a sleepy yawn, blinking against a flash of purple light. Turning to check on Ricky, her heart skipped a beat when she saw his empty sleeping bag.

She heard a voice call, "Coming Uncle Shimmer! Coming Ricky!"

Ricky?! Instantly awake, she yanked her sleeping bag off, grabbed her slippers, and went tearing down the hallway after the voice that had called her brother's name.

What's my idiot brother up to now? she thought with a mixture of anger and worry. She assumed the kid she was chasing had a purple flashlight, since she caught a glimpse of a bouncing purple light at the turn of every corner. The purple dot zipped down one hallway, then another, finally disappearing into the auditorium where she and Ricky had seen the constellation show.

Racing to catch up, Allie was nearly out of breath when she pushed open the theater doors. Her hands flew to her eyes, shielding them from the sudden burst of light. Peeling her fingers back, she was astonished to see a huge, glittering door hanging in the artificial sky. But her mouth dropped wide open when she saw a plump blue star standing next to her baby brother.

She was about to call Ricky's name when the star did something extraordinary; it started to spin, turning faster and faster as clouds of stardust pooled in the air. The star suddenly stopped spinning, puckered its lips, and gently blew. The clouds twinkled and twirled as they rose in the air, like enchanted spun sugar in a star-kissed sky. They spiraled up to the ceiling and bumped against the glittering door. A shower of stardust rained down upon the room as the door slowly slid open. There was a blast of thunder and a stream of dazzling colors spilled into the room.

Allie was bathed in a sea of rainbows when she opened her mouth to call her brother's name. But the instant she did, a strong gust of wind whipped out the open door, knocking her off her feet. Holding onto the back of a chair, she pulled herself up, fighting against the howling gale.

"RICKY!" she screamed again, only to be drowned out by the ear-splitting shrieks of the wind. It was so bright that she could just make out the silhouette of her brother against the glow of the star. Desperate to reach him, she pushed her way through the furious gusts, struggling to stay on her feet.

Through the hazy glare she saw the star tuck Ricky under its arm. "LET GO OF MY BROTHER!" she screamed as loud as she could, but her voice was lost in the roaring winds. Suddenly, the star began to move—*upward!* A growing dread consumed her as she fought her way toward them.

"OH NO YOU DON'T!" she shouted, flinging herself onto the star just as it started to fly. Allie hung helplessly from its bottom left-point as it continued to shoot up toward the door in the sky. Clutching the star as tight as she could, she was catapulted up at lightning speed. Her nightgown swirled around her as the winds raged even stronger. Certain the star was going to smash them all into the ceiling, she braced herself for the collision. But to her amazement, they continued to soar up. And up. And up.

Dangling several feet below her brother, she kept calling his name over the roar of the wind. But the words died on her lips when she saw the endless expanse of stars stretched out before her.

And they were flying straight into it.

Ricky was sure the shrieking winds were playing tricks on his ears, as he could have sworn he heard his name being called. Looking into the never-ending span of space, he grinned. The planets and moons became a hazy blur as Shimmer streaked faster and faster across the galaxy.

He was sorry that Twink was missing it, although he'd probably seen it countless times before. Both Shimmer and Ricky had been surprised when Twink had returned from the little star's room and zipped directly into Shimmer's pocket without even a word.

Ricky wondered how they could breathe in space, but they seemed to be traveling in some kind of invisible, air-filled vacuum. Shimmer had called it the *Interstellar Highway*. He said it was an express route through the universe created solely for use by celestial beings. He had mentioned that it was very popular with shooting stars in particular, as they were always in such a hurry.

A meteor shower lit up the sky, and Ricky once again thought he heard his name being called. He would have turned if he could, but Shimmer was clutching him much too tightly to move even an inch. So he just leaned back and enjoyed the fantastical ride through the galaxies.

Shimmer's bottom left-point felt like it was tethered to a weight nearly twice that of Ricky. Wondering if he had picked up some astral debris, he tried craning his neck to see, but flecks of space dust kept blowing in his eyes.

He turned off the Interstellar Highway at the Galdoren exit, but the unbalanced load he was carrying caused him to swerve into oncoming traffic. He crashed into a Pegasus and Ricky tumbled out of his arms. An instant later, the mysterious extra weight on his bottom left-point vanished as well.

Ricky fell through the outer rim of Galdoren's atmosphere, the sudden gravity dropping him like a rock. He landed roughly on the shiny curve of a moonbeam. His arms flailed at his sides as he tried to grasp the slippery surface. But it was no use—he slid down the moonbeam at breakneck speed, careening toward a jagged edge that ended abruptly in the middle of a dark nothingness.

Just as he was about to be hurled off, he grabbed hold of the edge, clutching his fingers tightly around the glowing beam. Dangling helplessly, he was shocked to see his sister barreling straight toward him.

Allie's feet smashed into Ricky, and they both plummeted through the air as it changed from the inky blackness of space to the hazy blue of a summer sky. They finally landed with a muffled thump on top of a fluffy white cloud.

"Oof," Ricky grunted, skidding to a halt in the thick haze.

"Ugh," Allie groaned, rubbing her backside. She looked up to see her brother standing before her in the mist. "Are you okay?"

Massaging his neck, he answered, "Yeah, I'm fine. How about you?"

"I'm okay," she replied as Ricky helped pull her up.

Assured that neither was hurt, the two siblings began arguing at once.

"What are you doing here?!" he angrily demanded.

"Saving your sorry butt!" Allie replied, shaking cottony fluff balls from her nightgown.

"My butt didn't need saving until you smacked into it!"

"I didn't smack into your *butt*, I smacked into your *head*! Or is it the same thing?"

Shimmer landed with a resounding plop beside them, splattering cloud fluff everywhere. Sucking in huge gulps of air he panted, "Are you ...," *gasp*, "... okay?"

"Yeah, we're both fine," Ricky grumbled, wiping bits of cloud off his shirt.

Shimmer staggered upright, then stared hard at the familiar-looking girl. Recognition suddenly dawned on him. "You're Ricky's sister!" he gasped.

Allie's eyes narrowed as she moved protectively between her brother and the star. "Stay away from him, you ... you ... kidnapper!"

Shimmer's face turned red as he sputtered, "Kidnap - ... kid - ... KID-NAPPER?!?"

"I wasn't kidnapped," Ricky insisted. "Unlike *you*, I was INVITED here!"

Allie looked around the blowing and drifting cloud. "And where, exactly, is *here*?"

"Galdoren," Ricky shrugged.

"Wait just a moment," Shimmer interrupted. "How is it that you're awake?"

"Yeah," Ricky grumbled. "How ARE you awake?"

"What do you mean, *how?*" Allie huffed, not knowing that she had been enchanted by a sleeping spell. "Some kid with a purple flashlight woke me up."

Shimmer's eyes grew wide. "A *purple* flashlight?" Bending his head to glare down at his invisible pocket he thundered, "TWINKLE! COME OUT THIS INSTANT!"

"Um, no thanks," a small voice answered.

"Twinkle, I'm waiting," Shimmer said firmly, tapping his foot-point.

The little star slowly poked his head out of the safety of his uncle's pocket. Allie gasped, thinking the star had appeared out of nowhere. Well, half a star anyway, as only his head was visible. Shimmer reached down and yanked his nephew all the way out.

Twink hovered nervously in the air, then, noticing Allie, he shyly mumbled, "Hello."

"Twinkle!" Shimmer scolded. "Why did you wake another Earth-ling? The invitation was only for Ricky!"

Twink chewed his lip nervously, then zipped over to his uncle's ear and whispered something.

Shimmer's gaze softened. "Her eyes? You had to know the color of her *eyes?*" Twink just dangled in the air, blushing. "Did you know that we were all nearly killed just because you wanted to know the color of her eyes?"

"Sorry," he muttered, shuffling his feet in the air.

Allie's heart melted at the sight of the lovesick star. "Well, no harm was done. We're all okay. Right, Ricky?" She nudged her brother.

"Huh?" Ricky was still trying to figure out why Twink would care what color his sister's eyes were. "Yeah, we're okay."

"So, what did you call this place again? Galdoren?" Allie asked, peering over the cloud tops toward the castle in the distance.

Shimmer sighed and began explaining to Allie all about Ricky's invitation, and how, inevitably, it seemed she was now invited too.

A short while later, as Shimmer was trying to figure out how to get them all to Galdoren Castle, Allie moved to get a closer look at the kingdom below. But when she took a step, she heard a muffled *squeak.* Lifting her foot, she saw a small ball of cloud fluff stuck to her slipper. Peeling it off, she heard another *squeak*. As the fluff began squirming in her hand, she shrieked and dropped it. The little puff ball continued to hover in the air, then slowly turned toward Allie. She was astonished to discover a face in the middle of the little cloud. Its lips were rosy pink and turned upward in a crooked smile. Two shiny black eyes blinked back at her.

"Squeak! Squeak!" the cloud chirped happily.

"Cirrus!" Twink yelped, surprised to see his friend. The little cloud bumped itself against Twink's outstretched hand-point in a kind of a high-five.

"What are you doing up here?" Twink asked.

"Squeak, squeak, squeak squeak," the little cloud answered.

"Babysitting?" Twink winced. "Are you at least getting paid?"

The little cloud shook back and forth in an angry "no!"

"Well, where's Nimbus? You didn't lose her, didja?" Turning to Allie, Twink explained, "This is my friend, Cirrus. Nimbus is his baby sister. He has to babysit her today 'cause their mom's at the cloudresser's getting pink highlights."

"Squeak!" Cirrus called loudly. A tiny voice answered from below. Cirrus floated down and nudged a teeny ball of pink fluff. The pink puff rose up to greet him, cooing and nudging against her big brother. The baby cloud gurgled and squeaked, its bright eyes blinking happily.

"She's so cute!" Allie gushed.

"Squeak squeak squeak?" chirped Cirrus.

"Cirrus wants to know if you wanna hold her." Twink translated.

Allie's eyes widened. "May I?"

Cirrus nodded. Allie reached out and pulled the baby cloud puff to her. She stroked its downy head, murmuring, "She's so soft ..."

Ricky was just about to pet her too when the baby puff squeezed her eyes shut and made a funny gurgling noise. Suddenly, little drops of rain fell onto Allie's hands.

"Ew!" Allie cried, letting go of the cloud to wipe her hands on her nightgown. "I think she just peed on me!"

Cirrus erupted in squeaky giggles. While Ricky joined in the chorus of laughter, Twink tried not to laugh since Allie looked so upset. "Well, at least she didn't have gas," he said comfortingly. "She farts lightning."

Both Allie and Ricky quickly scooted away from the cooing puff ball.

Peering over the edge of the cloud, Allie noticed a charming village below. She stared down at the old-fashioned rooftops, their quaint gingerbread shingles gleaming in the sun. The whole town looked like an illustration out of a children's storybook.

"Excuse me," Allie called to Shimmer, pointing down to the village below. "Can I get some clothes down there?"

Shimmer glanced at the Earth girl's clothing. "You don't like your dress?" he asked.

A smile played on Allie's lips. "Um, it's not a dress. It's a nightgown."

"Oh," the blue star replied, scratching his head. Having no experience with Earth clothing, he was completely baffled.

"It's just that I don't want to look stupid when I meet the king," Allie explained.

"I think you look pretty," Twink murmured.

"Well, regardless, we simply don't have time for shopping," Shimmer stated firmly. He peered over the top of the fluffy cloud, sighing wistfully. "It's been a long time since I last visited Village Square."

"But, Uncle Shimmer," Twink chirped excitedly. "We can get Rocket Dust down there!"

The older star's forehead wrinkled as he thought about Twink's suggestion. He suddenly realized that having Rocket Dust would indeed make their trip both faster and easier. "I believe you're right," he smiled, as Twink flipped with delight. "But only one store! And just for Rocket Dust!"

"What's Rocket Dust?" Ricky asked.

Twink's lips curved into a lopsided smile. "You'll see."

Allie sighed, staring longingly at the distant castle. The sun was beating down so that its gray turrets gleamed like silver. She could just make out slivers of stained glass windows sparkling in the sunlight. The castle stood at the edge of a never-ending sea, the turquoise water stretching into the distant horizon.

Between the castle and the town lay a lush forest. Allie tried to peer through the tangle of trees, but the thick layer of leaves covered everything in a canopy of green. On the far side, the forest gave way to a colorful patchwork of farmland. For a moment, Allie could have sworn she saw rows of gumdrops glittering in the bright sunshine. She rubbed her eyes, thinking it was a trick of the light.

Turning in the other direction, she stared off into the distance and a puzzled look crossed her face. As far as she could see, there was a swirling mass of white. A line of jagged mountaintops poked out of the blizzard, their rocky peaks covered in blankets of snow.

"Windermere," Twink whispered.

Something about the name caused Allie to shiver. "What *is* that place?" she asked, turning to face the little star. But Twink's mouth dropped open when he met Allie's eyes, and he temporarily forgot how to speak. He just hung in the air, smiling stupidly.

Allie turned her attention back to Galdoren Castle. Unable to believe that she was standing on a cloud, talking to stars and about to meet a king, she ruffled the stardust on Twink's head. "Thank you so much for waking me!"

"Yeah, right," Ricky muttered sarcastically as he came up behind them. "Thanks *a lot*."

"Well, time to get moving," Shimmer announced, clapping his points together. Turning to Allie and Ricky, he said, "I'll fly each of you down, one at a time." Far from the weightlessness of space, the dense gravity of Galdoren made carrying both of the children at the same time impossible—they would simply be too heavy.

Twink stomped his foot in the air. "But I can fly Allie down myself," he whined.

Shimmer raised a brow. "I think it might be best if *I* fly them both down."

"But Uncle Shimmer …," the little star protested.

Shimmer crossed his points over his chest. "Remember what happened when you tried to fly your friend Avalanche to the Wizardfest last week?"

"Oh, yeah." Twink mumbled, his cheeks turning a dark shade of purple. "Um, maybe *you* should fly them down."

Nodding his head in agreement, Shimmer asked, "Okay, who's first?"

Chapter Six

THE SPY
ON THE CEILING

Far from the lovely village that Allie had seen from the cloud tops, a large black bird hid within the shadows of Galdoren Castle. The Furvel fluttered her wings as she curled her talons tightly around a thick golden beam. It was one of many such beams adorning the ceiling of the king's private chamber. A smug expression crossed the bird's face as she looked down upon the luxurious room. It had been so much easier to sneak into the castle than she had thought possible—she'd simply flown in with the morning fog.

Careless creatures, she scoffed, preening her feathers.

Below those beady prying eyes, a small dragon slept peacefully on a velvet couch cushion. Lazy tendrils of smoke rose from his nostrils with each snore. Dark orange and black scales covered his little body, while a single orange wing rested peacefully on his back. It was precisely because he had only one wing that King Shevre had picked him from the litter. The king's heart had been touched by the sight of the flightless baby dragon, and he had taken him home that very day.

One of the many reasons the king had chosen this particular room as his private chamber was its location. Situated at the top of the castle's tallest turret, the room afforded spectacular views across his kingdom. There were many secrets hidden in this room, not the least of which was the window that faced west.

Up on the ceiling, the Furvel pulled her glossy black wings in closer when she heard the sound of footsteps approaching.

The heavy wooden door creaked open as someone entered the room. *The king himself,* the Furvel marveled. She nearly gave herself away with her startled intake of breath. She promptly closed her sharp beak. She had to be careful. *After all,* she thought, *what good is a captured spy?*

King Shevre strode across the gleaming marble floor and sank into his favorite chair. Turning to the nearby end table, he reached past his reading glasses and the latest edition of *The Galdoren Gazette* to lift a leaded glass decanter. He poured an amber liquid into a silver goblet and leaned back into the overstuffed cushions to take a leisurely drink. He much preferred this worn and tattered chair to the many sparkling thrones scattered throughout the castle. Precious metals like gold, silver and platinum were extremely hard against the Royal Buttocks.

A faun played a flute in a distant meadow and the sweet notes of its melancholy tune floated up to the turret, bringing a smile to the king's handsome face. Bright sunshine poured in through the open window, reflecting ribbons of light off a crystal statue that stood near his chair. Despite its beauty, the king's smile faded as he turned to stare at the magnificent statue. Glittering brilliantly in the morning sun, it looked as if it were made of diamonds. The glistening crystal had been sculpted into the shape of a beautiful woman. One of the woman's arms was reaching out, pointing at something. Her expression was so sorrowful that it was almost painful to gaze upon her lovely face. But by far the most achingly sad feature was the single teardrop frozen forever upon her cheek. A marble plaque was attached to her pedestal, on which the words *B'yardin Shatavna Myesto Troo* had been etched in gold. The king tenderly ran his fingers down her arm. As always, she was cold to the touch.

Dropping his hand, King Shevre stretched his long legs and set his goblet down. He removed his diamond cufflinks, carelessly tossing them onto the marble end table. Rolling up the loose sleeves of his white satin shirt, he once again regretted wearing formal attire on such a lovely spring day. The collar on his fur-lined cloak felt like it was choking him, and his velvet breeches made his legs itch. He wiggled his toes inside the knee-high leather boots, debating whether or not to remove them. Scowling, he remembered the hole in the toe of his right sock and opted to leave them on, lest his assistant, Roberts, catch him being "un-kingly." At least he hadn't worn his accursed crown. Roberts was always pestering him to wear the blasted thing. He had resigned himself to dressing the part of a king, but he drew the line at the crown.

Turning to face the western window, the king sighed heavily. Unlike the open window across the room, this one was made of a thick, clear glass. Years before, the king had ordered Alchemist Magnus to cast a spell upon it. Every time a certain flame-haired witch strolled through her faraway gardens, the glass was enchanted to mist over and clearly reveal her as if she were close enough to touch.

Frustrated when he saw that the view spilled all the way to the distant horizon with no sign of his lovely witch in sight, he slammed his fist on the table.

"Blast!" he shouted so loudly that the spy on the ceiling nearly lost her footing. She quickly dug her sharp talons more tightly into the golden beam.

Staring hard out the window, King Shevre willed the view to change. But the rolling meadows and faraway mountains remained the same.

His brow furrowed in worry. Weeks had passed since the glass had revealed his favorite witch, Serena. Brooding, the king yanked opened a drawer on the end table and pulled out a silver picture frame. He sank back in his chair, staring at the old photograph. Then a loud knock echoed across the room. Furious, he wondered who would dare to intrude on his privacy. Everyone in the castle knew it was strictly forbidden to disturb him when he was in this room, unless it was an emergency.

He tossed the picture back into the drawer, then angrily crossed the room. His heavy cloak billowed behind him as he stormed past the seldom-used throne, nearly knocking over an ancient silver mirror that wobbled unsteadily as he swept by. The little dragon squeaked a pitiful excuse for a roar, stretched his wing, and jumped down from the couch. He trotted over to defend his master against the intruder, then, thinking better of it, hid behind King Shevre's long legs.

On the other side of the door, the alchemist's young apprentice, Henry, stood trembling. He had only arrived at the castle a few minutes before, and had spent that brief time trying not to hyperventilate. Dark circles of worry ringed the young man's eyes.

The travel dust he had used was one of the alchemist's special concoctions. Before he retired, Magnus was required to spend the majority of his time at the castle. However, whenever he needed a moment to himself, he had secretly escaped to his beloved cottage in the woods. He had spent years perfecting a spell that would allow him to travel to and from the castle at lightning speed. Over time, he had tweaked the spell to enable him to materialize within several feet of the king himself (this was all very well and good until the time he materialized in the middle of King Shevre's bubble bath. Thankfully, the king was not in the tub at the time, but the incident did lead to additional tweaking of the spell).

And so it was that Henry found himself standing at the top of a long, winding staircase. Noting the curved walls surrounding him, he guessed he was in a turret. There was only one room at the top of those stone steps, and its door was currently closed. It had taken him several minutes to drum up the courage to knock on that door, as he knew the King of Galdoren must be on the other side.

The door in question suddenly swung open. Henry stared open-mouthed at the regal figure standing before him.

"Well? What is it?!" the king thundered. But as he stared down at the unfamiliar face, his eyes narrowed. Startled that an intruder had managed to slip past his elite squadron of knights, he quietly slid his hand over the hilt of his sword and asked, "Who are you?"

Henry gulped. "I'm Alchemist Magnus's apprentice, Henry." Staring up at the scowling face above him he quickly added, "Your M ... Ma ...," his voice suddenly cracked and went up an octave, "...je ... sty!"

Clapping the boy on the back, the king replied, "Ah, yes ... *Henry*. Magnus told me all about you. Said you were a natural—a born alchemist!"

Henry shrugged his shoulders modestly. "Um, may we speak in private, Your Highness?"

The little dragon trotted dutifully behind his master as the king led Henry into his quarters. "There is nowhere within the castle more private than this," King Shevre assured him. Curled up on the ceiling above, the Furvel's beak twisted into a cruel smile as she cocked her head to listen more closely.

The king motioned for the lad to sit, suppressing a smile when Henry sat on his hands to keep them from trembling. But his amusement ended the moment Henry stammered that the alchemist was dead. King Shevre had known Magnus all his life, and a lump formed in his throat at the news of his death.

But as Henry began telling his terrifying tale, a red rage boiled up inside the king. "Shadow," he breathed, clenching his fists. "There must be a crack in the Border Spell," he murmured, scarcely able to believe that Shadow had escaped Windermere.

"Um, Your Majesty? There's one more thing." Pulling the spell book from the folds of his tattered pocket, Henry held it out for the king to inspect. "I know what spell he took."

King Shevre flipped through the book until he came to the torn bits of parchment where the page had been ripped from its binding. His blue gaze settled upon Henry.

"It's called, 'The Spell of Spilled Secrets'," Henry started to explain.

"I know that spell," the king interrupted. Many years before, when he was a moonstruck teenager in love, he had begged Magnus to use it on Serena. The alchemist had refused, of course, insisting that the spell was too powerful to be wasted on adolescent crushes. But King Shevre had longed to know if his feelings for the witch were reciprocated. And the Spell of Spilled Secrets would allow whoever cast it to know any secret they desired …

The king's eyes widened as a chilling comprehension suddenly dawned on him. "The Serpent's Eye!" he bellowed. He leapt to his feet and crossed the room in three strides, stopping at a large mahogany dresser. He yanked open a drawer and began rummaging through it. "That spell can reveal where the gem is hidden. The Serpent's Eye must be moved from its current location at once!"

Unsure of how to help, Henry reached down and stroked the king's pet dragon behind the ears. As the dragon trilled contentedly, the king pulled a tarnished key out of the dresser drawer. He grabbed a gleaming silver box from the top of the dresser and opened it. A small statue of a woman wearing an emerald green cloak sprang up inside the box. The king fit the key into a hole in the back. As he turned the key, the statue began to spin, its green cloak billowing in the slight breeze.

Halfway across Galdoren, a bell began to chime in a modest home within the forest. An elderly woman bearing a strong resemblance to the woman in the green cloak gasped in surprise. She put down her teacup and stepped into her living room. There, on the mantel above the stone fireplace, stood an exact replica of the silver box in the king's chamber. She reached up, removed the box from the shelf, and opened it. The bell chimed more loudly as she searched the shelf for her key. The only difference between the two boxes was that when she opened *hers*, a miniature replica of King Shevre popped up. Finally finding the key, she turned it in the lock. The statue of King Shevre suddenly sprang to life.

"Hildy," the miniature king rumbled. "Assemble The Three and fly to the castle immediately."

Worry lines creased the old woman's ebony skin as she noted the fierce expression on the king's face. She quickly replied, "Of course, Your Highness. We will be there within the hour."

Back at Galdoren Castle, King Shevre nodded solemnly to the animated replica of the woman, then pulled the key from the lock. Her image suddenly stiffened and became a statue once again. He snapped the lid shut and tossed the key back into the drawer.

Henry's mouth fell open. *The Three?* Their powers were legendary. He had a sudden flashback to when Magnus had taken him to the Sorcerer's Convention the previous year. When his teacher had introduced him to The Three, Henry had been so star-struck he couldn't utter a word. After an uncomfortable silence, Magnus had apologized to the ladies, claiming Henry was suffering from the after-effects of a botched spell. Henry blinked back tears brought on by the unbidden memory. He was startled out of his daydream by the king's pet dragon, who jumped off the couch, landing on the floor with a soft thud.

As King Shevre moved past an exquisite tapestry of knights charging into battle, he couldn't help but think how ironically appropriate the image was. Shaking his head, he yanked on a thick gold cord that hung from the ceiling. Almost immediately, the hazy image of a man's face appeared in the air. The man looked up, and, noting the king, bowed slightly. "Yes, Your Majesty?" he inquired, dabbing his chin with a napkin. It was only the image of the man that floated in front of the king, as the man himself was actually seated in the castle kitchen, eating his breakfast.

"Roberts, ready the Blue Throne Room. The Three will be arriving shortly. Escort them there the moment they arrive."

Roberts' eyebrows shot up in surprise at the mention of The Three. But he merely nodded respectfully and said, "I will attend to it immediately, Sire." Although he enjoyed his job immensely, he wished that he could just once make it all the way through a meal before being summoned. Especially today, as the chef had prepared his favorite: chocolate chip waffles with maple syrup and whipped cream.

As Roberts' image began to fade, the king had a sudden thought and hastened to add, "Oh, and Roberts? Be sure to contact Shimmer and cancel that invitation to Galdoren."

"As you wish, Your Majesty," Roberts answered with a quick bow. His image hovered in the air for an instant more, then began to fade away, but not before the king spied his assistant sneaking a mouthful of waffles dripping in syrup.

King Shevre let out a long sigh, relieved that he had remembered to cancel that invitation. He shuddered to think how dangerous Galdoren would be for an Earth child with Shadow on the loose.

Turning to Henry, the king grabbed the stunned teen's hand and shook it firmly. "Galdoren owes you a great debt, young Master Henry. Thanks to your quick thinking, The Three should have time to move the Eye to a new location as well as devise an enchantment to trap Shadow or anyone else who tries to steal the gem."

Henry muttered an embarrassed, "I really didn't do much of anything."

The king placed a comforting hand on the boy's shoulder as a pained look crossed his face. "I'm sorry about your teacher. I had nothing but admiration and affection for that man." He smiled sadly. "He was like an uncle to me, you know. As far back as I can remember he lived here at the castle. Until recently of course ..." His eyes suddenly turned hard as he fixed Henry with a steely look. His voice became cold as ice. "I promise that we will catch the demon who murdered him." Through clenched teeth he added, "And he will pay dearly ... very dearly." In that moment, Henry almost felt sorry for Shadow.

Noting the dark circles that ringed the boy's weary green eyes, the king's voice softened. "It looks like you could use some rest. Why don't you stay? When you get to the bottom of the stairs, turn left. There's a modest bedchamber there that you are welcome to use. Now, if you'll excuse me, I have an army to ready." The king gestured for the boy to leave ahead of him as he whistled for his pet. "Come, Pookie," he commanded, wincing with embarrassment at the sound of the dragon's name. Why he had agreed to allow his advisor's nephew, Twink, to name his pet was beyond him. Unable to fly, the little dragon trotted obediently behind the king, his one wing flapping limply in the breeze.

Up on the ceiling, the Furvel began to dance in celebration and nearly lost her footing. *My queen will reward me greatly for this news*, she thought excitedly, hopping from talon to talon. Then she spread her wings and glided out the open window, turning to fly east—toward Windermere.

Chapter Seven

GOSSAMER'S GIFT SHOP

Village Square was the most popular shopping district in all of Galdoren. Unicorns clip-clopped down cobblestone streets and, every now and then, one would stop to nibble at one of the flowerboxes that hung from every window. Rows of charming shops stretched from one end of town to the other, with silver birds cooing from the awnings above.

Shimmer splashed his face with water from a nearby fountain, exhausted after the long flight. Far from tired, Allie and Ricky stood in the middle of the sidewalk gawking at the astonishing sights before them as Twink hovered in the air with a bored expression on his face.

"Cool!" Ricky gushed, racing toward the window of Harold's Heraldry and Sword Emporium. A poster stuck to the glass showed a handsome knight slaying a dragon as a swooning princess looked on. The caption read, "Make your next rescue one to remember with a Mach 1 series sword (a *Harold's* exclusive)." And there, just beneath the poster, was a gleaming sword.

"Wow," Twink breathed. Turning to his uncle he begged, "Can I add that to my birthday list?"

"The princess or the sword?" Ricky snickered.

"Both," Twink said with a smile, turning his hopeful eyes to Shimmer.

"You're too young for *either*," Shimmer answered, giving his nephew a hard look.

Allie laughed, then turned her eyes to the jars of *Sir Galoric's Sword and Armor Polish* stacked behind the sword. "Even a damsel in distress wouldn't want a knight in tarnished armor," she read aloud with a smirk.

Twink nudged Allie and pointed to the window of a nearby jewelry store. "If I could, I'd buy you one of *those*," he said shyly. Crowns, scepters and magic wands glittered beneath a sign hawking their "On-site wand repair."

"Ohhh, that's so sweet!" she gushed, ruffling the stardust on his pointy head.

Just then, the village clock began to chime. Ricky turned to Shimmer, his brow creased in thought. "I wish you hadn't stopped time back on Earth."

"Really?" Shimmer seemed surprised. "Why ever not?"

"Because then I wouldn't have to go to school on Monday—'cause I wouldn't be there!"

"*School?*" Twink snickered. "You actually have to go to *school?*" Then he doubled over with laughter, flipping in the air as he giggled.

Ricky's eyes narrowed. "You mean no one in Galdoren goes to school?"

Twink tried to say *no*, but he was still laughing too hard.

"Twinkle! This is not the way we treat guests in Galdoren! King Shevre would be very disappointed in your behavior. I know I am."

Twink's smile was instantly replaced by a look of remorse. "Sorry, Uncle Shimmer."

"Don't apologize to *me*," Shimmer replied, nodding toward Allie and Ricky.

Twink flew over to hover directly in front of the kids. "I'm sorry," he began. Biting his lip he added, "I'm sorry you have to go to school," and helplessly burst into another fit of laughter.

"TWINKLE!" Shimmer pursed his lips then explained, "You see, the children in Galdoren are all given Sleep Phones when they turn four."

"What are Sleep Phones?" Ricky asked.

"They're tiny earphones that are placed into children's ears just before they go to sleep. Then, during the night, the Sleep Phones teach them everything they need to learn for their age. For example, four-year-olds learn the alphabet, colors, shapes and numbers while they sleep. Five-year-olds learn simple addition, subtraction and spelling. As they get older, the lessons keep getting more challenging. Then, when a child turns eighteen, he or she chooses which career they would like to pursue, and they get the appropriate Sleep Phones. Except, of course, for the fields that require on-the-job training such as knights, alchemists and rune-makers."

The kids' mouths fell open. Ricky remained speechless as Allie turned to Twink and asked, "Do you have to wear them every night?"

"Nope," Twink bragged. "Only Monday through Thursday. And I don't ever have to wear 'em on holidays or summer vacation, right Uncle Shimmer?"

Shimmer smiled indulgently at his nephew. "Right, Twink," he answered, stopping in front of an old-fashioned door. "Ah, my favorite store in Galdoren, The Book Nook." Putting his hand-point on the doorknob he added, "I think we have time for one extra stop."

Twink stomped his foot-point in the air, loudly complaining, "Not the Book Nook, Uncle Shimmer! It's so B-O-R-R-R-I-I-N-N-G!"

Ricky smirked, "Maybe you should go to school to learn how to S-P-E-L-L!"

Twink glared at Ricky as Shimmer pushed open the creaky door and led the children into the musty-smelling shop.

"Welcome," a soft voice greeted from above.

Allie looked up and was surprised to see a woman floating on a small carpet.

"Are you looking for anything in particular today?" asked the shopkeeper, smoothing the fringe on her flying carpet.

"No, no. We're just browsing," Shimmer answered.

Allie marveled at the rows upon rows of bookshelves. One set of bookshelves displayed the Galdoren Times Bestseller List, along with all of the corresponding books. Allie noticed there were only two copies left of the number one selling book in Galdoren: *Breaking Dusk, (The Sunset Saga, Book 4)*.

Ricky glanced at the table of non-fiction books, intrigued by titles like *The Soothsayer's Guide to a Brighter Future* and *The Strange Disappearance of Duke Albert*. As he rounded a corner, he nearly knocked into a stand displaying the wildly popular *Witch's Brew for the Soul* series.

Shimmer pulled a book off a shelf in the children's section. "My friend's daughter loves this book!"

"Aurora?" Twink wrinkled his nose at the mention of her name. The Borealis Family were old friends of his uncle's, and Aurora was their only child. A year younger than Twink, she irritated him to no end.

Ignoring his nephew, Shimmer handed the book to Ricky.

"That's a baby book," Twink sneered, curling his lip at the picture on the cover. It was an illustration of several fluffy kittens pawing at the title, *Kitty and Company*.

Shimmer let out an exasperated breath. "What do *you* think, Ricky?"

Allie watched with interest as her brother opened the book. Two cats suddenly leaped out of the binding. Ricky was so startled that he dropped the book. Six more cats and three kittens fell off the open page, mewing loudly. Some of the kittens scampered up the aisle while the remaining cats began sharpening their claws on a nearby stack of dictionaries.

"Mrrrow! Meow meowrrr!"

"Mrowr meowr mrrowr meow!"

The noise was ear-splittingly loud.

The shopkeeper zoomed her carpet over to Ricky, shouting to be heard above the screeching cats. "CLOSE THAT BOOK AT ONCE!"

Ricky slammed the book shut. The moment it closed, all of the cats vanished and it was instantly quiet. Both Ricky and Allie just stood there, astonished.

"I expected better manners from Earth children," the shopkeeper sniffed. She gave them a stern look, then steered her carpet back toward the register.

"Hey, Allie!" Twink called, tossing her a book. "What do you think of this one? It's my favorite!"

Allie caught the book and read the title, *The Top Ten Beaches in the Universe*. It didn't look that interesting, but she didn't want to hurt the little star's feelings, so she opened it to the first page. A stream of green seawater sprayed out of the book and splashed her in the face.

"What the—" she sputtered as another wave gushed off the page, drenching her.

Blinking the dripping water from her eyes, Allie stomped over to a giggling Twink and shook the book over his head. Dozens of fish poured out of the binding, bounced off his points, and landed with a splat on the floor. When he opened his mouth to laugh, a huge wad of seaweed shot out of the book and got caught in his teeth.

"Blecchh!" he choked, spitting the seaweed onto the fish-laden floor. Ricky was laughing so hard that he dropped his copy of *Kitty and Company*. A dozen cats leaped from the book onto the helpless fish. Cats and fish were sliding down the wet aisle when the shopkeeper glided back into sight.

Pointing a shaking finger at the children, she yelled, "SHUT THOSE BOOKS THIS INSTANT!"

The children slammed the books shut, and all of the fish, felines and seawater instantly vanished. Allie was stunned to find that she was now completely dry. As the shopkeeper glared at them, Shimmer sheepishly wrapped his points around the children and quickly led them toward the exit.

In his haste to get out, Ricky nearly stumbled into *The Complete Set of the Encyclopedia Magicka*. The display wobbled and swayed, but luckily, only the ad proclaiming it to be "the perfect gift for the alchemist in your life" fluttered to the ground.

As they hurriedly made their exit, Twink stuck his head back into the open door. "Thank you very much," he called in his most polite voice. The shopkeeper slammed the door in his face.

"Well, er, I suppose we should go get that Rocket Dust now," an embarrassed Shimmer stammered.

Crossing the street, they noticed a small crowd gathered around a fountain. A cluster of fairies and wood sprites were chatting amiably, most of them carrying shopping bags.

"Twink!" a boy's voice called out from amidst the crowd. "Hey, Twink! Over here!"

Everyone turned in the direction of the voice, but all they saw was a stick waving behind the heads of some fairies.

"Avalanche!" Twink squealed excitedly, zooming toward his friend.

A little snowman moved out from the crowd to greet Twink. Staring intently, Allie realized Twink's friend was not a snow*man*, but a snow*boy*.

"Hiya, Mr. Shimmer!" the snowboy called cheerfully, pulling off his baseball cap and flipping it in the air.

"Nice to see you, Avalanche," replied Shimmer, patting the boy's smooth white back.

Noticing Ricky and Allie, the snowboy's licorice lips lifted into a crooked smile. "Who are your friends?" he asked Twink, catching his cap and putting it back on his head.

Twink sailed over to the kids. "This is Ricky, and this," he smiled adoringly at Allie, "this is ... this is ...," his sentence trailed off dreamily.

"Hi, I'm Allie." She extended a hand, which Avalanche shook enthusiastically. Allie let go quickly, worried she might snap off one of his twig fingers.

Twink beamed proudly. "They're from Earth!"

"EARTH!" Avalanche's coal eyes nearly popped out of his head. "Wow."

"Yeah, wow," Twink sighed, staring at Allie. He nudged his friend, whispering loudly, "Smell her hair, it smells like flowers."

Avalanche shot up a brow, then casually strolled past Allie while she pretended not to notice. When he was behind her, he leaned over and inhaled deeply. A funny look fell over his face. "Ah– " he squeezed his eyes shut as they began to water. "Ah– AH– ACHOO!" His carrot nose flew off his face and landed with a splash in a nearby puddle.

Allie's jaw dropped. She had never actually seen anyone sneeze their nose off before. But the snowboy just reached down, grabbed his nose, and stuck it back on his face. The carrot, however, was now placed in the middle of his cheek rather than the center of his face. Nobody said a word, however, as they were all much too polite.

Just then, a small white cat crawled out from behind the snowboy. The cat was made of two snowballs, with an icicle tail and whiskers.

"Aw," Ricky bent down to pet the little snowcat. She purred happily, rubbing her cheek against the boy's leg. "What's her name?"

Avalanche shrugged. "I dunno. She's a stray. She just wandered into my yard this morning."

As Allie leaned down to pet her, the cat flopped onto its back, hoping for a belly scratch.

"She's not even cold," Allie marveled, rubbing the cat's tummy.

Avalanche looked confused. "Why would she feel cold?"

"Because ...," she looked into the snowboy's questioning eyes. "Never mind."

The cat flipped over again and stretched. Then she stood up, wrapped herself around Ricky's ankle and purred loudly.

"Wow, she really seems to like you," Avalanche noted with surprise. He pulled a piece of coal off his midriff, blew on it and rubbed it against his chest. Satisfied it was shiny enough, he popped it back onto his belly.

Ricky lifted the little snowcat in his arms. She looked up at him and wrinkled her button nose. "Mrrowrr," she said in a friendly greeting. Nuzzling against him, she closed her eyes and fell asleep. "I like you too, Snoball," Ricky cooed softly.

"Oh no," warned Allie. "Don't name her. If you name her, you know you'll want to take her home."

"What's wrong with that? I think she'd be very happy at our house," Ricky stubbornly insisted.

"Don't you think Mom might notice that your new cat is made of frozen water?"

Just then, a large white-haired woman ran out of a nearby gift shop. As she ran, her enormous silver wings flapped behind her. Apart from her wings, she looked like a storybook grandma, with her round spectacles, flowered apron, and white hair piled atop her head.

"Shimmer!" she called, holding a hand to her chest as she fought to catch her breath. "Thank heavens you're here! I've been trying to reach you!"

"What is it, Gossamer?" Shimmer asked, his brow knitted in worry.

She reached into her apron pocket and pulled out a wad of tissue. "Oh, Shimmmmerrrrrrrrr!" she wailed loudly, then noisily blew her nose into the tissue.

Shimmer looked flustered. "Gossamer! What is it? What's happened?" His concern only seemed to make her cry harder. The kids shifted uncomfortably as Shimmer murmured, "There there now. Everything will be okay."

She dabbed at her watery eyes with the already wet tissue, and sniffled, "Shimmer, I really must speak to you." She finally seemed to notice they weren't alone. Smiling weakly at the children she said, "Hello, Twinkle dear. And hello Twinkle's friends." She reached into her deep pockets and pulled out several lollipops. "Would anyone like some candy?"

Shimmer shook his head *no* as Twink reached for a sucker. "Gossamer, I insist you tell me what's wrong!"

Smoothing her skirt, she nodded toward the children. "Perhaps we can talk in private?"

Avalanche interrupted, saying, "I've gotta go anyway. I promised my mom I'd shovel the driveway before lunch. Bye, Earth kids! See ya soon, Twink!" Then he raced off down the cobblestone street.

Shimmer turned to the children. "Twinkle, why don't you show our guests around Gossamer's shop?"

Gossamer nodded approvingly. "That's a wonderful idea! I just got in a batch of self-shuffling cards and there's a new exhibit in the Sea Nymph gallery at the back of the store."

Shimmer choked. "Gossamer! Those paintings aren't suitable for children!"

Turning to Allie and Ricky, Twink whispered, "Sea nymphs don't wear any clothes!"

"Actually, Gossamer," Shimmer said as the kids giggled behind him. "We were just on our way to your shop. We are in desperate need of Rocket Dust."

Gossamer beamed. "Then you're in luck. I got a new shipment in this week."

"Excellent," Shimmer replied, leading everyone across the street toward her store.

A wooden sign above the door spelled out the words *Gossamer's Gifts* in bright, hand-painted letters. Allie smiled at the quaint sound of a jingling bell when Shimmer opened the door.

Waking up with a yawn, Snoball jumped out of Ricky's arms and landed with a soft thud on the worn wooden floor. Gossamer reached into her pocket and pulled out a toy mouse. Tossing it to Snoball, she turned to Ricky and winked. "You're not the only one with a snowcat."

Snoball leaped at the mouse and began batting it across the floor. She chased it behind a nearby counter and disappeared from sight.

"Don't worry," Gossamer told Ricky. "She'll be fine." Turning to Allie she smiled. "That's a lovely dress, dear."

Allie resisted the urge to roll her eyes. "It's not a dress, it's a nightgown."

Gossamer raised a brow in surprise. "Really?"

Twink tugged on Allie's arm. "C'mon, let's check out the wrapping paper!" Then he zipped down an aisle lined with self-stirring teaspoons and bottomless cookie jars.

"Wrapping paper?" the siblings asked in unison. Shrugging, they followed Twink down the long aisle.

Sighing dramatically, Gossamer lowered her voice to a whisper, "Follow me." She led Shimmer down a musty hallway stacked with unopened boxes and through a door marked, "Private." Once inside, Shimmer had to navigate his way around the clutter jammed into her cramped office. The wobbly coffee table was overflowing with gossip magazines, porcelain unicorns, dusty crystal orbs, and several dishes of candy. Her desk was barely visible beneath the piles of invoices, receipts and file folders. A chipped coffee cup and an enormous bowl of candy served as paperweights atop a stack of bills.

Patches of faded pink wallpaper peeked through the crowded shelves lining her walls. Each shelf was packed with dozens of snow globes in every size, shape and color. Gossamer's extensive snow globe collection spilled over onto an enormous display case that rose to the ceiling, each of its shelves brimming with the round glass ornaments.

Shimmer carefully made his way to a cozy chenille couch and sank into its deep cushions. Tucking her wings in behind her, Gossamer eased into a chair then promptly reached for a handful of candy.

"Now, Gossamer, tell me what's made you so unhappy," Shimmer said worriedly.

"Oh, Shimmer," she began, swallowing a large gumdrop. "I'm just worried sick." Her lower lip began to tremble. "You remember my nephew, Egmund, don't you?" Shimmer nodded as she continued. "Did you know that he was promoted?" Seeing the surprised look on her friend's face, she nodded proudly. "He's now a colonel in the Royal Guard!" Shimmer raised his brow, clearly impressed.

"Shimmer," Gossamer's voice dropped to a whisper, even though they were alone. "He sent me a coded message this morning." She reached into her pocket and retrieved a small handful of shimmery dust. Her hand shook as she tossed it into the air.

The dust sparkled and twirled, then slowly formed itself into letters. Shimmer paled as he read the short paragraph glittering before him. Not believing his eyes, he read it again. "*Shadow? Escaped?*" Gossamer nodded as she blew her nose. "He must be mistaken," Shimmer breathed. "That's impossible."

"No," she said, pocketing her spectacles to dab her wet eyes. "It's not."

"But Gossamer, that would mean … it would mean …," he couldn't finish his sentence.

She placed a warm hand over his. "I know, dear. That's why I've been such a wreck." She moved her hand to grab another helping of candy.

Unable to sit still, Shimmer glided to the large window next to Gossamer's cluttered desk. Gazing out through the streaky glass, he saw the Galdoren flag fluttering in the breeze above the entrance to

Village Hall. Beyond the building, he could just make out the snow-capped peaks of the Windermere Mountains off in the distance. "Has the king been informed?"

Gossamer nodded. "That's how my nephew learned of it. King Shevre briefed his officers before dispatching the army to the Windermere border." She bit her lip. "How long until ...," she stared out the window in the direction of Windermere. "How long until *she* escapes too?"

Shimmer's eyes widened with concern. The room was silent except for the crunching of chocolate maltballs.

The children watched Twink zip along the shelves of wrapping paper. Finally finding one he liked, he pulled the roll off the shelf.

"Watch this!" he called.

He unrolled the gift wrap, displaying a pattern of chefs holding birthday cakes, followed by lines reading, *Happy Birthday.*

"What's the big deal? It's just wrap—" Ricky was interrupted by one of the chefs.

"Do you mind?" asked the chef, sticking his head out of the paper. "We were just about to begin the song. Now, who's the lucky birthday boy or girl?" he asked, turning from Allie to Ricky to Twink. The other chefs began lighting all of the candles on all of the cakes.

Twink pointed to Allie. "She is!"

Before Allie could say anything, the chefs began singing a rollicking chorus of *Happy Birthday.* When they had finished, they all stared expectantly at Allie.

Another chef leaned out of the wrapping paper and whispered to Allie, "You're supposed to blow out the candles."

Stunned, she bent down and blew on the paper. All of the candles on all of the cakes flickered off. The chefs suddenly went still, as the images returned to ordinary-looking wrapping paper.

Twink rolled it back up. "Wanna pretend it's *your* birthday this time, Ricky?"

"Um, no thanks."

Noticing the different designs on the many papers Allie asked, "Do they all do that?"

"Sing happy birthday?" Twink asked, confused.

"No, I mean, do they all move and talk?"

"Yeah, sure. Doesn't wrapping paper on Earth?" The kids shook their heads. "Your planet sounds boring," Twink observed.

Ricky grabbed a roll covered with pictures of dinosaurs, while Allie reached for a pink and blue paper decorated with babies and rattles.

Allie unrolled hers first. Dozens of babies yawned and cooed. "Aw, that's so CUTE!" Allie squealed delightedly. Then Ricky unrolled his. A stegosaurus bellowed as a T-Rex roared. Suddenly, all of the babies on Allie's paper began to cry.

"Shhh, shhh," Allie tried comforting the babies, but it was no use. The dinosaurs roared louder, which only made the babies scream harder.

"WAHHHHH! WAHHHHH!"

"RRROAR! RRROAR!"

The noise was deafening.

Twink dove under a shelf and Ricky covered his ears as Allie rushed to close her roll of paper. At last, there was only one baby showing. He sniffled then shoved his thumb into his mouth. Allie was just rolling up the end of her paper when a milky white liquid shot up from inside the roll.

"Ew, spit-up!" Twink said as he scooted away from the smelly white puddle.

Ricky hurriedly began rolling his dinosaur paper back up. Just as it was almost closed, a T-Rex stuck its head out and bit Ricky's finger. "Ouch!" he cried, dropping the paper. Twink sailed over, closed it up, and put it back on the shelf.

"Shimmer," Gossamer said softly, joining him at the window. "All those years ago, when we were watching over the Serpent's Eye, did you ever wonder what would happen if Glacidia escaped and—it's unthinkable, I know, but—what if she got hold of the Eye?"

Shimmer shrugged. "I tried not to think about it. I was just so relieved that she was finally banished from Galdoren and imprisoned along with that monster, Shadow. And besides, I was so proud that the king entrusted us with guarding an object so powerful."

"You never thought that they might find a way to get out of Windermere?"

Shimmer stared out the window toward the distant castle. "No, Gossamer, I didn't. I had complete confidence in the power of The Three to seal the border." He sighed. "Shadow will be after the Serpent's Eye now."

Gossamer nodded, chewing nervously on her bottom lip. "Do you think he'll find it?"

"I don't know, Gossamer. It's hidden very deep within the woods. And no one has ever been able to get past the Invisible Knights. Still ...," he sighed, turning away from the window and leaving the rest of his thought unspoken. He pulled a snow globe off a nearby shelf and shook it, trying to calm a growing sense of dread as he watched the snowflakes drift slowly toward the bottom.

Gossamer seemed torn between wanting to say something and remaining silent. Finally, she began, "Shimmer, when we were watching over the Serpent's Eye, before it was hidden ...," her voice trailed off. She played with the silver chain dangling from her neck. "I need to tell you—" she stopped suddenly, unable to finish her sentence. Her eyes began brimming with tears again.

"What, Gossamer? You need to tell me *what*?"

She moved from the window, her lip quivering as she fiddled with a key hanging from the end of her necklace. "Nothing Shimmer. Nothing at all." She turned her head so he couldn't see the tears slip from her eyes, falling into the bowl of chocolate maltballs below.

Chapter Eight

THE GUARDIANS
OF GALDOREN

King Shevre swept into the Blue Throne Room. "Forgive me, ladies, for summoning you on such short notice."

Three hooded figures stood around a sterling silver drink cart near the back of the lavish room. The two in emerald green cloaks sipped daintily from their teacups as the third gulped down the contents of a jeweled goblet. Something about the third one made the king's brow furrow. Why was she wearing a plain brown cloak instead of the trademark emerald green of The Three? He raised a brow at the hot pink boots she kept tapping nervously against the marble floor. Just as he was getting ready to ask about her strange attire, one of the women in green set down her teacup and pushed her hood back. Her weathered skin was covered in wrinkles, and her hair had long ago turned silver. She was short and plump and wore a brilliant smile on her face. She also happened to be his only living relative, as well as one of his favorite people in the entire world.

"Aunt Sharonna," he said, smiling for the first time since hearing Henry's horrifying news.

"Come give your favorite auntie a kiss," she beamed at him. He quickly complied, his long legs carrying him across the room in just a few strides.

"I've missed you," he murmured, opening his arms.

Sharonna buried herself in his tight embrace. "If you missed me so much, why haven't I heard from you in weeks? Is your Spell-O-Phone broken? Someone steal your writing wand?"

"Sorry, Auntie. I've been a little busy around here. You know, ruling the country and everything?"

"Hmph, too busy to call the old woman who raised you?" she scolded, even as she planted kisses on his cheeks.

"Oh, for heaven's sake, Sharonna!" groaned the second woman in emerald, as she too, threw her hood back. She was the spitting image of the little statue in King Shevre's silver box. The lines on her coffee-colored skin grew deeper as she furrowed her brow. "Stop nagging the boy! He's the King of Galdoren! Don't you think he might have more important things to do than to chat with an old fart like you?"

The king winced. "Now, ladies. Let's not say anything we'll regret."

Ignoring her friend's insult, Sharonna pinched her nephew's cheeks in her chubby fingers. "What a handsome boy! Haven't I always said what a handsome boy he is, Hildy?" She brushed a stray lock of hair from his eyes. "You need a haircut, dear." Standing back, she scrutinized him. "You look like you've lost weight. Are you eating enough?"

He let out an exasperated breath. "Aunt Sharonna, I have seventeen cooks in my castle."

Hildy snorted. "They're probably all using *your* recipes, Sharonna. THAT'S why the boy is malnourished."

The king gritted his teeth as he fought to control his temper. "I am *not* malnourished, nor underfed. Now, can we please get to the point of this meeting?"

"Yes, dear. What is this emergency you summoned us for?" asked Sharonna. "Is that leprechaun bothering you again? I told you before, just ignore him. Bullies are only looking to get a rise out of you. And for goodness sake, don't blast him with that vomit spell again!"

King Shevre leaned forward against a jewel-encrusted throne, tightly grasping its golden armrests in frustration. He took several calming breaths, and through clenched teeth replied, "Aunt Sharonna, I was twelve years old when that happened. I can fight my own battles now, thank you." He took another deep breath then crossed the room to the polished mahogany table and pulled out two chairs. "Aunt Sharonna, Hildy, will you please sit down?"

As she allowed her nephew to push in her chair, Sharonna whispered loudly, "Aren't his manners impeccable, Hildy?"

Sliding into the satin upholstery, Hildy asked, "This isn't about you-know-what again, is it, Shevre?" Laying an ebony hand upon his muscular forearm she quietly said, "We've tried everything, dear. I don't think there's enough magic in this world to bring her back."

An unreadable expression crossed the king's face as he pushed in her chair. "I agree. But that's not why I summoned you here." He pulled another chair out as he gestured to the third woman still hidden beneath the plain brown hood. "Edna? Will you join us please?"

Sharonna and Hildy exchanged worried glances. Hildy lowered her eyes. "That's not Edna." King Shevre raised a questioning brow.

Sharonna nervously played with a gold locket dangling from the delicate chain around her neck. Snapping the locket open and shut she averted her nephew's gaze as she explained, "Edna's magic has been slipping steadily this past year. It finally got to the point where she could no longer be an equal member of The Three. She retired last week. We've kept it secret until the Power Transference to our newest member can be completed."

"Your newest member?" The king looked stunned as he stared at the stranger in brown. "What do you mean, the Transference isn't complete?"

"Well dear," Sharonna replied patiently. "It means that instead of The Three, right now we're more like 'The Two-And-A-Half'."

The king placed his hands on the table and leaned forward, lowering his voice to a somber tone. "Certain events have occurred here, Aunt Sharonna. Dire events. It is vital that we have the full power of The Three."

"What is it, Shevre?" asked an alarmed Hildy. "What's happened?"

The king took a deep breath, scarcely able to believe the words he was about to say. "Magnus was killed last night." Both Hildy and Sharonna gasped. "And there's more ..." The room fell silent as he continued, "The murderer stole a spell from Magnus's personal collection."

"My heavens!" Sharonna blurted, sinking back into her chair.

"What spell was stolen, Shevre?" Hildy asked.

"The Spell of Spilled Secrets," he answered. Noting the wide eyes staring up at him he continued to relay the ominous news. "But that's not the worst of it. The murderer was none other than," curling his hands into tight fists he fought to control his temper. "*Shadow.*"

Hildy leapt from her chair. "That's impossible!"

"No, it's not," the soft voice of the newest member said from beneath her hood. "It's been many years since that Border Spell was cast. More than enough time for a crack to have formed."

King Shevre's head snapped up at the sound of her familiar voice.

Sharonna buried her face in her hands. "Oh my word! We kept meaning to cast another layer of spells, but we're always so busy that somehow we just never got around to it …"

The woman in brown moved toward the older woman, and placed a comforting hand on her shoulder. "It's alright, Sharonna. No one could have foreseen this. Well, maybe Edna could have, but you said yourself her Futuresight has been slipping lately." Keeping her face hidden beneath the brown cloth she continued, "We must leave for Edna's immediately to complete the Power Transference. Galdoren is in danger; it needs the full force of The Three."

King Shevre's eyes narrowed as she spoke. In an instant, he was by her side looming over her. He pushed her hood back and felt the air whoosh from his lungs as he stared at the young woman before him. She turned her pointed chin defiantly upwards as her hazel gaze settled upon him. A loose tendril of flame-red hair escaped the pearl clip that had held it back.

"Serena!" whispered the king.

Chapter Nine

THE WOMAN
UNDER THE HOOD

"*Y*ou're the newest member of The Three?" King Shevre asked incredulously.

"Why are you so surprised?" Serena snapped, yanking her cloak out of his hands. "I come from a long line of powerful witches and elves. Magic runs strong in my family."

The king crossed his muscular arms. "Yes, you're very good at running."

"For your information," she said, jabbing a finger in his broad chest. "I did NOT run out on our wedding!"

He raised a brow. "No? Then what do *you* call it when the bride-to-be leaves her fiancé's castle two weeks before her wedding?"

Serena started to answer with a sarcastic comment, but when she looked into the king's deep blue eyes, the words died on her lips. Blinking back tears, she simply turned away and crossed her arms angrily.

"Shevre dear," Sharonna said gently. "You make it sound as if she ran off in the middle of your vows!"

"HA!" Serena threw her head back defiantly.

"And Serena," the older woman continued. "You should have told him in person that you wanted to postpone the wedding to take a job with the Faerie Council."

"I left him a note," she muttered.

"Which I didn't find for TWO DAYS!" the king roared. "Two days of tearing the country apart, searching for you!" Turning to look out the window, he softly added, "Two days of torture, not eating or sleeping, worrying sick that you needed rescuing ... and I couldn't find you!"

Serena blinked and tried to swallow the sudden lump in her throat. "You couldn't eat or sleep?"

He slammed his fist on the table so hard that the chairs shook. "Wasn't being Queen of Galdoren challenging enough for you? You gave that up for *what*? To listen to the snooze-a-thon of complaints filed with the Faerie Council?"

"I didn't realize that marrying *you* meant I had to give up being *me*!"

The king thundered, "I never said you couldn't sit on the Faerie Council!" Scowling, he added, "I couldn't, as you never even gave me the chance to discuss it."

"The Council needed me to start immediately," Serena countered. "If I hadn't left that day, they would have chosen someone else! I didn't want to break off our engagement; I only wanted to postpone our wedding so I could take that job. Which I explained very clearly in my note!"

"Children, children," Sharonna said soothingly, trying to restore the peace. "This argument is better left for another time and place. Haven't we more important things to discuss right now?"

Serena tried glaring at King Shevre, but looking into the face that she dreamt of every night, found she couldn't. Their eyes locked and held each other, until she finally looked away.

The king took a deep calming breath, then shook off his bottled-up emotions. Moving back to the table, he once again pulled a chair out for the newest member of The Three.

Serena sat, and as he pushed in her chair, she mumbled, "Thank you."

"You're welcome."

Sitting at the head of the table, King Shevre addressed the three women. "When we adjourn, you are to fly directly to the Serpent's Eye. Get it out of there as fast as you can. But before you leave, cast an enchantment trap to catch anyone who tries to enter. Even in your weakened state, you could probably manage some sort of meager spell."

"Gosh," quipped Serena. "Thanks for the vote of confidence."

The king kept his temper in check and ignored her. Turning to his aunt he asked, "Do you think you can seal the crack in the border at your current level of power?"

She shook her head. "A spell of that magnitude requires that all three of our powers be at their highest levels. We won't be able to do it properly until the Transference is complete."

The king sighed and rubbed his weary eyes. "Then after you get the Serpent's Eye, fly as quickly as you are able to Edna's. Hide the gem somewhere on her farm under a layer of protective spells. How long will the Transference take?"

"Not long, only a few minutes," she answered.

His face reddened as he raised his voice, "A few *minutes*?!? Then why didn't you complete it to begin with?"

Sharonna patted his hand and patiently explained. "I told you, dear, Edna is weak. It's not the amount of time involved, it's the degree of energy. It takes enormous reserves of energy to completely transfer a power to another being. Since Edna has, or had, dominion over all water in Galdoren, that's quite a bit of power for her to transfer to Serena." Sharonna neatly folded her hands on the table. "And there's no need to shout, Shevre," she concluded primly.

Serena muttered something about his short temper under her breath.

"Serena," King Shevre stood and slowly walked around the table. When he came to her chair, he stopped. Towering above her he asked, "Can you do anything but undermine my authority?"

She smiled sweetly. "Why yes, I can."

She wiggled her finger and a stream of water poured from the ceiling right onto the king's head.

Hildy leapt to her feet. "SERENA! No matter your issues, he is still our KING!" The old woman swept her hand in an arc, and a stiff wind blew to the ceiling, plugging the leak.

A dangerous look crossed the king's face. As he leaned menacingly into Serena, she scooted out of her chair and wriggled past him. He quickly followed, backing her into the wall. Sharonna jumped from her seat and moved between them.

Dabbing the king's face dry with her sleeve, she stood on her tiptoes and whispered, "Control your temper, Shevre. She's just angry and hurt that you broke off your engagement."

"What was I supposed to do?" he hissed back in her ear. "Wait two years until she finished her obligation to the Fairie Council?"

"Ahem," interrupted Hildy, rising from her chair. "Since time is of the essence, shouldn't we leave now?"

Staring at the women he cared most about in this world, King Shevre suddenly found he could not send them on such a dangerous mission without additional protection. "Wait," he commanded. "I'm sending a battalion of knights to accompany you." Ignoring the surprised look on Serena's face he added, "On second thought, I will lead the battalion myself. You will follow us, and cast your spells when I have deemed it safe."

Sharonna placed a hand on her nephew's cheek and gently said, "Shevre, you know that is foolish. We move like lightning. No one in the kingdom can travel as fast as us. And no one in the kingdom wields as much power. Please, darling, don't worry."

"Aunt Sharonna …"

Cutting him off, she insisted, "Shevre, you are the king of this country. Your people cannot afford to lose you on such a foolhardy errand. Your place is here." She pointed out the window. "And our place is there."

The king took a deep breath then nodded. "You're right, of course." Crossing his arms, he muttered, "But don't tell me not to worry."

"I'm not as old as I look," Sharonna said firmly. "I still have a few tricks up this ancient sleeve." Casually, she pointed at an enormous potted fern in the corner and the plant instantly burst into flames.

"Show off," he mumbled as he kissed her cheek.

"Serena dear," Sharonna said sweetly. "Do you mind?"

Serena wiggled her finger and a stream of water splashed over the plant, extinguishing the blaze.

"Thank you," King Shevre said, staring at the charred leaves on the floor. "I never did like that plant."

Hildy marched to the window and drew the heavy brocade curtains back. She twisted her hands upward, creating a strong breeze. The gust blew the window open. "You're not the only ones who can strut their stuff!"

Sharonna gave her nephew a quick hug, again brushing the hair from his eyes. "You really do need a haircut, dear." Lowering her voice, she whispered, "When you say goodbye to Serena, use your charm. Then maybe when we get back, you won't need that enchanted window to see her anymore."

King Shevre gasped. "How do you know about that?" he whispered into her silver hair.

"I'm old, dear. Not blind," she replied. Then she joined Hildy at the open window. The breeze was blowing softer now as the two women climbed out onto the window ledge. Turning back to Serena, Hildy asked, "Coming?"

"Um, in a minute," the young woman answered.

Sharonna smiled knowingly. "We'll wait for you outside." Then she and Hildy leapt onto the swirling mass of air hovering just outside the window.

Serena turned to the king. "I just wanted to say ..." She rushed to his side, threw her arms around his shoulders, and kissed him.

Before he even had time to react, she was out the window and sailing on a breeze toward the Serpent's Eye.

Blinking, King Shevre sank into a nearby chair. He traced a finger along his lips and smiled.

Henry yawned and stretched. He couldn't figure out why his straw mattress felt so pillowy soft, until he remembered he wasn't at his farmhouse—he was at the castle! Blinking open his eyes, he took in his surroundings and was surprised to see sunlight pouring in through the half-drawn curtains. He glanced at a nearby clock. Only a short time had passed since he had entered the guest room. He had been so bone-tired that he had flopped onto the floating bed without giving even a cursory glance around, falling asleep before his head even hit the pillow.

The warm bed still enticed him, but he refused to go back to sleep. He jumped off the floating mattress, noting the hypnotic effect of sleeping on a cumulous cloud covered in satin.

Henry was determined to help save the kingdom and to bring Shadow to justice. He reached for Magnus's book of spells, which he barely remembered dropping on a nightstand. He was startled to see a package addressed to him sitting atop the worn leather book. Who even knew he was here? He carefully opened the card attached to the brown paper wrapping. It was from Edna! *Why would a member of The Three be sending me a gift?* Scratching his head in bewilderment, he read the card.

Dearest Henry,

I cannot begin to express how sorry I am about the loss of your teacher. I know you two were very close. It might please you to know that he thought of you as the son he never had. He often spoke of your kindness and loyalty. You impressed him greatly with your innate magical skills. Did you know that he was grooming you to become the Royal Alchemist?

Please accept this small gift from me. Take it with you on the journey I know you are planning to embark upon. You will find it useful.

Good luck!

Edna

Henry sucked in his breath. *Royal Alchemist? Me?* Surely Edna was mistaken. He quickly reread her letter. Had she truly guessed where he was going? He hadn't even decided himself until a few moments ago. Curious, he opened the package. He pulled out a hand-knit red and orange striped scarf and matching hat. Sitting down on the edge of the bed, he grinned. So she *did* know where he was planning to go!

Chapter Ten

GOSSAMER'S SECRET

Allie, Ricky and Twink fled the wrapping paper aisle as quickly as they could. Allie stopped to peer inside a huge glass case filled with Gossamer's handmade jewelry. Each piece sparkled with a different gem. The boys had little interest in Gossamer's jewels, preferring to toss a small china statue of King Shevre back and forth. The little statue kept yelling at them to stop. Ignoring its pleas, they continued to fling it back and forth until Ricky noticed that the statue was starting to turn green. He quickly put the moaning statue back onto the shelf. Had he turned back, he would have seen a tiny pile of china vomit appear near the king's feet.

As they continued to explore the store, Twink zoomed ahead. Finally finding what he was looking for, he screeched to a halt. Wearing a toothy grin, he pointed down an aisle. "It's here! It's here!"

"What's here?" asked Ricky.

"Come and see," piped the little star.

Allie and Ricky followed Twink toward a shelf filled with *"Never-ending Candy Bowls."* Each bowl was filled with a different candy, and all were guaranteed to refill themselves once empty.

"Not *those*," Twink said, rolling his eyes. "THESE!"

The shelves he was pointing to were stacked with small bottles. Each bottle was filled with assorted colors of some kind of jumping glitter. The glitter shot around inside the bottle, giving Allie the impression that the bottles were about to explode. The label on each bottle simply read, "*Rocket Dust.*" And in smaller print: "*Warning: Contents Under Pressure.*"

"What color do you want, Allie?" asked Twink.

"What's it do?" asked Ricky.

"Did you decide on a color, Allie?" Twink pressed, ignoring Ricky. He kept nodding toward the bottle whose purple glitter was the exact shade of purple as he was.

Allie laughed as Ricky again asked, "What's it do?"

"This color is nice, don't you think?" Twink suggested, pointing again to the purple.

"It's my favorite color," Allie fibbed, taking the purple bottle off the shelf. Twink beamed, then spun happily in the air.

"WHAT'S IT DO?" Ricky demanded, grabbing a blue bottle.

"Oh, don't you know?" blinked Twink.

"NO!" Ricky snapped.

A mischievous glint came into the little star's eyes. He took the bottle from Ricky and unscrewed the top. "See for yourself!" he squealed, shaking half the bottle over Ricky's head.

"Hey!" Ricky cried, shaking glitter from his hair. The glitter danced and jumped down his body. It skipped across his skin. "What's the big idea?!" he squawked angrily, brushing glitter off his shirt.

"Don't look down," the star advised, even as he giggled.

So naturally, Ricky looked down. His feet weren't touching the floor! Within moments, he was floating up. And up. And up.

"Ricky!" Allie yelled. "Watch out for the—"

SMACK!

"Light fixture," she finished too late.

"Ow," Ricky groaned, rubbing his head.

Twink soared up to his side. "Stretch your arms out! You know, so you can fly!"

"Aren't I flying now?" Ricky grumbled, bumping his head again on the ceiling.

"No, you're floating," answered Twink.

Ricky stretched his arms out. Nothing happened. He stretched even further. Still nothing. Then he stretched as far as his arms would go. He was now firmly wedged against the ceiling. He couldn't go forward. He couldn't go backward. He couldn't go down. And he certainly couldn't go up. He was stuck.

"Ricky, get down from there!" Allie scolded from below.

"I can't!" her brother shouted back.

"What do you mean, you *can't?*" she demanded.

"It means the opposite of *I can!*"

"Twink, get him down!" Allie huffed.

Twink surveyed the situation then chewed on his lip. "Uh-oh."

"What's uh-oh?" asked Ricky, trying hard not to panic.

"Um, I may have used too much Rocket Dust."

"You think?" Ricky answered sarcastically. "Let me see that bottle!" Twink hesitantly handed him the half-empty bottle.

Ricky read the label on the back out loud. "*Ages 5 to 10, one to two shakes as needed. Ages 10 and up, three to four shakes as needed.*" Turning to Twink he yelled, "DO NOT EXCEED REC-OMMENDED DOSAGE!"

"Um, I'll get my uncle," Twink chirped, starting to fly away.

"No, wait!" Allie called anxiously from the floor below. Twink skidded to a halt in mid-air. "I'll get him," she said. "You stay right next to my brother, and DON'T LET HIM FALL!"

"I don't think falling will be a problem," grumbled Ricky.

Allie raced past the cash register and down the hallway toward Gossamer's private office. She pushed open the door, her words spilling out in a frantic rush, "I'm sorry to interrupt, but my brother's in trouble!"

Shimmer soared off the couch. "Where is he?!"

"On the ceiling," she replied.

Shimmer stopped in the doorway and turned. His eyes narrowed. "Does this have anything to do with my nephew and a large amount of Rocket Dust?"

Allie nodded.

"TWINKLE!" he shouted as he flew down the hallway.

"Why don't you wait here, dear?" Gossamer suggested, patting the couch. She held up a bowl of gummy bears and offered it to Allie. "Candy?"

Allie nervously glanced at the door, unsure of what to do.

"It's really best to let Shimmer sort this out on his own," Gossamer advised. Seeing the concerned look on Allie's face, she added, "Don't worry. Ricky is not the first child Shimmer has had to rescue from my ceiling."

Reassured, Allie smiled and took a handful of gummy bears. She moved to the shelves of snow globes, running her hands across the cool glass. "These are beautiful," she breathed. "Where did you get them all?"

"I made them," Gossamer answered proudly.

"You made *all* of these?" Allie's eyes flitted from shelf to shelf.

Gossamer nodded. "I've been making them since I was a little girl."

"Can I shake one?"

Gossamer laughed. "You can shake them all!"

"I don't think I have that much time," Allie smiled, carefully lifting a snow globe off a shelf. This particular one was filled with flying horses. She turned it upside down and shook. "I collect snow globes," she murmured, watching the tiny snowflakes sink slowly toward the bottom.

"Really?" Gossamer answered, genuinely surprised. Watching the girl shake the snow globes, an idea began to form in her mind. "Allie, dear, are you planning to stay in Galdoren, or are you returning to Earth soon?"

Allie was puzzled by the question. "I'm definitely going back to Earth."

Gossamer nodded approvingly. Leaning forward in her chair, her eyes narrowed. "Are you sure? I mean, are you very, very certain you will be going back to Earth?"

Allie, who was absorbed in shaking a snow globe filled with shimmering fairies, answered distractedly, "I'm sure."

Gossamer chewed her bottom lip. Finally coming to a firm decision, she pulled out the long necklace that was tucked inside her dress. Attached to the end of the silver chain was a small, tarnished key. She walked to her desk and sat in the worn swivel chair, folding her wings in behind her. Looking up at the girl she sighed, then slowly fitted the key into a small hole hidden under the lip of the desk. A secret drawer suddenly popped open.

The only object in the drawer was a miniature snow globe. Inside the snow globe was a replica of Galdoren Castle, made entirely of crystal. The castle was so exquisitely carved that it sparkled from every angle. Near the bottom, elegant gold letters formed the words, *"Welcome to Galdoren."*

Gossamer stood, holding the small snow globe out to the girl. "Allie, I want you to have this."

When Allie saw how beautiful the dainty globe was, she refused. "No, I couldn't! It looks much too valuable." Admiring the intricate detail she added, "It must have taken you forever to make!"

Gossamer fidgeted nervously. "Not really. I believe I was in a terrible hurry when I made this one." She pressed the snow globe into Allie hands. "Please ... take it back to Earth with you." Then she quickly added, "As a souvenir of Galdoren."

Allie was tempted. "But, how can I carry it? I really don't want to lug a shopping bag around the kingdom."

Gossamer grabbed Allie's free hand and marched her out of the office. "That won't be a problem."

She led her to a small display unit next to the register. The sign above the seemingly empty shelves read, *"Invisible Pockets."* Gossamer felt around the top shelf, mumbling to herself, "Too small, too scratchy ..." She made a face. "Too sticky!"

She searched around another shelf. "Aha!" she smiled with satisfaction, grabbing what looked like nothing in her fingers. "Perfect!"

She peeled something off the invisible object she was holding, then smoothed her hand over Allie's hip. "Done!"

Baffled, Allie asked, "What's done?"

"Your new pocket. Try it!"

Allie looked down at her nightgown. Seeing nothing, she slowly moved her hand around the material. She suddenly felt something. Lowering her hand inside, she gasped. Her hand had completely disappeared! Quickly pulling it back out, she was relieved to see her hand was once again visible.

"That's amazing!" she breathed, unable to hide her pleasure.

Gossamer shrugged. "It's just an invisible pocket."

Allie smiled and slipped her snow globe inside the pocket. It instantly vanished. She turned her head at the familiar sound of her brother's footsteps.

"Flying's not all it's cracked up to be," Ricky declared grumpily as he stomped up the aisle toward the register.

"I told you," Twink said in a flustered tone. "You weren't *flying*, you were *floating*."

"Twinkle, I want you to apologize to Ricky this instant!" Shimmer angrily demanded.

"Sorry," Twink mumbled half-heartedly.

"That's okay," Ricky shrugged. "I guess it was kind of fun."

"Really?" Twink appeared puzzled. "Which part? The part when you knocked your head against the light fixture or the part when you were stuck on the ceiling?"

"Never mind," Ricky muttered, bending down to pet Snoball. She was curled up inside the display window, lying in a patch of sun.

"Mrrow," she said lazily, stretching her neck so that he would scratch under her chin.

Ricky suddenly noticed the bright sun shining across her frosted fur. "I've gotta get you out of there before you melt!" He quickly scooped her up and set her down in a shady spot near the register.

Gossamer gave him a questioning look. "Why would she melt, dear?"

"Because she's made of snow." Seeing the blank look on her face, he added, "And she was in the sun."

Gossamer just blinked in bewilderment.

"Maybe Galdoren snow is different than our snow back home," Allie suggested.

Gossamer looked horrified. "The snow-creatures on Earth *melt?*" She shuddered, picturing puddles of melted animals on every street corner.

Shimmer handed Allie and Ricky their bottles of Rocket Dust. He had replaced Ricky's half-empty bottle with a new one, and had given them firm instructions to follow the directions on the bottle. "You'll be needing these to fly to the castle. It's much too far to walk."

Allie squealed in delight. Shimmer gently placed a hand-point on her shoulder. "I'm sorry, Allie. But the first part of our journey is on foot. We're taking a shortcut through Galdoren Woods."

Gossamer's brows shot up. Shimmer winked at her as he added, "There's something I need to check on in that forest." Shimmer didn't notice the way Gossamer nervously fidgeted with her hands.

"Hey, is anyone else starving?" Twink asked.

Ricky vigorously nodded his head.

Gossamer reached behind the counter and handed the boys a deep bowl filled to the brim with chocolate bars. Shimmer intervened, placing the bowl back on its shelf. "Twinkle, what have I told you about junk food?"

The corners of Twink's mouth crooked up. "That it's a wonderful and delicious snack that should be eaten several times a day?"

"No, that's what you've told *me* about junk food," Shimmer said. "I've told you a thousand times that it's not healthy, it rots your teeth, and it makes you fat."

"Nuh-uh, Uncle Shimmer, you've only told me that ...," Twink's tongue went to the side of his mouth as he reached deep inside his invisible pocket. Pulling out a crumpled piece of paper he recited, "How many times Uncle Shimmer has told me how rotten junk food is—four hundred and thirty-two." Looking up from the paper, he tapped his foot-point in the air. "But that didn't count the time you just said it again, so now it's, um," grabbing a pen off the counter he scribbled, "four hundred and thirty-three!"

Crossing his arm-points, Shimmer firmly stated, "We'll pick spawberries in the woods. That should hold us over until we reach the castle and have dinner."

Twink's face twisted in revulsion. "Spawberries? Blech!"

Just then, a small flap in the front door opened. "Mrrorw," a snowcat called as he jumped through. Like Ricky's cat, he was made of two snowballs, an icicle tail and frosted whiskers, but his coloring was more of a splotchy brown.

"Fudgicle!" Gossamer cried, scooping up her pet. Covering his ears she told the kids, "He was made with muddy snow, poor dear."

"Mrrow mreowrr morrrw," Snoball called up from the floor.

Fudgicle leaped out of Gossamer's arms, and padded over to Snoball. They began taking friendly swipes at each other, rolling across the floor, tails swishing happily.

Watching them play, Ricky sighed. Should he leave Snoball here where she belonged, or selfishly take her back to Earth? *Allie's probably right,* he thought sadly. It would be hard to explain a cat made of magic snow to his mother.

Sensing Ricky's eyes on her, Snoball stopped playing and looked up at him. "Mrrowr?" she asked, cocking her head.

Ricky stroked her under the chin, whispering, "I'll miss you." She rubbed her cheek affectionately against his fingers, purring loudly.

Understanding Ricky's intentions, Gossamer was filled with admiration for the young boy. "What a kind and selfless child you are!" Smiling reassuringly she added, "Don't worry, I'll take good care of Snoball for you." Then she pulled Ricky to her ample chest, and hugged him tightly. Letting go, she plucked Twinkle from the air and hugged him as well. But the longest hug was reserved for Allie. "Be careful, dear," she warned.

Allie gave her a questioning look.

As Gossamer embraced Shimmer, he gave her a reassuring squeeze. "Don't worry," he murmured. "Everything will be fine." He only wished he could believe his own words.

The bell on Gossamer's front door jingled as the foursome left her shop. Her silver wings drooped sadly as she watched them disappear down the street, heading toward Galdoren Woods.

"Forgive me," she whispered as she closed the door, but not before a small white snowcat slipped out, following the boy she had grown to love.

Chapter Eleven

THE SPY RETURNS

A huge black bird swooped out of the sky. Preparing to land, she lowered her talons. But she was flying so fast that she skidded across the moss and smacked her beak into the invisible wall of magic that formed the Border Spell.

A strangled voice laughed harshly as a woman drifted into view on the Windermere side of the border. Bony hands clutched the collar of her fiery red cloak. Her face was hidden beneath her velvet hood.

"Your Majesty," the bird cooed, bowing deeply. Her beady eyes glittered with excitement. "I bring you important news—from the *castle*!"

Queen Glacidia admired her shiny fingernails. "Get on with it."

The Furvel puffed up her chest and began rattling off everything she had seen and heard in the king's private chamber that morning. Glacidia's eye grew wide as the bird relayed the king's orders for The Three to seal the crack in the Border Spell.

The queen took a calming breath. "No matter," she replied. "By the time they find the crack, I will be wearing the Serpent's Eye. And then *no spell can hold me!*"

The Furvel nervously batted an insect back and forth with her talons, afraid to relate the next bit of news. She cleared her throat and gave her mistress a sideways glance. "Oh, and there is one more thing …"

Glacidia raised a brow. "Yes?"

"The Three have been ordered to move the Serpent's Eye to a new, undisclosed location." The cautious bird took a few steps back when she noticed the queen's fingers begin to twitch. She swallowed hard and then quickly warbled, "And they will be devising an enchantment to trap Shadow and any goblins who remain loyal to you." She bowed curtly. "That's all Your Majesty," she chirped, spreading her wings in her haste to fly away.

"DO NOT *DARE* TO LEAVE BEFORE YOU ARE DIS-MISSED," Glacidia commanded. Her fur boots crunched in the snow as she paced. "THAT'S *MY* GEM!!!" she screamed with a murderous rage. *"MINE!!!"*

Her hair slithered and hissed beneath her hood as ice shot out of her fingertips. It hit the Border Spell with such force that it ricocheted off the invisible wall and hit a nearby tree, splitting it in two. The barren branches crashed into a snowdrift, and exploded into a mass of powdery white. Glacidia's eye glowed with a blind fury as she stalked toward the shaking Furvel. Tiny ice daggers dripped from her fingers, leaving a glittering trail in the snow.

Petrified, the Furvel flapped her wings, spraying a shower of black feathers across the mossy ground. She said a silent prayer of thanks that she was on the Galdoren side of the border, protected from the wrath of her mistress.

Queen Glacidia pointed toward the woods. "Fly to the ancient part of the forest and find Shadow. Warn him that The Three are en route and to make haste. I must have the Serpent's Eye at *any cost*! If he should fail me …" Left unspoken, the threat was even more terrifying. The white membrane of her empty eye socket began to bubble, like egg whites in a frying pan. The whipping winds blew the cloak off her shoulders as she screamed, "GO!"

Chapter Twelve

GALDOREN WOODS

Shimmer, Twink, Ricky, and Allie had been hiking down a well-worn dirt path for what seemed like ages. The deeper they moved into the forest, the more oppressive the humidity became. Allie's hair was starting to frizz, and her fuzzy pink slippers were covered in a fine layer of dirt.

Twink kept turning in the air, sneaking peeks at Allie, until he smacked into a leafy branch. As he thrashed his way out, a series of twigs rained down upon Ricky's head.

"HEY!" the boy yelped, pulling a twig from his hair. "Watch where you're flying!"

Shimmer was too lost in thought to even notice the scuffle. They were nearing the ancient part of the woods, where the Serpent's Eye was hidden.

Twink had just opened his mouth to speak when a loud growl erupted from the pit of his stomach. He clapped a hand-point over his mouth in embarrassment.

Allie smiled. "Hungry?"

"Maybe a little," he lied, as he was in fact, *starving*.

Looking up at the rapidly setting sun, Shimmer sighed. "I suppose we should stop and eat a little something."

"How about *a lot* of something?" Twink asked hopefully.

"I'm pretty hungry too," Ricky admitted.

Allie brushed some dirt from the bottom of her nightgown and shyly added, "I could eat."

Shimmer reached deep into his invisible pocket and pulled out two foldable baskets he had packed before leaving Gossamer's. "Allie and I will gather spawberries. You boys wait here."

Twink made a face like he had just chugged a gallon of sour milk. "Ew! I HATE spawberries!"

"Strawberries?" asked Ricky.

"No, SPAW-berries." Turning to Ricky he asked, "What's a *strawberry* anyways?"

Shimmer gave his nephew a stern look. "We're having spawberries for dinner, and that is that. They're healthy and easy to find in the forest." Seeing Twink opening his mouth to protest, he added, "And I don't want to hear another word about it."

"But ...," Twink started to say.

Shimmer held up a hand-point, interrupting his nephew. "I mean it, Twinkle, not one word!"

"Fine," Twink grouched. "Then I'll say *lots* of words. Blech, disgusting, puke, gross—"

"Twinkle!" Shimmer warned.

Twink clapped his mouth shut and angrily kicked a rock at a tree.

"Um, I'm kind of thirsty, too," Ricky added.

Shimmer turned to the Earth boy. "Oh, yes. Of course." He patted his invisible pockets muttering, "Now, where did I pack that canteen?" He searched around then cried, "Aha!" pulling a faded yellow canteen from his rear pocket.

Ricky eagerly took it and swigged what he hoped would be a giant gulp of water. But there was nothing to swallow except air. He leaned his head back and held the canteen upside down over his mouth, but not even one drop of liquid poured out. "Um, Shimmer?"

"Yes?" Shimmer answered, handing a basket to Allie.

"This is empty."

"That's impossible. I filled it before we ...," his voice trailed off as he took the canteen from Ricky. He shook it, hoping to hear something sloshing around. His face fell when he realized that there was nothing inside to slosh. "I can't believe it! How could I have forgotten to bring water?"

"So, there's nothing to drink?" Allie asked, trying to keep the worry out of her voice.

Shimmer peered through the trees, surveying the forest. He sighed with relief when he saw a familiar sign hidden behind a clump of leaves. "There's a brook at the end of this winding path," he said, pulling aside some overgrown brush to reveal a sign with a picture of water and an arrow pointing down a well-worn trail.

Twink brightened. "Ricky and I will go fill the canteen while you and Allie get our disgusting dinner."

As his uncle shook his head *no*, Twink pointed to the bits of indigo sky just visible through the canopy of leaves. "It'll be dark soon," he argued, "and then it'll be too dangerous to go."

With a weary sigh, Shimmer agreed. "I suppose you're right."

"Okay," Twink replied. "See ya!" As he turned to leave, Shimmer plucked him out of the air.

"Do not stray from this path, Twinkle! These aren't the gardens of Galdoren Castle. There are dangerous creatures out here who would like nothing better than to eat a little star for dinner."

Ricky couldn't help but joke, "Wouldn't he be more like an appetizer?"

"Ricky!" Allie scolded. Then, pulling her baby brother protectively to her side she added, "Um, Shimmer, maybe we should all stick together?"

Wriggling free of his big sister, Ricky was about to protest when the hair on the back of his neck began to bristle. He suddenly got the strangest sensation that someone was watching him. He spun around to peer into the forest. A nearby bush rustled and then the feeling of being watched was gone.

"Don't worry," Shimmer assured Allie. "They'll be perfectly safe as long as they STAY ON THIS PATH!"

"Did you hear that?" Allie asked her brother.

"It was kind of hard to miss," he replied. "C'mon Twink," he said as he set off in the direction the arrow was pointing to.

Floating backwards, Twink waved goodbye to Allie. "I'll see you soo—" THWAP! He knocked his head on another branch.

Allie bit her lip, trying not to laugh. But as she watched her brother and Twink disappear into the shadows of the forest, she was suddenly struck by a deep feeling of foreboding. Shaking it off, she followed Shimmer past the thick brush toward a grassy nook brimming with bright purple berries.

Chapter Thirteen

THE LITTLE MAN IN THE WOODS

"Spawberries, blecchh!" Twink grumbled. He kicked a pebble on the path, stirring up a small cloud of dirt in its wake.

"What's so bad about spawberries?" Ricky asked, fanning the cloud from his face.

As the path veered to the right, a small patch of purple berries came into view. "See for yourself," Twink suggested with a mischievous smile.

Ricky hadn't realized how hungry he was until he saw those berries glistening among the leaves. He ran ahead and leaped into the spawberry patch, reached down and yanked the fattest one he could find off its stem. He rubbed it on his shirt then popped it into his mouth.

As he bit into the purple fruit, a warm juice flowed over his tongue. At first, it tasted sweet. But then, as he began to chew the skin of the berry, a bitter taste exploded between his teeth. His eyes started to water as his stomach roiled. Spitting the foul tasting fruit on the ground he choked, "Ugh! It tastes like a blueberry threw up in my mouth!"

"Told ya so," Twink smirked.

Ricky suddenly stopped in his tracks, as he was once again overcome by that strange feeling of being watched. He carefully turned his head, scanning the forest. A pair of glowing eyes stared back at him from behind a tumble of leaves.

"Do you see that?" he whispered to Twink.

"See what? Your purple spit?" Looking at the wad of half-chewed berry on the ground, Twink grimaced, "Yeah, I see that."

"No, not that. I mean those glowing eyes in the leaves over there!"

"WHERE?" Twink said so loudly that he scared whoever was hiding. The leaves shook as something white streaked out of them and into the woods.

"Never mind," Ricky snapped.

The boys continued down the path, until they finally reached a rickety wood sign. Freshly painted letters spelled the word *Brook*, with a neat arrow painted underneath pointing toward a winding path. This new path snaked through a particularly thick grove of trees.

"I guess it's this way," Ricky shrugged.

"There's no way I'm eating spawberries for dinner!" Twink grumbled as they moved down the twisting path. "I don't care how hungry I get!"

"Me neither!" Ricky agreed. Just then, he heard a faint, scratching sound. He quickly turned and saw a little blue man wiping his footprints off the dirt path with a small, wooden broom.

"Hey, what are you doing?" Ricky called to the man.

Twink spun around and gasped, "A Leshy!" He zoomed toward the little man, shooing him away, "Get outta here!"

The blue man ignored Twink, and continued to brush Ricky's footprints off the path. The bristles on his broom were stirring up a tremendous cloud of dirt.

Ricky scrutinized the strange little man, from his tuft of blue hair to the numerous pockets covering his faded green overalls. He recognized some of the items sticking out of his pockets, like a hammer, paintbrush and saw. But he had no idea what some of the other things were. They all looked like tools of some kind, just not like any tools found on Earth.

Twink's eyes narrowed. "I know what you're trying to do, you Leshy! And it won't work!"

The Leshy began to babble in a high-pitched voice, "Meegle-dee beegle-dax spik spak zip zax—" He suddenly began to cough and wheeze, choking on the enormous cloud of dirt he had stirred up.

Ricky heard a deafening sneeze and watched in amazement as the force of that sneeze blew the little Leshy up from the path and flung him into the branches above.

"SPAGGLETY MEEGLE BLAX ZIPPITY BLONX!" the Leshy screeched from the tree. The leaves rustled furiously as the Leshy continued to rant.

Twink clapped a point over his mouth to stifle a giggle. "That's the most curse words I've ever heard in one sentence!"

Ricky laughed while trying to commit the foreign curse words to memory. "What's a Leshy, anyway?" he asked as they resumed walking down the path toward the brook, the sounds of the Leshy's ranting fading in the distance.

"Oh, they're these annoying little wood sprites. They live in the forest and they try to get travelers lost. That's why he was wiping your footprints—so you couldn't find your way back."

Ricky scratched his head. "But there's only one path," he pointed out. "So, what difference would it make if he erased my footprints or not? I'd still be able to find my way back."

Twink shrugged. "I didn't say they were smart. Just mean."

"Oh," Ricky replied. "Well, what else do they do?"

Twink wrinkled his nose, thinking hard. "Hmm. Oh, yeah. Sometimes they enchant all the trees to look alike. You know, to get you more lost."

Ricky looked around at the trees. They all *did* look alike. "But, we can still follow the path...and the sign."

"I told you they weren't smart."

But as the boys pushed their way through a tangle of branches and leaves, the path suddenly ended.

"What the—" Ricky whirled around, and saw the path disappearing before his eyes. His mouth hung open as the dirt beneath his feet began to fade away. The boys now found themselves stranded in the middle of the forest, with only twigs and fallen leaves on the ground and not a trace of the path remaining.

"What happened to the path?!" Ricky yelled.

High-pitched laughter filled the air. Ricky suddenly remembered the saw, paintbrush and hammer sticking out of the Leshy's pockets. His eyes narrowed. "He tricked us!"

Twink hung in the air, a guilty look crossing his face. "Oh, yeah. I just remembered something else Leshies do. They make fake signs and conjure fake paths."

Chapter Fourteen

THE TWO QUEENS

As Allie and Shimmer filled their baskets with spawberries, the curious star peppered her with a million questions about Earth. Allie was glad for the distraction, as she still couldn't shake that ominous feeling about her brother and Twink.

"So, what is this *Starbucks*, anyway?" Shimmer asked. "Twink and I noticed quite a number of them when we entered the Earth's atmosphere." He lowered his voice to a concerned whisper, "Have they taken over your planet?"

Allie was just about to answer when a rainbow of light danced across her hand. She wiggled her fingers, enchanted by the sparkling colors dancing across her fingertips. Expecting to see a huge rainbow arcing above, she looked up and was surprised to see nothing but a dusky sky peeking through the branches.

"That's strange," she muttered. Wondering where the tinted streaks of light were coming from, she dropped her basket and followed the trail of rainbows to an opening in the middle of an overgrown bush. A weathered sign sticking out of the bushes said, *"The Rainbow Gallery. Open daily to the public. Hours …"* Allie couldn't read the times, as they were so faded. A filmy curtain draped across the opening was printed with the words, *"Please wipe your wings."* The cloth was covered with hundreds of tiny dirt smudges. Curious, she poked her head through the curtain, amazed at what lay before her.

Misty paintings floated everywhere, drifting in the light breeze. The translucent artwork floated above a large clearing of green moss sprinkled with flowers. Tiny silver bells dangled from the center of each flower, tinkling in the breeze.

Feeling a bit like Alice in Wonderland, she pushed herself through the hole and fell into an ethereal garden. Brushing the leaves from her nightgown, she looked out across the clearing and sucked in her breath.

A handful of butterflies were dipping their wings into buckets filled with shimmering rainbows. Dots of color dripped across the garden as the butterflies flew to a painting suspended in the air. They brushed their wings across it, swirling the iridescent colors over the misty canvas.

"They're painting with rainbows," Allie breathed.

She stared at the portrait fluttering in the air before her. A beautiful woman was painted in the mist. She wore the most sorrowful expression Allie had ever seen. A single tear rolled down her cheek as she pointed a finger at some unseen presence. The words *B'yardin Shatavna Myesto Troo* floated in the wind. For some strange reason, the words seemed oddly familiar to Allie, like the foggy haze of a barely remembered dream.

Something soft and dewy bumped against her arm. It was another painting that had drifted over on the wind. She reached out and touched the canvas, delighted by the way the colors rippled beneath her fingertips.

This painting was of the same woman, only here she was smiling radiantly at a little boy. It was obvious that they were mother and child. Both shared the same black hair, although the woman's was pulled back in an elegant twist, while the boy's was in dire need of a haircut. Both had the same sapphire eyes. And both wore matching gold crowns.

"Her name is Queen Jacqueline." The sound of Shimmer's voice startled her, as she hadn't realized that he had followed her into the gallery. "And that's King Shevre, when he was, oh, about ten or so." Gazing at the paintings floating across the garden, he sighed. "I had nearly forgotten this was here."

Allie turned back to the portrait of Queen Jacqueline, lightly running her hand across the transparent image. Dots of colored mist rippled wherever she touched. "She's beautiful," Allie murmured. When she glanced back at Shimmer, she was startled by the sadness in his eyes. Allie chewed her lip nervously. "Did she, um, is she, er, still alive?"

Shimmer blinked, unsure of how to respond. He finally decided upon a cryptic, "She's neither dead, nor alive."

"Oooo-kay," Allie said, afraid to pursue it further.

As the painting spun in the light breeze, Allie found herself mesmerized by Queen Jacqueline's strange ring. A round diamond sparkled on her finger, but right in the center of the gem was a black diamond, giving it the appearance of a giant eyeball. "Spooky-looking jewelry," Allie said, unable to look away.

A knot of fear twisted in Shimmer's stomach. He could feel his heart beat faster with each passing moment. Gossamer's words echoed in his ear: *Did you ever wonder what would happen if Glacidia escaped?* "The Serpent's Eye," he murmured.

"Pardon me?"

"The ring," Shimmer answered, his eyes fixed upon the gem. "It's called the Serpent's Eye." Wondering how much he should tell the girl, he chose his words carefully. "It's a family heirloom, handed down from generation to generation. It was her mother's, and her mother's before her, and so on and so forth for many centuries. At one time it was a necklace, and then a pin, until finally the Eye was set in a ring. It's a fairie creation from another time … another age."

"Who has it now?" Allie asked, poking her hand through the mist. She arranged her fingers so that the ring appeared to sit on her knuckle.

"No one," Shimmer answered quickly. "It's been secreted away. Hidden forever." He said those last words with more conviction than he felt.

"Is it that valuable?" Allie asked, thinking it strange that anyone would want to own such a creepy piece of jewelry.

"No," he answered truthfully. "It's that powerful." Allie raised a brow while Shimmer tried to explain. "You see, if the person wearing it is not of fairie ancestry, then it's just a diamond. But if there is even one ounce of fairie magic coursing through their veins, then the gem will double … no, *triple* their powers."

"I still don't get it," Allie said. "Why is it hidden away?"

"Because the gem doesn't know good from evil." He paused, unsure of how to explain this next part. "And it has a history of wielding power over the people who wear it if they are not strong enough to control the magic inside the Serpent's Eye."

A chill ran down Allie's spine. She yanked her hand out of the painting.

"Gossamer and I had the honor of guarding it, you know."

Allie's eyes widened. "Did you try it on?"

"Certainly not!" Shimmer's thoughts were suddenly lost in a far-away time, as unbidden memories came rushing back. He spoke so softly that Allie could barely make out his words. "The Three were scouring the kingdom, looking for the perfect place to hide the Eye. Gossamer and I were in charge of its safekeeping until such a place could be found … the country was in turmoil … Queen Glacidia's rampage had left a path of destruction …" He sighed. "The weight of so many problems heaped upon the shoulders of such a young boy …"

Allie was confused. She had guessed that the young boy was King Shevre. *But who was Queen Glacidia? And who were The Three?*

Shimmer shook his head as if to clear it. Looking up at the splotchy patches of indigo gradually fading in the sky he said, "We should go."

They walked in silence back toward the opening in the bushes. Allie smiled at the butterflies as they sailed past, foregoing their painting for the evening. Her foot suddenly squished into something wet. She looked down, surprised to find that she had stepped into a puddle of spilled rainbows. As she pulled her foot out, she saw that one was stuck to the top of her slipper. She wiggled and shook her foot, but she couldn't shake the rainbow off.

When she looked up again, she found herself staring at the misty portrait of Queen Jacqueline. The wind had carried it over to hover in front of her eyes. She brushed her hand through the tear on the queen's cheek. "Why is she so sad?"

Shimmer fought back the memories of that dreadful evening. "It's a long story that's best saved for another time."

"But …" Allie couldn't draw her eyes away from the mysterious words floating in the wind—*B'yardin Shatavna Myesto Troo.* She cupped her hands around the letters and asked, "What does it mean?"

"It's a fairie spell," he sighed, staring at the letters captured in Allie's hands. "Those were the last words Queen Jacqueline ever uttered." His chin wobbled for a moment and then he cleared his throat, adding, "Everything but the last word, as she never got to finish the spell."

"Why not? What happened?" Allie knew that it must have been something terrible. Something unimaginable.

But Shimmer had already flown through the small opening in the bushes. Allie hesitated before following him back. She was strangely drawn to the words. She brushed her hand through the wispy letters. Wishing fervently she knew why the queen was never able to finish the spell, she whispered, *"B'yardin Shatavna Myesto Troo."* A stiff wind suddenly whipped through the garden. The bluebells began to chime as they swayed in the breeze.

Ting. Ting. Ting …

B'yardin Shatavna Myesto Troo, the wind whispered in her ears.

All at once, Allie felt terribly sleepy. She tried to walk toward the opening in the bushes, but her feet felt like clay. Her eyelids were impossibly heavy. Her lips began to move along with the whispers on the wind … *B'yardin Shatavna Myesto Troo.*

Overcome by her sudden wave of exhaustion, she lay down amongst the bluebells. She fought to keep her eyes open, but within moments she was falling into a strange slumber, still wishing she knew the mysterious story of the queen's fate.

A thick mist rose up from the ground. As the fog swirled around her, she shivered, the damp air startling her awake. Allie slowly stood, pushing her way through the foggy veil. When she finally stepped out of the mist, she found herself standing in a strange, round room. A velvet couch was flanked by a throne on one side and a worn and battered chair on the other. An ancient mirror stood beside an ornate grandfather clock that ticked softly in the silence.

The door suddenly burst open. Queen Jacqueline came running in, pulling a young and frightened King Shevre behind her. Allie gasped. "Your Majesties," she bowed. But neither the woman nor the boy seemed to see or hear her.

"Shevre, quick! Help me barricade this door!" Watching them struggle to push the heavy couch, Allie cried, "Let me help!" But again, they didn't seem to notice her presence. Allie rushed to help them push the heavy piece of furniture, but when she put her hand on the couch it went straight through, as if the object didn't exist.

Footsteps could be heard running up the stairs outside the room. "Shevre, quick!" the queen whispered urgently, pulling aside an ornate tapestry that hung on the wall. She pointed her finger at a crack in the stone and commanded, *"Onbregdan!"* The wall slowly slid open, revealing a room just large enough for a small boy to hide in.

"No, mother! Not without you!"

"Shevre, don't argue! Just go!"

As the sound of the footsteps grew louder, he drew a sword from beneath the folds of his cloak. "I can fight them, mother! I'm good! And Magnus charmed my sword to cut through goblin skin!"

Allie waved her hand in front of their faces. They never blinked. Realizing that she must be in some sort of dream, all she could do was watch helplessly as the events unfolded.

With a quick look at the door, Queen Jacqueline knelt and held Shevre's eyes in her own. "Shevre, you're very brave. But it's only a matter of time before they break down this door." She smoothed the hair back from her son's brow. "Queen Glacidia has cast a perimeter spell around the castle, making it impossible for anyone to transport in or out. She doesn't know you're still here. She's certain to think I magicked you out the instant the castle was attacked, before she had time to cast her spell."

Shevre fought hard to stave off the well of tears gathering in his eyes. "I'm sorry I put up that shield blocking you from transporting me, Mother. But I couldn't leave you here alone! I just couldn't!" He laid his head against his mother's shoulder. "Why couldn't you come with me?"

"Shevre, you know that she would follow me wherever I go. She wants the Eye and she'll stop at nothing to get it. I have to end this, darling. I have a sworn duty to protect our country." Looking out the window at the fires raging across the kingdom she narrowed her eyes. "She's left a trail of death through Galdoren that ends tonight."

Hugging his mother tightly he whispered into her lilac-scented hair. "I can protect you."

As the sound of the footsteps drew terrifyingly near, Queen Jacqueline held her son's cheeks in her soft hands, saying, "Shevre, I wield the power of the Serpent's Eye. You needn't worry about me. But if Glacidia finds you here, she will use you against me. She knows you are my one weakness. Please, Shevre," she pleaded. "Do this for me."

The prince reluctantly nodded his head.

Animal-like growls echoed outside the room. Both their eyes grew wide as the first thump landed on the door.

"Hurry, Shevre!"

The boy sheathed his sword and squeezed himself into the secret opening. Queen Jacqueline leaned down and brushed a tear from his cheek. She kissed him softly on the forehead and whispered, "I love you more than anything in this world."

"MOM!" the boy choked as she closed the secret door, leaving him alone in the dark.

She quickly smoothed the tapestry over the wall and walked to the center of the room. She calmly held her finger out, and aimed it at the door.

"The Serpent's Eye," Allie murmured, staring at the haunting gem glinting on the queen's finger.

Suddenly, the door exploded, blasting shards of shattered wood across the room. Dozens of half-man, half-beast creatures stormed in. Beads of sweat dripped down the coarse red flesh of their bare chests, matting their long hair to their skin. Allie recoiled at the sight of those greasy black tangles hanging off their heads, half covering their feral yellow eyes. They snarled at the queen, baring razor-sharp fangs. Allie's hand unconsciously went to her heart as she whispered, "Goblins." She briefly wondered how she could be so certain.

But then a harsh voice ripped through the room, "Remember, no one touches her before I get my Eye!"

A woman glided across the threshold, stepping over the fragments of shattered wood. The aura of evil surrounding her was so powerful that Allie took an involuntary step back, even though she knew she couldn't be seen.

As the woman swept past the goblins, her fiery red cloak billowed out behind her. Thick braids of crystallized hair slithered around her icy crown, hissing violently. Allie's heart nearly stopped when one of those frozen strands stood on end, reaching out toward her.

The icy braid recoiled, revealing Queen Glacidia's empty eye socket, covered in a bubbling white membrane. Allie had never seen anything so frightening in all her life. When Glacidia turned her gaze on Queen Jacqueline, her socket began to glow like ice under a full moon. To her credit, Shevre's mother stood bravely facing her enemy, never lowering her ringed finger.

When Glacidia caught sight of the gem, her fingers instinctively moved to her empty socket, tracing the outline of where her eye should be. Her breath caught in her throat, the object she had sought for so long finally close within her grasp. Fairly panting with greed, she opened her palm. "The gem," she demanded.

Queen Jacqueline laughed. "Do you really expect me to just hand it over?"

Green smoke curled from Glacidia's nostrils as she snarled, "I expect you to *die!*" Her hand whipped out of her robes, shooting razor-tipped icicles from her fingertips.

Queen Jacqueline pointed at the icy daggers as they streaked toward her heart, shouting, "*Acwencian!*" The icicles vanished into thin air.

Glacidia's voice dripped with malice, "Impressive." Turning to the door she purred, "Shadow! I need you, my pet."

Allie took a step back as a dark vapor blew into the room. It floated to Glacidia's side and transformed into a demonic-looking shadow made entirely of black mist.

The shadow growled as it leapt toward Queen Jacqueline. She pointed her finger and a slice of white-hot light pierced the shadowy figure, causing him to fall to the ground, writhing in agony.

"I'm losing my patience," Glacidia snarled, stepping over her fallen servant. "Hand over the gem—NOW!" With a flick of her wrist an arctic wind suddenly whipped through the room. Queen Jacqueline had to grab onto a nearby throne to keep from being blown over, all the while keeping her ringed finger trained on the evil witch.

The Ice Queen laughed, "Do you really think you stand a chance against *me?!*" She raised her arms high in the air and her hair began straining up from her scalp, growing to ten times its natural length. Still attached to the witch's head, the frozen locks slithered across the ceiling, hissing and spitting from above. Allie's face turned white with fear as each tendril grew a snake-like head made of solid ice, opening its mouth wide and exposing two sharp fangs.

Still holding tightly onto the throne, Jacqueline called out, "*Heora sweorde!*" A sword of silver light appeared in her free hand just as the crystal snakes began to lash down from the ceiling. She swung left and right, slashing the heads off each icy lock as the deadly serpents tried to strike her. But no sooner had she chopped one off than another began to grow.

Glacidia's eye blazed with a burning madness. "Enough! I grow tired of this game!" With a flip of her hand, the wind instantly stopped blowing. She ran her eye up and down the rightful Queen of Galdoren and with a cruel smile said, "Goodbye, Jacqueline." With that, one of the hissing tendrils lashed down from the ceiling and bit Queen Jacqueline on her neck.

Jacqueline screamed, dropping her sword to press the magic gem to her wound. It healed instantly, but as it did, her weapon flickered and faded from sight. At the sound of his mother's scream, Shevre burst out of the tapestry, wildly swinging his sword.

Glacidia's eye widened in disbelief. "The Prince! *SEIZE HIM!*"

As Shevre began slashing his way to his mother's side, Shadow rose from the ground. He flew at the young prince, but before he could reach him Queen Jacqueline pointed her finger at the demonic mist, shouting, "*Liflyess sceadu!*"

Shadow's body sizzled where the spell hit him and he again fell to the floor, but not before knocking the boy to the ground. Within moments, a dozen goblins had seized the young prince.

Panicked, Queen Jacqueline dared not throw another spell for fear of injuring her own child.

Shrill laughter pierced the air. "Why, Prince Shevre! What a delightful surprise!" Glacidia glided toward the boy. She pressed a sharp nail under his chin, smiling cruelly at Queen Jacqueline.

"LET HIM GO!" Queen Jacqueline commanded.

"Your son's life for the ring!" she hissed.

Queen Jacqueline looked from her child to the madwoman holding him. "What reason do I have to believe you will spare him once I have given you what you want?"

Glacidia's lips twisted upward. "You'll just have to trust me."

Queen Jacqueline stared into the other woman's soulless eye. And in that moment, she knew her son would die at the hands of this monster. Glancing from the horde of snarling goblins to the vicious shadow rising from the ground, she decided her only chance to save her child was to kill the evil queen. But how did one vanquish such a powerful witch? She raised her arm, pointing her ringed finger at the Queen of Windermere, and began reciting the most powerful spell she knew.

"*B'yardin ...*" The scene suddenly began to play in slow motion, as if watching a movie frame by frame. Allie watched in horror as Shadow flew at Queen Jacqueline. Allie leaped forward, trying to push the shadow out of the way, but her hands slipped right through him.

"*Shatavna ...*"

Queen Glacidia raised her arm. A stream of ice shot out from under her nail. Allie watched helplessly as the ice flew across the air.

"*Myesto ...*"

The shadow ripped the ring off Queen Jacqueline's finger just as the stream of ice pierced her heart. She opened her mouth to finish the spell, but no sound came out.

"MOTHER!" Shevre screamed. He broke free of the goblins and raced to her side. But even as he ran, ice snaked up her body, crackling as it transformed her limbs … her torso … and finally—her head. And by the time he reached her, the only thing that remained unfrozen was the single tear flowing down her cheek. And then, that too, was ice.

Flinging himself onto her frozen body, Shevre sobbed. And as Glacidia reached for the Serpent's Eye, Shevre reached for his sword. With murder in his eye he turned and charged, just as a thick fog began to rise.

"Allie!" She heard her name being called from a distance as the room became shrouded in haze. "Allie!" The voice grew louder and clearer as she felt herself being shaken. She fought to see what was happening, but the room was now completely misted over. Her eyes fluttered open and she found herself looking up into the face of a very worried-looking blue star.

Chapter Fifteen

THE DOOR IN THE TREE

As the sun finally sank below the horizon, Ricky and Twink wandered through the night-cloaked forest, lost and alone. More than once, Ricky thought he saw shadows moving among the tree limbs. And the trees themselves were shifting and changing. They were becoming taller and thicker … the entire forest had slowly transformed into an ominous maze of twisted limbs and gnarled branches. Soon they were surrounded by colossal trees, their bark withered and gray with age, their grizzled branches twisting high overhead.

Twink chewed on his lip. "Uh-oh."

"Don't say that," Ricky said. "Nothing good ever happens when someone says *uh-oh*."

"I think we're in the ancient part of the woods," Twink whispered.

Ricky's heart began to hammer. "What's in the ancient part of the woods?"

Twink swallowed. "Scary stuff."

"What kind of scary stuff? Scary stuff like owls hooting, or scary stuff like monsters leaping out of the trees?"

"The second one."

Just then, Ricky felt a presence. He turned to the woods and saw a familiar pair of glowing eyes staring back at him.

"Who are you?" he called out.

A shrill shriek suddenly sliced through the air, causing the glowing eyes to grow wide with fear. A huge and ferocious-looking bird swooped out of the branches above, scaring the creature with the glowing eyes into hiding. The bird streaked toward the boys, its sharp beak opening wide as it shrieked yet again.

"A Furvel!" Twink screeched in alarm. "RUN!"

Ricky ran as fast as he could, while Twink whipped through the air. They raced through the trees, knocking branches out of their way as they fought to stay ahead of the menacing bird.

"Over there!" Ricky shouted, pointing to a soft light shining on the forest floor.

Charging toward the light, they saw that it was spilling out of a mammoth tree. In his mad dash to reach it, Ricky tripped over a fallen branch and his canteen went flying. As he scrambled to get up, he saw that a door had been carved into the tree's massive trunk and that it was thrown wide open. Both Ricky and Twink sped toward the open door as the terrifying Furvel closed the distance between them.

As soon as they had crossed the threshold, they began shoving against the heavy door, trying to close it. They pushed with all their might, but the door wouldn't budge. The Furvel's shrill scream pierced the night, and Ricky could see its sharp talons ripping through the leaves as it sped toward them.

"Harder, Twink!" he yelled, hurling himself against the door with renewed strength. Inch by inch, it started to creak closed. And just as the Furvel was about to fly in, Ricky saw that a broken lance was stuck under the door, keeping it from closing. He kicked it out, and the door slammed shut. They heard a muffled thump and the sound of the bird's muted shrieking.

Out of breath, Ricky slid to the floor. He nudged Twink and pointed. The inside of the tree had been gutted, replaced by a stone staircase spiraling deep into the ground. Flickering torches lined the walls leading down the stone steps.

On the other side of the door, the furious bird spat blood from her mouth, having bitten her tongue when her beak hit the tree. Screeching with rage, she streaked up to the sky and out of sight.

A nearby bush rustled and a small creature leaped out. The glowing eyes that had been following Ricky all day grew wide with worry. The creature they belonged to grabbed Ricky's canteen in her mouth and then bolted back into the forest.

"Are you okay?" Shimmer asked as he helped Allie up. "You were screaming."

"I was?" Allie blinked. She felt woozy and confused. She was startled to see that the sun had already set. A full moon hung low in the sky. "I ... I think I fell asleep. But I had the strangest dream." As she told the star what she had dreamt, he paled to a light blue.

"That was no dream," he whispered. Goosebumps rose up and down his arms. *How could she have known what happened that night, all those years ago?* Narrowing his eyes he asked, "Are you sure you were born on Earth?"

Allie nodded her head vigorously. "Of course! And I have about a thousand baby pictures to prove it!"

As Shimmer paced through the air, trying to make sense of what had happened, Allie said, "That's what you meant when you told me Queen Jacqueline was neither dead nor alive, wasn't it?"

He sighed. "To this day, King Shevre keeps her icy form on a pedestal in that very room—he's made it his private chamber. He even had a plaque mounted on the base, with the spell she never finished etched in gold."

A thick cloud blew over the moon, momentarily plunging the garden in darkness. Allie inched closer to the shiny star, grateful for his soft, blue light. But when the cloud drifted away, hundreds of tiny flowers began to glow. The little buds slowly opened as they became drenched in moonlight. The pale yellow petals shone brightly, like a trail of tiny nightlights dotting the lawn. "Nightlilies," Shimmer explained.

Haunted by the young prince's grief-stricken face, Allie softly asked, "What happened, after ... after ... you know."

An owl hooted in the distance as Shimmer pondered how to answer her question. "That's a very long and complicated tale, and Ricky and Twinkle must be wondering where we are. We really must be going." He turned in the air and began leading her toward the opening in the bushes.

A wave of guilt washed over Allie. She hadn't thought about her brother or Twink since waking from her strange dream. Suddenly alarmed, she blurted out, "What if they're not there?"

Shimmer paled. The same thought troubled him as well. But not wanting the girl to sense his anxiety, he patted her hand. "I'm sure there's nothing to worry about. Twink knows these woods fairly well. And knowing my nephew, he's been keeping Ricky entertained with tall tales of Galdoren." Smiling, he added, "He does tend to embellish a bit."

Despite Shimmer's reassurances, Allie couldn't help but worry.

When they reached the bush leading back to the woods, Shimmer held out his hand-point to help Allie climb through. She placed her hand in his, then stilled. Looking up at him with fear-filled eyes she quietly said, "Please ... just tell me what happened to Queen Glacidia. And that shadow thing."

"They were imprisoned in Glacidia's homeland—Windermere. The Guardians of Galdoren cast a spell along the border to keep them locked inside."

"Forever?" Allie asked nervously.

Shimmer avoided her gaze. "Er, yes, forever."

Allie breathed a sigh of relief. She carefully climbed through the bush, but just as she reached the other side, a streak of white shot out, nearly knocking her to the ground.

"Snoball?" Allie couldn't have been more surprised. "What are *you* doing here?"

The little snowcat yowled dramatically as Shimmer flew to Allie's side. "What's she saying?" Allie asked. Mystified, the star shrugged.

"Meow! Mrrow, mrrrowr, meowrr meow!" Snoball mewed loudly, her tail swishing hard across the damp spawberries.

Allie stroked the agitated snowcat behind her ears and a shower of tiny icicles fell to the ground. "What is it?" Allie asked in a concerned voice. "What's wrong?"

"Mrrrowrr!" she answered. Frustrated, Snoball leaped into the tall grass that surrounded the spawberry patch, then emerged holding something clenched between her teeth.

Even in the pale moonlight, Allie could see that a faded yellow canteen was dangling from the strap in Snoball's mouth. Her eyes widened in recognition. "That's *Ricky's* canteen!"

Shimmer carefully took the canteen from the shaking cat. "Snoball, is Ricky in trouble?"

"MRRREOW!" the cat wailed miserably.

"And Twink?"

"Meow mrrrow," she whimpered.

"Can you lead us to them?"

Snoball jumped back into the tall grass, her ears pressed flat against her head, and the anxious star and trembling girl followed close behind. As the trio raced toward the ancient part of the woods, the rainbow on Allie's slipper glittered in the shards of moonlight peeking through the clouds. But she never once glanced down as she sped past the shadowy trees, desperate to find her brother and a little purple star.

Chapter Sixteen

THE ROOM IN THE TREE

Ricky and Twink carefully made their way down the long spiral staircase. When they finally crossed the last step, they stared at their surroundings. They were standing in a small circular room, enclosed by smooth stone walls. Other than the torches flickering against the walls, the room was completely empty. Their faces were mirror images of confusion.

"I don't get it," Ricky said. "Why would someone go to all the trouble of building a secret room inside a tree, and then not put anything in it?"

Twink shrugged. "I dunno. Stupid?"

They just stood there blinking, staring at the stone walls.

Twink's eyes grew wide. "Maybe there's a secret entrance to another room hidden somewhere!"

Ricky stared at the empty room. "Where? There's nowhere to hide anything!"

But the little star was excited about the possibility, so he began to investigate. He started to soar across the room, smacked into something in mid-air, and tumbled over backwards.

Ricky's lips twitched. "Well, that's the first time I ever saw anyone trip over the *air*!"

"I did NOT trip over the air!" Twink protested, holding his sore nose. "There's something there!"

"Yeah, right." Ricky smirked, making his way toward Twink. But with his next step, he promptly banged into the invisible object. "OW!"

"Told ya so!"

Ricky reached out and touched the solid mass. He felt something hard and cool beneath his fingertips, but could not see anything there. It was as if the object didn't exist. "There *is* something here!"

"I *know*!" Twink replied, rubbing his still-sore nose. "Hey—I've got an idea! I'll shake some stardust on it!" He soared above the spot where Ricky was standing. "Reach out and touch it again!"

"Okay," Ricky shrugged, stretching his arms out until he felt the invisible mass.

Twink soared above Ricky's fingers and began to spin. Thousands of specks of purple stardust rained down over the spot Ricky was touching. As it landed, an ancient-looking suit of armor began to take shape beneath. The boys stood open-mouthed, staring at the armor that had appeared under the blanket of stardust.

It rose from a tall pedestal and was arranged to look like a knight charging into battle. One arm was thrust forward, the gloved hand curled around the hilt of a glittering sword. In its other hand was a large chevron shield, emblazoned with the picture of a unicorn under a sprawling tree.

"Hey! That's the Galdoren Coat of Arms!" Twink squealed.

Ricky's eyes moved to the pedestal. He knelt down and read the strange words chiseled into it: *Segnian eard ac fira*. Pointing at the inscription he asked Twink, "Do you know what that means?"

Twink flew down and read the words out loud. "*Segnian eard ac fira*." He made a face. "Oh, that just Old Galdorish."

"What's Old Galdorish?"

"Those words."

"No, I mean, what's *Old Galdorish*?"

Twink gave him a funny look. "Those words!"

Ricky took a deep breath. "I get that the words are written in something called Old Galdorish, but what *is* Old Galdorish?"

"Oh. It's like New Galdorish, only older."

Ricky's teeth were set on edge. "What's Galdorish?"

"Duh! It's only the language we speak!" Pointing to the pedestal, Twink explained, "That's the name of the Galdoren national anthem ... it means, *Bless this land and all its people*... You *do* know what a national anthem is, don't you?"

Ricky shot him a withering look.

Scrunching up his face, Twink complained, "I hate that song! It makes me wanna puke!" He turned to Ricky. "Wanna hear it?"

"Not real—"

Twink cut him off and launched into singing the first verse at the top of his voice:

> *"Bless this land and all its people*
> *From the rich and strong to the poor and feeble*
> *From Galdoren's shores to its highest peaks*
> *May we live together in love and peace."*

He stuck a finger-point down his throat and made a vomit noise. As Ricky snickered Twink said, "I like my version better."

"Your version?"

"Yeah, I made up my own lyrics. Wanna hear?"

"Ummm …"

"Okay! I'll sing it to you!" He cleared his throat and in the same tune began to sing,

> *"Bless this land and all its folk*
> *From the dumbest girl to the stinkiest goat*
> *From Galdoren's shores to its highest peaks*
> *There's a big fat crack in my buttocks cheeks."*

Both Ricky and Twink dissolved into peals of laughter.

"How do you say—" Ricky tried to finish his sentence, but he couldn't stop laughing. "How do you say *buttocks cheeks* in Old Galdorish?"

Again, the boys dissolved into giggles. Twink was laughing so hard that he flipped over in the air and landed on the suit of armor's outstretched hand. The entire arm slowly began to creak downward toward the knight's leg. And as it did, the stone wall behind it slid open.

As Ricky stared open-mouthed at the secret entrance, Twink chirped, "Told ya so!"

Chapter Seventeen

THE SHATTERED BOX

Ricky cautiously moved into the dimly lit room. The charred torches lining the walls had all been recently snuffed out, leaving tendrils of smoke curling in the air. He glanced up in time to see the wall on the other side of the room sliding closed. *Another secret panel?* Just before it slid shut, Ricky caught a glimpse of a hulking creature retreating into the darkness. He turned to Twink and asked, "Did you see that?"

"See what?" the little star chirped. He was still very pleased with himself for discovering the secret entrance. As he flew across the threshold, the wall behind him suddenly slid shut, plunging the boys into near total darkness. If it weren't for the soft glow of Twink's starry light they would not have been able to see a thing.

"Don't worry," Twink said cheerfully. He wrapped his arm-point around Ricky's shoulder. "There's gotta be another secret door around here somewhere!" Before Ricky could tell him that he had just seen such a door, Twink began spinning around the room, squealing, "Isn't this fun?"

Fun?! Ricky thought, staring at the flickering shadows creeping across the dark stone walls.

"OW!" Twink suddenly yelled. He had yet again knocked into an invisible object. But this time, the object began to glow the moment the little star bumped into it. It was a crystal pedestal. And sitting atop the glowing pedestal was a shattered glass box, its jagged edges glinting in the mysterious light.

Ricky's eyes moved from the empty box to the glass shards scattered across the floor. "Whadya think was in that box?"

Twink chewed his lip thoughtfully. "A donut?"

Ricky turned to stare at the little star. "Why would anyone put a donut in a glass box?"

Twink shrugged. "To keep it fresh?"

Ricky suddenly whipped his head around, sensing movement behind him, but when he looked, all he saw were the murky shadows of a darkened corner. Turning back to the shattered box, he started to walk toward the pedestal. But the moment he moved his feet, he tripped over something and landed with a thud on the floor.

"Have a nice trip?" Twink snickered. But before Ricky could answer, Twink pointed at him and squealed, "Hey! You're floating!"

"Huh?" Ricky looked down and was surprised to find that he was indeed seated several inches off the floor. But it didn't feel like he was floating. It felt more like he was sitting on something.

He felt around beneath him. His fingers were met with something hard and cold to the touch. He looked down, but couldn't see a thing. *Another invisible object?* He spread his hands to touch the floor beneath him. His face suddenly went ashen as he scrambled to get up. With a shaking finger, he pointed to the ground. "There's something there! I think … I think …" He took a deep breath and whispered, "I think it's a *body!*"

"What kind of a body?"

"The DEAD kind!" Ricky snapped. A stunned silence hung in the air as the boys stared down at the seemingly empty floor. "Twink, shake some stardust over here!"

The little star quickly zoomed above the spot Ricky was pointing to and began to shake. As the sparkling flecks fell through the air, the outline of a knight's body began to appear beneath the layer of stardust below.

"Is that another invisible suit of armor?" Twink asked hopefully.

Ricky shook his head and quietly said, "No … it's a knight." Swallowing hard, he added, "A *dead* knight!" The knight's thick chain mail had not been strong enough to stop the dagger that was sticking out of his chest.

Twink scratched his head. "An invisible knight …" As soon as the words were out of his mouth, Twink felt like he knew something important, but couldn't quite recall what. It was as if the information was just beyond his reach.

Afraid to move another step, Ricky looked up at his friend. "Can you shake stardust *everywhere*?"

Twink nodded solemnly and then began flying around the room, shaking stardust onto all but the darkest corners. Within moments, the floor was glittering with the lifeless bodies of dozens of knights and a jumble of discarded weapons. Ricky's eyes scanned over the eerily glowing knights, maces, swords and crossbows scattered across the floor.

"An army of invisible knights," Ricky murmured.

Twink's head snapped up as he suddenly remembered. "The king's invisible army!" he breathed. "They guard only one thing ...," his voice trailed off as a sudden dread consumed him. He streaked toward the shattered glass box and gasped, "Someone's stolen it!!!"

Ricky instantly thought back to the hulking creature he had seen just before the door slid shut. He met his friend's horror-stricken eyes and asked, "What did they steal?"

"The Serpent's Eye!"

Ricky shook his head in confusion. "The Serpent's *what*?"

But before Twink could answer, a shadow suddenly peeled itself off the wall and flew at the little star.

"Twink! Watch out!" Ricky shouted. But it was too late. The cold fingers of the shadow's hands were tightly curled around Twink's neck. Twink struggled to break free, but he was rapidly turning a sickening shade of whitish-purple.

Ricky grabbed a sword off the floor so quickly that the layer of stardust covering it tumbled to the ground, rendering it invisible again. Had he not felt the weight of the hilt in his hand, he would have doubted he was holding anything. He charged toward the shadow, stabbing him in the shoulder with his invisible sword. The shadow howled a blood-curdling cry, dropping the tiny star.

Ricky watched helplessly as Twink fell to the floor. Eyes closed, the little star lay alarmingly still. Enraged, Ricky once again attacked the growling mist. But his enemy had already guessed that he was wielding an invisible weapon. In a flash, he kicked the boy's hand, knocking the sword from his fingers.

Tears blurred Ricky's vision. The shadow had broken three of his fingers. He felt nauseous as he doubled over in pain. The shadow flew at him from behind and wrapped his vice-like fingers around Ricky's throat. Ricky tried clawing at his tormentor with his good hand, but he could not pry even one finger loose. He gasped for air, but his throat was being squeezed so tightly that not even a single breath could slip through. Black dots danced before Ricky's eyes. His lungs burned like they were on fire. Within moments, he became so weak and dizzy that his arms stopped flailing and dropped to hang helplessly at his sides.

Then a brilliant explosion of blue light shattered the room. Ricky thought he heard his name being screamed as the shadow's fingers suddenly slipped from his neck. And the last thing Ricky saw before he lost consciousness was the shadow's hazy hand curled around a glittering eyeball.

Chapter Eighteen

HAUNTED MEMORIES

The Three swept into the ancient tree, eyes blazing, wands out. Expecting to thwart Shadow and his goblin assassins, they were stunned to find Shimmer, an Earth girl, and a mewing snowcat hovering over two unconscious boys.

Allie was sobbing against her brother's chest, while Shimmer fretted in the air above Twink. Snoball was curled between them, her tail swishing quietly against the floor.

Shimmer looked up at the three women, his eyes brimming with tears. "Shadow!" he cried. "He … he attacked the boys! I don't know how to revive them!" Choking over a sob he added, "He took the Serpent's Eye! I tried to stop him but—"

"How long has he been gone?" Sharonna interrupted.

"A minute, two at the most!"

"Serena, Hildy—after him! I'll heal the children." Unclasping her cloak, she called, "GO!"

She gently covered the fallen boys as Serena and Hildy flew out of the room, up the stairs and into the forest.

Shadow sped through the trees. Feeling the weight of his mistress's prize bouncing in his palm, he nearly laughed out loud. But as he stole a glance at the diamond sparkling between his fingers, he suddenly stilled and looked up at the sky. Two hooded figures circled above the treetops—he was being hunted.

He slid the gem into the folds of his cloak, cursing beneath his breath as he transformed into a dark mist. Traveling in his vaporous form would slow him down, but speed was not his primary concern at the moment.

My mistress will soon start wondering what is keeping me, he thought bitterly. *But she will have her prize before this night is over,* he vowed, melting into the thick fog already covering the forest floor.

✯ ✯ ✯

Serena and Hildy flew above the treetops, scanning the ground. Even by the light of the full moon, the woods were nearly pitch black, shadowed beneath the enormous branches and thick canopy of leaves.

"It's no use," Hildy sighed. "We'll have to search by foot."

"But that will take too much time!" Serena fretted.

"I know, but it's our only hope of catching him."

Their cloaks swirled in the wind as they glided between the branches, landing on the soft forest floor below. Pointing their wands at the ground they commanded, *"Leoht-bora!"* A large patch of earth was suddenly bathed in a soft, golden light.

"Oh, my stars!" Serena exclaimed. The ground was covered in a thick fog. "How do you find a mist within a mist?"

The two women exchanged worried glances. Hildy squared her shoulders as she stepped forward, pointing her wand. "Let us hope that good fortune is on our side."

✯ ✯ ✯

Not far ahead, a black mist moved quickly against the natural direction of the fog. The witch's enchanted light was nearly upon him. Shadow clung to the damp ground, continually glancing back. He sucked in his breath when he saw an emerald green cloak billowing in the breeze—*the Guardians of Galdoren!*

He redoubled his efforts to stay ahead as his mind drifted back to the last time he had encountered The Three. The foul memories of that fateful night came rushing back, unbidden. He clawed at the ground as that long-ago nightmare seeped into his thoughts, transporting him back to the dreadful evening that had changed his and his mistress's lives forever ...

Ice was rapidly crackling down Queen Jacqueline's arm as Shadow ripped the Serpent's Eye from her finger. Within moments, the Queen of Galdoren was nothing more than a frozen statue. The young prince fell upon his mother's body, weeping uncontrollably.

Shadow held the ring triumphantly in the air. But just as Queen Glacidia reached to claim the fabled gem, the prince suddenly turned. He charged toward the evil witch, his sword thrust murderously forward. Shadow dove between them, knocking the boy to the ground. He twisted the prince's wrist until he heard a loud crack. The boy screamed in pain, his sword clattering to the floor. Glacidia looked on with a malicious smile as her servant pinned the boy to the ground.

Shadow looked up at his mistress questioningly. "Kill him," she ordered.

But as he was reaching for the prince's fallen sword, a stiff wind blew in from the open window. The blast of air slammed into Shadow, knocking him off the boy and hurtling him against a wall. As a stunned Glacidia watched in horror, the wind lifted Prince Shevre in the air, carrying him out the window, and into the safety of the night.

Shadow slithered to the ground, half-conscious. When he hit the floor, the ring he had been clutching fell from his fingers and skidded across the marble floor, stopping at the frozen body of Queen Jacqueline.

"My ring!" the Queen of Windermere shrieked. But as she flew across the room, a wall of black fire suddenly lit up, dividing the room in two. Separated from the Eye by the wall of flames, she shrieked in rage.

The fuming queen turned to her band of goblins. "Fools! Why do you stand there and do nothing while my treasure sits unclaimed?!?" Pointing at the inferno, she screamed, "GO!"

The goblins hesitated, unsure if their fire-proof skin would be immune to this magical blaze. When they made no attempt to move, Glacidia's eye blazed with a murderous rage. "Get ... my ... RING!" She flipped her hands, flinging them into the fire. Their mouths began to melt even as they opened them to scream. Within moments, their flesh was burned from their bones, and they were nothing more than piles of ash.

Glacidia's hair stood on end, furiously straining out of her scalp, each frozen strand hissing violently. "That ring is mine! MINE!"

Shadow slowly rose from the floor, limping toward his mistress. "Allow me to try, my Queen."

But just then, three hooded figures flew in from the open window, their emerald green cloaks billowing in the wind.

Glacidia's glassy eye socket twitched dangerously as she snarled, "The Guardians of Galdoren!"

Sharonna fell upon her younger sister's frozen body, her heart breaking as she quietly wept. Hildy pulled out her wand, pointing it at the lifeless queen. She began to chant spell after spell, trying to revive her. Staring through the flames at Glacidia, Edna slowly moved toward the Serpent's Eye. Kneeling, she picked up the ring and slipped it into her cloak pocket, all the while keeping her eyes firmly trained on the wicked queen.

Glacidia moved as close to the wall of fire as she dared. In a murderous rage, she pointed a shaking finger at Edna, shooting a deadly spell through the flames. But the venomous magic was instantly consumed by the raging fire. "The ring for your queen's life," *she spat.*

"I do not strike bargains with murderers," *Edna shot back, raising her wand to point at her enemy.*

The witch's good eye flashed with pinpricks of red as she growled, "Then the prince's mother shall remain frozen—forever!"

"Perhaps," *Edna said cryptically.* "But who can foretell the future?" *Keeping her wand trained on Glacidia and Shadow, she turned to her fellow guardians and asked,* "What shall we do with them?"

Sharonna looked from the frozen Queen of Galdoren to the window. Staring at the pale boy shaking in the air outside, she sighed, "Let us ask our new king."

A twig snapped, startling Shadow back to the present day.

"What was that?" he heard a voice behind him ask.

He climbed up a nearby tree, and hid within the dark shadows of its branches. One of the witches pointed her wand and commanded, "Leoht-bora!"

The ground below him was instantly bathed in a golden light. He rose higher into the tree as the two women slowly moved forward, carefully waving their wands through the thick fog rising up from the forest floor.

He held his breath as they stopped just beneath him. They scanned the area, then continued walking on, never noticing the dark vapor clinging to the branches above.

Sharonna rubbed her palms together and pressed them against Twink's neck while commanding, *"Healian aberstan sweora!"*

The little star's neck began to glow, dimly at first, then little by little it glowed more brightly. His sickly pallor began to change from a chalky white to a faded purple. Worry lines etched Sharonna's face as she felt his pulse. She again touched her fingers to his neck, but his weak heartbeat and pale color remained unchanged.

Frowning, she turned her attention to Ricky. Pressing her hands lightly against his neck, she repeated the incantation. His skin glowed beneath her fingertips, and within moments, a flush swept across his cheeks, imbuing his face with color.

Sharonna then picked up the boy's hand. His fingers were blue and swollen and set at the wrong angle. Lightly touching them, she murmured, *"Healian aberstan folma!"* The bluish tinge instantly vanished along with the swelling. Allie watched in amazement as her brother's fingers straightened themselves back to their natural angle. Sharonna nodded in satisfaction.

Turning to Twink, she rubbed her palms together once more until they glowed a brilliant white. She pressed her shimmering hands firmly against his heart. Instantly, the little star's labored breathing became more normal. Exhausted, she dropped her hands to her sides, where they slowly stopped glowing.

She looked up at Allie and quietly said, "Your brother will be fine when he awakens."

Allie flung herself at Sharonna and embraced her. Unable to find the right words, she simply choked, "Thank you."

Sharonna patted the Earth girl's back comfortingly, then reached into her pocket, pulled out a handkerchief and handed it to the sniffling girl. As Allie blew her nose into the lacy cloth, Sharonna turned her attention to Shimmer. He hung limply in the air, staring worriedly at his unconscious nephew. Sharonna squeezed his hand and gently said, "I've done all that I can."

Hildy looked up at the moon looming high above. "It's no use. We're wasting valuable time—time that would be better spent completing the Transference and sealing the crack in that border."

"I agree," Serena replied.

The two women tucked their wands back into their cloaks, and then flew straight up through the trees, soaring into the sky.

Not far from where they had been standing, a black vapor peeled itself off a nearby tree. It swirled above the wet moss for a moment or two, then began to transform into the shadow of a man. The dark figure slowly rose from the ground, and moved quickly in the direction of Windermere.

Chapter Nineteen

UNEXPECTED GOODBYES

Ricky slowly opened his eyes. He was disoriented at first, but when he saw the shattered glass box sitting atop the glowing pedestal, the nightmarish memories came flooding back. His hands automatically flew to his neck. But it felt just as it always had. He sat up so quickly that the room began to spin. He took a few deep breaths to clear his head, then lifted his injured hand and turned it. He wondered why it didn't hurt anymore. Cautiously, he wiggled one finger, then two, and then he wiggled them all. It was as if his hand had magically mended itself.

"Twink!" he called loudly, his eyes darting around the well-lit room. He was surprised that all of the torches were now blazing brightly against the thick stone walls.

"TWINK!" he yelled even louder. He slowly pulled himself up to a standing position. Again, the world twirled. He leaned on the glowing pedestal to steady himself.

Still holding onto the pedestal for support, he took a step forward. He gasped when he saw the little star lying unconscious on an emerald green cloak. He fell to his friend's side, enormously relieved to see his chest rising and falling with each breath. At least he was alive. At least they were *both* alive! But how had they escaped that horrible shadow? And where were all the dead knights and their weapons? And who had cleaned up all those shards of glass?

"Did someone call me?" Shimmer's voice was shaky as the secret wall panel slid open. "Hello? Is anyone awake?" Ricky was stunned to see the once vibrant blue star hanging raggedly in the air, his brow etched with worry lines. He was so pale, he was nearly white. But the moment he saw Ricky, a huge smile split his face. He streaked across the room and wrapped the boy in a tremendous hug, clutching him tightly.

"Shimmer!" Ricky cried with relief, hugging him in return. He didn't see the spark of hope in Shimmer's eyes flicker and die when he saw his nephew still lying motionless on the ground.

As Shimmer's arms fell to his side, Ricky began to babble, the words flowing almost faster than he could say them. "We were attacked by this ... this ... shadow thing! And there were dead knights everywhere! And glass!" He pointed frantically at the shattered box. "And something important was stolen from that box! And ... and the knights ... they were *invisible*! Twink's stardust must have worn off!" His eyes were wild as he grabbed the star. "You've gotta shake more stardust across the floor!"

Trying to calm the boy down, Shimmer took his hand and patted it reassuringly. "The knights are gone, Ricky. They have all been moved."

Ricky's voice rose, "But how did that shadow kill *all* of them?"

"He didn't. Their weapons were covered in goblin blood. I suspect a fierce battle was fought in this room."

"But," Ricky ran his hand through his hair, "why was he trying to kill *us*?" His eyes moved to Twink. A lump formed in Shimmer's throat as he followed Ricky's gaze.

"Will he be okay?" Ricky softly asked.

Shimmer eyes were watery as he choked, "I don't know." Wiping his eyes, he continued, "As for your other question, Shadow attacked you because you stumbled upon him just as he was stealing the Serpent's Eye." He moved toward the shattered box, and gingerly ran a hand-point down its side.

"What *is* the Serpent's Eye?" Ricky asked.

Shimmer had nearly forgotten that the boy was from Earth. "It's an ancient gem resembling a serpent's eyeball—white with a glittering black gem in the center. It looks like a diamond, but it is really made of pure fairie magic. The wearer of the ring must be of fairie ancestry to wield its power."

"A glittering eyeball?" Ricky's blood ran cold. "I saw it, Shimmer! That shadow thing was holding it!"

Shimmer's eyes dropped as he stared at the floor. He looked like the weight of the world was on his shoulders. "I know," he said. "But my main concern when I confronted him was with saving you and my nephew. When I saw both of you lying there on the floor … so pale … your eyes closed …" Unable to complete his sentence, he turned from Ricky as he shook with a silent sob.

Ricky suddenly remembered the explosion of blue light that had caused Shadow to stop choking him. "It was YOU!" Unsure of what to say to someone who had just saved his life, Ricky stammered, "Thank … thank you."

"Think nothing of it," the star whispered in response.

"Uncle Shimmer?" Twink's tiny voice interrupted their conversation.

Shimmer streaked to his nephew's side, clasping him tightly to his chest. "You're awake!"

"Air," gasped Twink. "Can't breathe. Squeezing too tight."

Shimmer released his young nephew, some of the natural blue coloring returning to his cheeks. "Twinkle, I—" He broke off his sentence to pull the little star to his chest and hug him again, tears of joy slipping from the corners of his eyes.

"Hey! You're leaking!" Twink said, wiping the salty water off his head.

Just then, Allie walked into the room. When she saw her brother, she rushed to his side. Embracing him tightly, she sniffled, "Are you okay?"

He was surprised to see that she had been crying. "I'm fine." Noting the fresh tears watering her eyes, he insisted, *"Really!"*

Allie turned her watery gaze to the little star. "Twink!" He slipped out of his uncle's arms, smiling shyly at her. She plucked him out of the air and hugged him tightly. His mouth dropped open as he turned three shades of purple.

Releasing the stunned little star, she turned back to her brother. "Are you sure you're okay?" When he nodded in response, her eyes narrowed to slits. "Then I'm going to *kill* you! Why did you and Twink wander off that path?!"

"Yes, why did you?" Shimmer asked.

Twink and Ricky exchanged nervous glances.

"We got tricked! This little blue man—"

"MEOW!" A snow-white cat wrapped herself around Ricky's legs.

"Snoball!" he called happily, stroking the cat behind her ears. A shower of tiny icicles fell to the ground.

"She's the one you should thank," Shimmer smiled. "Without her, we might never have found you."

Ricky looked into Snoball's glowing eyes. As recognition dawned on him, he laughed. "So *you're* the mysterious creature who was following me all day!"

Snoball mewed in response, rubbing her check affectionately against his hand. When he bent to pick her up, he glanced out the open door. He was surprised to see a strange woman speaking to a blurry man's head floating in the air before her. "Who's *that?*" he asked, pointing at Sharonna.

"She's a member of The Three," Allie answered. Seeing the blank look on her brother's face, she laughed. "Don't worry. I'll explain everything later. Just don't say anything stupid. She's, like, really important."

Sharonna nodded to the fuzzy image in the air just before it disappeared. Tucking a wand back into her pocket, she stepped into the room. Seeing the boys up and about she smiled for the first time that evening. "Well, I'm glad to see you two looking so well. It will make traveling so much easier."

"Traveling?" Shimmer questioned.

"Hildy and Serena have just returned. They're waiting for us outside." Shimmer's eyes grew wide with hope, until Sharonna shook her head dismally. His shoulders slumped as she picked her cloak up off the floor and continued, "We must hurry! Shadow will be halfway to Windermere by now."

As she shooed everyone out the door she explained, "I've just spoken with the king." She shook her head, muttering, "The reception is terrible in this part of the woods—the spell kept breaking up. But I got the gist of his orders." She suddenly grabbed Ricky's shoulders. "Mind the antique, dear," she advised as she steered him around the invisible suit of armor. He had forgotten it was there. "Shimmer, King Shevre wants you to fly to the castle immediately. Hildy, Serena and I are to leave at once for Edna's to complete the Transference."

As they came to the base of the stairs, she waved her wand across the group, twirling it three times. "*Arisan!*" she commanded. All at once, everyone was carried up the steps on a stiff breeze. Snoball yowled the whole way up, but within moments, she was lowered back to the floor along with everyone else when they reached the top of the stairs. As Sharonna pushed open the door leading out of the tree, she cleared her throat. "Shimmer ... I was ordered to bring the children with us to Edna's."

His mouth hung open. "WHAT?!?"

"The king feels—and I really must agree—that they will be much safer tucked away on her little farm."

As Serena and Hildy greeted the children, Shimmer argued with Sharonna. "But the castle is heavily guarded, and I will watch over them every moment I am able. Twink will promise to be on his best behavior ...," he turned to his nephew who nodded enthusiastically. "And Roberts can—"

"I am afraid King Shevre gave a *direct order* that the children are to come with us." Her voice softened as she added. "I'm sorry, Shimmer. I know how you worry. But they really will be safer at Edna's."

Shimmer wished he could be certain of that. But a direct order from the king was not something that could be argued with. So he reluctantly nodded his head.

"Quickly, everyone!" Sharonna urged as she fastened the cloak around her neck.

Shimmer hugged each of the children, brushing a kiss across Twink's forehead.

"I'll miss you, Uncle Shimmer," the little star murmured.

"I'll miss you too." Shimmer assured him. As he turned to leave, he gave one last bit of parting advice to his nephew. "Stay out of Edna's crops. Remember what happened the last time?" Twink smiled crookedly, a guilty look crossing his face. Shimmer gave him one last hug, then streaked up to the sky. Within moments, he was out of sight.

"Ladies," Sharonna said, nodding toward the children. Each of the women wrapped a child within the folds of her cloak. Snoball shivered in Ricky's arms as they began to rise in the air. The next moment, they were rocketing up to the sky, soaring toward a little farm at the edge of the woods.

Chapter Twenty

LAUGHING AT THE MOON

A dark cloud drifted over the moon, cloaking the forest below in a velvety blackness. Shadow raced through the trees, heedless of the dark, for it was under the shroud of darkness that he could see most clearly.

At last he came to the edge of the woods. He scanned the mossy clearing that lay between the edge of the forest and the Windermere border. He looked up to the sky, half-expecting to see The Three flying above, waiting to ambush him. He sniffed the humid air, but the only scents he could detect were a mix of woodland creatures and insects. The hollow opening of his mouth curved upward in a gruesome smile.

He transformed into vapor and floated above the damp soil, careful to stay shrouded within the dark shadows lest anyone be watching. A breeze blew the cloud off the moon and the world was bathed in a golden light. Shadow covered his sensitive eyes against the sudden brightness. When he opened his lids, he saw his queen pacing back and forth on the Windermere side of the border. She looked worried—anxious even. He could hardly wait to see her face when she saw the prize he had brought her.

When at last he reached the Border Spell, he rose to a standing position as he changed back to his solid form, and bowed to his mistress.

"Show me," she growled.

He reached into his cloak and retrieved her treasure, slowly opening his hand to reveal it to his queen. Nestled in his palm was a stone of brilliant white, sparkling impossibly against the dark mist of his fingers. And in the center of that white stone was a black diamond. Glacidia's breath caught in her throat. She pushed her hands flat against the Border Spell, willing it to crack even further so that she might reach out and touch the magnificent gem.

"Bring it to me!" she commanded in a shaking voice. On the Windermere side of the border the icy winds howled, blowing her crimson cloak out behind her. She curled her hands into tight fists, her sharp fingernails digging deep into the tender skin on her palm.

"HURRY!" she shrieked.

The few moments it took for her shadowy servant to slip through the crack in the Border Spell stretched an eternity for her. It was agonizing to be so close and yet so far from the object she had sought for so many years. When at last Shadow materialized on Windermere soil, she found she could only stare at the sparkling creation in his hand.

"Take it, my Queen," he said in a raspy whisper, thrusting his hand toward her.

"Yes, YES!" she cried, her shoulders trembling with excitement. She reached out and curled her fingers around the stone. It felt warm against her skin.

"Break free, Your Highness! Galdoren is now yours for the taking!" Shadow's eyes gleamed supernaturally in the moonlight.

Queen Glacidia's lips curled into a twisted smile. She spread her arms wide and rejoiced in the feel of the icy winds, knowing she would soon be bathed in the balmy breezes of Galdoren. It was then that she caught sight of the moon, looming large and full in the sky. She threw her head back and began to laugh. And laugh. And laugh.

On the other side of the woods, Gossamer sat alone in her dark office, staring at an empty desk drawer. A soft breeze blowing in through her gauzy curtains caused her to look out the open window. When she saw the moon hanging over the distant mountaintops of Windermere, she too began to laugh. And laugh. And laugh.

Chapter Twenty-One

THE TRANSFERENCE

The Three glided out of the midnight sky and landed gently on a gingerbread rooftop, setting the children down before them. Serena grimaced as something squished beneath her shoe. She lifted her foot, making a face when she saw the layer of vanilla frosting coating the bottom of her pink leather boot. She heaved a sigh and mentally chastised herself for wearing her favorite pair of shoes just to impress the king. She let out an exasperated breath. *As if he even noticed!*

A white-haired woman stood waiting for them on the roof, buttoning her brightly patterned cardigan. A lacy apron stuck out from the bottom of her sweater. "We should take the children inside," she said worriedly. "They'll catch a chill out here!"

"Honestly Edna, you know we're in a terrible hurry!" Sharonna huffed. "You can take them inside after we complete the Transference." When Edna opened her mouth to argue, Sharonna cut her off. "You know that you'll insist upon giving them a steaming mug of hot cocoa with marshmallows once you get them in. I'm sorry, but time is one luxury we cannot afford right now!"

"Nonsense," Edna answered. "The poor little lambs must be freezing up here, and exhausted to boot! And have you forgotten how hot the sparks from the Transference are? No, it's much too danger-ous for them up here." She moved toward the children, arms open, wearing the warmest smile Allie had ever seen. "Welcome to my home," she beamed. Then she hugged Allie, Ricky, and finally Twink. As she bent to hug the little star, Allie overheard her whisper, "Guess what's in season?" Twink, in return, squealed with delight.

"Edna!" Hildy chastised. "Do hurry!"

"Oh, it's obvious we'll accomplish nothing until she gets her way. As *always*," Sharonna added in an irritated tone.

"Don't mind her," Edna whispered to the children as she led them to the edge of the roof. "She always gets cranky just before an important mission."

"What stuff and nonsense are you telling them?" Sharonna demanded.

Ignoring her, Edna plucked something off the side of the chimney. "I believe this is yours now, dear," she said to Serena as she tossed the object her way. Serena looked at the cloth in her hands; it was an emerald green cloak.

Edna reached into her apron pocket and pulled out a wand. She muttered an incantation under her breath and waved the wand above the children. A shower of sparkling flecks surrounded them as they were suddenly lifted into the air. They sailed off the edge of the gingerbread roof and into an open window below.

Even before Edna's spell floated them to their waiting beds, Allie's and Twink's eyes were starting to close. Ricky fought to stay awake, but the sleeping spell Edna had cast was simply too powerful. He heard the muffled sounds of footsteps on the roof as he was gently lowered onto a pillowy soft bed. A down comforter pulled itself over the yawning boy.

As Ricky snuggled into his fluffy pillow, he thought he smelled marshmallows. His eyes fluttered and shut just before a tremendous flash of brilliant white light lit up the sky above the rooftop. He was dreaming of s'mores by the time the Power Transference was complete. The curtains on his open window rustled lightly when three green-cloaked women streaked past, flying in the direction of Windermere.

Chapter Twenty-Two

THE IMPOSTER

"The moment has finally arrived, my pet." Glacidia's words sounded like silk on the wintry winds. Shadow knelt before her, tingling with anticipation.

The Ice Queen stroked the glittering eyeball in her palm, whispering a spell to separate the gem from the ring. It wobbled in her hand and then the diamond tumbled off the prongs that had held it in place. She tossed the useless ring into the snow and held the jewel up to the moonlight. Tears pooled in her good eye as she was flooded with emotion. From the moment she had learned of its existence, she had been obsessed with the fabled gem. She yearned to see the world through the sparkling facets of the Serpent's Eye. And the power the gem would bestow upon her ... Glacidia's heart raced at the thought.

She took a deep breath and then carefully began to press the jewel into her empty eye socket. With a loud slurping noise, it was sucked into the folds of her milky flesh.

"My Queen, what do you see?" Shadow breathed.

Glacidia blinked, stunned that she was still half-blind. She had been so sure that the Eye would instantly give her the gift of sight. *Well, no matter*, she thought, blinking half-shed tears away. Raising her chin in the air, she concentrated on her powers and the spell she needed to break.

"*Breotan sceard aberstan!*" she commanded, her voice choking with emotion. Jagged spears of ice shot out of her fingertips. Streaking toward the Border Spell, the razor-tipped icicles glistened in the arctic air. They smashed into the invisible wall of the Border Spell with a thunderous boom that shook the earth. The air above sizzled, then exploded with a blinding flash. But the next moment, all was calm, and the tightly woven Border Spell was as strong and solid as ever. Expecting to see a gaping hole, Glacidia was so startled that all she could do was stand there, blinking. In a daze, she reached out and traced her fingers over the solid wall of magic.

She fell backwards in the snow, her legs suddenly wobbly and weak, no longer able to support her. The jewel had had no effect on her powers whatsoever! She was still trapped in this frozen wasteland, barred from Galdoren forever. And she still had no sight in one eye. She slowly turned to face her quivering servant.

"You *fool!* YOU BROUGHT ME A FAKE! A *FORGERY!*" she screamed, clawing at the worthless gem in her eye socket. Rising to her knees, she howled with rage, twisting and pulling at the Eye until the gem finally snapped free of her membrane. She pointed a shaking finger at the jewel and the diamond exploded into a thousand shards of crystal.

She turned to Shadow, so angry she could barely speak. "Who has my gem?" she spat. "*WHO?!?*"

"My Queen, my Queen!" Shadow rasped frantically. "It is true that we have both been tricked. But so has the king himself! Someone in Galdoren must have the *real* Serpent's Eye. And if they have stolen it for themselves, then it cannot be very well protected. No guards ... no army of Invisible Knights ... think of it, my Queen."

Glacidia sucked in huge gulps of air. Kneeling in the snow, she turned her head to the sky. The wind blew a layer of ice crystals across her upturned face.

She thought about her servant's words, and with a horrified clarity she realized the mistake she had made when she first cast the Spell of Spilled Secrets: she had asked the wrong question. Instead of asking where King Shevre had hidden the Serpent's Eye, she should have asked where the Serpent's Eye was hidden. A small, but vital, distinction. The spell had worked; it had shown her exactly where King Shevre had hidden the fake gem. Shadow was right—the king had not known that the diamond his Invisible Knights were guarding was a forgery.

She squeezed her eye shut, focusing all of her energy on this one, all-important question: who had the Serpent's Eye? Her lid suddenly flew open. She turned to Shadow and hissed, "Who guarded the gem before it was hidden away in that tree?"

Shadow nervously flicked a black tongue over his lips, trying to remember. Glacidia's face suddenly hardened as a name sprang to mind. "Shimmer," she breathed, rising from the ground.

At the mention of the star's name, Shadow's pulse quickened. His hand touched the wound that still burned. Both the Earth boy and Shimmer had inflicted pain upon him that evening, and he vowed they both would pay.

"Shimmer was in charge of guarding the ring," she said with growing excitement. "I remember my spies reporting that bit of information. And there was a witch … no, a fairie, who guarded it with him. What was her name? The one with those ridiculously large wings?" She snapped her fingers. "*Gossamer!* Yes, that was it!"

"I do not believe that Shimmer has the Serpent's Eye, your majesty. He fought too fiercely for the fake diamond earlier this evening."

Queen Glacidia raised a brow. She had not asked Shadow the details of how he had obtained the ring, as she had not cared. "Then that woman, Gossamer, must still have it," she reasoned. "They were the only two who had possession of the gem before it was secreted away."

Just then, a large black bird swooped down from the sky on the other side of the Border Spell. The Furvel wondered why her queen had failed to use the gem yet to break free. Something must have gone wrong.

Glacidia rose and moved toward the border to address the Furvel. "Do you know of a fairie named *Gossamer?*"

"Gossamer?" the Furvel repeated. "She owns a shop in Village Square—Gossamer's Gifts. It's funny you should ask, because only yesterday I saw her talking to Shimmer and his bratty nephew. Oh … and those Earth kids." She fluttered her wings. "They were all there tonight, you know. In the tree."

The queen drummed her fingertips against the Border Spell. "Well, isn't that interesting?" A slow smile curved her lips. "I believe I am in the mood to do a little shopping. Could you and Shadow kindly bring the proprietor of Gossamer's Gifts to our little corner of the world? I am certain she will soon be *dying* to supply me with the one gift I crave above all others."

The Furvel flapped her wings excitedly as Shadow transformed into a black mist and flowed through the hidden crack in the Border Spell. Pouring himself into Galdoren, he changed shape into the shadowy image of a man. "We will return shortly, my Queen."

Gossamer sat alone in her office, staring out the open window as the moon slowly sank in the sky. The first beams of sunlight were beginning to shine over the village casting golden shadows on the cobblestone streets.

The bell jingled on her front door, even though it was locked. She was surprised by how calm she felt. She had been expecting this for so long; it was almost a relief now that the moment had finally arrived.

"You're too late, Shadow," she called. "It's gone."

The shadow flowed under her closed office door, reappearing on the other side. Gossamer shivered as the misty figure rose from the floor. She had never been this close to him before. There was almost nothing to see. Just a wisp of smoke, really.

His eyes swept over her crowded shelves. With a violent swipe of his hand, snow globes flew in every direction, crashing against the walls and floor. He leaned in close to her face. "Where is the Serpent's Eye?" he hissed. His breath felt cold against her warm cheeks.

Fighting to stop shaking, Gossamer held her chin high. "I told you, it's gone."

He whipped his other hand out, smashing more snow globes to the floor. Tears stung her eyes as she watched the glittering water pour out of the cherished ornaments she had so lovingly created.

"If you will not tell me," he rasped in her ear. "Then perhaps you will tell your queen!"

Gossamer's eyes flashed. "She will NEVER be my queen!"

A claw-like hand slapped the tender skin on her cheek, knocking the spectacles off her face. Blood dripped from the deep scratches, splattering onto her flowered apron. Shadow snaked his arms tightly around her body and lifted her. A huge black bird swooped in through the open window, grabbing Gossamer in the supernatural strength of its talons. Gossamer's screams were soon swallowed by the wind as she was carried far from her home, toward a wintry doom.

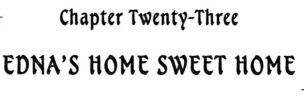

Chapter Twenty-Three

EDNA'S HOME SWEET HOME

Ricky awoke to the smell of chocolate and the sounds of crunching. Opening his eyes, he saw Twink propped up in the other bed, shoving a huge chunk of chocolate into his mouth. The growling in Ricky's stomach reminded him that he hadn't eaten in more than a day. He licked his lips hungrily. "Can I have a bite?"

"Glarph en thell dreshhurr," answered Twink, his mouth full of candy.

"What?"

Twink continued chewing as he pointed to a light brown dresser in the corner, which looked as if it had seen better days.

"It's in the dresser?" Ricky leaped out of bed. "Which drawer?"

Twink finally swallowed. "The chocolate's not *in* the dresser … it *is* the dresser! And the chair … and the nightstand …" Reaching for the object in question, he ripped a knob off and popped it into his mouth. He made a face and spit the half-chewed candy back into his hand. "Ew. Dark chocolate."

Ricky turned to examine his headboard. It *did* look like it was carved from chocolate! He moved closer and sniffed, inhaling the mouth-watering aroma. He snapped off a corner and shoved it into his mouth. "Mmmm," he sighed, savoring the sweet taste of the creamy chocolate.

Twink zoomed across the room and threw open the closet door. "Yummy!" he squealed. "Licorice hangers!" He pulled an empty hanger off the rod and took a giant bite.

Just then, the door opened. Edna smiled warmly at the boys. "Good morning! Did you have a good night's sleep?" She sniffed the air. Her eyes narrowed as she took in the boys' chocolate-smeared faces. She placed her hands on her hips and gave Twink a stern look. "Twinkle, what did you promise the last time you visited?"

Twink hung his head and kicked a foot-point in the air. "Not to eat the furniture."

Tapping her foot she added, "And?"

In a small voice he answered, "Not to drink the toilet water." Looking up at her with pleading eyes, he implored, "But Edna, it's Tropical Punch—my favorite!"

"Not anymore. All the toilets in this house now flush with Mocha Cappuccino."

Twink scrunched up his face. "Blech!"

Allie poked her head in the door. "Good morning! I hope I'm not being rude, but can I get some breakfast? I'm *starving*!" Sniffing, she added, "Can you hallucinate smells? Because I've been smelling chocolate since I woke up. I even dreamt I slept on a marshmallow pillow!"

Ricky and Twink exchanged bemused looks, as bits of marshmallow were indeed stuck to her hair.

"Oh, dear," Edna said apologetically. "I had forgotten that your pillow had sprung a leak. Well, never mind. You can clean up after breakfast."

Shooing the gang down the stairs and into the kitchen, Edna showed them to a large, wooden table. Her kitchen was filled with the sweet aroma of nutmeg and gingerbread. It was the most wonderful fragrance Allie had ever smelled.

Edna slipped on some oven mitts, opened the oven door and pulled out three steaming bowls. Setting them down in front of the children she ordered, "Now eat your oatmeal. It will make you grow."

Allie made a face and whispered to her brother, "Yeah, it'll make me grow sick to my stomach!"

He snickered quietly as Edna urged, "Go on, eat up!"

Allie was pleasantly surprised to find several gooey oatmeal cookies in her bowl instead of the mushy cereal she had been expecting. She eagerly ate everything and even asked for seconds.

"Oh, goodness, gracious," muttered Edna, blushing. "I forgot the fruit!" She grabbed a large bowl from the counter and set it down on the table. The bowl was filled with candy apples and chocolate covered raisins.

"Allie, I'll eat your fruit if you don't want it," Ricky offered cheerfully.

"That's okay. I wouldn't want to skip it, as breakfast *is* the most important meal of the day!"

Edna sighed contentedly, watching the children devour their food. "I just love to see growing boys and girls eat a nutritious meal!"

"I wonder what Shimmer's doing?" Allie mused, slurping the last drops of chocolate milk from the bottom of her glass.

"I wish we could have gone to the castle with him," Ricky said glumly.

"To the castle!" yelled Twink, zooming toward the open window.

Edna reached out and plucked him from the air. "Not so fast, young man. King Shevre has ordered you children to stay here, out of harm's way. He probably thinks the only trouble you can get into on a candy farm is a bad tummy ache."

"Candy farm?" blinked Ricky.

"You've never been to a candy farm?" Twink asked.

Ricky and Allie both shook their heads.

"Not even on a field trip?"

"We've never even *heard* of a candy farm. The candy on earth is made in factories."

Edna gasped. "Factories?" She looked horrified. "You poor dears." Shaking her head she added, "Right after breakfast, Twink will show you around. In fact, you can milk the cows and gather eggs for me!"

"Great," Ricky muttered. On his first visit to a candy farm, the last thing he wanted to do was milk cows.

"After that, you can pick some candy." Edna was overjoyed when she saw the children's faces light up. "But only the Red Hots," she added. Their faces instantly fell. "I'm sorry, dears, but it's the only crop that's in season."

"But Edna," Twink coaxed. "What about the lollipops? They should be ripe!"

Edna's expression hardened. "The lollipop field is strictly off limits to *you*, young man. Or did you forget what happened the last time you were here?"

"Oh, yeah," the little star giggled.

"What happened?" asked Allie and Ricky in unison.

Edna wiped her hands on her apron. "Let's just say that pre-licked and half-eaten lollipops do NOT sell well in the Village!" She walked briskly to the hall closet, opening the door while muttering to herself, "I know they're here somewhere." She pulled out an array of jackets, hats and scarves before she finally found what she was looking for. She came back to the kitchen carrying a pair of red and gold lizard-skin boots.

"You can't pick Red Hots without these," she said, placing them on the floor by the children.

"What are they?" Ricky asked.

"They're *beautiful!*" Allie gushed, picking up one of the boots and running her hand across the top. She looked down at her own worn slippers and sighed. Aside from the glittering rainbow that was still stuck to one slipper, they were so dirty that they looked more brown than pink.

"They're made from Salamander skin," Edna explained.

"*Salamander?*" Allie asked.

Edna nodded, but before she could answer, Twink began reciting from his third grade Sleep Phone lesson. "Salamanders are lizards who are born in lava pits. Their skin is impervious to fire." Enormously proud of himself for remembering the lesson word for word, he smiled smugly, showing almost all of his teeth.

"Very good," gushed Edna.

"Thank you," he replied. Holding his head high as he floated past Allie he boasted, "I don't need 'em. Those boots are just for girls and sissies." He tossed a boot to Ricky. "Here ya go!"

"Ha, ha." Ricky snapped, catching the boot in his hand. "Very funny."

"Twinkle, remind me," Edna began. "Whose burning foot-points did I have to soak in ice cream the last time you picked Red Hots?" Twink blushed a deep purple. She pulled the boot out of Ricky's hands and returned it to the small pile on the floor. "We'll sort out who is wearing what when you get back from doing your chores." She handed each child a bucket and shooed them out the door. "This is for the milk. There are baskets near the chicken coops for the eggs. Please bring back at least a dozen!"

Twink led the way to the barn. They followed him down a rock candy path past a crop of malted milk balls (they weren't nearly ripe, as they were still only the size of peas), a patch of gummy bears (whose heads were just beginning to poke up out of the ground), a field of cotton candy, some jelly beanstalks, and a gumball tree.

"Here it is!" Twink said, pushing his way through the red barn door.

There were four stalls inside, each containing at least one cow. In the first stall was an ordinary looking black and white bovine. The sign on the wall behind her said "White Milk."

One stall over, a brown cow was grazing on some hay. The sign on her wall said "Chocolate Milk."

At first, the kids couldn't see any cow in the third stall. They heard mooing, but saw nothing. Then suddenly, there she was! She was rail thin, so slender that when she turned, she disappeared completely. The sign dangling from the hook in her stall said "Fat-Free Milk."

The last stall was larger than the rest. Three cows were penned inside, each a different color. They were all wearing earphones, swishing their tails in time with the beat. One cow suddenly started break-dancing, spinning on her head so fast that straw flew in every direction. The sign tacked to the wall behind her said "Milk Shakes."

Allie chose the brown cow to milk, while Twink took his bucket over to the Fat-Free cow. Ricky decided to gather eggs.

On the other side of the barn was the chicken coop. Ricky laughed when he looked into the large cage and saw a dozen chocolate chicks running around. He grabbed a nearby basket, lifted the rusty latch and opened the cage door. He reached in and found several eggs resting on a bed of straw. They were all made of marshmallow.

Just as he was putting the last egg in his basket he heard a crash and the familiar sound of his sister yelling. He closed the cage door and walked back to the stalls. Allie was sitting on a stool drenched in chocolate milk. Her bucket lay upside down in the straw. She sputtered a string of nonsensical words as she wiped dripping milk from her eyes. Ricky burst out laughing.

"Uch! I'm outta here!" she yelled, stomping out of the barn. She left a trail of milky footprints all the way back to the house.

A short while later, the boys returned with their baskets and buckets full. In his haste to find Allie, Twink set his bucket down so fast that milk sloshed over the rim onto Edna's freshly washed kitchen floor.

"Allie! Allie?" the little star called hopefully.

"She's in the shower, dear," Edna said, pulling a mop from a nearby closet. "Next time, do be more careful when you're carrying a full bucket!"

"Sorry," Twink mumbled, flopping into a nearby chair.

"That's alright." She smiled warmly at the boys. "Thank you for all your help. There's so much work to do on a farm, I can barely keep up! But thanks to you, I'm almost done. Now I just have to wrap that pile of chocolate bars on the kitchen counter. They're not going to wrap themselves, you know." Patting the wand in her apron pocket, her eyes twinkled. "Then again, maybe they will!"

Edna put the mop aside and picked up the pair of Salamander boots she had set near the back door. She handed them to Ricky, saying, "Why don't you and Twink go pick those Red Hots?"

As Ricky slipped his protective footwear on, Twink casually asked Edna, "So, um, shouldn't we wait for Allie?"

"No, dear. I have other plans for her. Just remember, Red Hots are only ripe if they're smoking. But do be careful—if they're overripe they'll explode. Now you boys have fun!"

When Allie was cleaned and dressed again, Edna knocked on her door. "Allie, I'd like to show you something."

Back to her usual good cheer, Allie opened the door smiling. "Okay, sure!"

Edna led her past the bedrooms, down a long hallway. She stopped at the end of the hall in front of a red and white striped wall. It smelled faintly of peppermint.

She rubbed her hands together, and closed her eyes. Her fingers began to shimmer. As her hands glowed more brightly, she pressed them against the wall. Within moments, the wall began to fade from sight, until it completely vanished. Allie watched in stunned silence as a stone staircase materialized where the wall had just been.

"Come along, dear," Edna said, leading the way up the steps.

When they got to the top, Edna was winded. She was so full of life that Allie had nearly forgotten how old she was.

"Phew!" Allie said, fanning her face. Pretending to be out of breath so that Edna wouldn't feel bad, she added, "That was quite a workout!"

An unreadable look passed over the old woman's face. Tears welled in her eyes for a moment as she whispered, "You're so like him, in so many ways ..."

"Like who?"

Blinking back tears, Edna ignored her question and led her into the lone room before them.

Allie's eyes grew wide when she stepped across the threshold. Huge tapestries adorned every wall but one, which featured a tall, arched window that looked out toward the nearby mountains. Numerous tables were littered with cauldrons of varying sizes, each filled with a different colored liquid. Some of the cauldrons were bubbling, some were spitting, and some were being stirred by wooden spoons suspended in the air above. There were dozens of shelves, each stacked to the ceiling with potions and powders. Lined up across a table beneath the window were several gleaming wands, arranged by size in descending order.

"Don't look so surprised," Edna said, sniffing the contents of a silver cauldron. "I was an active member of The Three for the better part of my life. You don't think they give that job to just anyone, do you?"

Allie shook her head distractedly, dazzled by all the wonders within the room.

"I may be old, but I'm not completely useless," Edna chuckled, pulling a bottle labeled *Baby's Breath* off a shelf. She took the lid off, and poured it over a vase filled with wilting roses. A little whoosh of air poured out, followed by a tiny burp. All at once, the flowers stood erect, their petals instantly changing from a faded pink to a fiery red. "These flowers were given to me on my 25th birthday," Edna said proudly as she put the bottle back on the shelf.

"Your 25th birthday?" Allie asked incredulously. "But that would make them ... er, um..."

"Very old!" Edna laughed. Noting Allie's blushed cheeks, she kindly added, "You needn't be embarrassed, dear. I know I'm old. But I still am a fairly powerful witch. It may not be as clear as it used to be, but I still have the power of Futuresight!"

"What's Futuresight?" Allie asked as she watched a wand tap itself against a jar of wand cleaner.

"No!" Edna snapped at the wand. "That jar is nearly empty and it's the third one I've had to conjure this week!" Dejected, the wand slumped over, pathetically tapping its tip against the lid over and over. Edna cupped her hand over her mouth and whispered to Allie, "It has a cleaning fetish, poor thing." Feeling badly for having scolded the brooding wand, Edna picked it up and inspected it. "My, don't you look sparkly today?" The wand straightened itself proudly, then leaped out of her hand and hopped across the floor. As it jumped back onto the table, Edna asked, "Now, what were we talking about?"

"Futuresight."

"Oh, yes. Futuresight is exactly what it sounds like; the ability to read the future."

Allie's jaw hung open. Snapping it shut she asked, "So, you know what's going to happen? Before it happens?"

"Not always. Sometimes the future is too cloudy. But the important thing to remember is that I can see what *might* happen, not necessarily what *will* happen. A small, but significant difference."

"What's going to happen to Queen Glacidia? To Galdoren? To my love life? Will I get a date for the prom?"

Edna wrapped her arm around the girl, laughing. "So many questions. As for Galdoren, that's a future too murky to see. As for your love life, let's just say that when you're in the dressing room and can't make a decision about your prom dress, choose the blue one. It won't stain as easily as the gold."

"I'll have a date?" A wide smile spread across Allie's face. "What's he like?"

"Clumsy. Remember, choose the blue dress!" Reaching into a bubbling cauldron, she pulled out a piece of neatly folded paper and handed it to Allie.

Allie stared at the paper in her hand. In a shaky scrawl, the word *"Allie"* was written across it. Heart hammering, she unfolded the note. The words, *"B'yardin Shatavna Myesto Troo"* floated just above its surface. Startled, Allie dropped the paper, but the words continued to float in the air.

"Those are the last words Queen Jacqueline ever said," Allie whispered.

Edna nodded approvingly. "Very good. I knew that you would be familiar with that spell."

"But ... but what does it mean?"

"It's an ancient fairie spell."

"I know, but I thought that only fairies could use it!"

"Perhaps," Edna said cryptically. "Just remember, it's very powerful magic. And it has many uses."

Confused, Allie asked, "But how can I use it if I'm not a fairie?"

"I'm certain you will figure that out, all in due time. In the meanwhile, why don't you pick up that note? The words should slide right back onto it. Then you can tuck it away in your invisible pocket. It should fit nicely between your Rocket Dust and that snow globe."

"But how did you know ..." Allie sighed, wondering if she would ever get used to this strange world.

Chapter Twenty-Four

FROZEN IN FEAR

Henry landed face first in the dewy moss near the Windermere border.

"Oof," he grunted, as the travel spell dumped him onto the soft earth. He had used the last of Magnus's travel dust to get here. He lifted his head and looked around. *No sign of The Three. Well, it's a very long border,* he reasoned.

He pulled himself up, wiping his muddy hands on the sides of his pants. He had never been this close to the border before. He moved slowly toward it, fascinated by the snowy landscape just a few feet away. And yet, the weather on the Galdoren side was balmy and warm. He couldn't help smiling. It was such a perfect piece of magic. As an alchemist in training, he had a special appreciation for the intricacies of complex spells.

He held his hands out in front of him, moving more quickly now. His fingers itched to touch the fabled Border Spell. Out of nowhere, his hands smacked against something hard.

"Amazing," he whispered.

Everywhere he looked, he could see nothing but air. And yet, everywhere he touched, he felt the hard shell of an invisible wall. He felt humbled and a little frightened when he realized that this spell was all that separated Galdoren from the Queen of Windermere.

He pressed his nose against the spell, searching for any sign of the evil witch. Seeing nothing but snow and ice, he set about doing the work he had come to do.

He was determined to help save his kingdom and seek justice for Magnus's death. To that end, he needed to find the crack in the Border Spell. He had enchanted the travel dust to deposit him as close to the crack as possible, but he had no way of knowing if his spell had worked. The one thing he did know was that the crack was Shadow's only way in and out of Windermere. His eyes narrowed when he thought of the monster that had murdered his teacher.

He gritted his teeth. "Queen Glacidia!" he shouted into the swirling blizzard on the other side of the border. "As of now, your plans have officially changed! Your servant will no longer be able to deliver the Serpent's Eye you were expecting, as he will have to go through *me!*" He banged a clenched fist against the invisible wall.

His eyes suddenly grew wide when he felt a trickle of freezing air against his fist. He had found the crack! Instantly, however, his elation at having succeeded gave way to cold terror. For when the blizzard briefly died down on the Windermere side of the border, a glistening block of ice suddenly came into view. Encased within those thick sheets of ice was a woman. Her huge silver wings were crushed behind her. Deep gashes ran down her cheeks. Her chocolate-smeared mouth was wide open, as if in mid-scream, a look of terror literally frozen on her face.

As Henry reached into his pocket for Magnus's book of spells, his fingers brushed against fuzzy wool. Knowing it was never wise to ignore a clairvoyant witch's gifts, he wrapped the scarf Edna had given him around his neck and pulled the woolen hat over his ears, all the while keeping his eyes on the terrified-looking woman inside the block of ice.

"Hang on," he whispered. "I'm coming to get you."

He stuck his hand back into his pocket and grabbed the alchemist's book of spells. With shaking hands, he flipped through its yellowed pages, at last finding the spell he sought. He closed his eyes and said a silent prayer, wishing for the power to complete it.

He placed his palm against the crack in the Border Spell, and was surprised that the air against his skin no longer felt bitterly cold. Shrugging, he began to chant the incantation from the charred and yellowed page before him.

"Henry!"

He turned his head at the sound of his name being called in the distance. A woman in a green cloak was running toward him. He recognized Serena immediately. He had met her only once a few months before at one of Magnus's garden parties, but who could forget that mane of fiery red hair? Magnus had told him in confidence that she would soon be replacing Edna as the third member of The Three. But he was still surprised to see her wearing the trademark green cloak.

"HENRY!" she shouted again. "DON'T DO IT! IT'S A TRAP!"

At the same moment, a movement inside Windermere caught his eye. A black mist rose above the pristine snow. Shadow.

With renewed vigor he raced to finish the incantation, desperate to break through the border and get his hands on the monster who had murdered his teacher. All rational thought left his head—his only focus was to rescue the woman in ice and to avenge his teacher's death. And so he ignored Serena's frantic shouts of warning, concentrating solely on smashing through the border.

As the last word of the spell left his lips, a tremendous blast of arctic air whipped out of the hole he had just blasted. With not a moment to lose, Serena waved her wand, casting a spell to stun him just as he charged into Windermere, the first human to enter in decades.

Chapter Twenty-Five

THE TRAP

Serena's stunning spell narrowly missed its target. "Blast!" she shouted in frustration.

She hesitated for a moment, unsure of what to do. She looked behind her. Hildy and Sharonna were fast approaching, wands at the ready. She knew that they would try to seal the hole the instant they got close enough, whether Magnus's teenage apprentice was inside or not. Poor Henry, he really believed that Gossamer was truly in Windermere. She knew it was only an illusion—a trap to lure them into blasting a hole in the Border Spell large enough for Glacidia to escape through. She had no doubt that Gossamer was encased in ice somewhere, just not in Windermere.

She nervously chewed on her bottom lip as she watched Henry's hand slip right through the image of Gossamer. His brow creased angrily when he realized that he had been tricked. He turned his attention to Shadow and charged. Serena knew she had no other choice: she simply had to save the young alchemist. She could never live with herself if she stood by and watched him die at the hands of that vile creature.

She briefly wondered if hers would be the shortest career in history as a member of The Three, as she had no doubt she would be fired after the stunt she was about to pull. She shrugged, took a deep breath, and leapt into Windermere.

"Serena, NO!" both Sharonna and Hildy shouted. They reached the hole in the Border Spell just as Serena reached Henry.

They looked at each other in disbelief. "What do we do?" Sharonna asked in a stunned voice.

Tears glittered in Hildy's eyes as she whispered, "We have to seal it."

Sharonna looked horrified. "We can't! Serena ... Henry ... And we need the full power of The Three to seal a hole that size!"

"We have to try."

Sharonna looked toward Serena, her beautiful red hair blowing in the wind. The young woman had grown up at the castle, and Sharonna felt like she was part of the family. And what of Shevre? He was like a son to her, and she knew how deeply in love with the girl he was.

Hildy placed her hand upon Sharonna's shoulder. "We must stop Glacidia from escaping..." Hot tears streaked down her face as she choked, "Whatever the cost."

While Sharonna tried to come to terms with her duty, Shadow easily dodged Henry's attack. Serena jumped between the unevenly matched combatants, yelling an incantation. She looked shocked when only a few sparks trickled out of her wand.

"She doesn't know how much our powers are weakened inside Windermere," Sharonna breathed.

Henry grabbed Serena and shoved her protectively behind him. Everyone was stunned when he hurled Shadow into a nearby snow bank with a mere flick of his wrist. They had no idea that Magnus's apprentice was so powerful. But no one was more startled than Henry.

"His powers don't seem to be diminished at all," Sharonna observed.

Expecting to see the black shadow rise up from the snow bank, they were all shocked when the Queen of Windermere ascended instead.

"Sharonna, *now!*" Hildy yelled, unable to seal the hole on her own. But when Sharonna saw the witch point her blood-red nail at Serena, her maternal instincts took over. Unwilling to let Serena meet the same fate that had befallen her sister, Jacqueline, she charged across the border, wand blazing. Glittering streaks of silver shot out of her wand, hurtling straight toward Queen Glacidia.

The evil witch laughed, easily repelling Sharonna's spell. "Did you forget?" she sneered. "You wield no power here. You are in *my* kingdom now!" Her look was venomous as she sailed across the snow toward Sharonna. With the evil queen's back to her, Serena shouted an incantation and pointed her wand at their enemy. The spell froze in mid-air, well before it ever reached its target, and only served to bring the queen's attention back to the youngest member of The Three.

Glacidia whipped around, pointing her finger at Serena. Chains of ice shot forth and flew at the young woman, twisting around her body. The chains were so bitterly cold that they burned, and Serena screamed as they curled around her, tearing the bare skin on her hands.

Sharonna barreled toward the witch. But the queen shot a spell that lifted the old woman off the ground and flipped her over, suspending her upside down in the air. The howling winds ripped the protective cloak from her shoulders, leaving her exposed, shivering and spinning in the arctic winds.

Shadow rose from the snow bank, a murderous look in his gleaming eyes. As Henry sped toward Glacidia, Shadow leapt at him from behind. But Henry repelled him with a strong, unseen force that sent Shadow hurtling backwards through the air. He landed with a thump in a grove of pine trees, their sharp needles piercing the layer of mist that formed his body. He lay unmoving within the snapped branches and twigs.

"YOU WILL PAY FOR THAT!" Queen Glacidia shrieked. She turned in Henry's direction and pointed a shaking finger at him. Now the icy chains shooting out of her fingertips whipped around the young alchemist's body, imprisoning him. He opened his mouth to shout an incantation, but with the flick of her wrist, a rope of ice slipped between his lips and wrapped itself around his head, gagging him.

"You're as weak as your teacher," she sneered. "But he has an excuse—*he's dead!*" Henry shot her a murderous look as she laughed cruelly. Then she flipped her hand and Henry went soaring backwards through the air, crashing into the branches of a nearby tree. His chains got tangled on a jagged limb so that Henry was caught in the tree, bound to the barren branch like an icicle. He writhed and twisted, fighting furiously to break free. But as he struggled, the ice sliced across his bare skin, the arctic temperature burning his flesh. And yet, Henry didn't feel a thing. He suddenly realized that he hadn't felt cold since the moment he had slipped on Edna's hat and scarf. His eyes snapped open—*Edna! The material must be enchanted to produce heat!* He quickly wriggled to adjust his position so that the scarf fell against the ice binding his hands. He had been right: as soon as the material came in contact with the ice, it began to melt. *Hurry!* Henry thought desperately, willing the ice to melt more quickly. He shouted incantations over and over again in his mind, but he was still only an *apprentice* alchemist, and had not yet mastered the art of casting spells using only his thoughts.

Hildy stood on the border, unwilling to cross the threshold, knowing that once she entered Windermere she would be as powerless as her sisters-in-arms. She aimed her wand at Glacidia and fired.

The silver spell rocketed out the tip of her wand and streaked toward its target. Glacidia was blasted backwards when it hit her full force. Furious, the enraged witch rose in the air, the milky membrane in her empty eye socket beginning to bubble ominously. She chanted an incantation, crooking her index finger as she spoke. With each tiny motion of the witch's finger, Hildy was yanked a little further over the border.

Unable to stop herself from being sucked into Windermere, Hildy continued to shoot spell after spell. But the further she was pulled over the border, the weaker her spells became, until at last, she was standing knee deep in snow. Powerless now, she struggled to move, but with a wave of her hand, Glacidia bound her within an invisible web of magic, paralyzing her in the snowdrift.

The Ice Queen's hair stood on end, hissing. Suddenly, the ground began to shake. A distant rumble turned into a thunderous roar as an avalanche crashed down the side of a mountain, barreling straight toward The Three. Within moments, they were buried in snow, the white powder rising into the sky like smoke.

Glacidia's snake-like tendrils slithered around her head, whispering in her ear. She nodded in agreement and waved her hands in an arc, summoning the full strength of her power as the Queen of Windermere. The avalanche rumbled once more, and began moving *backwards* up the mountain, carrying the trapped women inside. The roaring mass finally came to a stop at the top of a distant peak, the frosted white tower disappearing into the clouds above.

A cruel smile split her lips as Glacidia drifted back to the ground. Crunching across the frozen earth she spied the green cloak that had been ripped from Sharonna's shoulders. She picked it up and stroked the velvety material.

A black mist floated out of the pine needles. It drifted over the snow to hover before its mistress, slowly reforming into the shape of a man. Bowing before her, Shadow rasped, "My Queen."

She dragged her fingers affectionately across the top of his head and purred, "Rise, my pet." Dropping Sharonna's cloak, she ground her foot into it, sneering, "I won't be needing this. I hear the weather in Galdoren is *to die for!*"

Henry jerked violently against the thick chains imprisoning him, but Edna's scarf had not melted the ice enough for him to break free. Tied to the barren branch, all he could do was watch helplessly as his enemies slipped through the hole he himself had blasted in the Border Spell.

And then Shadow and Queen Glacidia stepped into Galdoren.

Chapter Twenty-Six

ROCKET DUST

Ricky burst through the door of Edna's house, carrying a smoking and sizzling basket filled with freshly picked Red Hots. Twink followed close behind, carrying his own sizzling basket of candy. The two boys were in high spirits following their candy-picking adventure.

"Allie!" Twink called loudly. "Want some fresh Red Hots?"

Allie was sitting on the living room couch, reading a magazine called *"Confection Projections: The Premier Candy Quarterly."* She looked up from the periodical to see Twink smiling shyly at her from behind a haze of smoke.

She smiled. "Shouldn't we wait for them to cool off?"

"Nah," Twink said in a swaggering tone.

Allie shrugged, put the magazine down, and followed the little star into the kitchen.

"I'll try one first, so you know it's safe," he said with bravado, sticking a hand-point into the hissing basket. His eyes widened as his face turned a deep purple. He yanked his hand-point out, faked a smile for Allie, and then zoomed straight to the freezer. He threw open the freezer door and flew in, holding his burned hand-point out in front of him.

Just then, Edna entered the kitchen. Seeing the open door she tsked, "Children, you must remember to close the freezer so everything doesn't melt." With that, she shut the door.

Allie yanked the door open again. "Twink!" she yelled. But there was no reply. She stuck her head in and looked around. All she could see were several cartons of ice cream, frozen cookie dough, two pies and a box of popsicles. Confused, she stood on her tip-toes, trying to peer over the pies. "Twink?"

Edna let out an exasperated breath. "Allow me, dear." She pulled out the ice cream and pies. When she pushed aside the box of popsicles, a little purple star could be seen shivering in the back. The top of his head was already covered in ice crystals.

"Twinkle," Edna scolded, hands on her hips. "You come out of there this instant!"

Twink slowly flew out with his arm-points wrapped around himself. His teeth were chattering and his skin looked blue.

"How many times do I have to tell you," Edna began as she moved the baskets to the kitchen table, fanning smoke from her eyes as she spoke. "Wait until the Red Hots cool before you eat them!"

Ricky held back a chuckle as he started to pull off his boots. Edna turned to the boy and firmly said, "Keep those on, dear. You may need them again." Ricky gave her a curious look, then shrugged and sat down at the table.

Allie moved to Twink's side. "Are you okay?" she worriedly asked.

"I'm f-f-f-fine," he shivered.

"Aw, you poor thing! You're freezing!" She wrapped her arms around the little star, trying to defrost him.

Twink's mouth fell open. The ice chips on his head instantly melted. Within moments, he went from cold to warm. However, he pretended he was still chilled to the bone so that he could stay in Allie's arms.

"Better?" Allie asked.

Twink shook his head *no*, and tried gnashing his teeth to make them chatter. Faking a shiver he said, "I-I-I'm still f-f-f-freezing!"

Edna raised a brow. "Really?" Twink nodded his head earnestly. "Then I have just the thing for you," she said smoothly. She plucked him from Allie's arms, and headed up the stairs. "Nothing warms the body like a nice, hot bath."

"A BATH?!?!" Twink gasped in horror. "But I don't need a bath! I just had one last week!"

The sounds of their argument became muffled as they moved further up the stairs.

"So, did you have fun today?" Allie asked her little brother, pulling a chair out to join him at the kitchen table.

Ricky's face became animated as he rattled off the details of his day. "It was amazing! There were rows and rows of Red Hots. Some were smoking and some were sizzling! And some were just lying on the ground, sort of sputtering. But those were the ones you *really* had to watch out for, 'cause they were overripe. And they would just BLAM, blow up in your face!"

Allie looked horrified. "Are you serious? That sounds really dangerous!"

Ricky rolled his eyes. "Allie, even *Mom* doesn't think candy is dangerous."

"Yeah, well, Mom's never been to Galdoren."

The two of them fell silent, both experiencing a sudden bout of homesickness. Moving her hands to her lap, Allie's fingers brushed against her invisible pocket. A smile slowly curved up her lips.

"Hey, Ricky," she said, pulling something from her pocket. "Wanna race?" She waved her bottle of Rocket Dust in the air.

Ricky's eyes lit up. He reached into his pocket and retrieved his own bottle. Both their smiles grew wide.

Allie looked up at the light fixture. "We'd better go outside," she teased. "There's no ceilings for you to get stuck on out there!"

"Ha, ha," he said, following his sister out the back door.

Edna's yard was breathtaking. Candy canes grew wild amidst a sea of rock candy. A gumdrop path led to a small grove of caramel apple trees near the back of the garden, while sunlight glinted off the shiny peanut brittle fence surrounding the yard.

"I'm dropping out of school," Ricky announced, "and moving here."

Allie laughed. She looked up at the sky and shielded her eyes from the sun. "Stay clear of the clouds," she advised. Then she turned the bottle in her hands to read the directions. "Three to four shakes as needed." She opened the bottle, and carefully shook it four times over her head, slipping it back inside her invisible pocket when she was done. The glitter skipped down her hair and jumped across her skin. She gasped when she felt her feet leave the ground.

Intent on beating his sister in their first-ever flying contest, Ricky quickly opened his bottle and shook four times. He shoved it back in his pocket so fast that he missed the opening and the bottle dropped into Edna's yard. He watched it bounce across the grass as he was lifted into the air, soaring higher and higher into the sky.

Allie sailed upon the breeze, arching her back and spreading her arms. The wind blew through her hair as she skated across the sky, gliding through the air as though she had been born with wings.

Ricky sped after his sister. Gaining altitude at a ridiculous pace, he soon whipped right past her.

Allie was feeling so serene that she couldn't muster up even a drop of competitiveness. Never before had she felt so free. All her troubles seemed tethered to the ground, too heavy for her to carry to the clouds. Sailing gracefully, she closed her eyes, and let the wind carry her where it may.

Meanwhile, in Edna's upstairs bathroom, Twink was just getting out of the tub. Wrapping himself in a fluffy mint-scented towel, he glanced out the window. His jaw dropped when he saw his two friends fly by. He dropped the towel, opened the window and took off after his pals, smelling faintly of mocha cappuccino.

"Hi, Allie!" he chirped as he flew to her side.

"Oh Twink, you're so lucky," she gushed. "You can do this any time you want! If I could fly, I'd never ask my mom for a ride again!"

Unable to see what the big deal about flying was, Twink simply shrugged. Wanting to impress the girl, he waggled his brows, saying, "Wanna see a trick?"

"Okay," she answered. Then she called out to her brother, "Ricky! Slow down!" He turned his head and smiled in response. Allie pushed herself to fly faster so she wouldn't lose sight of him.

In an effort to show off for Allie, Twink zoomed ahead, turning to fly backwards. He casually crossed his arm-points behind his head, smiling a huge toothy grin. He continued soaring backwards until he smacked into Ricky, sending the boy into a downward tumble.

Allie shrieked as she helplessly watched her brother topple through the sky until he smashed into a fat pink cloud. He somersaulted across the cloud puff, finally skidding to an upside-down halt—his head literally stuck in a cloud.

Allie soared to her brother's rescue, Twink trailing just behind. "Ricky!" she cried, frantically pulling at his legs. "Are you okay?!"

She heard a muffled, "Yeah," and watched as her little brother righted himself, then pulled his head out of the pink fluff. She clapped a hand over her mouth to stifle a giggle when she saw that his entire face was covered in sticky pink goo.

Twink took one look at Ricky's cotton-covered face and burst out laughing.

Assured her brother was fine, Allie couldn't help herself and dissolved into peals of laughter.

"It's not funny!" Ricky grumbled, rubbing goo from his eyes.

"Yes …," Twink managed to choke out between laughs, "… it is!"

"Then see how *you* like it!" Ricky smiled, grabbing a huge handful of pink fluff and flinging it at his friend.

Allie wisely moved away from the ensuing fluff fight. She walked to the edge of the cloud and peered over the side. Letting the wind blow through her hair, she smiled down at the spectacular view of a rugged mountaintop. A rocky path circled its craggy peak, ending at a jagged ledge. Sandwiched between the ledge and the side of the mountain was the mouth of a dark cave.

Just then, three figures emerged on the path, heading toward the cave. Allie recoiled at the sight of the lobster-red creatures. Their sharp fangs glinted in the sunlight, their long knotted hair trailing behind them as it blew in the wind—goblins.

Chapter Twenty-Seven

THE CLAURICAN

Allie slowly backed up. Stumbling into Twink, she let out a small yelp.

"What's the matter?" he asked.

Seeing his sister's trembling lips, Ricky wiped his sticky hands on his shirt and moved to her side. "Are you okay?"

Allie shook her head, eyes wide with fear. Pointing toward the mountain she stammered, "G-g-goblins!"

Ricky and Twink crawled to the edge of the cloud, careful not to be seen. Peering over the side, they saw several goblins assembled at the mouth of the cave.

Allie dropped to her knees, joining the boys as they spied on the creatures below. "I'll bet this has something to do with that horrible witch," Allie muttered as she watched the group of goblins enter the cave.

"Hey, those are the guys from inside the tree!" Ricky exclaimed, remembering the hulking creature he had seen retreating through the secret panel. "We should find out what they're up to!"

Allie was about to agree, when she turned to look at her brother. His face was still covered in pink cloud fluff. Suppressing a smile, she dug into her pocket and pulled out the handkerchief that Sharonna had given her.

"I don't have to blow my nose!" he protested.

Allie rolled her eyes, pressing the lacy linen into his hands. "Your face is covered in cloud fluff, you moron!"

"Oh," he said. With one wipe of his face, every bit of goo magically disappeared. Allie gasped in astonishment, wondering if she'd ever cease to be amazed by all the wondrous things in Galdoren. But just as Ricky was handing it back to her, a stiff breeze blew the handkerchief out of his hands. Allie tried grabbing it before it flew off the edge of the cloud, but she couldn't catch it in time.

"I'll get it!" Twink cried, flying after the cloth as it fluttered gracefully in the air. But Allie held him back.

"Don't bother," she sighed. "We've got bigger things to worry about." They all peered over the cloud at the goblin cave below. "I'll fly down and check it out," Allie said with more bravado than she felt. "You two stay here!"

"But—" Ricky started to argue.

Allie cut him off. "No buts! I'm the oldest and I'm telling you BOTH to stay up here!" She looked from her brother to Twink. "Promise?"

Ricky shrugged noncommittally while Twink crossed his points behind his back. Only then did he nod.

Allie leaned over the edge of the cloud, looking both ways. Satisfied that no more goblins were climbing up the path, she dove off the cloud toward the mountain ledge. No sooner had she landed than she heard two muffled thumps behind her. Narrowing her eyes, she turned. "I knew it!" she hissed, glaring at her brother and Twink.

"There's no way I'm letting you face goblins alone," Ricky said, careful to keep his voice low so the goblins couldn't hear.

"I'm not planning on facing them," she whispered back. "I'm just going to do a little spying."

"And we're gonna spy with you," Twink whispered. "We're like that candy bar from your planet ... The Three Musketeers!"

"Hey, that's my favorite candy!" Ricky smiled.

"Shhh," Allie said, holding a finger to her lips. She motioned for the boys to follow as she moved toward the mouth of the cave. They stood outside, listening. They heard the muffled sounds of faraway voices.

Suddenly, loud music blared behind them. Startled, they each jumped several inches in the air. They turned in unison to see a little man sitting on a rock, playing a golden flute. Large pointed ears stuck out from the sides of his blue top hat, a wilted red feather bobbing in the breeze. The bright color of his bushy orange beard clashed with the emerald green of his one-piece jumper. The buckles on his pointy shoes jingled as he tapped them against the rock, keeping time with the music he was playing.

"A Claurican!" gasped Twink.

Allie wrapped her hand around the end of his flute to muffle the sound. "Shhhh," she whispered urgently to the strange little man.

"Ach!" he answered loudly. "Those goblins cannae hear us! 'Tis so loud in there they could nae hear a thundercloud if it burst right over their heads!"

"If you don't mind, I don't want to take any chances," she snapped, still holding onto his flute.

Raising a bushy brow he replied, "Aye, that's a smart move, lassie. 'Tis powerful sharp teeth those goblins have."

"That's why we're trying to be QUIET!" she hissed.

Jumping off the rock, the Claurican licked his lips. "I'll tell ye what, lassie. I'll be real nice 'n quiet if ye give me a meal. Perhaps a nice roasted turkey with creamed corn?"

"Do we LOOK like we're carrying roasted turkeys and creamed corn?"

The Claurican ran his eyes up and down each of the kids, inspecting them carefully. He stroked his beard, replying, "I cannae see anythin' outright, but that dinnae mean yer nae hidin' somethin' in that invisible pocket o' yours, lassie!"

"What's the point of having an invisible pocket if everyone can see it?" Allie complained.

The Claurican laughed. "Only magical folk with the power of *Sight* can see it."

"What's a Claurican anyway?" Ricky asked.

The little man leaped into the air, clicking his heels. "A Claurican, my fine young man, is the best kind o' sprite there is! We're cellar sprites! Bringin' luck and good cheer ta those kind folk who share their food and drink with us." He narrowed his eyes. "But *beware*, if ye don't share yer food, you'll soon feel our wrath!"

"Cellar sprites? Then what are you doing way up here?" Allie asked suspiciously.

He looked surprised. "Isn't it obvious? I'm movin'!"

"Moving where?"

"Why, inta the goblins' cellar, o' course!"

The kids shifted their feet, unable to look the poor Claurican in the eye. Tapping him on the shoulder, Ricky asked, "You do know that this is a cave, right?"

"Aye. What's yer point, laddie?"

"Caves don't have cellars."

The little man's mouth opened and closed. He blinked in surprise. Then he put his hand over his heart and fell back on the rock. He looked up at the kids and whispered, "No cellar?" They all shook their heads. "Now what am I ta do?" he wailed. Burying his face in his hands, he began to sob. "So far from home! And here I spent the entire day walkin' up this bleak mountain! I'm too old and too tired ta go walkin' back down again." His small shoulders shook as he cried.

Everyone felt sorry for the pitiful little sprite. Then Allie got an idea. Sitting down next to him, she gently asked, "Do you like candy?"

Looking up through red-rimmed eyes he sniffled, "Aye, o' course I do!" Then he added hopefully, "Do ye have any?"

"No, I don't. But I know someone who does." Pulling him off the rock, she pointed down the mountain, toward Edna's house. "See that little house? It's part of a candy farm! I'm sure if you ask nicely, the lady who lives there will be happy to let you live in her cellar. She's very generous, and she has loads of candy."

He jerked away. His eyes narrowed to slits. "A *lady*? So THAT'S what this is all about? I may be hungry, but not hungry enough ta be tradin' me bachelorhood fer a wife!" Crossing his arms defiantly he huffed, "I'm not the marryin' kind."

Twink flew over to the little man. "We're not trying to trick you into marrying her! She's like, a thousand years old!"

The Claurican looked horrified as Allie snapped, "TWINK! She is NOT a thousand years old!"

"Five hundred?" he asked innocently.

The Claurican recoiled.

"NO ONE IS TRYING TO MARRY YOU OFF!" Allie yelled, forgetting where she was.

"Shhh," the little man put his finger to his lips. "The goblins might hear ye!"

"Arggghhhhh," Allie fumed.

The Claurican peered back over the edge of the mountain, looking down at the candy farm in the distance. The sun sparkled on the gumdrop fields, fairly glistening with sugar. He stroked his beard thoughtfully, and then clapped Allie on the back. "I'll make ye a deal, lassie. I'll court her, I jest will nae marry her. A Claurican knows how ta show a lady a good time. That ye can be sure of," he winked mischievously.

"Fine, whatever," Allie mumbled, distracted by the loud hoots of laughter drifting from the cave. "We really have to be going, Mr. Claurican."

As he turned to leave, the little man stopped abruptly. His eyes ran up and down Allie, lingering on her invisible pocket. Moving to her side he said, "I can tell ye have a good heart, lassie, so I want ye to have this. It may come in handy." He slipped his flute inside her invisible pocket as he whispered, "It's magic."

Twink's eyes narrowed. "What kind of magic?"

"The best kind!" he said with a wink. "Claurican magic!" Then he tipped his hat, and sprinted down the path, whistling a merry tune.

"No, wait!" Allie called, pulling the flute from her pocket. "I don't want ..." But it was too late. The little man had disappeared.

Twink tapped Allie on the shoulder. "Um, Allie? I don't think Edna has a cellar."

"Oh. Well, I'm sure she'll figure something out." Dropping the flute back into her pocket, she led the gang inside the goblins' cave.

Chapter Twenty-Eight

THE SNOW ANGELS

Henry thrashed violently against his icy bonds. With one last powerful push, he snapped the chains that held him, the sound of cracking ice echoing across the frigid valley. He yanked the gag out of his mouth and leapt down from the tree, landing with a muffled thump in the soft snow below. He started to race toward the Border Spell, determined to catch Queen Glacidia and Shadow before they could inflict any damage on Galdoren. But then he stopped and turned around to gaze toward the distant mountain.

He shielded his eyes from the swirling blizzard and tried to make out the mountain peak. Blinking back the snowflakes from his eyes, he felt utter despair when he saw how far the avalanche had carried The Three. He couldn't just leave them there to die. Setting his jaw, he began running toward the foot of the looming mountain. But then something caught his eye, bringing him to an abrupt halt. He knelt and picked up the emerald green cloak that was half-buried beneath a pile of sleet. Glacidia's boot print was still on its back. Scowling, he wiped it off, tied it around his waist, and continued to race toward the mountain.

As he ran, a series of disturbing thoughts clouded his mind. He knew that all of the cloaks worn by The Three were enchanted to protect them against extreme weather conditions. But would Sharonna be able to survive the sub-zero temperatures without her cloak? *At least she has her wand,* he comforted himself, knowing that it was connected to her life-force and would help to keep her heart beating as she lay buried beneath the suffocating mound of snow. But a witch's wand could only keep her alive for so long, and although this particular witch was especially powerful, surely even *her* wand had its limits. The same was true of Hildy and Serena.

When Henry reached the base of the mountain, these grim thoughts inspired him to move even faster as he began to climb toward the icy summit. But the mountain was so steep and so slippery that climbing it was proving to be treacherous. Refusing to turn back, he pulled himself up the jagged rock in a race against time. Stopping to rest on a craggy foothold, he again peered up at the snowy peak. It looked even farther than it had before. He leaned his head against the rock, breathing heavily. He feared he would never reach the women in time. And what of Galdoren's fate without its guardians?

As he cursed himself for blasting a hole in the Border Spell, a gust of arctic wind suddenly whipped down the mountain, knocking him off the snowy slope. He narrowly clung to a jagged piece of icy rock, his feet dangling in the air.

As he hung high above the frigid valley, his fingers slowly slipping off the frozen rock, he scolded himself: *You are an alchemist in training—make your teacher proud!* He closed his eyes and searched his mind for an incantation. All at once his eyes flew open. *Could it work?*

His hands continued to slide as he cast his spell. *"Ic ceallian eard scimcraeft!"* he commanded

His body swayed in the air as another gust of wind shrieked across the mountain. "I CALL UPON THE MAGIC OF THIS LAND!" he shouted above the whistling winds.

No sooner had the last word left his mouth, than his fingers slipped from the icy rock. But as he tumbled through the air, the snow on the ground below began to move. Within moments, a dozen snow angels had risen from the frost-glazed earth. Their crystal hair flowed behind them as their gowns of sparkling white billowed in the breeze. They reached their arms out, clasping each other's hands as they rose, forming a floating circle. And it was within this circle of magic that Henry fell.

Henry was stunned to be caught by a current of sparkling air. He was even more shocked to find himself surrounded by a circle of angelic faces smiling serenely at him. Cradled within their protective spell, he felt himself being lifted. They rose higher and higher, flying rapidly toward the top of the mountain.

Made entirely of ice and snow, the angels sparkled brilliantly, their icy halos glittering like diamonds. Henry shouted a thank you to his rescuers, then laughed out loud, amazed that his spell had worked.

At last they came to the peak, and Henry felt himself being lowered upon the ice-crusted rock. As the winds shrieked around him, he pulled down his hat and tightened his scarf, whispering a silent thanks to Edna for her magical gifts.

But then he turned and saw the giant tower of snow that The Three were buried beneath. He stared open-mouthed at the insurmountable task before him. How could he possibly clear all that snow?

Turning to the snow angels he asked, "Can you help?"

They shook their heads no, and rose in the air to sit on a branch, sadly looking on.

Henry turned back to the soaring mass of snow and began to dig with his bare hands. After several minutes, he leaned back on his heels and surveyed his work. He had hardly made even a dent. Just then, another howling gust of air whipped across the mountain top, blowing fresh snow into the small hole he had just dug.

"Blast!" he shouted into the wind. Determined to save the three Guardians of Galdoren, he reached into his pocket and pulled out Magnus's spell book. He doubted there was a spell in there that could help, but he was desperate.

The wind blew the book open, furiously flipping its pages. Fearing that the powerful gusts might rip the pages from their binding, Henry pressed his hand firmly against it. But when he looked down at the spell he was touching, he blinked in surprise.

It was a spell that Magnus had taught him the first day he had arrived. It was so simple, even a novice alchemist could perform it. And the only ingredient required was a handful of grass. Magnus had invented the spell after constantly running out of his most common potion ingredient: violet petals. The old alchemist tended to use them in almost every potion, as he liked the way they smelled.

The spell transformed each blade of grass into a single violet petal. It had quickly become one of Henry's weekly duties to keep Magnus's violet jars fully stocked. He had performed the spell so often that it was permanently ingrained in his memory.

He stared down at the page in his hands. He hadn't realized that Magnus had ever bothered writing it down. But now that he looked at it, he saw that the spell didn't require blades of grass at all: it only called for "any substance commonly found in nature."

A slow smile curved up his lips. *Snow is a substance commonly found in nature!*

With renewed hope, he leapt toward the enormous mass of snow and held his arms wide before it. "*Awenden florisc!*" he commanded.

He could scarcely believe it when the snow actually began to change colors from a pristine white to lavender, and finally to a deep purple. The snow angels looked down from their perch in the tree, grinning, as all of the snowflakes slowly transformed into violet petals. Soon, there was a small mountain of purple flowers. And as another arctic wind shrieked across the cliff, the petals were lifted into the air, swirling in the snow. Henry laughed out loud as a million purple petals cascaded down the icy cliff, tumbling down toward the powdery valley below.

And then all that remained were the three women who had been buried beneath.

Chapter Twenty-Nine

THE SURPRISE ATTACK

The children carefully made their way through the slimy tunnels of the goblins' cave, following the path of torches lighting the way to the heart of the dark cavern. More than once Allie thought she saw the shadowy outline of bats hanging from the ceiling. The sound of dripping water was slowly replaced by the loud clamor of goblins as they drew ever nearer to the creatures' hideout.

Suddenly a loud cheer erupted. "We're getting close," Allie whispered to the boys. "Stay behind me." She moved quickly and quietly over the damp limestone floors of the passageway. As the deep voices and feral growls grew louder, Allie motioned for the boys to stop. They had come upon a set of huge stone columns stretching from the ground to the ceiling. Within the craggy columns were a series of gaps, just big enough to peek through.

Allie pressed her face against the damp rock, looking through one of the small holes. Hundreds of goblins were gathered around a roaring fire in the center of the cavern, their scarlet skin dripping with sweat. She turned to the boys, pressing her finger to her lips, then signaled for them to spy through the gaps within the rough rock formations. They drew a collective breath as they watched the scene unfold before them.

Countless goblins surrounded the bonfire, their fangs dripping saliva as they snapped and snarled loudly. They were packed so tightly together that they were nearly shoulder to massive shoulder.

They soon began shoving each other and cheers erupted as fights broke out. A vicious punch knocked a nearby goblin to the ground and he landed within inches of the children's hiding place. As he pulled himself up, his yellow gaze turned in Allie's direction.

"SILENCE!!!" A deep voice bellowed from amidst the noisy throng. Allie sighed with relief as the sound of that echoing word drew the goblin's attention away before he could catch her peeking through the stone. A hush fell over the crowd as a hulking creature moved to stand dangerously close to the crackling fire. A tattoo of a lethal-looking snake crawled across his sweat-soaked chest.

"Our time draws near," he growled. Hoots and whistles erupted from the boisterous crowd as he stepped directly into the center of the bonfire. He reached down and literally pulled a handful of flames from the heart of the blaze. He dipped a finger into the fireball cupped within his hand and began to trace a design in the air.

"What's he doing?" whispered Twink.

"I think he's drawing with fire," Allie answered, unable to tear her eyes away.

He twisted and bent the flames until an outline of Galdoren Castle appeared in the air. "We have been far too patient for far too long!" he spat. The goblins cheered, growing rowdier by the minute. "Hiding in caves … scrounging for food … THOSE DAYS ARE OVER!" The crowd went wild. Holding his hand up for silence, he continued, "I have received a message from Queen Glacidia. At long last, SHE IS FREE!" The crowd rose in a standing ovation as the children's eyes grew wide with fear.

Again, he motioned for the audience to be silent. "Our queen has given us the order we have been waiting for …" When all eyes were upon him he thundered, "Tonight … WE ATTACK THE CASTLE!" He threw a handful of burning embers at the outline of the castle, engulfing it in flames.

The crowd erupted in ear-splitting cheers and applause. The goblins howled and whistled, banging their weapons against the craggy floor. Some began pounding their fists against their bare chests, hollering battle cries at the top of their lungs.

"We've got to get out of here before they see us!" Allie whispered frantically, pushing her brother toward the exit.

Twink soared above them as they raced for the mouth of the cave. "We need to warn the king!"

"Edna will know what to do," Allie said between breaths, running as fast as her legs could carry her. Just then, a final cheer rose from the blood-thirsty throng. Within moments, the sounds of approaching feet began to echo off the cavern walls.

"C'mon!" Twink urged in a frightened voice as the goblins drew closer. "FLY!"

Both Allie and Ricky leaped into the air at the same time, and were startled when they tumbled back to the ground.

"The Rocket Dust!" Ricky said in a panic. "It must have worn off!"

Allie shoved her hand into her pocket, reaching for her bottle. "Hurry!" she told Ricky. "Get your bottle out!"

Ricky colored. "Um, I sort of dropped mine in Edna's yard."

"Just take some of mine!" She feverishly searched her pocket, but couldn't seem to find her bottle.

"Hurry!" Twink called worriedly as he hovered in the air.

Allie gasped. "It's not here!" Brushing her hand against the flute, her eyes narrowed to slits. "That double-crossing Claurican stole my Rocket Dust!"

The pounding of approaching feet drew nearer. Allie and Ricky had no choice but to run as fast as they could. Twink kept stopping, waiting for his friends to catch up. As the trio sped toward the mouth of the cave, the flute in Allie's pocket suddenly began to play! Allie quickly covered it with her hand, but it only played louder.

"What's that awful noise?!" bellowed a goblin not too far behind. As he rounded a corner, he saw the children ahead in the distance. "SPIES!" he roared. The entire horde of goblins reached for their weapons.

"KILL THEM!" thundered their leader.

The children dashed forward on a renewed burst of speed. But the goblins were stronger and faster, gaining ground with every step. The kids bolted out of the cave and into the sunlight with their pursuers close on their heels. But in their panicked haste to escape, they took a wrong turn and abruptly found themselves at the edge of the mountain.

The mob of wild-eyed goblins spilled out of the cave and rushed forward. The children were caught between the savage creatures and a sheer drop off the edge of the cliff. Having nowhere to run, they were trapped on the mountain ledge. Ricky cursed himself for leaving his bottle of Rocket Dust behind.

Tears stung Allie's eyes as she cried, "Twink, you can fly! GO!"

The little star stubbornly shook his head. "No! I won't leave you! I won't!" He bravely flew between his friends and the murderous throng.

Certain the children had no chance of escape, the goblin leader smiled cruelly. "Kill them quickly," he ordered. Licking his tongue across his sharp fangs he added, "I don't like anyone playing with my food!"

The flute was playing so loudly now that it sounded more like screeches than music. "Why won't that thing shut up?!" Allie cried as the goblins moved forward, with murder in their eyes. She pushed her hand into her pocket with the intention of flinging the screeching flute at the advancing mob. But then she felt a piece of paper brush across her fingertips.

The note! Having nothing to lose, she pulled it from her pocket. She quickly scanned the words and began chanting, "*B'yardin shatavna myesto troo.*"

She felt her feet lift off the ground. Quickly grabbing her brother's hand she continued to chant. A goblin lunged at Ricky, raking his claws across his back. Allie stumbled over the words when Ricky screamed in pain. She swallowed hard and began again. "*B'yardin shatavna myesto troo.*" She rose higher, pulling her brother along. But just then, the goblin wrapped his claw-like hand around Ricky's ankle, holding him back. Twink pummeled his points across the creature's thick, red-skinned knuckles. The goblin howled, losing his grip on Ricky to cradle his injured hand.

Allie continued to chant the magic words over and over as she pictured Edna's farm in her mind. Suddenly, she was gliding with her brother in the air, streaking toward the little gingerbread house. Twink cheered as he zoomed happily beside them.

The goblins threw rocks and boulders their way. Some began shooting arrows while others hurled razor-sharp lances, but it was no use: the children were already halfway to Edna's. Coasting on a breeze, Allie aimed for the open upstairs window. They sailed through, landing in a tangle of arms and legs on the floor of Edna's secret room.

Edna was hurriedly stirring a bubbling cauldron. Rather than looking surprised to see them, she seemed angry.

"It's about time you got here, there's not a minute to lose! Quickly, into the cauldron!"

Ricky leaned over to look inside the bubbling brew. An image of Galdoren Castle was spinning wildly within the big black kettle. Edna gasped when she saw Ricky's torn and bloody shirt. She grabbed a potion bottle off the shelf. Rubbing the greasy contents on her fingers, she waved her hands above the cuts on his back. They healed instantly.

"Twinkle!" Edna urged, wiping her fingers on her apron. "You first!"

Twink smiled reassuringly at Allie. "See ya soon!" he called as he jumped into the bubbling concoction. The castle continued to spin as Twink disappeared within the brew.

"Ricky, you're next!" Edna ordered, pushing the boy toward the cauldron. Unsure of what to do, he looked at his sister questioningly. Just then, the sounds of goblin howls floated through the open window. "Hurry!" Edna implored.

"It's okay," Allie said. "Go!"

Shrugging, the boy leaped into the brew and disappeared.

"You knew this was going to happen, didn't you?" Allie demanded, staring hard at Edna.

The old woman sighed, pushing Allie toward the cauldron. "I told you dear, I'm old, not feeble."

"But how was I able to use that fairie spell?" Allie asked, slipping the note back into her pocket.

"There's no time for explanations. Hurry!"

The goblins' war chants grew louder as they closed in on Edna's house. Allie suddenly grabbed the old woman. "Come with me!" she begged.

Edna kissed the girl's cheek and squeezed her hand. "My part in this has been played. You still have much to accomplish. Your destiny lies within this cauldron. Now, go!"

Allie ducked as a large stone was hurled through the window. Taking a deep breath, she leapt inside the swirling mass of liquid and disappeared from sight.

Chapter Thirty
THE KING'S JUNK CLOSET

*A*llie landed with a thud on a gleaming marble floor. She grabbed hold of a golden pillar and pulled herself up, nearly knocking into the suit of armor standing on a pedestal beside her. She grabbed hold of the wobbling armor, terrified it would crash and fall. She could just picture a headless helmet rolling down the length of the long hallway. Her eyes grew wide as she took in her surroundings—numerous suits of armor lined the walls in the cavernous hall, the light of a dozen torches reflected in the polished steel. An enormous tapestry depicting a unicorn standing beneath an amber tree hung from above, the colorful fabric standing out against the drab stone walls.

She quietly called, "Ricky? Twink?"

Something moved behind her, but when she turned, all she saw was another suit of armor. But this one was vastly different from all the others. Its highly polished steel was black as coal, and as she gazed upon it, she felt as if she couldn't turn away from that endless sea of glossy darkness.

"Allie!"

She jumped at the sound of Twink's voice. Turning, she smiled with relief at the sight of the little star and her younger brother. A very worried-looking Shimmer had his points wrapped around both boys. Allie flung herself at the three of them, hugging them tightly.

"Welcome to Galdoren Castle," Shimmer murmured, hugging her back.

A heavy wooden door suddenly swung open. A powerfully built man stepped out, his sapphire eyes narrowed to slits. He moved so quickly that the cloak blew off his shoulders, exposing the shiny white satin of his loosely tied shirt. Allie pulled her brother in close when she saw the man's fingers brush against the hilt of his sword.

"Blast it all, Shimmer!" he bellowed. "What is the meaning of this interruption?!"

When he turned in Allie's direction, so intense was his gaze that she felt his eyes were actually boring holes into her head.

"These are the Earth children I was telling you about, Your Majesty," Shimmer hastened to explain. Twink nudged his uncle. "He knows who *you* are," he whispered to the little star.

The king's scowl melted into a smile when Twink bowed so deeply he accidentally flipped over.

Moving his gaze back to Allie and Ricky, the king's voice softened. "I truly apologize for this mess I have landed you in. I had hoped our first meeting would be on a less solemn occasion. I am King Shevre."

"Your Majesty," Allie bowed, kicking Ricky on the ankle until he bowed as well. "I'm Allie, and this is my brother, Ricky."

"Lady Allie," he murmured, taking her hand and lightly kissing the back of it. Allie blushed, the bristles of the king's short beard tickling her knuckles. "Sir Ricky!" the king smiled broadly, clapping Ricky on the back. "You are the first guest who has ever invited his sister along!"

"But I didn't ..."

The king laughed warmly as he winked at Ricky. Pulling a silver cord that hung on the wall, he continued, "I'm afraid it's impossible to provide you with all of the entertainment promised on your invitation, but the least I can do is provide you with a feast."

"But, King Shevre," Allie began. "We came because—"

A man suddenly appeared amidst a cloud of garlic-scented smoke. He straightened the spotless apron tied around his thick waist, then removed his towering chef's hat. "Your Highness?" he said, bowing deeply.

"Ah, Chef Braeden! We have some unexpected guests. Prepare one of those mouth-watering meals you're so famous for. We shall dine in the ...," he stroked his beard thoughtfully, "in the Great Hall."

The chef nodded respectfully and bowed again. As he turned to leave, Twink called, "Don't forget the dessert! And the Jello!"

"Jell–*Jello?!?*" he sputtered, raising his nose snootily in the air. Opening his mouth to berate the tiny star, he snapped it shut when he saw the king's warning look. "As you wish, Sir Twinkle," he said through clenched teeth.

After the disgruntled chef had disappeared in an aromatic puff of smoke, Ricky blurted, "Your Majesty, we overheard—" A streak of white shot out of an open doorway, skidding into Ricky's leg. "Snoball!" the boy squealed happily, lifting the little snowcat into his arms. "How did *you* get here?"

"Edna sent her just before you arrived," Shimmer explained.

"Edna?" The king knotted his brow. "Is *she* the reason these children are here against my DIRECT orders?"

"No sir," Ricky squeaked. "The goblins are the reason we're here."

"Goblins?" the king replied, squeezing the hilt of his sword.

The children quickly explained what they had overheard in the cave.

The king's eyes blazed dangerously. "Shimmer, we will convene in the War Room to plan the defense of the castle."

"Should I call General Nobling to join us, Sire?"

The king cleared his throat. "General Nobling and our troops are en route to the Windermere border."

Shimmer sucked in his breath. "Who is left to guard the castle, Your Majesty?"

"A small unit of knights and a handful of servants." Striding confidently toward the War Room, he added, "I will order the army back at once. They can't have traveled far. They should be able to make it back before dawn."

As the king's heavy footsteps echoed down the hallway, everyone was thinking the same thing: *would dawn be too late?*

Suddenly remembering the children, King Shevre stopped and pulled a gold cord hanging from a nearby archway. Noting Allie's and Ricky's disheveled attire he said, "My personal assistant will find some clothes for you while you wait for your meal to be served. Guests of the king do not wear dirty slippers or tattered shirts to dinner." Allie blushed at his words, while Ricky really couldn't have cared less.

A faint buzz could be heard coming from the direction of an adjoining hallway. Rounding the corner, a man appeared. His long blonde hair had been neatly tied into a fashionable queue. A worn leather scabbard hung at his side, the gleaming hilt of a sword sticking out of its top. He was sitting in a shiny red chair that flew through the air, the sleeves of his muslin shirt billowing in the breeze. On the arm of his chair was a control pad and joystick that looked just like Ricky's video game controller back home.

"Roberts," the king began. "Please show our visitors to the Royal Suite. They had a run-in with some goblins earlier this evening." Roberts raised a brow as the king continued. "They can rummage through my junk closet for something more suitable to wear, although they might have better luck with the armoire. I leave it in your capable hands." Crooking his finger he said, "Shimmer?"

The blue star smiled apologetically at the children, then flew down the hallway to join the king.

"Good evening," the man in the floating wheelchair smiled. "I'm Roberts."

Ricky set Snoball down as he gaped. "That chair is awesome!"

"Ricky!" Allie nudged him, shaking her head.

Roberts laughed. "I agree: it is pretty *awesome*. Maybe later I'll take you for a spin. But for now, let's find you some clothes."

The children followed Roberts as he glided down a series of hallways.

"What happened to your shirt?" a deep voice boomed from above. Ricky looked up to see a stone gargoyle blinking down at him.

"It looks like an animal attacked him," another gargoyle observed.

Roberts cupped his hands and called up, "Not an animal. *Goblins!*" There was an audible gasp from the ceiling. He leaned in close to Ricky, whispering, "That'll give them something to gossip about."

Before he had even finished his sentence, all of the gargoyles up and down the length of the hall began talking at once.

"GOBLINS?!?"

"Rubbish!"

"Vile creatures."

"Terrible breath. They really ought to brush their fangs more often."

The children were relieved when Roberts turned off the main hallway into a much smaller, gargoyle-free one. Here, each wall was covered in portraits, from floor to ceiling. The paintings were of the Royal Family, spanning hundreds of years.

A portrait near the bottom of the wall grabbed Allie's attention. It was a painting of a young man with brown hair and hazel eyes. He wore a gold crown adorned with sapphires and rubies. The frame, like most in the gallery, was gilded gold.

There was something about the man in the picture that caught her eye. "Ricky," she said, nudging her brother and pointing to the portrait, "Doesn't he look familiar?"

Ricky knelt to get a closer look. There *was* something familiar about him. "Who is he?"

Roberts steered his chair to the painting in question. "He was King Shevre's great-uncle, the Duke of Margolia. He was a great favorite of the people—kind and friendly, with a wicked sense of humor. When he was a teenager, he snuck into the queen's privy chamber and squeezed glue all over the royal toilet seat." His eyes crinkled at the memory of Edna's stories. Roberts hadn't been born yet when Duke Albert's legendary reign of practical jokes began. But Edna was much older that Roberts. She had been a young girl at the time, an apprentice witch at the castle. She and Albert had become fast friends.

The kids all giggled. "What happened?"

"Hmm? Oh, the queen had to soak in the tub for nearly half a day until the toilet seat finally became separated from her, uh, er ... well, needless to say, she was quite angry with the young duke."

"Is he still alive?" Allie asked, wondering where she had seen his face before.

Roberts shrugged. "No one knows. He disappeared many years ago."

Ricky's eyes grew wide. "Disappeared?"

"Yes. Edna was the last to see him. She was on holiday at her family's candy farm. Albert came to visit one evening, and by the next morning, he was gone. For days, everyone assumed it was just another one of his practical jokes. But then, days turned to weeks, weeks turned to months. He was never seen again."

The children turned from the portrait, saddened by the strange mystery. Roberts led them down another hallway, which finally brought them to the Royal Suite.

The room they entered was exquisitely decorated with a grandeur befitting its regal-sounding name. The crown moldings near the ceiling were literally inlaid with hundreds of gilded crowns. A huge four-poster bed floated several inches above the marble floor, its luxurious bed linens shining beneath the candlelight of a crystal chandelier.

As Allie moved further into the room, she was warmed by a fire crackling within a large stone fireplace. Her eyes moved past a softly-ticking grandfather clock to a huge mahogany armoire standing in the corner.

Noting the direction of her gaze, Roberts smiled. "Allie, why don't you see if there's something in that armoire for you to wear?" He pointed to an adjoining room, adding, "You can change in that dressing room over there." Then he led the boys to the rear of the lavish bedchamber where he threw open a set of double doors. "We'll be here in the king's junk closet when you're done."

"Whoa," Allie heard Ricky say. "This is the king's *junk*?"

As she walked past the floating bed, Allie couldn't help poking it. It felt vaguely familiar; soft, fluffy … *wait a minute*, she thought with a wry smile. She pulled back a corner of the satin coverlet. *Just as I suspected*, she grinned, eyeing the fat cloud puff drifting beneath the covers.

She turned to the enormous armoire and wondered how many clothes it could hold. She eagerly pulled open its massive doors then stood motionless, blinking at what lay inside. The armoire was empty except for a beautiful ball gown and matching shoes that were floating gently within its folds.

Allie gingerly lifted the dress from the cabinet. Holding it up to herself, she twirled with delight, the long gown swishing across the floor as she spun. It was the palest of blues, glittering with the light of a thousand silver sequins. Layers of satin slid across her skin as she folded the gown over her arm. She plucked the shoes out of the air, dangling the whisper-thin ankle straps from her fingers.

As she headed toward the dressing room, she suddenly remembered her invisible pocket. She set down the gown and shoes, then felt around her nightgown until she found the familiar bulge of her pocket. She stuck her hand inside, relieved to find the contents still there, except for the stolen bottle of Rocket Dust. Her eyes narrowed when she felt the Claurican's flute. But when her fingers brushed against cool glass, she couldn't resist pulling out the snow globe that Gossamer had given her.

She gently shook it, smiling at the tiny snowflakes suspended in the liquid. She watched them sink past the crystal castle to land softly on the golden words etched across the bottom, *Welcome to Galdoren.*

Allie slipped the little glass souvenir back into her enchanted pocket. She peeled the pocket off her nightgown and pressed it onto her new dress. Holding the gown up to the light, she ran a hand over the shimmery material, double-checking that her invisible pocket was really there. She then scooped everything into her arms and raced into the opulent dressing room to try it all on.

While Allie was changing clothes, Ricky and Twink were exploring the king's junk closet. Ricky picked up a battered-looking copper lamp. "Is this a genie's lamp?" he gasped. Roberts glanced at the object in his hand and nodded. Ricky looked baffled. "Then what's it doing in his *junk* closet?"

"It's used," Roberts shrugged. "There's only one wish left." As Ricky excitedly rubbed the lamp, he added, "Don't bother. The genie belongs to the king, and will only answer to him."

Twink rummaged through a pile of jewels thrown haphazardly on a bottom shelf. There was a solid gold unicorn with emerald eyes; an assortment of rings bearing every imaginable precious gem; a pearl-and ruby-encrusted scepter; two ceremonial swords; and several crowns, all set with scores of sparkling stones.

He pulled a glittering crown from amidst the pile and carefully placed it on Ricky's head. "All hail King Ricky," Twink said grandly, performing a mock bow.

"I command you to do my homework!" Ricky ordered.

Twink knocked the crown from his head, snickering, "You make a rotten king!"

"Boys!" Roberts scolded. "Those are the Royal Jewels! Please handle them with the utmost of care. They are, after all, symbols of our monarchy."

"Sorry," they mumbled.

Ricky's eyes fell upon a large box sitting on a middle shelf. Lifting the lid, he peered inside. It was filled with dozens of stone tablets, all engraved with strange symbols. "What are these?"

Roberts smiled. "That's the king's ancient rune collection from when he was a kid. He was obsessed with them. Had to have them all!"

Ricky creased his brow. "Ancient runes? Aren't those magical or something?"

"Each rune is a different spell. But you have to know how to decipher the symbols in order to use them."

"Does King Shevre know how?"

"He got as far as levitation, and then lost interest. I think he got into amulets after that."

Allie stepped into the closet and Twink's jaw dropped nearly to the ground. In her long shimmery gown, she looked like a princess.

Roberts smiled warmly. "That dress looks like it was made for you."

"I think it was," Allie answered.

"Mrrowr." Snoball had dragged something out from under a shelf. Batting the two small objects between her paws, she purred happily.

"So *that's* where he hid them!" Roberts exclaimed in surprise. He pushed on the joystick so that his chair floated down. Plucking the objects off the floor, he laughed out loud. "The king's old Sleep Phones." Shaking his head, he continued. "He missed the entire fifth grade! Claimed he couldn't find them. Every time Sharonna would buy him a new pair, they would mysteriously disappear. He never did like school." Turning the Sleep Phones in his hands he arched his brow. "His aunt was really angry when he lost *these*. They're interactive. Very expensive."

"Fifth grade?!" piped Ricky. "That's the grade *I'm* in! Can I try them?"

"Why not?" Roberts said with a smile. "Sleep mode or quiz mode?"

"What's the difference?"

"Quiz mode is interactive. You answer questions, which you listen to later on while you sleep."

Ricky thought about it, then said, "Sleep mode."

Roberts adjusted the volume, then slipped one in each of Ricky's ears.

Ricky sat on the floor and listened. A soft, female voice spoke in a soothing monotone: *Lesson One, Grade Five: parts of speech. A verb is an action word, like run, jump and walk. Adjectives are description words, like pretty, smart and kind. A noun can be a person, place, or thing, like mermaid, Utopia, or wand. Now, you try!*

Before Ricky could say anything, a different voice began speaking. It sounded like a kid, someone around his own age. Ricky realized this must be King Shevre's voice, recorded when he was just a boy.

Verbs, the young King Shevre answered, *are action words, like vomit and burp. Adjectives are description words, like ugly and stupid. Some examples of nouns are boogers, diapers, and toilets.*

Very good, answered the monotone teacher. *Now use them in a sentence.*

The boy's voice said, *Serena is stupid and ugly. When I see her I want to vomit. Her face looks like boogers and her hair smells like diapers.*

Excellent, answered the teacher. Laughing, Ricky pulled the Sleep Phones from his ears.

A small oriental carpet suddenly zoomed off a shelf, then began tapping Roberts on the shoulder with its tassel.

"Uh-uh. No rematch. I beat you fair and square," Roberts said firmly. The carpet slumped over, hanging sadly in the air.

"A magic carpet!" breathed Allie. "Can I have a ride?"

The carpet nodded vigorously until Roberts reached his hand out, holding it back. He whispered to Allie, "I don't think that's a wise idea."

"Why not?" she whispered back.

"He doesn't have a very good sense of direction. In fact, it's terrible."

"What do you mean?"

"King Shevre once sent him to his bedchamber, and he didn't turn up for months! When we finally found him, he was in an upstairs bathroom playing cards with the bathmat."

"So?"

Sighing, Roberts turned to the carpet, speaking once again in a normal tone. "I have a job for you." The carpet nodded, looking at him expectantly. "Could you please bring me that wand over there?" He pointed out of the closet to a tarnished wand sitting atop a nightstand.

The carpet gave him a two-tassel salute and zoomed out of the closet. Allie watched in dismay as the carpet flew straight past the wand, through the door and out of sight.

Allie was choking back a laugh when she saw something move in the shadows at the rear of the closet. Curious, she walked past the boys as they giggled over an old wood nymph poster, wishing for a flashlight as she was swallowed by the darkness. She tripped, and a set of strong arms caught her before she could hit the floor. Looking up to thank whoever it was, Allie's mouth went dry when she stared into the black eyes of a misty shadow.

"Call the guards!" she screamed, backing away. "It's Shadow!"

In a split-second, Roberts had his sword drawn. But when he saw the familiar mist blinking back at him, he relaxed and sheathed his sword.

"Doppelganger?" Roberts gasped in surprise. "What are you doing in here? King Shevre has been looking everywhere for you!"

Twink cupped a hand-point over his mouth and whispered, "That's the king's shadow."

Doppelganger pointed to a dark corner. Roberts turned to a candelabra sitting on a nearby shelf and politely asked, "Would you mind?"

The candelabra hopped across its shelf, then leaned over, illuminating the dark corner with its flickering light. A hand shadow looked up from a game of chess.

"Ah, I see," said Roberts. Turning back to Doppelganger, he sternly said, "I'll let you finish your game, but when it's over, I must insist you return to the king. He finds it very disconcerting to be without a shadow." Doppelganger nodded curtly, then turned his attention back to the chess board.

Twink suddenly squealed from above. Sticking his head out from the highest shelf he chirped, "This is just my size! Can I have it Roberts? Can I?"

Roberts pressed his joystick and his chair climbed to the ceiling. Pausing to look at what the little star was holding, he chuckled. "I'm sure the king won't mind. He hasn't worn it since he was a toddler."

"*Awe-some!*" Twink said, repeating the strange Earth word that Ricky had used. "Don't look!" he called to everyone. Turning his back, he fiddled with something, and then finally yelled, "Twink to the rescue!" He zoomed through the air, wielding a tiny wooden sword.

"Don't worry, fair damsel!" he called to Allie, waving the sword valiantly in the air. "I'll save you!" Then he lunged at the candelabra, accidentally knocking it against the wall. Wearing a lopsided smile, he turned back to his friends. The candelabra streaked across the shelf, smacking Twink in the head.

"Ouch!" yelled the star. The candelabra lit all of its candles at once, as if to say *Hmph!*

"Show-off!" Twink shouted, rubbing his head.

"It doesn't look like we'll find anything for you to wear in here, Ricky." Roberts sighed. "Why don't you try the armoire?"

"It's empty," Allie replied.

Roberts smiled. "Try anyway."

Ricky crossed the room to the armoire. He opened its massive doors and was surprised to see a shirt floating inside. He pulled it out. It felt heavier than his usual clothes, probably because the bottom was embroidered with 24 karat gold thread. He made a face when he saw that each "button" was actually a precious gem.

"What's wrong with my own shirt?" he complained, even as the strips of cloth hung from his back.

"Just put it on!" Allie ordered in her big sister tone.

"Fine!" he grumbled, stomping into the dressing room and slamming the door shut. Muttering to himself, he pulled off his torn shirt and slipped the jeweled one over his head. Staring at his reflection in the mirror he shook his head. He kept pulling at the hem of the heavy satin shirt, unused to the feel and weight of it. Plus, the gold thread was itchy.

Sighing, Ricky reached for the doorknob and rejoined the others in the bedchamber. Just as he opened his mouth to complain about the fancy clothing, a servant entered the room. "Dinner is served," he announced.

Allie leaned over and whispered in her brother's ear, "If you spill on that shirt, you're dead."

Roberts led them down several hallways to an enormous dining room. They all sat down around a table that twinkled under a glittering chandelier. Then they were served a meal that was fit for a king. Literally.

As servants filled their crystal goblets with sparkling water, Allie glanced up. A familiar-looking carpet zoomed past the door and out of sight.

Chapter Thirty-One

THE MAGIC OF WINDERMERE

The bitter winds of Windermere whipped across the mountain-top, but Henry took no notice of their icy sting as he raced to Sharonna's side, quickly draping her cloak around her shivering body. The moment the enchanted material touched her skin, she stopped shaking. He stared down at her face, alarmed at the bluish tinge in her wrinkled skin. Her eyes were closed, and her cracked lips were open just enough to form a little "o." Her chest barely rose and fell with each shallow breath. Unsure of what to do, he turned to the other two women. They also lay unmoving upon the frozen rock, but their color was good and they appeared to be breathing normally.

He tried every spell he could think of, but nothing seemed to wake the women. If not for the bright glow of Serena's and Hildy's wands, Henry might have feared the worst. But it was Sharonna he was most worried about. She looked nearly frozen to death. He carefully unwrapped the scarf from his neck and gently lifted her head to place it between her and the frozen rock. At least the blinding blizzard had died down to an occasional trickle of snowflakes.

Feeling utterly useless, he sat at their feet as the sun continued to sink on the horizon, painting the sky with ribbons of purple. Frustrated, Henry started to flip through Magnus's spell book once again when a sparkle in the ice caught his eye.

He dug beneath the icy crust and pulled out a gold locket attached to a long, delicate chain. He turned the locket over and was surprised to see an inscription: *To my wonderful aunt, who is more like a mother to me.*

As he brushed the snow off the clasp, the locket suddenly clicked open. Inside was a picture of a teenaged King Shevre with his arm tightly wrapped around a beaming Sharonna. Henry leaned back on his heels. He had nearly forgotten how Sharonna had moved into the castle to raise Shevre after her sister, Jacqueline, had been frozen by Queen Glacidia. He pocketed the locket safely inside his cloak, praying he would get the chance to present it to Sharonna when she awoke.

"Henry?" Serena's groggy voice interrupted his thoughts. He quickly turned to face the young woman, who was stretching and yawning as if merely waking up from a nap.

"You're awake!" Henry called happily.

"Just barely." Pulling her cloak more tightly around herself she shivered. "It's freezing up here!"

"What are you babbling on about?" Hildy asked as she, too, sat up. "Oooh," she moaned softly, rubbing the back of her neck. "Maybe I should have retired with Edna."

Serena snorted, rising stiffly to her feet. "Puh-leeze! You wouldn't know what to do with yourself! At least Edna has the candy farm to look after." She cast a quizzical look in Henry's direction as she brushed a handful of violet petals off her cloak.

"I suppose you're …" Hildy's breath caught in her throat when she saw Sharonna's nearly lifeless body. She stumbled across the icy rock and fell to her side. Serena joined her an instant later.

Hildy took Sharonna's hand in her own. She blanched when she felt the frozen skin against her palm. She reached into Sharonna's pocket and pulled out her wand, gasping when she saw how dim its glow was. She placed it upon Sharonna's heart. The wand flickered and died. An instant later it began to glow again, but so weakly that it was barely visible. Hildy blinked back tears and turned to Henry. "What happened?"

He shook his head. "I don't know … she was buried under all that snow without her cloak … I found it in the valley below."

Serena stared up at him. "But without it, she could …" Unable to finish her sentence, she tucked Sharonna's cloak more tightly around her.

It was then that Hildy noticed the snow angels hovering nearby, all of them staring down with concerned faces at Sharonna.

Choking back the lump that was lodged in her throat, she stood and addressed them. "Please," she implored. "If you know of *any* magic that might help ..." Her tears turned to ice as they slipped down her cheeks. "I know how most of the magical beings in Windermere have gone into hiding since Queen Glacidia's reign of terror began." The angels nodded their heads in agreement, and a shower of snowflakes fell from their sparkling halos. "If you help us, I promise that we will vanquish her, and Windermere will be free from that evil witch once and for all! But we will need my friend's help to complete such a monumental task."

The snow angels looked from one to the other and then flew toward a barren tree near the edge of the cliff. Each angel reached up and touched an icicle dangling from the frost-covered branches. As their fingers brushed against the ice, the icicles began to spin. Faster and faster they twirled, until they finally snapped off the branches like twigs. They whirled through the air, glistening like pale moonlight as they spun. And as they slowly stopped turning, each icicle began to transform into a tiny, glittering fairie, made entirely of ice.

"The crystal fairies," Hildy breathed. She had heard of them, of course, but had never actually seen them.

The snow angels pointed to the deathly pale woman lying still as stone on the ground near Hildy's feet. The crystal fairies all began trilling at once, their tiny voices sounding like the tinkling of a thousand tiny bells.

A single fairie flew out from the cluster, her glittering wand leaving a trail of sparkles as she soared through the air. She stopped to hover above Sharonna's sickly face. A hush fell over the mountaintop as the tiny fairie pointed her wand at Sharonna's parted lips. Then all at once a silver liquid poured forth from the tip of her wand into Sharonna's mouth. And as the magic elixir trickled down her throat, the old woman's skin began to glow.

It glowed brighter and brighter until it became so blinding that Serena, Hildy and Henry were forced to shield their eyes. And when they were able to look up again, the glow had been replaced by a healthy tinge to her rose-colored cheeks. Hildy heaved a sigh of relief, smiling with joy when she saw the tip of Sharonna's wand suddenly light up, shining brilliantly against her emerald green cloak.

Sharonna's eyes fluttered open. The first thing she saw was Serena's hot pink boots. "I don't believe those are part of our standard issue uniform," she said, slowly sitting up. "Otherwise, I want a pair."

Serena laughed as she knelt down and hugged the old woman. When Serena finally let go, Hildy clasped her dearest friend to her chest. Clutching Sharonna tightly, she choked, "I swear, if you *ever* scare me like that again …" The two women held each other tightly.

When at last they parted, Sharonna cleared her throat and said, "Well, what are we all sitting around for? Don't we have a witch to capture?" But when she stood up, she blinked in surprise. She had never seen a sight quite as beautiful as the one before her.

Caught between the setting sun and the rising moon, the frost-glazed cliff was bathed in a magical light. The tiny crystal fairies sparkled with lavender, their icy wings reflecting the ribbons of purple streaking the sky. The snow angels' halos glittered with bits of orchid, and the snowdrifts twinkled in moonlight as if made of fairy dust.

Sharonna reluctantly turned from the magical scene at the sound of Henry clearing his throat. "Um, I think this is yours," he stammered, dangling a locket on his fingertip.

Sharonna's hands flew to her neck. Finding it bare, she reached out and reclaimed her necklace with shaking fingers. "Thank you," she breathed. "It's my most precious possession."

He shifted his feet uncomfortably. "You're welcome," he mumbled.

As she slipped the necklace over her head, she saw Henry reach down and pick up an orange- and red-striped scarf off the ground. "Wait a minute," she said, recognizing the knitting. "That's Edna's scarf!" Her eyes traveled to Henry's head. "And her hat as well!"

Just as Henry opened his mouth to respond, Hildy interrupted, "Oh, my stars!" she exclaimed. "Look how far away that valley is!" She was peering off the edge of the cliff, pointing down below. Everyone joined her to stare at the great distance they would need to travel.

"Glacidia and Shadow must have left hours ago," Hildy said dejectedly. "I fear Galdoren may already be in grave peril."

Serena huffed angrily. "And here we are stuck on this mountain top! It will take us *forever* to get back down!" She smacked her wand on a nearby frosted rock. "Blast! Why don't our powers work here?!"

The crystal fairies all began trilling excitedly, their jingling voices carried on the wind as they breezed past to hover above the valley. They formed a floating circle and touched the tips of their wands together. A moment later, the air on the cliff came alive. Waves of turquoise flickered in and out, until at last, four magnificent unicorns appeared before them in the snow.

"Our transportation, I presume?" Hildy asked with a smile.

The unicorns whinnied and shook their manes, tossing the silken strands of silver and blue from their eyes.

Serena sighed dreamily. She couldn't resist brushing her hand down the nearest unicorn's shiny coat. His spiral horn glistened like fine sterling as he lowered his head to nuzzle her. "Can I take you home?" she whispered in his ear.

Hildy approached one of the magical beasts and asked, "Can you transport us back to Galdoren Castle?" The unicorn stomped his hoof, shaking his head no. "Are you able to magic us into Galdoren at all?" Again, he shook his head.

Sharonna patted a nearby unicorn on its flank. "These unicorns are Wild Windermerians. They cannot leave their land." Looking into the unicorn's sea-green eyes she asked, "Can you get us as close as possible to the hole that's been blasted in the Border Spell?"

Henry winced at her words, feeling miserable for being the cause of such a catastrophic situation. The unicorn nodded in response to Sharonna's question. "Excellent," she smiled. Clapping her hands she firmly said, "Climb aboard everyone. Time is of the essence!"

The unicorns all bowed down, waiting for their passengers to mount. Sharonna was still a bit unsteady on her feet, so Henry lifted her onto the unicorn's back. "I ... I'm sorry about ... well, about *everything*," he said with raw emotion.

Sharonna watched the miserable-looking teenager move toward his own steed, his shoulders slumped in shame. "Henry," she began, "as you age, you will learn that all things happen for a reason. Everything unfolds as it is meant to be. For better or worse, fate gave you a part to play in this. But from what I have seen, you have played that part bravely. Oh, I admit, blasting a hole in the Border Spell was foolish and brash, a mistake born of youth and inexperience. But the important thing is that your heart was in the right place." She placed her hand on his shoulder and smiled down into his eyes. "It took great courage to cross that border, knowing you were about to face the greatest evil of our time."

Surprised and touched by her kind words, Henry blinked, then expertly mounted his steed, having grown up with horses on his farm. But since he had never traveled by unicorn before, he nearly fell off when the cliff suddenly became a wavy blur.

Sharonna turned, smiling slyly at him, lowering her voice so that only Henry could hear. "I'll tell you a little secret. Edna predicted that you will someday ..." but the rest of her words were lost in the whistling winds as the group disappeared off the mountaintop.

Chapter Thirty-Two

AN UNLIKELY ARMY

As a servant lifted the silver lid off his plate, Ricky wondered what kind of food they served in Galdoren. So far, all he'd had was cookies and candy. Although he would never admit it to his mother, he found to his great dismay that he actually craved real food. But what kind of real food would be under that silver lid?

"Your dinner, sir."

Ricky was enormously relieved to find his favorite meal sitting on his plate; hot dogs, chicken strips, fries, onion rings, cheeseburgers and nacho chips. *Finally*, he thought, *a healthy meal.*

Allie was equally happy to see a large salad on her plate. *That's just what I was hoping for,* she thought. She was a little concerned over how much weight she might have gained at Edna's candy farm. Ricky snorted when he saw his sister lift a forkful of vegetables to her mouth, while under the table Snoball munched contentedly on a plate of frozen fish.

A little orange dragon trotted into the dining room, stopping next to the king's feet. He trilled hungrily, staring up at his master.

"Awwww, he's so cute!" Allie gushed, bending to pet the dragon's scaly back. "What's his name?"

The king grimaced. "Pookie," he answered, placing a bowl of meatballs on the floor. The dragon gobbled them up.

"I named him myself!" Twink said proudly, lifting the lid off his plate. He squealed with delight at the giant glop of lime-green jello jiggling before him.

"Children," Shimmer said, clearing his throat. "King Shevre and I have decided that when the goblins attack, you are to go directly to the king's private chamber."

Twink's jaw dropped. "But I have a sword!" he whined.

The king's lips twitched. "Then you may protect our Earth guests."

Twink was torn between wanting to fight in the big battle and longing to protect Allie.

"But I'm a yellow belt in karate," Ricky protested. "I don't need protecting!"

"What's carroty?" asked Twink, sticking his hand-point deep into the jiggling mass of Jello. "Do you fight with vegetables?"

"*Karate,*" Ricky corrected. "It's a kind of martial arts." Seeing the blank look on Twink's face he added, "You know, self-defense?"

Shimmer gave his nephew a severe look while pointing to his spoon. The little star reluctantly pulled his hand-point out of the gelatin, then began slurping the green goo off its tip.

Ricky's diamond cufflinks got dunked in ketchup, and Twink burped milk from his nose, but other than that, the rest of the meal was relatively uneventful. Toward the end of dinner, everyone's spirits began to sink along with the sun in the sky. *How long until the goblins attack?* Although no one said it out loud, it was the one thing on everyone's minds.

King Shevre was just slipping the last of his steak to Pookie when the door to the Great Hall swung open. Chef Braeden stood in the open doorway, loudly clearing his throat. When he had everyone's attention, his hand flourished dramatically in the air as he announced, "The dessert you requested, Sir Twinkle ..."

All eyes turned to the numerous tables being wheeled in. On the first was a line of sterling silver bowls, overflowing with every kind of ice cream imaginable. Smaller dishes sat to the side, filled with chocolate, caramel and marshmallow toppings. The next table was brimming with bowls of creamy puddings, followed by one loaded with freshly baked pies. Two burly servants struggled to push an overstuffed table piled high with platters of warm cookies, gooey fudge brownies, sugar-sprinkled donuts, and plump cinnamon rolls.

The chef waved a wand in his chubby fingers, and rows upon rows of chocolate cupcakes flew under the archway, stacking themselves into a tower that spiraled to the ceiling. Just as everyone started to clap, he held his hand up for silence. He waved his wand once more and a single cherry floated into the room. It flew to the top of the teetering tower, then plopped itself into the frosting on the uppermost cake.

The snooty chef raised his brow, waiting for a response from the awestruck dinner guests. Allie began clapping, kicking her brother under the table until he applauded as well. Soon the room was filled with the sound of thunderous applause.

As the chef bowed and left, Allie turned to say something to Ricky, only to find herself addressing an empty chair. He was already in line behind Twink at the extravagant dessert bar.

Allie slumped in her seat. *What was the point of having salad?* she thought bitterly, staring at the thousands of calories awaiting her on the mouth-watering tables. She wondered how much her magical dress would stretch before it ripped.

While the boys eagerly crammed as much dessert as they could onto their plates, Allie fidgeted with her hands, stealing looks at the king and Shimmer. Absentmindedly watching a servant pour hot liquid into the king's china cup, Allie tried to find the words she wanted to say. "Um ... back at the goblin cave ...," she began in a small voice. But just then, Ricky returned, balancing a plate stacked two feet high. "Ricky," she huffed, "you're going to burst!"

"What were you saying about the goblins?" King Shevre prompted.

Allie glared at her little brother, amazed at how ten pounds of dessert could fit into an eighty-pound body. Turning back to the king, she continued, "Remember how I told you that we escaped off the mountain by flying to Edna's?" Both King Shevre and Shimmer nodded their heads. "Well, I never mentioned that we were out of Rocket Dust."

Shimmer wrinkled his brow. "But then, how were you able to fly?"

Allie twisted the napkin in her hands. "That's the thing. I don't really know. Edna had given me this spell ..." She reached into her invisible pocket and pulled out her note. As she opened it, the words floated into the air above the table. "I repeated these words and pictured her house in my mind. The next thing I knew, we were flying straight toward Edna's farm!"

King Shevre sat transfixed, staring at the all too familiar words hovering above Allie's plate. He narrowed his eyes. "That's impossible. Only those with faerie ancestry can use that spell."

Allie stuck her chin out. "Well *I* used it, and I'm from Earth!" Shimmer continued to stare thoughtfully at the girl. "Allie, try the spell now."

Allie took a deep breath and cleared her mind. She closed her eyes and began to chant the magical words. Just as Ricky was about to bite into a large cupcake, it floated out of his hands and hovered above his overloaded plate. Then all of the desserts rose off his dish, spun in the air and coasted across the table to float above King Shevre's coffee cup.

"Hey!" Ricky snapped, leaping up from his chair. "Give 'em back!" He lightly shoved his sister, breaking her concentration. All of the goodies plopped into the king's cup, breaking it in two and spilling its contents across the table.

The king stared at Allie in utter disbelief, only moving when Shimmer began throwing napkins onto the dripping mess in front of him.

A servant entered the room and cleared his throat. "Pardon the interruption, Your Majesty." He paused to cast a disapproving glance at the pile of soggy napkins and broken china. "A visitor has arrived who insists upon being seen. He says it is urgent."

"We'll continue this conversation later," the king said to Allie as he rose from his chair. "You may show him in."

The servant shifted his feet. "Er, he did not ask to see *you*, Sire," he said uncomfortably. "He wishes to have a word with Lady Allie."

All eyes turned to the Earth girl. She hastily pushed the enchanted words back onto the parchment, shoving the whole thing back into her pocket. *Who even knows I'm here?* she thought in bewilderment.

The servant motioned for the visitor to enter, who had clearly been waiting impatiently. The buckles on his pointy shoes jingled as a small man marched into the room, glared at Allie, and pointed an accusing finger at her. "I'll be havin' me flute back now, lassie!"

Allie threw her napkin on her plate and stood. "YOU!" she yelled at the Claurican. "Your stupid flute nearly got us all killed!"

His brows lifted in genuine surprise. "Dinnae it warn ye of approachin' danger?" His eyes grew wide as they fell upon the scrumptious dessert bar. He licked his lips hungrily,

"It started screeching uncontrollably!" Allie fumed.

The Claurican laughed as he slipped an empty pouch off his belt loop and moved toward the sweet tables. "'Tis just what it's supposed ta do, lassie," he said with a smirk. He lowered his voice while scooping a plate of cookies into his pouch. "It blows when danger is near."

Allie cocked her head. "Well, that would have been useful information to have, don't you think?"

"Aye." The little man nodded his head in agreement, causing the feather in his hat to bob. He dropped a handful of donuts into his pouch and turned to face Allie. "That old bat ye tried marryin' me off ta dinnae even have a cellar!"

"Edna?" Waves of guilt washed over Allie as she realized she hadn't given Edna a thought in hours. "How is she? Did the goblins ..." She couldn't bring herself to finish her sentence.

"Ach, ye dinna have ta worry about that wily witch," he said, trying to shove a coffeecake into his over-stuffed bag. The material was stretched so thin, it looked about to burst. "She threw an explodin' spell that sent those greasy-haired devils runnin' fer cover, she did!" Everyone in the room let out a sigh of relief.

The servant cleared his throat again. "Excuse me, Sire. May I clear the table?"

The king nodded his approval. The servant pulled a wand from his pocket and pointed it at the mess. "*Cleannis lea-oor!*" he commanded.

The dishes spun, and then rose into the air. The tablecloth folded itself neatly over the spill, then slid off the table and sped out the door on its way to the castle laundry. The dishes followed the tablecloth, turning down a different hall on their way to the kitchen. The servant bowed and then left the room.

The Claurican continued his tirade. "Since the crone dinnae have a cellar fer me ta live in, I'll be takin' me flute back now!" Winking at Twink, he whispered, "I think ye were right, lad. She IS a thousand years old!"

"I heard that!" Shimmer said, insulted. "And I'll thank you to speak kindly of Edna in my presence. She has done more good for this country than anyone I know!" The king's eyes twinkled as he gave Shimmer a pointed look. The flustered star hastily added, "Present company excluded, naturally."

"Naturally," said the bemused king.

"Good fer the country?" the little man's voice rose as he struggled to tie the bulging pouch back onto his belt. "That's a laugh! 'Tis a fact there are more homeless cellar sprites now than there've been fer centuries!"

"Homeless sprites?" the king asked, clearly concerned. "This is the first I've heard of that."

Finally managing to hang the heavy pouch from a side loop, the Claurican sighed, "Aye, there are hundreds of us wanderin' the countryside. No shelter ... no food. 'Tis the trend these days ta convert the cellars into playrooms for the wee ones. Why, before I moved out of me old cellar they had put a barrel of blocks where me bed use ta be, and a wooden train on top of me dinin' room table! And the lady of the house kept yellin' at me not ta drop crumbs on her new carpet!"

Ricky nodded in sympathy. His own mother was always nagging him not to bring food to the basement. She simply didn't understand that a boy needed to keep up his strength while he played video games.

Allie pulled the golden flute from her pocket and turned it over in her hands. "I'll return this to you if you give me back my bottle of Rocket Dust."

The Claurican colored. "Oh, it's the BOTTLE ye be wantin?" he said slyly. He pulled an empty bottle of Rocket Dust from his pocket. A lone piece of glitter bounced off the lid.

Allie's mouth fell open. "How could you have used an entire bottle?"

The buckles on his shoes jingled as he shifted his feet. "I may have shared it with one or two o' me homeless friends," he said, nodding toward the window. "Our poor feet grow weary of walkin' the countryside in search of a cellar."

The king crossed the room and pulled the heavy curtains back from the window. More than a hundred Clauricans stood illuminated in the torchlight. As the rest of the guests joined him at the window, the king stroked his beard thoughtfully. Turning to the Claurican he asked, "What's your name, sprite?"

"The name's Tibbly," he answered proudly.

"Tibbly, do you think that you and your friends would be interested in striking a bargain?"

The sprite's eyes twinkled. "That depends on what kind of a bargain, dinna it?"

"I'll allow all of you to stay in *my* cellar for as long as you wish ..."

The Claurican gasped. "The castle cellar? 'Tis the finest in all the land!" Then his eyes narrowed. "What would ye be wantin' in exchange?"

"Only to help defend this castle until my army returns in the morning," the king replied. Shimmer's head whipped around to stare open-mouthed at him.

"Defendin' the castle against *what*?" the Claurican shrewdly asked.

"Goblins," the king answered, crossing his arms over his chest.

"Goblins, eh?" Tibbly pulled a donut from his pouch and began to munch on it as he contemplated the king's offer.

King Shevre smiled. "Naturally, your meals will be prepared by my staff of chefs. And all of you will have access to my extensive wine collection. Where is that stored again, Shimmer?"

"In the cellar, Your Majesty," Shimmer answered, holding back the smile that tugged at his lips.

Tibbly leaped for joy, clicking his shoes in the air. He jumped upon the window ledge and shouted to the crowd below. "How'd ye like ta live in the *castle* cellar?" A roar of approval floated through the open window. "Would ye be willin' ta fight goblins this night for the privilege?" A low murmur could be heard as the Clauricans argued amongst themselves. Within moments, another roar of approval came from below. Tibbly turned from the window, a broad smile on his face. "It looks like ye got yerself an army, Yer Majesty."

"Then it looks like you've got yourself a new home," the king said, extending his hand in friendship.

"Now, if only I had a flute ta go with me new home," the Claurican mused as he shook King Shevre's hand.

"Alright, already! I never wanted the stupid thing to begin with!" Allie huffed as she tossed the flute to him. But when he caught it, a new sound drifted through the window.

The Claurican's back stiffened as he whispered, "Danger."

The low hum of a hundred flutes whistled from below. "Shimmer!" King Shevre yanked a golden cord. "The children!"

Shimmer gathered the kids in his points and hurriedly ushered them out of the room just as a unit of guards rushed in. Snoball padded so close to Ricky's feet that he nearly tripped over her.

"But I don't wanna go to the king's chamber!" Twink whined as they raced down one hallway after another. "I wanna fight!"

Shimmer's voice was firm. "It is not up for discussion, Twinkle. You will remain in the king's chamber for the duration of the battle. It's the safest place in the castle. There is only one way in and one way out—the spiral staircase."

"What's happening?" a gargoyle called from above.

"Goblins are attacking the castle!" Twink said dramatically.

"GOBLINS?" shrieked a frightened gargoyle from an adjoining hallway.

They sped down a labyrinth of hallways, until finally coming to a stop at the base of a long, spiral staircase. "The king's private chamber is at the top of this turret," Shimmer explained as they raced up the winding stairs. "It's the highest part of the castle. No arrow could possibly make its way up there."

When at last they reached the top step. Allie and Ricky sank to the floor, trying to catch their breath.

Twink stared down at his friends. "What's the matter?"

Ricky glared up at the little star. "It's a lot easier," gasp, "*flying* up those stairs than," he paused to suck in another mouthful of air, "*climbing* them!"

The siblings pulled themselves up from the floor, their breathing starting to return to normal. When Shimmer pushed open the door to the king's chamber, Allie's mouth fell open. The room was identical to the one in her vision. Her heart skipped a beat when she saw the frozen body of Queen Jacqueline in the center of the room.

"Remember, you are to stay here until either the king or I come to tell you it's safe to leave," Shimmer was saying. "I need your promises." Staring sternly at Twink he added, "*ALL* of your promises!"

Allie pulled her eyes from the frozen statue and exchanged a resigned look with Ricky. "We promise," they said half-heartedly.

Shimmer flew to his nephew's side and tapped his foot-point in the air. "Twinkle?"

Twink pouted. Pulling his little wooden sword form its sheath he whined, "But I can help, Uncle Shimmer!"

"Stop waving that thing around! You'll poke someone's eye out!" Twink's lip started to wobble. Shimmer sighed and wrapped a point affectionately around the brooding star. "Remember what King Shevre said? You have a solemn duty to protect our Earth visitors."

Allie moved to Twink's side. "I'd really feel a lot safer if you stayed, Twink."

As Ricky looked at her questioningly, Allie winked. Then she nodded her head in Twink's direction, silently imploring Ricky to help persuade Twink to stay. Ricky rolled his eyes. "Yeah, Twink," he said unconvincingly. "Help us. Save us. Protect us." Allie shot her brother a dirty look and kicked him on the shin.

"OW!" he yelled.

Twink puffed up his little chest. "Don't worry, Allie," he said valiantly, swinging his little sword. "I'll protect you!"

Shimmer sighed in relief and kissed the top of his nephew's head. As he turned to fly out the open window, Twink zoomed to his side, and wrapped his arms around him. "I love you, Uncle Shimmer," he said softly.

"I love you too," Shimmer choked, hugging him back. Then he gently pushed away from his nephew's tight grip and flew out the window, joining the battle about to erupt below.

The children rushed to Twink's side, peering out the window. But the turret was so high, all they could see was the distant glow of torchlight within a vast darkness.

While Shimmer was escorting the children to the turret, the king had ordered his few remaining guards to surround the perimeter of the castle. Most of the servants insisted on helping to defend it as well. Roberts led them all to the armory as the king quickly strode from the Great Hall, the small Claurican close on his heels.

As they made their way down the long hallway, the Claurican whistled at the sight of the numerous suits of armor lining the walls. "Jest a minute! I have an idea!" Then he blew a tune into his flute. As he did, all of the suits of armor but one clamored to attention. The eerie black armor continued to stand stiffly against the wall.

The other suits of armor all came alive as Tibbly continued to play. They stepped down from their pedestals, each grabbing a sword and a shield from the wall behind and promptly lined up in formation behind the king.

The king's eyebrows shot up in surprise. "I wonder who made the better bargain?" he asked, clearly impressed.

Despite the dozens of armored feet marching behind him, the king couldn't help but wonder how long his makeshift army would be able to stand up against the might of a full-blown goblin attack. He only hoped that the other Clauricans were as handy with their magic flutes as Tibbly.

Shimmer flew to a stop near the king, just outside the castle's portcullis. The drawbridge had been raised hours earlier, and the king briefly wondered how the Clauricans had been able to cross the moat. Then he remembered—they had flown in on Allie's Rocket Dust.

As the king barked orders to his ragtag army, Shimmer stared into the dark forest. He shivered, knowing that all that stood between the castle and the dangerous creatures was the murky waters of the deep moat.

What was that? Shimmer wondered, squinting at the thick growth of trees. Something was moving. The flutes were whistling more shrilly now, and the king ordered the Clauricans to quiet their musical instruments. Shimmer tapped the king on the shoulder and pointed into the woods. King Shevre narrowed his eyes, trying to see into the darkness.

The next moment, a flaming arrow shot over their heads and bounced off the stone wall behind them. Suddenly, hundreds of goblins raced out from the cover of the trees, their blood-red skin glowing eerily in the torchlight.

The battle had begun.

Chapter Thirty-Three

SHATTERED DREAMS

*A*llie couldn't resist running her hand down Queen Jacqueline's arm. She was amazed at how bitterly cold the frozen queen felt beneath her fingertips. Then she was distracted by a muffled grunt and turned to see her brother struggling to pull off his Salamander boots. Allie glared at him. "Do not even *think* about taking those shoes off! There's not enough fresh air in all of Galdoren to blow away the smell of your stinky feet!"

Ricky huffed, then sank back into the velvety cushion of the throne he was perched upon. As Twink practiced sword fighting with his reflection in the antique mirror, Allie turned her attention back to the tragic figure. "I can't believe it's really her."

"Who?" asked Ricky.

"Queen Jacqueline," she sighed.

Ricky gave the sparkling statue a cursory glance. "Who's Queen Jacqueline?"

"The king's mother," Allie explained. She was about to tell Ricky and Twink about the terrible scene she had witnessed in her vision, the one that had taken place in this very room, when Ricky asked, "What's she pointing at?"

"Your ugly shirt!" Twink giggled.

Ricky ripped a gem off his shirt and threw it at the little star. Twink blocked it with his sword, smacking the diamond across the room. It ricocheted off the mantle and bounced off a tapestry.

"Ten points!" Twink squealed. Ricky gave the little star an enthusiastic high-five.

Allie rolled her eyes, muttering something about boys. But in truth, they were all on edge, trying to keep their minds off the battle that was raging below.

Ricky reached across the end table and picked up a copy of *The Galdoren Gazette*. He flipped past an article on wand safety and one about lowering the speed limit for magic carpets. He skipped through the entire first section, as it seemed to be filled only with boring news stories.

He liked the second section much better. It had an interview with a famous siren, a recipe for Fairie Cake, an advice column for lovelorn mermaids, and a slew of personal ads (*"Single Fairie Godmother seeks Knight in Tarnished Armor," "Divorced Dragon, Non-Smoker, Seeks Same"*). As he skimmed past a scathing review of *"The Ugly Stepsisters Tap Dance the Classics,"* something at the bottom of the page caught his eye.

"Hey! There's an ad here for The Four Faeries Floating Follies!" He remembered the name from his invitation. "I was supposed to see that show!" He read the bold print splashed across the ad, *"Now in Fly-O-Vision!"*

"Aw, this looks really fun," he said disappointedly. "Do you think there's a chance I could still see it?"

Allie went to the window, trying in vain to see the assault on the ground. "Don't count on it."

Trying to distract himself from the distant sounds of combat, he got up and walked across the room to a large mahogany dresser. "Maybe there are some cards or something in here."

He slid open the top drawer. Inside were a tarnished key, a few sheets of royal stationery, a thick *Spell-O-Phonebook*, and several half-empty bottles of Rocket Dust. The glitter inside no longer bounced, as the expiration dates had come and gone.

Pulling open the next drawer he found a stack of old bills, a coupon for *"Half-off your next purchase at Gossamer's Gift Shop,"* and an old letter from Sharonna. Curious, Ricky went back to the throne and started to read:

> *Dear Shevre,*
> *Edna, Hildy and I took some well-deserved time off. We just got back from Wanda's World of Bargains. I found a gorgeous*

designer wand case and a pair of glass slippers. I bought you two new satin shirts. I hope I picked the right size, as these designer knock-offs sometimes run small.

When am I going to see you? I know you're busy, but I don't think it's too much to ask for you to take a few minutes each week to call your old aunty. Just a reminder, we changed our spell-o-phone. The new number is 1000–6–200–000.

Love and kisses,

Aunt Sharonna

P.S. – Don't forget to floss!

Ricky laughed. Sharonna sounded a lot like his own mother.

"You shouldn't snoop in other people's personal belongings," Allie scolded in her big-sister voice. Staring at the letter in Ricky's hands, curiosity got the better of her and she snatched it from him.

A smile dimpled her cheeks as she finished reading the old letter. When she tucked it back into the drawer, she noticed a glint of silver peeking out from under a pile of papers. She pulled out a silver picture frame, surprised by the old photograph inside. In the picture, a beaming King Shevre had his arm draped around Serena. Her hair was much shorter and the king had just begun to grow his beard. Allie wondered why the king would have buried it in the back of a drawer. Shrugging, she put it back where she'd found it.

A silver wand sitting on the mantle caught Ricky's attention. Curious, he went over to the fireplace to get a closer look, leaving Allie to rummage through the bottom drawer alone.

The drawer was empty except for an old article clipped from *The Galdoren Gazette*. It had been neatly folded and was so old it had yellowed and was starting to curl at the corners. Allie carefully unfolded the paper. It was an article on the capture of Shadow and Queen Glacidia. There were several pictures that accompanied the article, but it was the last one that held Allie's attention. It was a close-up image of the Ice Queen herself. Allie began to tremble as she stared into the depths of that soulless eye.

"Allie," Ricky said, tapping her on the shoulder.

She jumped, dropping the paper into the drawer. "Don't do that!" she snapped.

"Do what?"

"Sneak up on me!"

195

"I didn't sneak up on you! I just wanted to show you something."

Turning from the mirror, Twink sheathed his sword. He was surprised to see Ricky waving a wand in the air. When nothing happened, Ricky waved it again.

Twink snorted, "You have to say a spell first, doofus!"

"Oh," Ricky replied. "Wait, whadja call me?"

"Ricky, I don't think you should be waving that thing around," Allie said.

"So *you're* the only one who's allowed to do magic?"

Allie sighed, wondering how to explain what she felt to her brother. "You're messing with stuff you don't understand. What if you were to say a wrong word? I'm afraid something terrible might happen!"

"Well, *I'm* not afraid," he said firmly. Then he concentrated on remembering the spell the servant had said in the Great Hall. *How did it go again?* He pointed the wand at the cushion Snoball was sleeping on.

"*Cleannis lea-oor!*" he commanded. Sparks shot out of the tip of the wand. A very surprised Snoball was suddenly lifted into the air as the cushion rose from the couch. She leapt off just as it flew out of the room and down the stairs, speeding toward the royal laundry.

Twink doubled over in laughter. "That's a cleaning spell! What are you going to do if Shadow attacks us? Shampoo him to death?"

Ricky's eyes narrowed. He pointed the still-sparking wand at Twink. The little star ducked, so that the spell struck the crystal decanter behind him. The amber liquid sloshed inside the decanter as it wobbled in the air, then, it too, flew out the door and down the stairs.

"Put that wand down!" Allie yelled at her brother. But he kept trying to blast Twink, who continued to laugh at him. As Twink streaked around the room dodging spells, Ricky accidentally blasted a candelabra, a scepter, two oil paintings, and a pair of reading glasses. All of the objects zoomed out of the room and down the stairs to the laundry.

"STOP IT!" Allie yelled.

To her surprise, Ricky listened. Then she realized it was only because the wand had stopped working: the spell had finally worn off.

"I wonder if that candelabra will fit into the washing machine?" Twink asked with a giggle.

Ricky laughed.

"You see, *that's* why I don't think we should mess with magic!" Allie huffed.

Twink pointed to the plaque on Queen Jacqueline's pedestal. "Hey, Allie! Isn't that *your* spell?"

Allie knelt to examine the golden words etched across the plaque. Goosebumps crept up her arms. "Yeah, that's it."

"Are you sure?" Ricky asked.

Allie nodded. She reached into her pocket and pulled out her note, not realizing that she had knocked the snow globe to the edge of her pocket. She unfolded the paper and watched as the golden words flew off the page to float in the air.

Seeing the spell gave Ricky an idea. *At least this is a real spell and not some stupid laundry one.* He waved his wand, reciting the words hovering before him, "*B'yardin Shatavna Myesto Troo!*"

Suddenly, the wand began to smoke. Allie narrowed her eyes. "What did you do?" she demanded, pressing the words of the spell back onto the parchment.

The wand quickly became so hot that Ricky flung it from his hands. It hopped across the floor, sizzling and popping, until it finally burst into flames. Allie dropped her note and grabbed a nearby vase. She quickly yanked the flowers out and dumped the water over the burning wand.

Ricky stared open-mouthed at the charred remains.

"COOL!" Twink exclaimed. "I never saw anyone kill a wand before!"

As Allie leaned over to examine the smoking remnants, the snow globe fell out of her pocket and crashed onto the hard marble floor. It shattered into a hundred pieces.

"My snow globe!" Allie cried. Her heart broke along with the toy. It was her only souvenir of Galdoren. And besides, Gossamer had made it herself!

"Do you think we can glue it back together?" Twink asked.

Ricky looked at the shattered glass swimming in the pool of snowy water. "I don't think there's enough glue in all of Galdoren." He patted his sister's back, trying to comfort her. "You can have my invitation," he said gently. "That could be your souvenir."

Choking back a sob, she picked up the jagged crystals that were once a miniature replica of Galdoren Castle. As she lifted it, something slipped out of the broken turret. It was a ring! *Why would Gossamer have hidden a ring inside the castle?* she wondered.

She held the diamond in her hand. Drawn by the unearthly brilliance of the stone, she looked at it more closely. And when she saw what she was holding, her hand began to shake. The sparkling gem looked exactly like an eyeball.

Chapter Thirty-Four
A CHILLING DISCOVERY

The air near the Border Spell buckled in blurry waves as four unicorns and their passengers materialized into view. The sun had finally sunk over Windermere and the moon was looming large over the snow-capped valley.

Henry and the three Guardians of Galdoren leapt off their steeds and raced toward the border. But they stopped cold when they came upon the mirage of Gossamer. They had all but forgotten about her.

"*Leoht-bora!*" Sharonna commanded, pointing her wand. The life-like image of Gossamer instantly lit up.

Henry knelt to examine something that had caught his eye as Serena brushed her hand through Gossamer's crushed wings. The air rippled where her hand went through it.

Sharonna tapped her wand thoughtfully against her hip. "I believe that Gossamer may well be the key to discovering what Glacidia is up to and where she is headed. We must find the *real* Gossamer at once."

"But we don't have time!" Serena insisted, her voice rising as her emotions got the best of her. "Galdoren may already be—"

"Serena," Sharonna interrupted, "you will soon learn that knowledge can often be the most powerful weapon we wield."

Hildy raised a hand to cut off Serena's imminent protest. "Sharonna is right. It would be unwise to proceed without first learning what information Gossamer was forced to give the Queen of Windermere."

Serena reluctantly nodded her head in agreement.

"Now, where could she be?" Hildy murmured, running her hand across the glowing image.

Henry stood from his crouched position near Gossamer's feet and smiled. "I know where she is!"

"You do?" Hildy blinked. "But how?"

He pointed to a pink and orange spotted mushroom that had been trapped inside the block of ice along with Gossamer. "Magnus needed those mushrooms for a potion once. There's only one place in all of Galdoren where they grow—and I know where that is!" he finished triumphantly and started to run toward the hole in the Border Spell, calling over his shoulder, "It's not far from here!"

The three women trailed close behind as Henry leaped out of Windermere and back onto Galdoren soil. Surprised by the sudden warmth, he pulled off his hat and scarf and tucked them back into his pocket.

The instant Hildy crossed the border, she waved her wand, creating a strong current of air that lifted everyone off the ground. "Which way?" she asked, as they hovered in the air.

Henry rattled off the directions, grateful that Magnus had required those particular mushrooms for his spell. A lump suddenly formed in his throat, and he knew then that the loss of his teacher had left a hole in his life that would never quite be mended.

Within moments, the wind they had been riding on lowered everyone to the ground as they arrived at their destination. Even by the dim light of the low moon, Henry could see that the block of ice before him was the real thing, and not another illusion. Knowing that the woman trapped inside was real as well sent a cold shiver down his spine. He couldn't help but stare at her horror-stricken eyes, wondering what torture she had endured.

Sharonna tapped the ice with her wand. "Just as I suspected. She has only been temporarily frozen. Since Glacidia shot the spell through the crack, it was not powerful enough to freeze Gossamer permanently." Turning to Serena and Hildy, she said briskly, "Ladies ... wands out!"

Hildy and Serena pulled their wands from the folds of their cloaks. The three women pointed the tips of their wands at the ice block while Sharonna commanded, *"Awendan brim!"*

Henry watched with fascination as the ice began to melt. Within moments, the icy block had turned to slush. Shivering from her glacial imprisonment, Gossamer fell forward and Henry lunged to catch her in his arms.

Serena felt sick at the sight of the fairie's battered wings. Gossamer's bruised face twisted in pain. Frantically, her eyes sought Sharonna's. "The Serpent's Eye," she breathed, wincing as her broken wings involuntarily began to beat.

"What about it?" Sharonna replied, gently brushing Gossamer's ice-crusted hair from her forehead.

Gossamer swallowed hard, barely able to talk. "It's not where you think …"

Hildy, Serena and Henry all exchanged puzzled looks. "Where is it?" Serena urged.

"Earth girl …," she panted, closing her eyes against the pain.

Sharonna looked confused. "Allie? What about her?"

Gossamer ignored the black dots dancing before her eyes, struggling to stay conscious. "It's … in … her …," she willed her eyes open as she fought to finish her sentence. "… snow globe." Then she fainted in Henry's arms, her crushed wings going into spasms behind her.

"Hildy!" Sharonna snapped. "Get us to Edna's. NOW!" Turning to Henry she explained, "That's where the Earth children are."

He looked at the injured woman in his arms. "But what about—"

"Edna can heal her." With that, the group rose upon the gust of air that Hildy had conjured. Sharonna shouted to be heard above the shrieking winds. "Our only hope is that Edna foresaw this and put both Allie and the Serpent's Eye out of harm's way. If not, I fear it may already be too late—for both Galdoren *and* the Earth child!"

Her voice was soon swallowed by the whistling winds as they sailed past the moon, soaring toward the little candy farm near the edge of the valley.

Chapter Thirty-Five

THE TRAPPED
AND THE HUNTED

Ricky stared, unblinking, at the ring in Allie's palm. Twink dropped his sword. Their eyes moved from the gem back to Allie.

Ricky gulped. "So, is that …?"

Speechless, Allie just nodded her head.

"The Serpent's Eye?" Twink squeaked. "But …," he hung in the air, bewildered. "But *how*?"

Allie dropped into the velvet chair behind her, thinking. She tried to unravel the mystery as she spoke. "Shimmer told me that he and Gossamer had shared the duty of guarding the ring while The Three were looking for a safe place to hide it." Twink nodded his head enthusiastically, having heard the story countless times before. "Since they had shared guard duty," she reasoned, "Gossamer would have had plenty of time alone with the Serpent's Eye."

"But how did it get inside your snow globe?" Twink asked.

Allie thought back to the conversation she had with Gossamer about this particular snow globe. *I believe I was in a terrible hurry when I made this one.* "She must have hidden it inside when Shimmer wasn't with her." Allie's voice trailed off as she thought of something else—the way Gossamer kept pressing her about whether or not she was planning on staying in Galdoren.

"She must have wanted me to have the ring so I'd take it to a place where Queen Glacidia could never get her hands on it ..." The kids all looked at each other, and in unison said, *"Earth!"*

Gossamer's parting words rang in Allie's ears: *Be careful, dear.*

"Allie," Ricky said softly. "What should we do?"

"We should tell King Shevre," she said with certainty. Closing her shaking fingers around the gem she added, "Now!"

They all looked toward the window, where the distant sounds of the battle rang from below.

Excited at the prospect of doing something courageous, Twink squealed, "I'll go!"

"No, Twink," Allie said firmly. "It's too dangerous."

Setting his jaw, Ricky bravely volunteered. "I'll go." When Allie opened her mouth to argue he countered with, "I have Salamander boots!"

She gave her brother a funny look. "So as long as the goblins are on fire, you'll be okay?"

Twink swept his sword up from the floor and heroically cried, "Fair not, fear maiden! I mean, fear not, fair maiden!" And then he flew out the open window.

"TWINK!" Allie called. She raced to the window alongside her brother. They both stuck their heads out, straining to see in the dark. "Come back!" she yelled. But it was too late. The little star had already streaked out of sight.

The grandfather clock ticked steadily as Allie and Ricky stared blankly at each other.

"So," Ricky joked. "Got any more stolen jewelry on you?"

On the other side of the castle and across the moat, a goblin crouched in the tall grass. He ignored the flaming arrows streaking past his head, concentrating instead on the task at hand. He uncoiled the thick rope he had carried since the attack order had been given. Pulling his gnarled hair from his eyes, he peered across the moat toward his target. His yellow gaze lingered on the raised drawbridge and the iron lever that controlled it.

Instead of the large battalion of knights he had been expecting, a lone Claurican stood guard, shadowed beneath the head of a stone gargoyle. Two knights lay dead near the Claurican's feet.

The goblin wondered: *Where is the king's legendary army?* They were nowhere in sight. He curled his lips into a twisted smile, exposing his fangs. *This will be even easier than I thought.*

He swung one end of the rope in the air, spinning it like a lasso. He hurled it across the moat, snapping it taught as it cracked against the wall, causing it to whip around the stunned gargoyle's neck. The Claurican turned at the sound of the gargoyle's choked screams.

Dropping the rope, the goblin grabbed his bow and arrow, leering in the dark. *Just the distraction I needed.* He pulled back on the bow and fired.

Zing!

The Claurican fell onto his stomach, an arrow sticking out of his back. He writhed in pain, slowly raising his flute to his mouth.

The goblin cursed and aimed again, shooting the flute from the Claurican's fingers.

"HELP! HELP!" the Gargoyle shrieked hoarsely. "The drawbridge," he cried, "It's unprotected!" But no one could hear his raspy warnings above the loud din of battle.

The goblin shoved his weapon back into its harness, and quickly tied the other end of the rope around a nearby tree trunk. Then he leapt up, grabbed hold of the rope, and began to make his way, hand-over-hand, across the moat.

He landed with a soft thud on the other side, smiling cruelly as he kicked the gasping Claurican.

"Please," the shaking Claurican pleaded.

The goblin slowly twisted the arrow from his back, causing the little Claurican to shriek in pain.

"Shhh," the goblin whispered. With a gleeful look, he thrust the arrow into the Claurican's neck, killing him instantly.

Struggling for breath, the gargoyle tried in vain to shout for King Shevre. When the goblin heard his strangled cries, he pulled a heavy club from his belt. The gargoyle's eyes grew wide as the goblin whipped it toward his head. The blow knocked the stone gargoyle clean off the castle wall where he had hung for over a hundred years. As his head rolled across the dirt, the loyal gargoyle continued to shout a choked warning to the king's men. The last thing he saw was the sneering goblin poised above him, his heavy club raised high in the air. He squeezed his eyes shut just as the club smashed down, shattering him into a hundred pieces. One broken piece of rock carved with the gargoyle's lips continued to cry softly for help. The goblin ruthlessly swung his club down, smashing it to dust.

Caught up in a rage of bloodlust, the goblin swung his club at the iron lever that held the drawbridge up. It lurched, and then began to turn. And as it did, the drawbridge slowly began to lower.

A deafening cheer rose on the other side of the moat. Within moments, hundreds of goblins were running across the bridge, their heavy boots trampling the freshly planted flowers at the entrance to Galdoren Castle.

"I can't see anything from up here, can you?" Ricky asked, staring out the window into the black nothingness below.

Allie stood on her tip-toes, leaning her head out the window as far as she could. "All I see are those red streaks," she answered, not knowing that the glowing streaks lighting up the sky were flaming arrows.

"Any sign of Twink?" he asked anxiously.

She squinted her eyes as tightly as she could, hoping to catch even a glimpse of something purple. Sighing, she turned to her brother and slowly shook her head *no*. She leaned back against a tapestry and nervously began rolling the Serpent's Eye back and forth across her palm.

Ricky turned from the window and made his way toward his favorite piece of furniture. "Do you think this chair would look good in front of our TV?"

Allie gritted her teeth. "It's a *throne*, not a chair!"

He sank back in the throne, absent-mindedly playing with the threads from an empty button hole, where another gem (a ruby this time) had fallen off his shirt. He sat in silence, worrying about Twink and the violent conflict he was flying into.

Ricky was so lost in thought that he didn't notice his sister's eyes suddenly glaze over. "*Accennan mec se breag ... Bring me the ring ...,*" a soft voice whispered in Allie's head. "*Accennan mec se breag ...,*" it whispered over and over.

She moved as if in a trance toward the icy statue of Queen Jacqueline. "*Lecga binnan min leawf ... Place it upon my finger ...,*" the voice urged as Allie inched ever closer.

Silently obeying the pleading voice, she opened her palm. But just as she was about to place the ring on the frozen queen's outstretched finger, an icy breeze swept through the room, breaking whatever spell she was under.

She shook her head, trying to clear it. Then without thinking, she pushed the ring over her own knuckle. Curious to see how she looked, she walked over to the ancient mirror. But then a movement in the tarnished glass caught her attention. Something had swooped in through the open window. Smiling with relief, she happily called, "Twink!" But when she turned, the smile died on her lips. Shadow leered at her from across the room. And standing beside him—staring at Allie through one glittering eye—was the Queen of Windermere.

The goblins were laying siege to the castle. The handful of remaining guards and knights were ambushed at every turn. They fought fiercely, but were so severely outnumbered that they were quickly falling, one by one. And the king's servants were no match for the strength and cunning of the goblins. The enchanted suits of armor were rapidly dwindling in numbers as well. Ironically, it was the little Clauricans who held the one advantage: their magic flutes.

Three goblins cornered a shaking Claurican near the castle's portcullis. The Claurican's hands were trembling so badly he could barely lift his flute to his mouth. As the flute moved closer to his lips, one of the goblins kicked it from his hand. It landed in the dirt near the lifeless body of a fallen knight.

The goblin laughed, baring a set of broken fangs. Bending to retrieve the flute, he noticed the buckles on the Claurican's pointed shoes. His lips curled into a cruel smile as he sneered, "Nice shoes, twinkle-toes!" All the goblins laughed and jeered.

The cellar sprite set his jaw and through trembling lips stammered, "'Tis a fine Claurican tradition to wear these shoes, datin' back thousands o' years."

One of the goblins pushed his face right into the Claurican's. "Well, guess what, little man?" The cellar sprite turned his face away from the goblin's foul breath. "I think your little tradition is about to be *axed!*" Snarling, he pulled a huge axe from a harness attached to his back. As the other goblins cheered him on, he lifted it in the air, preparing to chop off the helpless Claurican's foot.

But then the notes of a nearby flute trilled loudly. The goblins turned in the direction of the music. Tibbly held a flute to his lips, and as he played, the axe was yanked from the goblin's hand. It hovered in the air above, its sharp edges glinting in the moonlight.

"Faith and begorrah!" the rescued Claurican sputtered, wiping his sweaty brow. "Never have I been so happy ta see a fellow cellar sprite!"

Tibbly clapped his friend on the back. Turning to the growling goblins he roared, "Go back ta where ye came from, ye hairy ...," he paused for a moment to think of the perfect word. As he spat the name out, his friend colored, never having heard Tibbly use such foul language before.

The goblins turned their bloodshot eyes upon both Clauricans, dangerous expressions crossing their faces. With a collective growl, they lunged at the little men, their large fists nearly the size of the Clauricans' heads.

"Did ye nay hear me?!" Tibbly shouted, dodging their blows. "I told ye to *run*!" Then he lifted his golden flute. As the notes began to play, the hovering axe began swinging savagely at the goblins' heads.

WHOOSH! The blade tore through the air, cutting half the hair off the nearest goblin's head. *WHOOSH, WHOOSH!*

The cowering creatures fled with the murderous axe hot on their trail. The enchanted weapon chased them all the way back across the drawbridge and into the dark forest beyond.

Tibbly was wiping goblin spit off his friend's flute when a little purple star streaked out of the sky.

"Have you seen King Shevre?" Twink asked, nearly out of breath.

"Aye," Tibbly answered. He pointed toward the gardens. "He's over there."

"Thanks!" Twink called, speeding off in the direction of the king.

Allie quickly moved to the throne Ricky was perched upon, pulling her shocked brother protectively to her side. The two siblings clasped each other tightly as Shadow and Glacidia moved toward them.

"You have something of mine," the queen snarled. "And I want it back!"

Ricky carefully covered his sister's ringed finger with his hand. Allie's eyes darted to the open doorway, their only means of escape. But the queen caught her look and smiled cruelly. "Tsk, tsk," she said icily.

"That stairway looks dark and dangerous. It would be a tragedy if you were to slip and fall. Allow me to light your way!" Her hand moved in a flourish as she pointed a bony finger at the staircase, yelling, *"Scima fyr brond!"* Sparks flickered across the top step, igniting a fire that swept all the way down the stairs, until the entire staircase was engulfed in flames.

As Snoball dove under the throne, Ricky nudged Allie and whispered, "You can use the ring to escape out the window!" Lowering his eyes to his Salamander boots he added, "I can go down the stairs!"

The fire hissed and crackled loudly, masking the sounds of their hushed whispers. The witch cocked her head as Allie whispered back, "I don't think I can make it past them. You go! Get help!"

"No!" Ricky insisted. "I won't leave you!"

"SECRETS?" Glacidia snarled. "I *loathe* secrets. Shadow, make them tell me what they said!"

Shadow moved toward Allie and Ricky. "With pleasure, my Queen."

"GO!!!" Allie screamed, pushing her brother toward the stairs. Ricky gave her one last pleading look, then bolted down the burning staircase.

"GET HIM!!!" Glacidia shrieked.

Shadow sped from the room in pursuit of the boy.

Ricky's heart hammered in his chest as he leaped through the flames. He took the stairs two at a time, sensing Shadow's looming presence behind him.

The fire ended abruptly on the last step. Ricky peeled down a long hallway, desperately searching for help.

A sick thrill shot through Shadow as he watched the boy try to outrun him.

"There is no escape," he hissed, gliding after the boy.

Queen Glacidia's eye flashed dangerously when she spied the shattered snow globe lying on the floor. "So it's true," she whispered, bending to run her finger along a jagged piece of glass. "And where, I wonder, is my prize?" She raised her glittering pupil to Allie's hands, hidden behind her back.

The witch's lips curled into an angry sneer. "You couldn't resist trying it on, could you, little Earth trash?" As she moved toward

Allie, the trembling girl took a step back. Each time the witch advanced, Allie moved backwards, until she finally bumped into the frozen body of Queen Jacqueline.

"*She* didn't obey my command!" Glacidia snarled, nodding toward the statue. "Now give me the Serpent's Eye or spend eternity in ice by her side!"

"Stand back!" Allie ordered, pointing her shaking ringed finger at the witch. "Or I'll use the gem on *you!*"

Queen Glacidia was so startled that someone so insignificant would challenge her that she stopped in her tracks. She blinked, then threw her head back and roared with laughter. "Idiot girl! Only those with fairie blood coursing through their veins can wield the power of that gem!" She clicked her sharp nails against a marble table. "Now, the one question that remains is whether I freeze you, or burn you?" The strands of ice growing out of her head twirled madly in the air, and Allie could have sworn she heard them hiss, "*Freeze her, freeze her, freeze her...*"

✵ ✷ ✷

Twink rocketed into the garden, frantically searching for the king. Instead, he found his uncle laying face down on a bed of trampled flowers.

"UNCLE SHIMMER!"

A goblin stepped out of the shadows. "Is this your uncle?" When the little star nodded tearfully, he pulled a spiked club from the harness tied to his back. He gave Twink a feral grin as he raised the club high in the air, poised to strike Shimmer as he lay helpless on the ground.

Twink streaked through the air, smacking the goblin in the eye with his little wooden sword.

"AHHHHH!" the goblin screamed, dropping his weapon to cup his injured eye.

Twink hovered protectively above his fallen uncle, his sword thrust out in front of him.

Growling furiously, the creature charged. But then a swarm of Claurican shoes dove down from the sky. The jingling footwear savagely kicked the goblin up and down the length of his sweat-soaked body. He ran off howling for help, the pack of shoes streaking behind.

Shimmer moaned softly as he rolled over, rubbing his head. As his eyes fluttered open, Twink worriedly asked, "Are you okay?"

"I'm fine, Twinkle. I just got the wind knocked out of me, that's all."

Twink smiled in relief, and then squealed with glee, "Guess what? You were right, Uncle Shimmer! I *DID* poke someone's eye out with my sword!"

Shimmer pulled the little star to his chest. The two stars hugged tightly while the sky above them lit up with flaming arrows.

Shimmer pulled away and scowled down at his little nephew. "What are you doing here? You promised that you would stay in the king's chamber!"

"But Uncle Shimmer! You'll never believe what was hidden inside that snow globe Gossamer gave Allie …"

Ricky raced down the empty hallways, wondering where everyone had gone. The castle was deserted. His spirits sank when he realized they must all be outside, fighting. He had to find help for Allie, fast. *But which way to the main entrance?*

He knew it was only a matter of time before Shadow caught up to him, and then there would be no hope at all for his sister.

Racing into the portrait gallery, he skidded to a halt. Three hallways connected here—but only one led to the main entrance. *But which one?* He prayed for someone to show him the way. His eyes were suddenly drawn to the familiar-looking man in the portrait, Duke Albert. The duke's eyes seemed to be staring in the direction of the left hallway. Taking it as a sign, Ricky bolted down that hallway just as Shadow entered the gallery.

Shadow's eyes fell upon the boy's back as he darted around the corner. The hollow opening on his face tilted upward in a twisted imitation of a smile. *You will soon pay for stabbing me with that invisible sword, Earth boy.* A black tongue flicked hungrily as he imagined all the ways he would torture the child before killing him. But just as he turned to follow the boy, a confused-looking carpet careened into the hall, knocking Shadow off his feet. The carpet sped out of sight, leaving Shadow to curse at it from the cold marble floor.

As Ricky fled down the long corridor, he passed a familiar-looking room. *The Royal Suite!* He skidded to a stop, snuck a quick glance behind him, then raced into the enormous bedchamber. He hoped to lose Shadow by hiding in the king's junk closet—he knew if that monster should catch him before he got help, his sister was doomed.

The room was dark, but he dared not turn on a light. He found his way to the closet by using the little shaft of light spilling in from the hall. He opened one of the closet's double doors and crept inside, quietly closing it behind him.

Inside the closet it was so dark that he could not even see his hand when he held it in front of his face. *Good,* he thought, *if I can't see anything, then neither can he.*

Little did Ricky know that Shadow saw best in the dark.

Shadow rose from the floor. He crept down the hallway, turning left as he had seen the boy do. He closed his eyes and inhaled deeply. He smelled something ... *fear.* The boy was near.

Shadow's pulse quickened with the thrill of the hunt. *Hiding, are you?* He almost laughed. He slithered down the long hallway, stopping to sniff at each door. Suddenly, the smell of fear was overpowering. It was drifting out of a large bedchamber at the end of the hall. He silently crept into the room, the scent of his prey making his nostrils flare. Turning his head toward the closet, he moved soundlessly toward the double doors. Curling his fingers around the doorknob, he started to twist it open. But then his hand stilled. With a cruel smile, he transformed into mist and melted under the closet door.

The hairs on the back of Ricky's neck suddenly bristled. *I'm not alone in this closet.* His heart was hammering so hard he thought it would burst from his chest. He stood perfectly still in the shroud of darkness. Icy breath suddenly blew across his cheek. Ricky lashed out blindly, his punches only striking empty air.

He felt a sharp claw rake across his shoulder, tearing his shirt and ripping his skin. He whirled around, screaming in pain. He snap-kicked the air, but again, his blows were lost in a black nothingness.

"Show yourself, you coward!" he shouted with a courage born of desperation, his bloody shoulder beginning to burn. How could he fight an enemy he couldn't see?

A pair of icy hands suddenly wrapped around his throat. "Soon I will finish what I started back in that tree," Shadow whispered.

Ricky kicked and punched blindly into the blackness as disembodied laughter filled the air.

The king's old candelabra suddenly lit itself, bathing the room in light. Shadow released Ricky from his clutches, shielding his sensitive eyes from the sudden brightness. At last Ricky could see his assailant. He smashed his fist into Shadow's stomach and shuddered as his hand sliced through what felt like a frozen mist.

Shadow howled in pain. In a blind fury he tackled the boy to the floor. "My queen should be freezing your sister about now," he rasped in Ricky's ear, pinning the boy to the ground.

"NO!" Ricky's choked cry rang through the enclosed space. The image of his sister frozen forever fueled his strength and he sank his teeth into the shadow's arm. Ricky gagged on the foul taste, spitting the poisonous mist from his mouth.

A tortured sound filled the room as Shadow screamed in agony. He grabbed the boy's neck, squeezing as tight as he could.

Ricky's world began to spin. Black dots blotted his vision. Shadow's image blurred into *two* shadows. But then, the second shadow put his finger to his lips, imploring him to be quiet. It was Doppelganger!

The king's shadow pulled the evil wraith off Ricky and threw him against a wall. Ricky sucked in huge gulps of air as the shadows fought behind him. The large closet soon looked like a war zone—boxes, scepters, vases, and lamps were knocked from their shelves, littering the floor with broken glass.

Ricky pulled himself up, his eyes darting across the contents of the overturned boxes. *If only there was some weapon here that I could use!*

Shadow smashed his fist into Doppelganger's jaw and the king's shadow tumbled backwards, colliding into a solid brass coat rack. Shaking off the blow, Doppelganger hurled himself at the monster and the pair crashed to the floor. Shadow smashed Doppelganger's head with a candlestick, and then the brave shadow lay unmoving on the floor.

With smoke oozing from his cuts, Queen Glacidia's servant raised a jagged knife in the air, poised to strike Doppelganger's heart. From the corner of his eye, Ricky spotted the box of ancient runes. *If only I knew how to use them,* he thought desperately. Staring longingly at the box of heavy stone tablets, he suddenly realized that he *DID* know how to use them! He reached up and grabbed the box, nearly falling backwards with the unexpected weight. Using every ounce of strength he possessed, he raised the box high in the air and smashed it over Shadow's head. The monster collapsed in a heap on top of Doppelganger, his knife clattering to the floor.

Ricky pushed the unconscious shadow off Doppelganger and watched with satisfaction as he slid to the cold, marble floor. Breathing heavily, Ricky smiled with relief when he saw the king's shadow open his eyes. He held his hand out, helping the heroic shadow to his feet, surprised at the warmth that tingled against his skin. The opposite of Shadow's icy touch, it felt like the warm mist of a hot shower.

"You saved my life," Ricky said, staring up into his rescuer's hazy features.

Doppelganger nodded down at the boy, then sat on an overturned box, still woozy from his fight.

Suddenly remembering, Ricky cried, "My sister!" The shadow cocked his head in confusion as Ricky explained in a rush, "Queen Glacidia … she's got Allie trapped! I've been trying to get help, but everyone's outside! *How do I get out of this castle?!?*"

Doppelganger quickly led Ricky through the bedchamber and out into the hallway. He pointed straight, and then signaled for Ricky to turn right. Ricky yelled his thanks as he bolted into the hallway, streaking toward the castle entrance.

Staring at the demon collapsed on the floor, Doppelganger wondered what to do with him. Being made of mist himself, he knew that no ordinary bonds could hold him. Scanning the shelves, an idea suddenly came to him. He began sifting through the clutter, searching for the one container he knew Shadow could not escape from. The candelabra hopped ahead to light the darkest corners of the closet.

At last he found what he had been looking for. He pulled a large box out from under a stack of old alchemy books. In a child's scrawl, the words, *"Private—Hands Off!"* were written across the lid. Doppelganger smiled. Long ago, the king had charmed it so that it couldn't be opened without first entering a secret code. Doppelganger fervently hoped that he remembered it correctly after all these years. He took a deep breath and then lightly tapped the tune of the Galdoren National Anthem across the top of the box. He sighed with relief when there was a loud click and the lid popped open. He quickly emptied the box, dumping the king's long-forgotten childhood treasures onto the floor. Then he lifted Shadow and dropped him none too gently inside. He closed the lid and tapped the tune again, charming the box shut. He tugged on it several times, just to be certain it was secure.

His work done, he slid to the floor, mopping the dripping moisture from his forehead. He glanced at the broken slabs near his feet and half-wished that Shadow would try to escape so *he* could get a turn at using those ancient runes.

Chapter Thirty-Six

THE WITCH OF WINDERMERE

Allie stood bravely facing Queen Glacidia, her ringed finger trembling as she held it before her.

"Now you will see what *real* power feels like," Glacidia snarled between gritted teeth. The snake-like tendrils of ice growing from the witch's head were standing on end, reaching out for Allie as they hissed. The evil witch pointed at the terrified girl and a stream of ice shot out of her finger. Allie fell back against Queen Jacqueline, squeezing her eyes shut. But just as the spell was about to strike, a ball of white leaped up between the enchantment and Allie, absorbing the full force of the attack.

Allie's eyes flew open at the sound of the mangled screech. She watched in horror as Snoball tumbled to the ground. "Snoball!" she cried, unable to believe that the cat had sacrificed her life for Allie's. Seeing the motionless cat lying rigid on the floor made something inside her snap. She glared at the witch, her eyes flashing furiously. She stepped forward, pointing her ringed finger at the witch, chanting the now familiar spell, *"B'yardin Shatavna Myesto Troo!"*

A shocked Glacidia's jaw fell open as a fog began to form. The fog quickly took the shape of a knight in full armor. His hazy sword drawn, he charged toward the wicked queen. She flew out of the way so that his sword merely nicked her arm, tearing the velvety material of her sleeve and ripping the skin beneath. But instead of blood, her cut oozed only smoke.

She screamed in pain, holding a hand over her smoking wound. Her eyes narrowed to slits as she shrieked, "YOU'LL PAY FOR THAT, YOU LITTLE BRAT!!!"

Panting heavily, the witch pointed a finger at the foggy knight. As he moved to strike her again, she blasted him with a spell and he evaporated into nothingness. "I don't know how you were able to use that spell," she hissed, "but you won't get a chance to use it again! No putrid Earth scum is going to get the best of *me*!"

She twirled her hand and Allie was suddenly lifted into the air. The wicked queen threw her head back and laughed. "Did you really think you stood a chance against ME?" She twisted her hand and Allie flipped in the air. The witch's eyes blazed with venom as she moved to stand nose to nose with the girl. "I was going to kill you quickly," she whispered. "But now," she stood back and shrieked, "Now I will make you *suffer!*"

Ricky sped toward the castle's main entrance, the sounds of the battle echoing throughout the empty castle. When he finally reached the massive arched entryway, he raced under the open portcullis and straight toward a small unit of castle guards.

"My sister needs help!" he yelled breathlessly, bending over his knees to suck in air. "She's alone in the king's chamber with Queen Glacidia!"

"This is no time for games, lad!" a guard snapped as he ran his sword through an attacking goblin. "Go back inside! It's not safe out here!"

"IT'S NOT A GAME!" Ricky shouted. Picking up the dead goblin's club, he added, "She needs help!"

Just then, two more goblins screamed a war chant as they leaped over the hedges. Ricky took a step back when he saw the mad gleam in their eyes. Their faces were streaked with war paint, their red bodies glistening with sweat. One of them was whipping a lethal-looking flail over his head while the other charged forward wielding an iron mace.

"RUN!" the guard called to Ricky as his sword clanged against the spiked head of the flail's thick chain.

Ricky was desperate; he didn't know where to turn for help. Then he saw a familiar red chair in the distance, glowing in the moonlight. *Roberts*! Ricky darted in the direction of the king's personal assistant.

He saw Roberts sheath his sword, a dead goblin on the ground near his feet. "My sister! Please—she needs help *now!*" Ricky yelled as he drew near.

Roberts' head snapped up. "What's happened?"

Out of breath, Ricky skidded to a stop when he finally reached him. "Queen Glacidia flew in through the turret window! Allie's alone in there with that witch!"

"Hop on," Roberts ordered. Ricky jumped onto the chair and they took off. The wind screamed in Ricky's ears as they streaked upward toward the lone room at the top of the castle's tallest turret. As they climbed higher and higher, the chair moved slower and slower, until it finally lurched to a stop a good fifty feet from the turret window.

"It's no use! I can't get my chair any higher than this," Roberts yelled over the howling wind. "We'll have to go back to the front ... there's no other way in!"

"NO! That'll take too much time!" Ricky cried, feeling like he was stuck in a never-ending nightmare.

But then Roberts spied the king on the lawn below. He quickly lowered his chair to the ground. "King Shevre knows of a secret entrance," he told Ricky as they landed.

A goblin growled at the king as the two enemies stood facing each other, unmoving, like deadly snakes coiled to strike. The goblin's muddied fingers squeezed the leather shaft of his axe and then he suddenly lunged, taking a vicious swing at the king's head. In a flash, King Shevre raised his heavy broadsword, blocking the attack. The loud clanging noise echoed across the lawn.

The king grunted as he swung his sword with all his might, knocking the goblin's weapon from his hands. An unholy sound tore out of the demon's throat as he bared his fangs and made a suicidal leap at the king. An instant later, a sickening gurgle bubbled out of the creature's mouth as he fell dead in the grass, the king's sword sticking out of his chest.

Ricky felt nauseous. But seeing the light at the top of the turret, he ignored the grisly scene, yelling, "GLACIDIA! She's in your chamber—alone with my sister!"

A murderous look crossed the king's face as he yanked his sword free of the goblin's lifeless body. "Follow me!" he thundered. As they raced toward the turret, Ricky's eyes were fixed upon the window looming high above them and he prayed for his sister's safety. *Hang on, Allie. We're coming!*

The king placed his hand on the turret wall, sliding his fingers across a single orange stone hidden amongst the grey ones.

"This stone is enchanted to recognize only my hand," he explained as the stone began to glow. A crack suddenly appeared in the side of the tower, revealing a secret entryway. He kicked the door open and stormed inside. They stood at the base of the spiral staircase.

The long stairwell twisted before them, its stone steps charred black from the recent flames. Wisps of smoke still clung to the air, floating up the impossibly tall tower.

The king thrust his sword in front of him, a determined gleam in his eye. "Your sister will *not* meet my mother's fate," he vowed as he charged forward, taking the steps two at a time.

Roberts and Ricky followed on his heels as they sped upward in a desperate bid to defend a fifteen-year-old girl against one of the most powerful witches in history.

Allie struggled to move, but she was caught within the evil queen's spell, bound by invisible strings of magic to float face-down in the air.

Possessed by a dark madness, the witch raised her outstretched arms to the ceiling, chanting in a strange language. She rose in the air, circling Allie while she continued to chant. Her hair crawled from her head, pulling out of her scalp as it hissed at the terrified girl. The serpent-like strands lashed out with lightning speed, biting Allie's flesh as she hung in the air. As if caught in a nightmare, she heard herself scream, the sound so anguished she barely recognized it as her own.

Streaks of ice shot out of the witch's fingertips, so bitterly cold that they burned Allie's skin. The deranged enchantress became lost in a murderous rage, shooting spell after spell at the screaming girl. Her nails glowed white-hot as Allie writhed and twisted in the air, the pain becoming more unbearable with each passing moment.

Suddenly, with a flip of the witch's hand, Allie was dropped back to the ground. She fell against the frozen body of Queen Jacqueline, doubled over, tears streaming down her face.

Glacidia's boots clicked against the marble floor as she stalked toward the cowering girl. Kneeling so that her mouth was right up against Allie's ear, she whispered, "I've only just begun."

Allie whimpered and tried to make herself as small as possible, curling up in a ball against the marble pedestal.

Admiring her fingernails, the sorceress purred, "I wonder how Shadow is going to kill your brother? Slow and painful, or *quick*, with a simple twist of a knife?" Allie's eyes flashed with anger. Ignoring her pain, she rose to her feet and glowered at the witch. Glacidia smiled cruelly and taunted, "I think I'll keep you alive for a little longer, so you can hear *all* the gory details."

"Call Shadow back *now*," Allie demanded through clenched teeth. "Because, I swear, if my brother has been hurt in *any* way, I'll … I'll …"

The witch threw her head back and laughed. "You'll do *what?*"

Allie closed her eyes and imagined she was holding a sword. "*B'yardin Shatavna Myesto Troo!*" Suddenly, the foggy outline of a long sword took form in her hand. Although it looked like mist, it felt heavy and substantial beneath her fingertips.

Queen Glacidia's demented cackle filled the room. "You can barely *stand*, little brat, do you really think your pathetic sword can hurt *me?!*"

Allie lunged, but she was so weak that the blade merely sliced the fur off the witch's cloak. Glacidia's eye narrowed to a slit as the torn material floated back up to her waiting hands. She pointed a shaking finger at Allie's sword and it vanished in a puff of smoke.

"That was my favorite cloak," she snarled, throwing the fur at Allie. "I am going to make you *very* sorry you did that!"

Red light streaked from her fingertips, striking the girl's bare arms. Huge red welts swelled up and down Allie's tender skin. Then the sharp cords of a hundred icy ropes wrapped around her body. She clawed at them, desperately trying to break free, but her hands were suddenly jerked behind her back and tightly bound. *The ring*, a soft voice whispered in her mind. *You wield the power of the ring!* It was the same voice she had heard earlier.

With a flick of Glacidia's wrist, Allie was once again raised high into the air. Floating face-down, her long hair swung in the breeze. The witch grabbed a handful and yanked. "Such a pretty girl," she sneered. "What a shame to meet such a tragic end." Then her lips tilted into a cruel smile. She opened her hand slowly, watching Allie's silken strands slip from her fingers.

As Allie's tears fell from above, the witch's lips began to move. "*Liflyess mal morto*," she whispered, and a long trail of green smoke curled out of the corners of her mouth.

Allie knew with utter certainty that this spell was meant to kill her. *Use the ring,* the voice urged. *Close your eyes and concentrate.* She squeezed her eyes shut, tapping into the ancient fairie magic on her finger.

That's it! Now imagine you're safe while you chant your spell. Allie's trembling lips began to move as she murmured, "*B'yardin Shatavna Myesto Troo.*"

Say it again! And remember to imagine that you're safe! Allie pictured herself inside a protective bubble, healthy and strong, as she softly chanted, "*B'yardin Shatavna Myesto Troo.*" The searing pain began to lessen and she repeated more firmly, "*B'yardin Shatavna Myesto Troo!*"

The witch's whispers rose in the air, carried on a trail of green smoke. "*Liflyess mal morto,*" the smoke whispered over and over as it twisted around Allie's torso.

Allie's throat began to constrict, and strange wheezing sounds came out of her mouth as she struggled to breathe. With her last wisp of breath she rasped, "*B'yardin Shatavna Myesto Troo.*" She rocked in the air with a sudden jolt of power that shook the room. Then an unseen force began to pull at her bonds. With a loud snap, they were broken, and she fell through the air. The deathly green smoke hissed into nothingness as she landed with a thump against the statue of Queen Jacqueline.

The maniacal queen shrieked. "It can't be! IT CAN'T BE!" She pointed a glowing finger in Allie's direction and shouted, "*Acwellan fira!*" A glittering orb of white flames streaked forward as Allie continued to chant. But just as the fireball was about to strike, a faint blue bubble began to glow around the girl. The spell bounced off the bubble, falling harmlessly to the ground.

"NOOOOOOOOOOOOO!" the witch screamed in a blind fury.

You're doing wonderfully, the soft voice spoke louder in Allie's mind. *Keep chanting!*

"*B'yardin Shatavna Myesto Troo!*" As Allie continued to chant, the blue light continued to glow more brightly, strengthening the protective bubble around her. The painful red welts dotting her skin turned pink, and then faded away. Little by little, she regained her health until all of her injuries were healed.

Glacidia was seized by a fit of uncontrollable rage. She blasted the blue light with spell after spell, but nothing could penetrate Allie's protective shell. The light began to expand, covering not only Allie, but Queen Jacqueline as well.

The rabid witch flew to the ceiling, sparks dripping from her fingertips. Her empty eye socket bulged out of her head, the white skin bubbling dangerously. Her good eye glittered with flashes of red. Steam sizzled and popped out of her twitching body as her frozen hair twirled madly in the air. She was in such a fit that she failed to notice what had begun to happen inside the glowing bubble.

Even Allie didn't notice, so intensely was she concentrating on her spell. But Queen Jacqueline's hands had begun to turn from clear ice to the natural color of her flesh. Her frosted gown began to melt into a soft pink. And as her face began to thaw, the tear that had been frozen for so long upon her cheek, finally fell to the ground.

Allie, the voice was strong and clear. "I'll take my ring back now."

Allie turned and looked up, startled to see Queen Jacqueline stepping down from her pedestal. As if in a dream, Allie slowly pulled the ring from her finger and handed it to the lovely woman. When the rightful queen slipped it on, the blue bubble flickered and vanished.

In her shock, Glacidia fell to the ground. Shaking with anger she cried, "You can't be alive … *you can't!*"

"Oh, but I am!" Queen Jacqueline insisted, inching toward the evil witch. "And now, I am going to finish something I started years ago." The Serpent's Eye glittered brilliantly as she raised her hand, calling out, "*B'yardin Shatavna Myesto Troo!*"

The witch's feet suddenly turned the color of granite and within moments they had changed to solid rock. The sorceress covered her face with her hands as she screamed. Rock quickly climbed up her legs, then her spine, and her arms, until everything but her head had turned to stone. "THIS IS ALL YOUR FAULT!" she shrieked at Allie. "I'LL GET YOU FOR THIS!"

"Oh no you won't!" Queen Jacqueline said with certainty, pointing her ringed finger once more. A stream of silver light flowed from her fingertips, wrapping around the madwoman's head. Glacidia's hair hissed violently, then went eerily silent as it transformed into rock. The deranged sorceress closed her eye and began to chant, "*Cwalu … deab … forofor …*" but the half-finished spell died on her lips when her tongue changed to stone in mid-sentence. With a thunderous roar, the last of the evil witch was transformed into a stone statue.

"A fitting end, don't you think?" Queen Jacqueline said, lifting her chin in the air. Her gown rustled as she turned to Allie. She held out her hand, and when their eyes met, they fell into a tight embrace. The queen's voice cracked as she whispered, "Thank you."

Allie was confused. "For what?"

"Why, for releasing me from Glacidia's spell, of course!"

Just then, the door was kicked wide open. King Shevre's eyes blazed murderously, his teeth bared as he slashed his sword. Ricky raced out from behind the king, swinging a goblin's club high above his head. Roberts followed just behind, charging into the room with his weapon drawn. They all stopped in their tracks, their eyes moving from the statue of Glacidia to Queen Jacqueline.

King Shevre blinked, unable to believe what he was seeing. "Mother?"

She held her arms open, tears glittering in her eyes. "Shevre," she whispered.

His sword clattered to the floor as he raced into his mother's arms. Towering above her, he cradled her gently against his broad chest.

"My little boy," she wept, as they rocked in each other's arms.

Ricky dropped his club and rushed to Allie's side. "Are you okay?" Allie nodded her head, shaking with relief that her little brother was unharmed. The siblings hugged tightly, both too choked up to say anything more.

A soft mewing sound floated up from the floor.

"Snoball?" Allie sniffled, pulling away from her brother. The little snowcat purred, rubbing her cheek against Allie's ankle. Allie picked her up, nuzzling her snow-white fur. "You're alive!" she laughed. "But I thought you were …"

"Glacidia's spell had no effect on her," Queen Jacqueline explained from the warmth of her son's arms. "Since she was already frozen to begin with, the spell merely knocked her out."

"Snoball was hit with a spell?!?" Ricky gasped, examining his cat as she purred in Allie's arms.

"She saved my life!" Allie grinned. "She's a hero!"

A loud voice suddenly shouted, "I'll save you, Allie!" Twink streaked in through the open window, waving his little sword wildly in the air.

Shimmer flew in just behind him, wearing a warrior's look on his shiny blue face.

The two stars skidded to a halt. Twink's eyes nearly popped out of his head when he saw the stone Glacidia. Shimmer's mouth fell open when he looked from the empty pedestal to Queen Jacqueline. He stared in disbelief at the healthy tinge in her rosy cheeks.

"Shimmer!" the queen called happily. "It's so good to see you again!"

He hung limply in the air, his mouth gaping open. Blinking rapidly he stammered, "Er... a-a-a guard said that Queen Glacidia was up here. H-he thought it was a joke, but we—"

"We knew it wasn't!" Twink interrupted. Pointing to the fossilized Queen Glacidia he asked, "Is that a new statue? 'Cause I don't like it."

Everyone laughed as King Shevre explained, "That's the *former* Queen of Windermere. She is no longer a threat." With this last sentence, he smiled proudly down at his mother.

The queen moved from her son's embrace to stand before Shimmer and his nephew. "And this brave young star I believe is called *Twink*?" Twink blushed, bashfully kicking a foot-point in the air. Jacqueline turned to Ricky, smiling radiantly at him. "And *you!* I can scarcely believe that you faced Shadow and lived to tell the tale. You must be a very special boy indeed!"

"You battled *Shadow*?" Shimmer asked incredulously.

Ricky nodded, blushing awkwardly. "It was no big deal." Suddenly remembering, he turned to the king, "Oh, yeah. Doppelganger's guarding Shadow in your junk closet."

The king laughed as he reached for Ricky's hand. "Do you know how many knights have failed to capture that monster? How did you finally manage it?"

"With Doppelganger. And your ancient runes!" Ricky answered, proudly shaking King Shevre's hand.

The king looked surprised. "You know how to use them?"

Ricky smirked. "Sorta."

Just then, the sound of a hundred horns trumpeted through the air. Everyone raced to the window, squishing together to try and see. A thousand knights were silhouetted against the dark sky as they soared upon their armored steeds. The troops flew across the hazy glow of the full moon, galloping on the wind.

"The army," King Shevre breathed. "They've returned." A grin spread across his face as he watched them glide to the ground, charging forward against the already retreating horde of goblins.

"Only The Three could have conjured magic strong enough to carry the entire army on the wind," Queen Jacqueline shrewdly observed.

"It's only a matter of time now, Your Highness," Roberts said with a smile. "No enemy can stand against the might of the Galdoren Army."

"I agree," said the king. "Nevertheless, I shall soon rejoin what is left of the battle. My place is with my troops. But before I go— Roberts?" The king's assistant looked up. "Find a spare battalion and send them to help guard Shadow." He lowered his voice to a dangerous tone, "I will see to that monster personally when this battle is over." Roberts bowed respectfully, then steered his chair out of the room.

The king turned his eyes back to his mother. When he spied the glittering eyeball adorning her finger, he gasped in astonishment, stumbling over his words. "How … where … how did you—"

"It's a long story, Shevre," she smiled, noting the direction of his eyes. "I promise to tell you everything—later. But for now, I believe you have more pressing matters to attend to?"

He nodded as if in a daze, still staring at the sparkling gem.

The queen took Allie's hands in her own. "How can I ever thank you? You are the reason I am finally free from Queen Glacidia's spell. Your magic must be very strong."

"But … I don't understand." Allie said, confused. "How am I able to use fairie magic?"

Queen Jacqueline sighed. "I don't know, Allie. But you were the only one who could ever hear me. The only one who could break the spell. Perhaps we'll never know. And how was your brother able to use that wand?" She pointed to the wand Ricky had exploded. "Only magical beings can cast enchantments."

Ricky shuffled his feet in embarrassment as everyone stared at the charred wand on the floor. King Shevre narrowed his eyes as he surveyed the room. "Wait a minute … Where's my candelabra? And my decanter?" Spying the nail holes on the bare walls he demanded, "And where are my paintings?"

"And your glasses!" Twink added helpfully. Ricky shot him a dirty look.

Queen Jacqueline laughed. "You'll get them all back, Shevre. And I guarantee they'll be sparkling clean!"

"Mother," he replied, putting his arm around her. "How do you know all this?"

She placed a soft hand upon his cheek. "While I was frozen, I was still aware of everything that happened in this room." Tears welled in her eyes as she softly murmured, "I am so sorry for giving you such unhappiness … for being the cause of so much sorrow."

He smiled sweetly as he brushed a tear from her cheek. "The only thing you have ever given me was joy. The unhappiness was caused by *her*," he said, nodding in the direction of the fossilized witch, "not you."

Three women and a young man suddenly swooped in through the open window. They gasped in surprise, surveying the scene before them.

When Sharonna saw her little sister standing there in the flesh, she nearly fainted. She fell back against Henry, holding her heart. She had long ago given up hope that her beloved sister would ever be returned to life. "Jacqueline?" she whispered.

The queen smiled radiantly as she rushed forward. "Sharonna!" Hugging her tightly, she murmured, "Thank you for taking such good care of my son."

King Shevre locked eyes with Serena. His look was so penetrating that she had to turn away.

"And whom do we have to thank for *this*?" Hildy grinned, motioning toward the stone Glacidia.

"I'm afraid that's my handiwork," Queen Jacqueline said with a hint of pride. "But I couldn't have done it without this amazing young lady." She smiled warmly at Allie.

Henry found he couldn't take his eyes off the Earth girl. No matter who was talking, he kept stealing glances in her direction. When their eyes met, he nervously looked away, his heart hammering in his chest.

"I'll leave you all to sort this out," King Shevre said. "I must return to the battle." He turned to address the Guardians of Galdoren, "Ladies, I am once again impressed by the depth of your powers. Thank you for getting my army here so quickly."

"Well, when we got to Edna's and found that the children had left …," Hildy started.

"I thought my heart was going to stop right then and there," Sharonna added. Turning to her sister, she dabbed her eyes, still unable to believe that she was no longer a frozen statue. She quietly slid her hand into Jacqueline's, relishing the warmth of their intertwined fingers.

"Edna told us that she had sent the children to the castle," Hildy continued. "On our way here we saw the army traveling at top speed. We stopped to talk to General Nobling and he informed us that he had received an urgent message ordering the troops back to the castle and that an attack was imminent! We feared they would never arrive in time ..."

"So, we decided to give them a little help!" Serena finished, giving the king a dazzling smile.

King Shevre's heart skipped a beat. Serena had always had that effect on him. When he was a teenager, her smiles had given him butterflies in his stomach, and now that he was a full-grown man, well, they were just bigger butterflies. He cleared his throat, motioning to the statue of Glacidia. "Ladies, if I may impose upon you yet again?"

"Of course, dear," Sharonna said, pulling the wand from her cloak. "Where do you want her?"

"The dungeon—for now." Craning his neck to see out the window, he was frustrated when all he could see was the distant flickering of torchlight. "Ladies, gentlemen, please excuse me. I will return as quickly as I am able." He leaned over and gently kissed his mother's cheek.

"Be careful," both Queen Jacqueline and Serena said at the same time.

A smile played across the king's mouth as he turned to leave. He had only gone a few steps when the exuberant sounds of cheerful conversation drifted out of his chamber, filling the empty hallway. He stopped and paused to listen to the unfamiliar sound of his mother's and Serena's laughter. And for the first time in years, he found himself whistling a merry tune as he bounded down the spiral staircase.

Chapter Thirty-Seven

A STORMY ROMANCE

Within the short time it had taken King Shevre to return to the battleground, the Galdoren forces had already captured what was left of Queen Glacidia's army. Most of the goblin mercenaries had retreated back into the forest upon seeing the king's legendary knights swoop down from the sky. After General Nobling repeatedly assured him that his presence was no longer required, King Shevre sprinted through the castle gardens, eager to be reunited with his loved ones.

When he reached the base of the turret, he grinned as he looked up at the window and saw the lights still blazing brightly. Reaching for the magic stone that opened the secret entrance, the sound of a snapping twig made him turn around. A goblin leaped out of the tall hedges wielding a bloodied battle axe. The king's hand flew to his sword. But just as the goblin was about to strike, a dark cloud appeared in the air above his head. Suddenly, a jagged bolt of lightning scorched the ground beside the goblin's feet. He yelped, jumping two feet in the air. An instant later, a loud clap of thunder shook the earth. Water gushed from the swollen cloud, plastering the goblin's knotted hair to his head. He raised his axe in a feeble attempt to shield himself from the huge rocks of hail that had begun to pelt him.

Meanwhile, King Shevre remained perfectly dry. In fact, other than the storm raging above the goblin's head, there wasn't a cloud in the starry sky.

The goblin turned and ran for the safety of the forest, his large feet splashing in ankle deep puddles. The thundercloud continued to attack him all the way back to the woods.

King Shevre roared with laughter. Sheathing his sword, he called out to the darkness, "Serena? You can come out now!" When there was no response, he crossed his arms over his chest and smirked, "I know you're there, oh goddess-of-all-things-wet." He tapped his foot impatiently, again calling out, "You don't honestly expect me to believe that was an act of nature, do you?"

Serena shyly poked her head out from behind the turret. "Well, I couldn't very well let a goblin assassinate the King of Galdoren, now could I?" She stuck her chin out defiantly, saying, "Don't take it personally, I would have done the same for any—"

The king cut her off by pulling her into his arms.

"Oh, my!" Serena gasped.

"What were you saying?" he asked, holding her closely.

"I-I, can't quite remem—"

"Something about saving my life not being personal? That you would have done the same for any old king?"

"Well ... I ... "

He abruptly released her from his tight embrace and bent down on one knee. Staring deep into her hazel eyes, he took one of her hands in his own. "Serena Cynthia Fey—will you marry me?"

She sighed as she smoothed the hair back from his brow. "I thought you'd never ask."

A castle guard rounded the corner just then. Having seen the strange thundercloud from a distance, he had come to investigate. "Your Majesty—" he stopped mid-sentence when he saw the couple before him. "Er, I-I'm sorry, I didn't mean to interrupt," he stammered. With a quick bow he turned and fled as quickly as he was able. But he needn't have bothered apologizing. The King of Galdoren and his future queen were so lost in their kiss that they never even heard him.

Chapter Thirty-Eight

THE CELL
BENEATH THE CASTLE

I n the king's chamber high up in the turret, Queen Jacqueline was just finishing the bowl of chicken soup that Sharonna had conjured for her, joking that it was the best meal she'd had in years.

"Queen Jacqueline," Twink began, stifling a yawn. "Did King Shevre ever pick his nose when he was alone up here?"

Shimmer reddened as he gasped, "Twinkle!"

The queen laughed, her smile faltering when she caught sight of her reflection in the tarnished mirror. She rubbed a hand across her cheek, startled by the unfamiliar face staring back at her. After so many years, she had nearly forgotten what she looked like.

"You haven't aged since the day you fell under Glacidia's spell," Sharonna said softly. Staring at her sister's smooth skin she sighed, "Being the eldest, I always knew that I would wrinkle before you, but this is truly unfair!"

Hildy made some sarcastic comment about Sharonna's vanity, then continued the lesson she was giving Ricky on how to use a wand properly without exploding it. All the while, Allie and Henry kept stealing looks at each other as they sat in awkward silence on the couch.

Just as Sharonna began catching her sister up on all the local gossip, King Shevre burst through the door. "The battle is over," he announced. A loud cheer rose from the group.

"In that case," Hildy beamed. "Come join the party!"

"Party?" the king arched his brow. "What a wonderful idea!" Pulling Serena in behind him, he grinned. "We have much to celebrate. Galdoren is finally free from Glacidia, my beloved mother has been returned to us at last, and ..." He lifted Serena's hand to show the ring of twigs he had hastily made for her. "Serena and I are engaged to be married!"

There was a collective gasp and then Sharonna burst into tears. The queen kissed her son's cheek. "I couldn't be happier! You two were made for each other." Taking Serena's hands she beamed, "You have always been like a daughter to me—now it will be official!"

As Sharonna dabbed her eyes on the sleeve of her cloak she sniffled, "You'd better buy her a whopper of a ring, Shevre. Members of The Three simply do not wear tree scraps on their fingers."

"He can buy me a hundred rings," Serena sighed as she played with the twig circling her slender finger, "But none will ever be as special as this." Turning to the king she coyly added, "Although, I *am* partial to diamonds!"

Ricky yanked a loose diamond off his shirt and tossed it to Serena. "Happy wedding."

Serena laughed while Allie eyed Ricky's bloodstained shirt. In a burst of emotion, she pulled her little brother in close for a hug.

"What?!" Ricky asked, wriggling out of his sister's embrace.

The king grew serious as he turned to Allie and Ricky. "Galdoren owes you both a great debt. What can I offer to show my country's appreciation?"

Ricky's eyes lit up. "I've always wanted my own kingdom!"

The king's lips twitched. "Perhaps something a bit *smaller*?"

"A city?"

Allie glared at her little brother. "What is wrong with you?" she hissed. Turning to the king she insisted, "We don't need anything, Your Majesty. Our reward is seeing Galdoren safe and sound, and your mother alive and well."

Ricky's mouth hung open. "That might be *your* reward, but I want a city!"

The king's eyes twinkled as he replied, "I'll work on that, Sir Ricky. But in the meanwhile, can you think of nothing else you desire?"

Ricky's lips lifted into a slow smile. He reached over and grabbed the *Galdoren Gazette* from off the end table. Everyone looked on with curiosity as he thumbed through its pages. Finally finding what he was looking for, he held the paper up for the king to see.

"*That's* what I'd like!" Ricky grinned, pointing to an ad.

"An excellent suggestion!" King Shevre laughed. "I've been wanting to see the Four Fairies Floating Follies myself." Looking more closely at the ad, his eyes widened in surprise. "It's in Fly-O-Vision now?" He whistled in appreciation. "Then we really must see it." Wrapping an arm around his fiancé he announced, "The celebration will be held tomorrow evening."

"Don't forget the fireworks for the children's Royal Sendoff, dear," Sharonna reminded him.

Allie and Ricky turned to each other, their smiles fading. That meant that the next day was to be their last in Galdoren.

"Lady Allie, are you certain there is *nothing* you desire?"

Allie looked down at her once-beautiful gown, now tattered and torn. "Well, a new dress might be nice."

The king smiled. "Consider it done."

A little snoring noise interrupted the conversation. All eyes turned to the fireplace where Twink had fallen asleep on the mantle.

Shimmer gently shook him awake. "Come on. Time for bed."

"But I'm not tired," the little star protested through half-closed eyes.

Ricky was also finding it increasingly hard to keep his own eyelids open.

Seeing the boys' weary faces, King Shevre faked a serious tone. "Twinkle—you would do me a great service by allowing Sir Ricky to share your bedchamber tonight. With so many unexpected guests at the castle, I fear I may soon run out of rooms." In truth, there were several dozen unused bedrooms scattered throughout the castle, but he knew that the little star wouldn't be able to resist showing off his own.

Twink puffed up his chest. "I would be honored, Your Majesty," he replied, bowing deeply. But he bowed so deep that he fell off the mantle, catching himself just before he hit the floor.

Allie stifled a laugh. "Goodnight, Twink. Goodnight Ricky."

Ricky waved goodnight with a yawn as Twink babbled, "Wait'll you see you my room! I've got all the latest collections of ..."

As the boys' voices trailed off, Allie and Henry once again locked eyes, then quickly turned away. Their obvious chemistry was not lost on Sharonna. Ever the matchmaker, she slyly suggested, "Henry, dear? Why don't you teach Allie a little alchemy tomorrow? She seems to be a natural."

His eyes lit up. "Wow, that would be *amazing!*" Suddenly embarrassed by his over-eager reaction he lowered his voice to a blasé tone. "Yeah, okay … whatever."

Allie smiled shyly. "Thanks. That sounds like fun!"

King Shevre pulled on a gold cord. "It's getting very late, and it's been a long day. Roberts will escort you to your room, Lady Allie." Turning to Henry he added, "I assume you remember the way back to yours?" Henry nodded in response, then hastily said his goodnights and made his exit.

Shimmer was exhausted and achy. With a sleepy wave, he glided out of the room, on his way to a hot bubble bath before bed.

Queen Jacqueline was delighted to learn that her son had kept her room exactly as she had left it, and couldn't wait to finally finish the book on her nightstand. It was a mystery, and she'd waited twenty years to find out the ending.

Hildy and Sharonna insisted that Serena stay behind with her fiancé while they dealt with what was left of Glacidia. They disappeared in a puff of smoke, bound for the bowels of the castle.

When at last they were alone, the king's eyes danced with mischief. He crooked his finger at Serena. "Come here."

She sank back into the couch cushions and teased, "Don't you dare start thinking that just because we're getting married I'm going to jump at your every command."

He laughed, waving his hands in mock surrender. "I wouldn't make that mistake twice!"

She giggled when he settled on the couch next to her, pulling her into his arms. Serena rested her head against his strong shoulder, and they both sighed in contentment.

Several stories below the happy couple, Hildy and Sharonna held their wands before them, lighting their way through the dark and drafty dungeon. Sharonna pulled her cloak more tightly around her shoulders. "This place always gives me the willies," she shivered, her footsteps echoing on the slimy floor.

They finally stopped before a decrepit cell covered in cobwebs. Queen Glacidia lay in the shadows behind the rusty bars. Knocking the cobwebs aside, they touched their wands to the grimy iron, chanting an incantation. The bars began to glow a sickly green.

"There," Sharonna said, tucking her wand back into her cloak. "That ought to hold her."

They stood in silence, staring at the nightmarish expression frozen on Glacidia's face.

"Come on," Hildy said, linking arms with her dearest friend. "Let's get some hot cocoa and marshmallows."

"That does sound nice," Sharonna replied, turning away from the ghoulish statue.

They snapped their fingers and disappeared in a puff.

On the other side of the dungeon, the prison guards were trading stories about the evening's battle. Their laughter drifted into the dank hallway housing Queen Glacidia's cell.

As their laughter subsided, the only sounds left were the dripping of a rusted out pipe and the squeak of a nearby rat.

Only the rat witnessed the single flash of red light that blazed for a fleeting moment in Glacidia's eye.

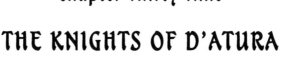

Chapter Thirty-Nine

THE KNIGHTS OF D'ATURA

The next day passed in a blur of activities. Twink and Ricky set off to find every secret room in the castle, while Allie spent the day learning basic alchemy with a besotted Henry. When at last the sun began to set, everyone returned to their rooms to prepare for the evening's gala.

Allie squealed with delight at the surprise that was waiting for her in her closet: a magnificent ball gown and matching shoes. True to his promise, the king had ordered the Royal Dressmaker to deliver a new gown to Allie that morning, rescuing her from a potential wardrobe disaster, since she once again had been left with nothing else to wear other than her nightgown. Her new evening dress was the exact shade of gold as her hair and had been spun with flecks of real gold so that it shimmered every time she moved.

Ricky was overjoyed to see his mended orange tee-shirt neatly folded on his bed. A tag attached to his freshly laundered tee-shirt read: "*Scrud's Tailors and Cleaners, specializing in the removal of hard to clean stains such as frog guts, gremlin snot, and dragon scorches.*" A hand-written note beneath said:

> *Thought you'd be more comfortable wearing this,*
> *Roberts*
> *P.S. – Are there any jewels left on that shirt you were wearing last night?*

Ricky grabbed the tattered cloth from off the floor where he had tossed it the night before and looked. There weren't.

Allie, Ricky and Twink had been asked to meet Roberts in the Imperial Hall. As honored guests, they were to be escorted into the party by a member of the Royal Staff. While they waited for Roberts, they wandered down the long corridor, inspecting the battered suits of armor that had returned after the fierce battle the night before. Some of the pedestals were empty—not all of them had made it back in one piece. But there was a single suit of armor that remained unscathed. The eerie black armor had nary a scratch on its highly polished steel.

When Roberts floated into the hallway, he noted the direction of the children's gazes, and his lips curled in disgust. "*That one* didn't fight."

"Why not?" Ricky asked.

"'Cause it belonged to the Knights of D'atura," Twink answered. "And that armor is *wicked.*" Hovering nearly nose-to-nose with Ricky he wailed in a dramatic ghost-like voice, "*Evilllll … deeeemonic!*"

Roberts and Allie laughed as Ricky swatted him out of the way. "Knock it off!" Careful to direct his question to Roberts, Ricky asked, "So, who were the Knights of D'atura?"

But just as Roberts was about to answer, an enormous grandfather clock at the end of the hallway began to chime. "I'm afraid that story will have to wait until another day," he replied. The kids all groaned in unison. "The celebration is about to begin and I have no desire to provoke the king's anger by bringing his honored guests in late." He held out his hand. "Lady Allie? Will you grant me the honor of escorting you into the party?"

Allie blushed. "Of course," she replied, taking his hand.

"Sir Ricky?" Twink snickered, extending his own hand-point. "Will you do me the honor of—"

"No way," he yelped, knocking Twink's hand away.

As Roberts led Allie into the Hall of Mirrors, she suddenly stopped. Pointing in the opposite direction she asked, "Isn't *that* the way to the Great Hall?"

"Indeed it is, Lady Allie. But this is the way to the Royal Gardens, which is where tonight's gala is being held."

Twink twirled in the air. "Yippee! Outdoor food!"

While Allie waited for her brother to catch up, she smoothed her satin skirt in one of the dozens of mirrors lining the long hallway. The reflections of a hundred Allies did the same.

Ricky was still lingering in the Imperial Hall, mesmerized by the glistening ebony armor. He couldn't resist reaching his hand out to touch something once worn by the mysterious Knights of D'atura. But the moment his fingers brushed against the cold steel, a blood-red dagger began to glow within the helmet. It instantly became so hot that Ricky whipped his hand away. He jumped back as a man's face suddenly appeared within the shiny steel. Seeing Ricky, he blinked in surprise then disappeared.

"RICKY!" Allie yelled from the other room. "Hurry up!"

Ricky stared open-mouthed at the gleaming steel for another moment, and then quickly rejoined the others.

Across the sea and above the sky, the phantom from the armor scowled. Enraged that his face should appear to a boy not of the Order, he stormed off to speak to the sorcerer responsible.

The phantom and his famous ancestor shared one trait: they did not tolerate mistakes.

Chapter Forty

A PARTY UNDER THE STARS

The Honor Guard sounded their trumpets as the children entered the enormous garden. The crowd rose to their feet in thunderous applause.

Allie felt like she had stepped into the pages of a fairytale. Knights in shining armor stood guard beneath stone pillars, while fairie lights twinkled in the white roses climbing above.

Allie lifted her skirt so that it wouldn't drag across the fairy-dusted lawn. Staring out at the ethereal garden, she wished she had a camera, and yet she knew that the picture of this magical place would forever be painted in her memory.

Roberts led them toward a table perched high above all the others, overlooking the entire garden. Tiny fragments of shooting stars streaked inside crystal jars scattered across the long table. Dozens of Galdoren flags floated in the air above, fluttering in the breeze.

Allie gasped. "We're sitting at the *Royal Table*?"

Roberts nodded with a warm smile as a knight raised a gloved hand to his helmet.

King Shevre motioned for the crowd to sit while the children climbed the steps leading up to the majestic table. The king was standing at its center, with his mother seated to his right, and Serena to his left. Sitting next to Queen Jacqueline were Sharonna and Hildy, leaning forward to smile brightly at the children. On the other side of

Serena, Shimmer beamed proudly, gesturing to the three empty seats beside him.

As Allie slid into her seat, she searched for Henry amidst the crowd, but the Clauricans were standing on their chairs, blocking her view.

Roberts kissed the back of Allie's hand, then heartily shook Ricky's and Twink's, before he directed his chair back to the lawn. He flew over to an empty spot at a nearby table, sitting alongside Tibbly, Doppelganger, and a beaming Gossamer. Other than her heavily bandaged wings, she looked the picture of health as she stood clapping and smiling radiantly up at the children.

The king silenced his guests by tapping a silver spoon against his goblet. The rowdy Clauricans finally settled down along with the rest of the crowd. Setting his goblet back on the table, King Shevre addressed the audience, his voice magically amplified to carry across the garden. "Friends, honored guests … mother." The crowd burst into applause. Queen Jacqueline blushed modestly as her son continued, "We are here tonight to celebrate many wondrous things, not the least of which is the return of our beloved Queen!" He turned to his mother as the crowd roared, and held his hand out. She took it as she stood, letting go to wave at her loyal subjects, smiling radiantly. Even after she sat back down, the applause continued.

"We are also gathered tonight to celebrate the capture of one of the most despicable monsters in Galdoren's history … Shadow." Raucous cheers and whistles rose up from the noisy throng as the king leaned across the table, his voice dropping dramatically, "And at long last, we are able to celebrate the end of a foul and sinister witch who has plagued our country for decades…" Raising his fist in victory, he roared, "THE ICE QUEEN HAS BEEN VANQUISHED!" The crowd went wild. Everyone leapt to their feet, cheering, hooting and howling. The knights banged their lances against the ground as the Clauricans danced upon the tables.

King Shevre raised his goblet along with his voice, "So now let us all drink a toast to everyone who fought in last night's battle … everyone who helped bring an end to that despicable witch!" Allie, Ricky and Twink clinked their goblets along with the rest of the crowd, and then sipped the sparkling beverage inside.

"Mmmm," Allie licked her lips. "It tastes like fizzy tropical punch!"

"Mine tastes like carbonated lemonade," Ricky grinned, gulping the rest down.

Twink scowled at the fizzing liquid in his cup. "Bubbles make me hiccup."

King Shevre turned to the children, smiling broadly. "And now, let us drink a toast to two children who came from another world, only to save ours. To Lady Allie and Sir Ricky!"

Everyone raised their goblets as a chorus of voices echoed, "To Lady Allie and Sir Ricky!"

Twink nudged Ricky, wearing a lopsided smile. "To Sir Icky!" he hiccupped. Ricky laughed, elbowing his friend in the ribs.

While the crowd continued to clap, the king got up and slipped Ricky a small package, whispering in his ear, "I'm sorry that I was unable to get you that city, but I heard you might be interested in these."

Ricky opened the box and laughed out loud at what he found inside—the king's old fifth grade Sleep Phones!

Just then, a familiar-looking carpet zoomed across the garden. It soared above the audience, landing with a thump next to Roberts' chair. It unrolled one of its tassels and proudly presented him with an old, tarnished wand. The people around him looked confused, as Roberts and the kids burst out laughing.

King Shevre raised his arms high in the air. His cloak swirled in the wind as he nodded to the chief steward and announced, "Let the celebration begin!" A line of waiters wearing crisp white uniforms entered the garden carrying trays laden with delicious smelling appetizers, while the court musicians began to play.

Gossamer rose from her chair and moved toward the stairs. Even the thick bandages wrapped around her wings couldn't stop them from fluttering excitedly as she approached the children. She hugged Allie, tearfully sniffling, "I'm so sorry dear, can you ever forgive me?"

Hugging her back, Allie answered, "Of course!"

She handed Allie a beautifully wrapped package, then turned to blow her nose.

Allie gazed down at the wrapping paper, amused by the tiny illustrated choir singing, *"For She's a Jolly Good Fellow."* She pressed her ear against the magical gift wrap to hear the song better just as a fat tenor suddenly belted out the last line in a deafening operatic voice, "Which nobody can de-NYYYYYYYYYYYYYYYYYY!" Her ears rang so loudly that she nearly dropped the package.

"Careful dear!" Gossamer cried. "The contents are very fragile!"
Allie opened the box and pulled out a sparkling snow globe.
Inside was a familiar-looking castle, made entirely of crystal. Across
the bottom, the words, *"Welcome to Galdoren"* were etched in gold.

"It's an exact replica of the other one I gave you," Gossamer whispered. "Only minus the Serpent's Eye!"

With one last hug, Gossamer returned to her seat. Just as Allie
was reaching for a cheese puff, someone tapped her on the shoulder.
"Lady Allie?" She turned, surprised to see a knight standing behind
her. "I was asked to deliver this to you." He handed her a sealed letter, then curtly bowed and left.

Allie's brow creased in bewilderment as she took the message and
opened it. *"Meet me in the king's chamber."* It was signed, *"A
friend."*

Thinking it must be Henry who had sent the note, Allie quickly
slipped out of her chair, and raced toward the turret.

Chapter Forty-One

AN OLD WOMAN'S REFLECTIONS

Two burly knights stood guard at the base of the stairs leading up to the king's chamber. As she approached, they silently crossed lances across the bottom step, barring her way.

"Excuse me," Allie said politely, "but I'm supposed to meet someone up there."

When they still didn't move or even utter a word in response, she dug into her pocket and pulled out the message the knight had given her. When the guards saw the Royal Seal, they raised their lances, allowing her to pass.

"Thank you," she murmured, lifting her skirt as she began climbing the never-ending series of steps. "Great atmosphere," she muttered halfway up, stopping to take off her heels. "But would it kill them to get an elevator?"

When at last she reached the landing, she leaned against a wall to catch her breath. She slipped her shoes back on, smoothed her hair, then knocked on the door. When there was no reply, she slowly turned the doorknob and stepped inside.

She looked all around, but there was no one there. Confused, she scanned the room again, thinking how different it looked from the night before. Everything that Ricky had magicked to the laundry had been returned, sparkling clean. The framed picture of Serena had been moved from the dresser drawer to a place of prominence on the mantle, and the broken fragments of Allie's snow globe had been swept up. Most reassuringly, all traces of Queen Glacidia had been removed.

Allie sank into the couch, jumping up when something squeaked beneath her. She reached between the cushions and pulled out a scorched dragon chew toy.

"I thought you might have some questions for me, dear."

Allie spun at the sound of Edna's familiar voice. Confused, she realized she was still alone. She looked all around, but could find no sign of the kindly witch anywhere.

"Over here, dear. By the grandfather clock."

As Allie walked past the antique mirror, a movement within it caught her eye. She was startled to see Edna's reflection inside the tarnished glass. But the room reflected in the mirror was not the king's chamber, it was Edna's cozy kitchen.

Allie pressed her hands against the cool glass. "Edna?"

The old woman smiled at her from inside the mirror. She was seated at her kitchen table, peeling the shells off a bowl of freshly picked chocolate candies.

"Edna, how was I able to use the Serpent's Eye? And how did I work that faerie spell?"

"Excellent questions," the old woman answered, her fingers deftly separating the chocolates from their hard shells. "Now I have one for you! Have you heard about the long-ago disappearance of Duke Albert?"

Allie nodded her head as she pulled over a nearby chair. "Roberts mentioned it when we saw his painting in the portrait gallery. But what does that have to do with *me?*"

"A great deal," Edna answered. Pushing her work aside, Edna took a deep breath and then began her story, "When I was a young girl, I came to the castle as an apprentice witch. Duke Albert was around my age, and we became fast friends. My, but he was such fun to be around!" Allie remembered how Roberts had described the familiar-looking man in the portrait. He *did* sound like fun!

Edna sighed, thinking back on days gone by. "He was always getting into trouble over one joke or another." She laughed, shaking her head as she continued to reminisce, "The summer before Albert disappeared, a girl came here on an invitation. As I recall, she wasn't much older than you. And, like you, she too was from Earth. She was enchanting. So much so that Albert fell hopelessly in love. He was heartbroken when she had to return to her own planet. Months went by, and still he pined for her. No more jokes … no more laughter …" Sighing, Edna pushed her chair from the table and stood.

Her eyes glazed over as she thought back to another time. "I'll never forget the last night I saw him. I was visiting my family, here, at our candy farm. There was a terrible storm that night—quite unusual weather for Galdoren. Albert was soaked to the skin. I wrapped a blanket around him and led him to the fireplace. And there, before the crackling fire, he poured his heart out to me. He said he couldn't go on without her. He begged me to find a spell that would send him to Earth."

She leaned across the table, her wise eyes peering intently at Allie. "So after my parents had gone to sleep that night, we snuck up to the secret room at the top of the house. We searched through every spell book, but there was nothing. It broke my heart to see Albert so upset. By morning, I had written a spell of my own. Obviously, it had never been tried before, and I was worried it might be dangerous. But he insisted that he didn't care."

Her eyes welled with tears as she recalled that fateful day. "He said he would rather die than live without her. He made me swear that if it worked, I would never tell a soul where he had gone. He was afraid that someone from the royal family would come after him and bring him back home."

She dabbed her eyes on her apron. "But my spell *did* work! I sent him through three galaxies and out of my life … and I never saw him again." Her chin wobbled as she softly added, "I kept my promise. I never told anyone Albert's secret—until now."

Allie's heart ached for the kindly witch. Wishing she could reach her arms through the mirror, she pressed her hands against the glass instead. "I'm so sorry you lost your best friend, Edna."

The old woman looked up at Allie, a sad smile on her face. "There's no need to be sorry, dear. I helped someone I cared for deeply find happiness, and isn't that what true friendship is all about? Albert was reunited with the girl he loved. They eventually married and had many blissful years together. They even had children. And their children had children …" She leaned in so close that her head nearly touched the glass. "And *those* children had children."

Edna then settled back into her chair and began shelling chocolates again.

When it became clear that she was done speaking, Allie was more confused than ever. "That was a beautiful story," she said. "But it doesn't explain how I'm able to wield fairie magic."

Edna looked surprised. "Doesn't it?"

Allie shook her head, baffled.

Edna laughed, "Haven't you guessed, dear? Albert Davidia Brian Jacobi, the Duke of Margolia, was your great-grandfather!"

Allie fell back in the chair, utterly stunned. "Great-grandpa Al?" she squeaked. Her head was swimming with questions. "That means that my great-grandma Mae was the girl who came here on an invitation? Just like Ricky?"

Edna eyes twinkled as she nodded her head. "You see dear, you *do* have fairie blood coursing through your veins! Ricky too!"

So THAT was how Ricky was able to use that wand! "But, why didn't they ever tell anyone in the family?"

Edna shrugged. "We all have our secrets, dear."

"But ..."

"Go back to the party now. You don't want to miss the Four Fairies Floating Follies. I hear it's in Fly-O-Vision!"

Allie stood and moved to the window. She stared up at the starry sky, trying to grasp everything she had just learned. "Edna," she began. But when she turned, all she saw was her own face reflected in the glass. Edna and her cozy kitchen had disappeared, and the mirror was once again just an ordinary mirror.

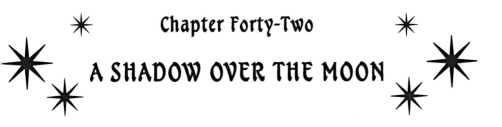

Chapter Forty-Two

A SHADOW OVER THE MOON

Four guards sat at a small table playing cards as their prisoner looked on through narrowed eyes.

"'E's awfully quiet, ain't 'e?" a guard inquired, nodding his head in Shadow's direction.

Another guard glanced up from his cards to look at the prisoner. The wall of magic containing him in his cell made Shadow appear blurry. In a cruel tone the guard teased, "Awwww, poor thing. He don't have nobody to play with, now that his boss has been turned to stone and chucked into the dungeon, eh?"

The four burly men laughed as a low growl rose in Shadow's throat.

"Oooh, we don't want to go makin' 'im angry, now do we? 'E might slash our necks with them long claws!" The men laughed harder as Shadow pulled his freshly clipped nails in to his sides.

"So, tell me again, why ain't he in the dungeon with that other piece o' garbage?"

"The king don't want them anywhere near each other," answered the third guard, studying the face-up cards on the table. He slid two cards from his hand, picking one up from the deck.

So intent were they on their game that they failed to notice how their prisoner's eyes kept darting to the window.

Tossing another coin into the pot, the guard continued, "The Three are workin' on some kind o' enchanted cell, clear on the other side o' Galdoren. Won't be ready till tomorrow, though." He lowered his voice. "I hear that the king wants a piece o' him before he's moved. Said he *wants some time alone with the prisoner.*"

The other guards grunted, nodding their heads appreciatively.

"Read 'em and weep," the biggest guard boasted, laying his winning hand down. His buddies moaned as he scooped up the pile of coins in the center of the table.

One of the guards stood to stretch, then moved to the window. Pulling the curtains aside, he called, "Eh! Do you think we'll be able to see the fireworks from here?" The other guards shrugged as they counted their money. "Oi! I think a see one!" His eyes grew wide as the burning red ball in the sky streaked straight toward him. It crashed through the window, knocking him unconscious as shattered glass exploded across the room.

The other guards' hands flew to their weapons. Three swords were suddenly pointed at the hissing red orb that had landed on the floor. On the other side of the room, the shadow rose in his cell, slowly backing up against the wall.

"What do we do?" a bewildered guard asked, pressing his sword against the mysterious object.

"Smash it!"

"No! Don't!" the burliest guard commanded, staring at the red vapor swirling inside the orb. But as he reached to pick it up, the orb began to hiss. He backed up a pace then once again reached his hand out. But just as he was about to grab it, the orb suddenly exploded in a blinding flash of light.

A putrid red smoke flooded the room. The guards instantly began to cough and wheeze, doubling over as they retched.

The lethal gas butted against the blurry wall of magic, instantly melting the spell that had kept Shadow imprisoned. He leapt from his cell just as a huge black bird swooped in through the broken window. The Furvel soared above the writhing guards, grabbing Shadow in her sharp talons.

A knight, alerted by the guards' screams, kicked the door open. He drew his sword, slashing at the prisoner clutched tightly in the Furvel's claws as she raced toward the open window. He sliced off the end of her tail and a shower of feathers sprayed the room. Her unholy shriek pierced the night as she flew past the broken glass and into the velvety sky.

The deadly fumes finally overpowered the knight and he fell to the floor, cracking his chin against the cold marble floor as the sword slipped from his lifeless hands. Then the only thing left moving in the deathly silent room was the wisp of red smoke curling up to the ceiling.

"Nice bit of sorcery back there," Shadow rasped approvingly, watching the castle grow smaller and smaller in the distance. "How did you fix it so that we weren't affected?"

A smug look crossed the bird's face as she replied, "I had a little help." She winced, the damp evening air stinging the fresh wound on her tail.

Shadow suddenly stiffened as they flew past the forest and away from Windermere. "Where are you taking me?" he demanded.

"To our new master," she answered, streaking ever higher into the starry sky.

Their bodies were silhouetted against the hazy glow of the full moon as they sailed toward a mysterious destination.

An instant later, they vanished.

Chapter Forty-Three

THE FOUR FAIRIES FLOATING FOLLIES

*A*llie walked back to the party in a daze. Edna's words kept echoing in her mind. No wonder she had felt so at home in this strange land, she thought. A part of her had always known—she *was* home!

When Henry saw her step into the garden, he pushed through the crowd in his eagerness to reach her. The court musicians had just begun to play a haunting tune when he finally arrived at her side.

"I've been looking for you," he said, pushing the shaggy hair from his eyes.

"Hmmm?" Allie blinked distractedly. "I'm sorry, did you say something?"

Henry's confidence plummeted and he shifted his feet nervously. "Would you like to, um, dance?"

She toyed with a loose thread on her dress, trying to hide her smile. "I'd love to." But just as she gathered her skirt in her hands, the sound of a dozen trumpets blew through the air. Dinner was served. A knight escorted Allie away from Henry as he dejectedly returned to his own table.

Sometime later, as the guests were finishing dessert, hundreds of cardboard eyeglasses drifted down from the sky. Twink leapt from his seat, squealing, "THE FOUR FAIRIES FLOATING FOLLIES! IT'S STARTING!"

Everyone reached up, plucking the 3-D glasses from the air. Ricky flipped his over, reading the words printed on the back, *"Fly-O-Vision."* Underneath it said, *"Please wait for instructions."*

Loud music blasted as four pint-sized fairies streaked through the air above them, sliding under each other's legs. One of the fairies waved his wand and hundreds of whipped cream pies instantly floated above everyone's heads.

A glowing sign lit up the sky. *"Glasses on,"* it read.

Ricky shoved his glasses over his nose. The moment the lenses covered his eyes, it looked like he was flying in the air alongside the fairies. One of them waggled his brows then threw a pie at his face. It splattered all over his glasses. But when he went to wipe them, they were dry! He took them off and saw that the entire crowd was wiping their own dry glasses. He smiled, finally understanding. *So THAT'S what fly-o-vision is!*

He pushed the glasses back on his nose and laughed along with the rest of the audience. Pies were flying in every direction, and even though he knew he wasn't really going to be hit with one, he still couldn't help ducking.

"Glasses off," the sign flashed.

Ricky removed his glasses just as four bicycles popped into the sky above. Smoke shot out of the tires as the fairies jumped on. They pedaled wildly up a dangerous track glittering in the sky, its treacherous ramps climbing up to the moon.

"Glasses on."

Ricky eagerly slipped his glasses back on, and suddenly *he* seemed to be soaring through the air, riding one of the bikes. The wind screamed in his ears as he climbed upward, a series of dizzying ramps looming before him. He streaked onto the track, pedaling across the dangerous curves into a death-defying leap. But just as he was about to smash into the top of the castle's highest turret, his bike swerved and he pedaled into the stars, leaving a trail of lightning bolts behind him.

A series of screams rose from the audience. Some of the older guests had already removed their glasses, many of them turning a putrid shade of green.

"Glasses off."

The audience erupted into thunderous applause, with the exception of those staggering green-faced to the bathrooms. The fairies all jumped down from their bikes and bowed. But then a huge orange dragon swooped in from behind the trees.

"Glasses on."

Ricky quickly pushed his glasses back on. The dragon instantly appeared to be nose-to-nose with him, growling and snarling, streams of smoke pouring out of her nostrils. Her rough scales glistened in the moonlight as she opened her mouth wide, baring razor-sharp teeth. Fire shot up from her throat and Ricky instinctively ducked. But then the flames she was blowing formed burning letters in the sky, spelling out the words *The End.*

Ricky leapt out of his seat along with the rest of the crowd, clapping loudly. Cheers and whistles filled the garden. Ricky took his glasses off and continued to clap as the giant dragon took a bow.

There was a loud *boom* and an explosion of light lit up the sky. The Four Fairies quickly withdrew as a dazzling array of fireworks burst overhead.

A floppy-haired figure ran up the stairs to the Royal Table and skidded to a halt behind Allie's chair. "I wanted to say goodbye," Henry said, nearly out of breath.

Allie lowered her eyes as she murmured, "I thought that maybe you had forgotten about me."

He looked so surprised for a moment that all he could do was blink. "I don't think I could forget you if I tried!" A dizzying spiral of fireworks burst overhead as Henry smiled down at her.

"Ahem," Shimmer loudly cleared his throat. "Allie, Ricky ... I'm afraid it is time to leave."

Henry's smile faltered as he helped Allie up. Shimmer led them down the stairs to where a small crowd was waiting to say goodbye.

Queen Jacqueline was the first to step forward. "What can I say? You helped save my life and my country." A string of perfect pearls slipped out of her gown as she bent to hug the children. "Have a safe journey home."

King Shevre kissed the back of Allie's hand, and then heartily shook Ricky's. "I hope your next visit is not quite as ... eventful." As he escorted Serena toward the dance floor, she turned, calling, "You can expect another invitation very soon!"

"For what?" Rick asked, confused.

"For their wedding, doofus!" Allie laughed.

Roberts steered his chair over to Ricky. "Forget something?" he asked, pulling a yowling cat from the folds of his cloak. Snoball was terrified of the loud explosions bursting overhead. She jumped into Ricky's arms, digging into his shirt with her sharp claws.

Roberts pressed a small package into Allie's hands. "Your personal belongings," he explained. Allie would have been perfectly happy to never see her nightgown again, but she had to admit she was pleased to get her fuzzy slippers back. They had been washed to a spotless pink and the cleaners had even buffed the rainbow still stuck to the top of one slipper so that it now glowed brighter than ever.

Sharonna pushed her way through and hugged each of the children to her ample chest while Gossamer blew her nose loudly behind her. Pocketing her handkerchief, Gossamer sniffled, "I hope you'll both stop by my shop the next time you're in Galdoren!"

"We will," Allie promised.

A loud whistle followed by a deafening boom turned everyone's eyes upward.

A cluster of gold and silver stars burst across the sky, dissolving into a glittering trail.

The audience cheered appreciatively at the spectacular display of fireworks. And as a sparkling pattern of colored lights flashed above, Allie heard a muffled sob. She followed the sound to a little purple star hanging limply in the air. Fat teardrops splashed to the ground as he hiccupped, "I'll miss you."

"I'll miss you too," Allie assured him. Wiping a tear from his eye she gently said, "But we'll see each other at the Royal Wedding. I promise!"

He nodded his head miserably as a distant clock began to chime.

"Midnight," Shimmer sighed, gliding forward. "We really must be going."

"See you soon, buddy!" Ricky called to Twink as the little star wiped his nose with his arm-point.

Allie grabbed Twink and hugged him tightly. Looking down at his tear-streaked face she couldn't resist kissing him on the cheek. Twink's eyes grew wide as he turned from purple to scarlet to red. And just as a shimmering pattern exploded across the sky, he fainted.

"Twink!" Allie cried.

"Don't worry about him," Shimmer said, pulling her up. "He'll be fine. But we really must hurry!"

When Allie turned to Henry, he looked at her in a way that made her heart pound. "Well, good—" but before she could finish her sentence, Shimmer had wrapped his arm-points around both her and Ricky and was streaking up toward the stars.

Henry jumped onto a chair. Cupping his hands around his mouth he shouted, "I'll miss you!"

Allie tried yelling back, but her words were lost in the series of loud bangs splitting the sky. And as the clock chimed its last note, Shimmer, Allie and Ricky disappeared behind Galdoren's golden moon.

Chapter Forty-Four

THERE'S NO PLACE LIKE HOME

Ricky woke up with a sore back. *This bed is so uncomfortable,* he thought, rolling around the lumpy mattress. He glanced at his clock through half-lidded eyes—the digital numbers were glowing 9:00 a.m. Shimmer had done it! Time was indeed ticking again back on Earth.

As Ricky yawned and stretched, he could scarcely believe that only the evening before he had been dining at a castle, watching fairies and dragons skate across the sky. *That was a really good show,* he thought with a sigh, climbing out from under his blankets.

When he swung his legs off the bed, he stepped into a small puddle. Making a face, he muttered, "Snoball." He had forgotten that she shed icicles. At least he *hoped* the liquid he was wiping off his toes was melted ice.

He looked around his messy room and smiled. It might not be as elegant as Galdoren Castle, but it was home. He carefully pulled two round objects from his ears, then tucked the king's old Sleep Phones into the back of his nightstand drawer.

He scrambled out of bed and headed toward the stairs. Although he'd never admit it, he had really missed his mother.

When Shimmer had delivered him and Allie to the Space Museum the night before, they had both realized that there was only one place in the whole world where they wanted to be—home. Shimmer had waited for them to pack, then deposited the siblings on their very own doorstep.

They had raced up the stairs to their mother's bedroom and had leaped into her bed. Hugging her tightly, they had told her how homesick they'd been. A bleary-eyed Mrs. Austin assumed they were referring to the few short hours they'd been at the museum. Still drowsy from the after-effects of Shimmer's sleeping spell, she had mumbled an incoherent response and promptly fallen back asleep.

Hungry for breakfast, Ricky bolted down the stairs, grateful for the short eleven steps in his house. As much as he loved Galdoren, he wouldn't miss climbing those never-ending spiral staircases.

He ran into the sunlit kitchen, nearly knocking his mother over as he dove into her arms. "MOM!"

Hugging him back she laughed, "Welcome home!"

Ricky looked around the cozy kitchen and smiled—not a demented shadow or evil witch in sight. "You have no idea how good it is to be back," he murmured into her warm embrace.

"I missed you too," she replied, kissing the top of his head. "Now, what do you want for breakfast? Cereal or toast?"

He made a face. "Is that all we've got?"

She gave him a funny look. "What were you expecting—a feast?"

He laughed out loud as he moved to the table.

"So, what's it gonna be? Cereal or ...," her eyes narrowed as she took in his disheveled appearance. "Did you fall asleep in your clothes?"

Ricky looked down at his favorite tee shirt and shrugged sheepishly. "I guess I'll just have some toast," he mumbled, already missing the six-course meals he'd become accustomed to.

Allie entered the kitchen wearing her favorite pajamas. Unlike her brother, she had changed out of her clothes the night before. She had tucked her beautiful gown in the back of her closet and put her slippers in an old shoebox, but the bright glow of the rainbow still shined through the cardboard top.

"MOM!" she cried, launching herself at her surprised mother. "It's so good to be home."

Mrs. Austin hugged her daughter back, relishing the display of affection. "Maybe I should send you two away for the night more often," she joked.

Allie moved out of her mother's arms and crossed the room to the fridge. Pulling out an apple, she sighed, thinking if she were at Edna's, it would be be covered in caramel.

Mrs. Austin's brow creased in worry. "Are you sure you've been eating enough?"

Both Allie and Ricky snickered. "Trust me, Mother," Allie replied.

After putting two slices of bread in the toaster, Mrs. Austin joined her children at the table. She leaned in on her elbows, smiling warmly. "So, how was your little adventure?"

"Awesome!" Ricky gushed.

"Amazing," Allie said. "And a little scary."

"Scary? You two didn't do anything dangerous, did you?"

The kids exchanged amused looks. "Nah," Ricky said.

"So, what are we doing today?" Allie asked.

"Well, your brother needs to study for his grammar test and—"

"No, I don't!" Ricky interrupted. "I already know everything!" He winked at Allie, pointing to his ears.

Mrs. Austin raised a brow. "You know *everything*?" She gave him a doubtful look as she pushed her chair out to get the toast that had just popped up.

"Hey, Ricky," Allie smiled. "What's an adjective?"

"Adjectives are descriptive words, like pretty, smart and kind."

His mother looked up from buttering the bread, clearly impressed.

"And what's a noun?" Allie asked.

"A noun can be a person, place or thing. Like boogers, diapers or toilets!"

"RICKY!" Mrs. Austin swallowed a laugh as she set his breakfast before him.

Allie lowered her lids, playing with the stem on her apple. "So, um, I was thinking that maybe we could go to the library today? I want to get some books about alchemy."

Ricky snorted.

"What? I happen to be very interested in the subject!" she said defensively.

"Interested in the *subject* or the *alchemist*?" he muttered under his breath.

She shot him a dirty look as their mother sat down. Mrs. Austin leaned back in her chair, sipping her coffee. "It's funny you should say that, Allie. I don't know why, but I've always been fascinated with magic myself." Staring out the window she added in a wistful tone, "Ever since I was a little girl."

Allie grinned, thinking, *It must run in the family.*

After breakfast, Allie went down to the basement. She opened a cabinet and rummaged through a stack of old photo albums. Finding the one she wanted, she brought it with her to the couch. She flipped through the yellowed pages, sucking in her breath when a familiar looking face stared up at her.

She touched the grainy photograph, gently rubbing a rip in the corner. The man in the faded picture was wearing a fedora instead of a crown, and a suit jacket in place of a cloak. But his face was the same as the man in the portrait back at Galdoren Castle. *So it was true!* Her great-grandpa Al really was the Duke of Margolia! If only she'd had a chance to know him, she thought sadly. He had died when she was just a baby. She turned the page and smiled at the sepia-toned wedding picture. Her great-grandparents looked so happy, as if they were bursting with joy. Staring into her great-grandfather's twinkling eyes she thought of Galdoren, and of another person whose eyes twinkled. Sighing, she slipped the picture out of the cracked leather album and went upstairs to change.

"Snoball?" Ricky whispered, sticking his head under his bed. The little snowcat lazily opened one eye. "Remember—we have to keep you a secret!" She opened her mouth wide in a sleepy yawn. "I'll get you some litter and stuff later today. Do you think you can hold it till then?"

She mewed in response. He looked over his shoulder, then whispered back to her, "If you can't wait, then go in Allie's room. It's right down the hall!"

"What are you telling her?"

Ricky jumped at the sound of his sister's voice, bumping his head on the bed frame. "Ouch!"

Allie pulled her brother up and pushed him toward her room. "Come on, I want to show you something."

Snoball padded down the hall after them, slipping into Allie's room just before she shut the door.

Allie grinned at her brother as he flopped onto the bed.

"What?" he asked.

"I have something to tell you …"

She pulled a faded photograph from under her pillow just as Snoball leaped onto her dresser. The little snowcat rubbed her cheek against a snow globe and then curled up in a patch of sun. The glass in Allie's window cast glittering rainbows over the crystal castle inside the snow globe. Sunlight sparkled off the golden words etched across the bottom:

Welcome to Galdoren

Coming Soon

The Knights of D'atura

The Door in the Sky, Book Two

By Sandy Klein Bernstein

Acknowledgements

To the real Queen Jacqueline — You've supported me and cheered me on in every endeavor, every day of my life. You made me believe that I could accomplish anything and that miracles could and would happen. You always believed in me and thus made me believe in myself. Without you and Shevre, these pages would be empty. And now it's my turn to slip money into *your* pushke!

To the real King Shevre — You've always been my hero. You are a true king and a knight in shining armor in real life as well as in fiction. You have the strongest shoulder I've ever leaned on, and the kindest heart of all.

To the real Sharonna—who is more like a mother to me—and her Prince Charming. If not for you, the cover would be a stick drawing of King Shevre. Thank you for helping turn my dreams into realities.

To the real Roberts and Serena — Thank you for always being there and for supporting me in every way possible. Without you, I would have been ousted from my castle years ago.

To the real Ricky — You bring me joy and laughter and piles of laundry. Without your superb PR skills, my book never would have been read aloud at school, which led to an abundance of wonderful reviews, which inspired me to publish. I have every confidence that one day you will fly without the help of Rocket Dust.

And to the real Allie — Without your help, my manuscript would still be gathering dust atop a stack of papers on my office floor. And a fairie would be dead. Thank you for your tireless editing, unwavering support, and the smile you bring to my face every single day.

To my editor extraordinaire, **Elizabeth Schwaiger** — I have always suspected that you are really a fairie godmother in disguise. You waved your magic wand and—*poof*—my manuscript was sprinkled with fairie dust. Your razor-sharp edits and enthusiastic support sparked my imagination and rekindled my love of writing. And like the chocolate icing atop a homemade cake, I made a wonderful new friend in the process (although your personality may not be quite as delightful as I think, since everyone sounds more interesting with an accent).

To my fabulous proofreader, **Susan James** — You went above and beyond the duties of a proofreader. Thank you for catching all those little details and for offering excellent editorial suggestions. Your sage advice about the publishing business was priceless. I will never forget your kindnesses, and am proud to call you a friend.

To my exceptionally gifted graphic designer, **Michael Leadingham** — You are an exquisite artist and one of the nicest people I know. If my readers have any artisitc or graphic design needs, look no further than michaelleadingham.com His work speaks for itself.

And to my remarkably talented editor/proofreader/shrink, **Allison Bernstein** — Your superb edits were always spot-on, and your discerning proofreader's eye caught mistakes that everyone else missed. If not for you, spell books would have been left behind, Ricky would have flunked 5th grade, and the *Book Nook's* bestseller list would have been embarrassingly outdated. You read my manuscript more times than all the girls in the graduating class of 2012 have read *Twilight*, and yet you never once complained (except about my nagging, but that's an entirely different subject).

About the Author

Sandy Klein Bernstein loves magic and castles and chocolate and dragons (but not chocolate-covered dragons as they give her indigestion). Ms. Klein Bernstein holds a Master's degree in Special Education which she should really put down since holding it makes it extremely difficult to type. She lives with her two children, the *real* Allie and Ricky, and hopes if they are ever whisked away to an enchanted kingdom that they remember to brush their teeth. Ms. Klein Bernstein is currently working on the sequel to *The Door in the Sky* called, *The Knights of D'atura*. It is a delightful book which you should definitely buy when it becomes available.

CPSIA information can be obtained at www.ICGtesting.com
Printed in the USA
BVOW021135030912

299438BV00002B/66/P